Further praise for *The Ugly*

"*The Ugly* is the funniest, smartest novel I've read in a long, long time; its protagonist, the inimitable and lovable Muzhduk, is a literary creation for the ages."

—Pete Duval, author of *Rear View: Stories*

"Here is a hero's journey like you've never read before. It's a wild ride that shows us the irrational underbelly of our supposedly rational world."

—Gibson Fay-Leblanc, author of *Death of a Ventriloquist* and poet laureate of Portland

"Seldom does one encounter a book that balances so much intelligence with so much heart. Muzhduk the Ugli belongs among the great heroes of fiction, alongside Bellow's Augie March and Dostoevsky's Alyosha. It's only after you stop laughing that you realize how much you've learned."

—Mark Powell, author of *The Sheltering*

"*The Ugly* hit me like a giant, knee-bending, stomach-emptying boulder."

—Stefan Sagmeister, author of *Things I have learned in my life so far*, and two-time Grammy award-winning designer

THE UGLY

THE UGLY

ALEXANDER BOLDIZAR

The Ugly

ISBN-13: 978-1-936767-47-2

Cover design by Alban Fischer. Interior by Benjamin DuVall.

Published in the United States of America by:
Brooklyn Arts Press
154 N 9th St #1
Brooklyn, NY 11249
www.BrooklynArtsPress.com
info@BrooklynArtsPress.com

LIBRARY OF CONGRESS CATALOGING-IN-PUBLICATION DATA

Names: Boldizar, Alexander, author.
Title: The ugly / Alexander Boldizar.
Description: First edition. | New York : Brooklyn Arts Press : Distributed to the trade by Small Press Distribution, 2016.
Identifiers: LCCN 2016008435 | ISBN 9781936767472 (pbk. : alk. paper)
Subjects: LCSH: Russians--Fiction. | Harvard Law School--Fiction. | Slovaks--Fiction. | Siberia (Russia)--Fiction. | Africa--Fiction. | GSAFD: Bildungsromans. | Adventure fiction. | Black humor (Literature).
Classification: LCC PR9199.4.B655 U55 2016 | DDC 813/.6--dc23
LC record available at https://lccn.loc.gov/2016008435

10 9 8 7 6 5 4 3 2 1
First Edition

For Samson. And in memory of Oliver.

Man's deepest social instinct is his antisocial instinct.
-Robert Musil

Credo quia absurdum est.
-Tertullian

THE UGLY

PROLOGUE

I, Muzhduk

Muzhduk stepped into the path of the flying boulder. It was the size and shape of a small woman curled up in a ball, but much heavier, and it came at him like a canon shot.

Muzhduk leaned forward to meet the boulder, knees bent, hoping to absorb the impact with his legs. He staggered backward with the force of the blow, but did not drop the big rock.

The audience erupted with cheering, and a cloud of yellow butterflies scattered from the noise. His opponent was Hulagu, arguably the strongest Slovak in the tribe, and all six villages were present for the Dull-Boulder Throw. All the Slovaks who lived in the mountains of northeastern Siberia were there, lined up along the edges of the saddle-shaped ridge. Even those so old or sick they knew the trip would kill them. Two had died on the way.

The audience watched Muzhduk. He knew some of them wondered whether he would disqualify himself. He hadn't moved out of the way, of course, but no one had ever tried to absorb the shock with his legs before. Arms and chest were normal, but bending the legs was almost like ducking and he could see Hulagu bite his fat lips, wanting to make a charge of dishonor, which would itself be dishonorable.

Muzhduk decided not to disqualify himself. Honor was about avoiding cowardice, not change. At only three hundred pounds, he was much smaller than his father, who was smaller than his father. The blood of the Uglis was becoming diluted, as they took women from the Mongols, Yakuts, and Russians, but Hulagu was inbred, huge, and dumb. If Hulagu won, the entire tribe would suffer.

It was Muzhduk's turn. He picked up the boulder, lifted it over his head, and launched with both arms. It flew straight, and Hulagu jumped forward to meet it. The boulder hit him high on the shoulder, ripped his bearskin pelt, and bobbled as he tried to keep it from falling. It fell anyway. He hadn't flinched, so the contest wasn't over, but Muzhduk would get to throw again. They traded places on the ridge and Muzhduk picked up the boulder. Hulagu leaned forward in anticipation, but his right arm hung limp at his side.

"Your arm is hurt," Muzhduk said. "We'll finish tomorrow."

"I can see past the end of my nose. Throw the rock, little Muzh."

The audience roared its approval, but Muzhduk didn't have the stomach to throw a boulder at a man with one good arm. Not even Hulagu. "Tomorrow is better."

"You give up?" Hulagu asked, grinning. If he won, he would climb the highest mountain right away, not wait for years as Muzhduk had done. Then he'd have both eyes and be chief. The first thing he'd do would be to exile the Ugli men and rape the Ugli women. As for Muzhduk, him he'd drag over sharp rocks until he was flayed alive. Then he'd stake him to the ground and spray him with urine. It would be the end of three generations of Ugli rule.

Muzhduk threw the boulder. Hulagu couldn't catch it with one arm, but he still managed to get his chest in front of it. The big rock broke his sternum, pushed his ribs into his lungs, and he collapsed. The contest was over. Bells rang to announce the end. Everyone cheered and came to congratulate Muzhduk for holding onto his title. He had gained another year to find and climb a mountain higher than the one climbed by his father or by any other Slovak chief before him. Then he would have two eyes—two claims to the chieftainship, one objective and one subjective. Then the chieftainship could pass to him undisputed.

Muzhduk found his father, Muzhduk the Ugli the Third.

"You won," his father said. "And that is good. But I don't know about your method."

"Mind if I take Hulagu to Fred the Political Officer?" Muzhduk answered. "It's better if he's healthy. For when the Reds come."

Ugli the Third shrugged and turned to watch the start of the long, slow procession of men, women, and animals back to their villages. Most were dressed in furs, though some of the younger women wore traditional red-and-white lace collars. From a distance, the line of waddling shapes had a self-protective, huddled look.

It was a terrible day to climb a mountain. The air was grey and wet—not quite rain, but damp and miserable. Still, it was the day after the Dull-Boulder Throw, and Muzhduk wanted to climb Mount Baldhead. It was the highest mountain in the Verkhoyansk Range, much of it covered in knee-high Arctic pine. He followed the river past the giant rock with the overturned Red tank, up through the first pass where the real trees ended, and then the second where the dwarf-trees turned to lichen, past where the lichen turned to scree, and on to the broken wall. It was only this last part that was difficult, where the mountain folded into sharp cliffs and jagged chasms. Muzhduk had climbed it many times, probably more than any other Slovak in the six villages. He did it for practice and in the hope that from the vantage of his grandfather he'd be able to see something higher. Baldhead had been the second eye of Muzhduk the Ugli the Second. What a simple test it now seemed.

But Muzhduk also climbed Baldhead because mountaintops were the place for introspection. And though it wasn't the actual top of the mountain, Muzhduk had a special spot that he preferred. It was a boulder about twice the size of a man, wedged between two cliffs, a few minutes from the summit. Under the boulder, the sheer cliffs continued down for half a mile, parallel, less than ten feet apart the whole way. He reached it by inching along a foot-wide ledge that dropped off just before the boulder. Crossing the gap required a little jump that always terrified him. He sometimes tried to imagine where the boulder had come from, but the only possible answer was that it had fallen from the sky.

He'd started coming here because he was scared of heights. As a child, he thought that if he made the jump often enough, the fear would go away. Every time his head spun, his stomach rose, and his chest constricted until he couldn't breathe. The fear never went away.

Instead, it got worse. He became convinced that he'd been born with a given store of luck, and each time he came to the rock he used up a little more. One day it would be done and he would slip and fall between those endless parallel cliffs. The fear never went away, and so he kept coming until the boulder from the sky became his favorite place.

He needed to find his second eye soon, to stop these annual challenges. His father had faced a similar problem at his age. Back then no one had known of a mountain higher than Baldhead; everyone wondered how Third would surpass Second. Third wandered up and down the northern coast of Siberia, staying with the Chukchi and Sakha tribes or spending months alone, with no luck. And then, like the boulder where Muzhduk now sat, like the Chukchi shamans in their sixty-pound coats whom the Reds sometimes threw out of helicopters, his father's answer fell out of the sky. During a winter so cold that the plum brandy turned to syrup and you could eat it on toast, so cold that logs gave off blue sparks when you chopped them and healthy trees exploded with cracks like tank-cannon, the Red Army dropped Spetsnaz paratroops into the valley of the Slovaks. Confused by their own maps, the Reds couldn't get out. They froze. Only one man survived, and when he reached the river Lena, the Uglis caught him. He was Frederick Vladimirovich Ekatin, the platoon's Political Officer. Born in an observation station on Wrangel Island in the Arctic Ocean, the son of two doctors, he'd spent decades as a spy before becoming a Political Officer. He knew the world. The Uglis kept him in the basement, and, as a child, it was little Muzhduk's job to clean and feed him. Fred's cot hung from two chains attached to the basement wall and it could be flipped up when there wasn't enough room. Muzhduk usually sat on a mound of potatoes that he could shape into a chair, or on the pile of loose grain that sometimes forced Fred to sleep on a slant. Neither of them could stand upright, because the permafrost ground had made digging difficult.

Fred said that he'd once stayed in a room even smaller than the Ugli basement at harvest. It was in Japan, and his body had touched all six walls at the same time. The higher the capsule-room, Fred said, the more expensive, because fewer people climbed the ladder past your head. Fred knew more languages than the Uglis, who read every book they could steal, and he told Muzhduk wonderful stories about the world beyond Verkhoyansk: America, Africa, Europe, and other odd places. He even knew the answer to Muzhduk's childhood question about the shamans that fell out of the sky—proof that he knew more than the big library in Yakutsk that his father and uncles had raided in the hope of getting Muzhduk an answer.

Fred said they fell out of the sky because of their coats. Everyone knew shaman coats were covered with metal antlers, iron bars, and chains hanging down the back—that's what made them jangle—but they also had bird-shaped pendants that, when dipped in reindeer pee, gave the shamans the ability to fly. The Reds were embarrassed by their lack of Progress, so they threw them out of helicopters and said, "Use the coat."

That's what Fred said, and Fred knew, because he'd thrown some out himself.

Muzhduk absorbed all the lessons, but when his father climbed down into the cold, shallow basement, lit by empty knotholes and gaps in the floor above, he asked Fred about only one thing—whether there was anything higher in this world than Mount Baldhead. Now, sitting on the wedged-in boulder and searching for an even higher point, Muzhduk understood why his father had been so obsessed.

Fred had told Muzhduk's father about Mount Communism, the greatest mountain on the planet, compared to which Baldhead was only a foothill. Immediately, Muzhduk the Ugli the Third set out for the Tadzhik Soviet Socialist Republic to climb Mount Communism, 7700 meters, 24,590 feet, the highest mountain on the planet.

When his father returned seven years later, he brought wondrous tales of Communism and of a beautiful country to the south called Afghanistan, where he'd stayed for a year to rest and fight some Reds. Having climbed the highest peak, he could now be objectively proud. He could use his spittle to paste money onto the broad foreheads of Slovaks he passed in the valley. His valley. This forehead-pasting was the weakness of the Ugli line and it impoverished the family, but it was the custom for one who had earned the right to be objectively proud. Upon seeing this, the original Ugli, Muzhduk the First, was satisfied. He died. Muzhduk the Second became old, Muzhduk the Third became chief, and young Muzhduk began planning his own quest. This was the way the generations cycled in Verkhoyansk on the river Lena.

But Muzhduk had been planning now for well over a decade, and he doubted that an answer would fall out of the sky the way it had for his father. There was only one top to the world. So long as he kept winning the annual Dull-Boulder Throw he would be the rightful heir. But the village would always say that he was a man with one eye leading a village of the blind. It could be done, but there was no pride in it. He would be challenged every year, until one day Hulagu or some other muscular dummy would defeat him and lead the tribe to ruin.

Enough thinking, he decided. He stood up carefully, unable to fully straighten his knees as the vertigo hit him. From the rounded top of the boulder he extended one leg onto the foot-wide path carved by nature into the cliff. For a second he straddled a thousand-meter drop. He fought off the nausea, a lifting-gut feeling like he'd leaned too far back in a chair, and pushed off with his other leg. On the path, he pressed himself up against the cliff with the irrational fear that his ass would pull him over the edge, or that he'd lose his mind for a moment and jump. He slid along the cliff until the path wound out and he was safe. He thanked the boulder and the path with a sigh of relief.

The true summit of Baldhead was around the corner. As he walked up for a quick look, for the formality of it, he heard a helicopter. It wasn't military; it was the sound of the new helicopters that had been circling the six villages for several months. They didn't shoot, didn't drop bombs or shamans, and only landed when there were no people nearby. No one knew why they circled. Muzhduk ran to the top of the enormous rounded rock that formed the summit and arrived just as the helicopter was landing.

Two women and three beardless men stepped out. They all, even the men, wore shiny pastel clothes made of cloth, not skins or the wool greatcoats of the Russians. All five were small and thin, the heaviest couldn't have been more than a hundred kilos—light enough for the wind to blow them away. Two of the men were obviously guards, despite their flimsy outfits, and the third was in charge, though he wore a red noose around his neck by which anyone could hang him. They all had clean, mild faces unlike any he'd ever seen.

Muzhduk picked up a boulder and said, in Russian, "Are you Reds?"

All five turned. They stared at Muzhduk and he stared back, until one of the women said, "Hello." She spoke Russian with a strange accent. Then she repeated the greeting in Slovak.

"You're not Slovak." Muzhduk knew everyone in the six villages, of course.

"I'm an anthropologist. From America."

"America?" Muzhduk said, wary. Fred the Political Officer had told him about the evil wizards of technology and the alienated factors of production and consumption, about the cities that scraped the clouds. And his father had met Americans in Afghanistan. He said they all sold shoulder-fired missiles.

"Jesus," said the man in the noose to the other woman, in English. "It's André the Giant."

"I speak English," Muzhduk said, and all of them started in surprise. It would have been fun to pretend he didn't understand them while they spoke to each other, but they already seemed a little helpless. "Fred the Political Officer taught me. Who is André the Giant?"

"My name is John." The man held his hand out. It looked like a woman's hand.

Muzhduk dropped his boulder. "Here in Verkhoyansk, it is rare to meet a stranger on a mountaintop," he said. "Normally there is only space for one. This means no empty greetings are required. So long as the mountain is high enough. Usually, that means above the clouds, but today is a bad day. We can't go by the clouds. Is this okay for you?" But he wondered whether the mountaintop rule applied to people who sat in a helicopter instead of climbing all day.

The man looked confused as well.

"Yes," the first woman, the one who'd called herself an anthropologist, said for him. She squeezed a closed green notebook, and that seemed to calm her. "Yes. That's okay."

"Good. Why are you here?"

The noose-man said, "We're surveying our property."

"Baldhead is your property?"

"Everything you see," the man gestured in a circle. "This whole part of the Verkhoyansk range. We bought it six months ago from the Russian government."

Muzhduk laughed. "The Reds tricked you. I hope you didn't pay very much."

"What do you mean," the man scowled, "they tricked us?"

"My father is the chief, and he didn't sell anything."

The man nodded. "We were told that there was an insurgency. When the Wall fell they released the old files and corrected their maps."

"Which wall fell?"

"Communism."

"Communism fell?" Muzhduk couldn't hide his amazement. Communism was his father's second eye. If it fell, did his father's chieftainship fall as well?

"Look," the man said, "we're fully aware that your people fought off the Soviet Army. But this is our land now, so we want to make an arrangement. We have no problem with your people living here."

"Thank you," Muzhduk said, picking up his boulder again.

"Wait," the man said, waving his hands in front of him. "We can work this out. All I want is to run some tours. Nothing intrusive. I don't want to mine or build cities or anything like that. Quite the opposite. You have a very rare breed of butterfly that lives only here. I want to set up a conservation area and fly in wealthy tourists. One hotel, that's it. Butterfly lovers who'd spend money and do no harm to the environment."

"Butterflies?" Muzhduk nodded at one that had landed not far from them. It had a stubby, juicy body, shaggy like a sheep dog, with long sleek wings that were transparent in the center but trimmed on all sides with thick yellow velvet. "We eat them."

"Eat them?" gasped the woman who was not the anthropologist, eyes wide. "They're endangered!"

"We eat them when they're still worms."

"For God's sakes, why?"

Muzhduk smiled. "They taste good."

The five Americans objected. Muzhduk told them they were wasting their time talking to him, since he only had one eye. They should object to Ugli the Third.

After checking with their Russian pilot on how much the helicopter could lift, the Americans offered Muzhduk a ride down to his village. On the way, they asked how Slovaks had ended up in this hidden valley in far northeastern Siberia. The Americans had read about the Czechoslovak Legion of 50,000 men who broke through Russian lines during World War I and refused to turn back despite cowardly orders to do so. They said that historians knew about the

Great March East, when the entire Legion walked from Central Europe to the Sea of Japan, but they thought the Legion had stayed in Siberia for only three years. The history books said they had captured eight train cars of gold bullion and bought passage on Europe-bound ships in Vladivostok, making it back to Czechoslovakia after a full circumnavigation of the planet, proud that they'd never had to retreat.

Muzhduk explained that while most of the Legion had continued east, his great-grandfather Muzhduk the Ugli the First had stopped here on the edge of the Verkhoyansk Range, on the banks of the river Lena, and shouted, "Big people do not walk so much!" He was a huge man with a forehead like a promontory and a neck like an amphitheater, and when he shouted the echo set off three avalanches. There had been a quarrel. General Stefanik, the leader of the Czechoslovak Legion, insisted that the world was round, and that eventually they would come home to their beloved Tatra Mountains, to villages nestled in cleft valley passes and their women warm within. He said that it was too cold in Siberia, that the Reds were winning the Russian civil war and Reds believed that all men were equal, regardless of how much they could lift. He said that Czechs were not mountain people and that the Czech philosopher Masaryk was waiting for them all in Prague, capital of a new Czech and Slovak Federated Republic.

Muzhduk's great-grandfather and six thousand men said no. The Verkhoyansk Mountains were similar enough to the Tatras, their feet were tired, they no longer remembered their wives. The six thousand stayed while the rest marched on.

The Reds defeated the Whites, but many years passed before they turned to face their Slovak problem. Mostly, they were occupied with other business. But by the late 1950s, they had established a worker's paradise, secured world peace, and were well on their way to the Moon. It was then that they decided it was finally time to clean out Verkhoyansk.

They invaded the valley every five years, but, needless to say, they failed. The Slovaks are strong and brave, a people who'd stopped the Roman Empire two thousand years earlier, holding off phalanx technology, onagers, and civilization with little more than large boulders. From the time they can stand unsupported, Slovak children are taught to throw oak logs and large rocks at each other. They have honor. In the end, the Red Army finally solved its Slovak problem by printing maps that didn't show the valley. And so, everyone lived in peace.

Muzhduk explained all this, and as much more as he could manage during the short flight. In exchange, the Americans told him about Mount Everest, K2, Kanchenjunga, Lhotse, Nuptse, Makalu, Dhaulagiri, Nanga Parbat, and Cho Oyu.

"Those are all higher than Mount Communism?" Muzhduk asked, shocked and delighted. After more than a decade of trying to find a higher mountain, here was a whole pile of them.

The anthropologist crouched around her notebook and wrote furiously, mumbling about lost tribes and colonial peripheries and her publisher, while Muzhduk talked about how, when he would return from his quest, they'd spot him when he crossed the river Lena. By the time he reached his village there'd be a hundred girls, each with a bottle of *slivovica,* using every wile known to Verkhoyansk woman in trying to force some down his throat, and the men would crowd at the Ugli home, jumping drunkenly to give Ugli the Third the honor of breaking his top step under the weight of all his guests. Then, after he'd clapped all the women courteously on the ass, after the top step was broken, and after the girl whose bottle was the emptiest was declared the winner—

The anthropologist cursed when they touched down in the center of the village and Muzhduk stopped talking.

Ugli the Third greeted them before the blades had stopped spinning by knocking unhappily on the window. "What do you want," he said, then grumbled that he didn't like helicopters. The Americans stared. He had a hundred pounds and six inches on Muzhduk.

Muzhduk's father led them back to the house, a square cottage with the tallest and widest roof-tree in the six villages. All the guests could fit in the central room, though they had to pause to let their eyes adjust to the weak light coming in through small fret-shuttered windows and their lungs to the sour smell of pine, earth, and lanolin that mixed with faint smoke from an iron wood-fired stove. Flypaper coils hung throughout the room, heavy with dead Siberian bugs, and tapestries covered the log walls. The only other real room in the house was the attic, where they slept, held up by rough branches that wove through the ceiling to the plank, tar, and scavenged-metal roof. Most of it was tank armor. But all the furniture was carved of wood, good wood that did not creak when you sat on it, and every crossbeam was engraved with scenes of men challenging each other to single combat or relaxing in various positions with women and *slivovica* afterward. And there were great battles against the Reds, as well as the objective-eye exploits of the family, scenes of walking and Baldhead and Afghanistan.

Muzhduk's mother quickly chased out the smell of earth and smoke with that of strong coffee. She shook bearskins, plumped bolsters, replaced the short nettle-cloth on the table with a white lace tablecloth from Austria-Hungary, and stacked meat and cabbage onto blue-onion china. Everyone sat, and the man in the noose introduced himself again as John. He added that he was an attorney and introduced the two women as an anthropologist and a biologist.

"How did you get these titles?" the Third asked, shaking a thick bottle toward his guests. They declined, so he poured it into his own coffee. "And why do you throw them around?"

The attorney looked at the anthropologist. She hesitated, then wrote in her notebook one word: "status." She underlined it for John's benefit.

"Status," Muzhduk said. The anthropologist winced.

"You think we cannot read?" the Third asked, incredulous, pointing at the upside-down English word. "When we steal women from the Red camps, we take their books too."

"I'm sorry," the attorney said. "I use my anthropologist to avoid offending you."

"Avoiding is the only thing that will offend me. Talk without help or crawl back into your metal shell and fly home."

The attorney didn't know what to say. He straightened his tie.

"And take that off. It makes me want to hang you from the ceiling just for fun—and then I can't concentrate. It's like if she," he stuck out his bottom teeth at the anthropologist, "pulled down her pants during our whole conversation. How could I think?"

The anthropologist stared back at the Third and stopped writing. For a few seconds the only movement was the biologist slapping at a black fly that had found its way through all the flypaper coils.

John took off his tie and jacket and rubbed his hands together. "Okay, you asked about my title. I'm the attorney for, and a partner in, a company called SiberTours—"

"I asked *how* you got your titles. They mean nothing if I don't know how you got them."

"Well," he hesitated, "I graduated with a *Juris Doctor* from Harvard Law School, first in my class, and I'm a member of the New York bar."

"Those still mean nothing."

John paused to think before each answer, and this was beginning to annoy the three hosts.

The anthropologist added, "Harvard is the top law school in the world, and—"

"It's the highest?"

"Yes."

Ugli the Third nodded. "And you graduated. So you climbed to the top of the steps of the highest law school. That is respectable, though it means nothing to us. I know what laws are. Fred the Political Officer has explained the world well. They are for the weak-willed. We don't believe one person needs to tell another how to live."

"You don't have laws?" John asked in disbelief. "What if someone murders your sister?"

Muzhduk's father made an enormous fist. "Then it's between my family and his. We don't bring strangers into such a personal thing."

"There must be something your people look down upon as a whole," the anthropologist said. "In the abstract. Otherwise you wouldn't have a culture. Do you understand what I mean?"

Ugli the Third pursed his lips, though the movement was hardly visible under his beard. "Dishonor. Ducking a boulder instead of trying to catch it. Too much introspection in the valley." He pointed a thick finger at his son. "Thinking about things instead of acting. But these are not laws. They are honor."

"Fine," John said curtly. "But your enemies have laws. Anyway, Harvard Law teaches more than laws. It teaches how to think and use language."

"Words are toys. You can't throw words."

"Of course you can. That is exactly what law school teaches. How to throw words."

"How do you weigh them? What's the most powerful word? It's nonsense."

"*Harvard*. In my life, that has clearly been the most powerful word." He paused again. "Like Communism was for you."

"Enough of this," Ugli the Third slammed his open hand down on the foot-thick table. His hand was as big as the anthropologist's notebook, and hairy. "What do you want here?"

John the Attorney explained his plan to fly in tourists to look at the butterflies. For the first time since the helicopter landed, Muzhduk's father smiled. He had big teeth, each as big as John's thumbnail.

"You are a funny man, John the Attorney. Take some *slivovica*."

This time John accepted, and Third filled John's coffee cup so it was half coffee, half 160-proof plum brandy.

"The butterflies are okay," the Third said. "But you keep the helicopters away from the villages and make the tourists walk the last hour."

"Great," John said.

"But you have to stop killing the worms," the biologist added.

"The worms taste good," Muzhduk the Ugli the Third said. "And if we don't eat them, they'll eat everything else. They never stop eating, especially the mulberry leaves. They make silk for us and then, on the first day in their cocoon, we pick some and have a feast. And after the rest grow, the women use the yellow from the wings for eye paint. This will not change."

"It must," she insisted.

"It will not change." Ugli shook his head somberly. "People who do not eat butterflies will wear their clothes the wrong way, and people who wear their clothes the wrong way are inviting lemmings inside."

"Our company owns this land now," the biologist said, her face white. The anthropologist squeezed her arm, but it was too late.

"Then I hope you are more powerful than the Reds. I withdraw my grant. We will kill your tourists and you."

"Even if we are not armed?" the anthropologist asked.

Ugli the Third frowned. It would make no sense for them to come unarmed to a battle; but if they did, if they were crazy, then what? He couldn't kill someone who was both crazy and unarmed. "Go away," he said.

"Wait," the attorney interrupted. "I can see that you're an honorable people, with your own sorts of rules. The rule of Lore instead of the rule of Law." He smiled and the Uglis stared at his perfectly straight teeth. Like a horse. "I get it. And you're right, this land is yours and only yours. To give or not to give, as you will. We were naïve to trust the Russians. The, um, Reds. But as a token, I ask that you grant me land the size of…" he looked around, finding the rug under the table, "…of a bearskin. Just one bearskin. To be mine, to not be interfered with no matter what, on your honor."

Muzhduk the Third laughed, finding John funny again. "What could you do with land the size of a bearskin? Even for a small man like you, that's barely enough space to lie down."

"A token."

Muzhduk the Third winked at his son. He was chief. He had both eyes, objective and subjective. Muzhduk the Fourth hadn't told him yet about the collapse of Mount Communism. "Fine," the Third said. "I grant you land the size of a bearskin anywhere in our domain. Now go away, but leave your anthropologist."

"Can you sign this paper?" John asked, handing Ugli the Third a contract.

"My honor!" the Third boomed. He spat on the paper and stuck it on John's forehead.

They left, taking the anthropologist with them, loaded down with gifts of plum brandy, mountain wool socks that Muzhduk's mother had knitted, a newborn goat, and enough apple strudel for a week of desserts. Had they left on warmer terms, there would have been too much for the helicopter to carry.

Two weeks later, Muzhduk saw the helicopter circling the six villages. When it landed in front of the Ugli home, Muzhduk the Ugli the Third was waiting, angry. "I told you not to fly this noisy thing so close."

"But you gave us this land," John said.

"Where is your bearskin?"

"I cut it into a fine thread. I took the thread and placed it in a big circle that surrounds the six villages. Now this area is all mine."

The Third's neck swelled and turned red.

"On your honor," John the Attorney said, backing up.

Ugli the Third pulled on his ears, rubbed his forehead, and looked dangerously close to indecision. Finally, he said, "If I kill you, then the person I gave my word to no longer exists."

"That sounds like ducking."

Ugli the Third growled. "You've learned too much." He stormed into his house, pulled up the trapdoor and climbed down into the dungeon where the family kept Fred the Political Officer. Muzhduk followed him. Fred looked terrible. He was lying on his cot, gaunt and pale and blind. And old. Ugli the Third should have listened to his son, but he'd been too stubborn.

"Fred the Political Officer," the Third said by way of greeting.

"Yes?" Fred answered. His voice was ragged and dry.

"Tell me about words."

"What words?"

"Words and attorneys. How do you fight words?"

"I can't tell you anything about them. I am almost dead."

"Yes," Ugli the Third said and went back upstairs. He told Muzhduk to sit across from him at the large table. Muzhduk's mother joined them, and the three drank coffee. They drank for hours, until it made them sweat and shake and hallucinate in their peripheral vision.

"I was wrong," the Third finally said. "Words are not just toys. They are heavy but not straight. You caught Hulagu's rock by doing strange things with your body, and you used to move the rug to give Fred the Political Officer more light when nobody was here. So maybe you will succeed with these people who want the butterflies to spread until they eat every bush and tree. Go to that place where John the Attorney learned to throw words. To fight Reds, we had to understand metal. To fight Americans, we need words. Pick up the word *Harvard* and learn it better than John and bring it back. It will be your second eye, more like that of the First, but still objective."

"Why not just kill John the Attorney? Then the promise dies with him."

"There will be more like him."

There would be others on Mount Harvard, surely, thought Muzhduk, other future chiefs of "niches," as the Americans called their tribes, learning to use words as weapons. Harvard wasn't really a mountain, but the first Ugli had only walked to Siberia and stopped. He hadn't climbed anything. And according to John, others had climbed Baldhead and Communism before the Uglis had ever even seen them. The whole family's second eye was at risk.

And chasing a word to its peak couldn't be wrong. The Verkhoyansk Slovaks had changed a lot living in the mountains of Siberia, but they were still Slovaks. And the word *Slovak* literally means *people who use words*. As opposed to, say, the word for Germans, *Nemtsi*, meaning *people who don't speak*. For a Slovak, even a Verkhoyansk Slovak, it couldn't be wrong to understand words. Could it?

When Muzhduk had pressed John for more information, he'd told them strange things like: "Objective success changes, though you must quickly forget that it does," and "The top's always changing. That's why it's hard to stay there. Power comes from many tiny micro-interactions, not broad sweeps. You keep your nose to the market, watch fluctuations, ride the wave. That's the only way to remain the big chief." And he'd told them that the name of Mount Communism had changed to Ismoil Somoni Peak.

"Ismoil Somoni Peak!" Muzhduk's father repeated for days, shaking his head.

The fall of Communism overshadowed everything. The six Slovak villages of Verkhoyansk wondered whether Ugli the Third had lost half—the objective half—of the family's claim to the chieftainship. Then, on top of everything, Fred actually started to die.

He'd been coughing blood for months, but everyone thought it was just because he lived with the grain and that wheat dust bothered him. And normally when people coughed more than the usual amount of blood, they went to see Fred. Everyone assumed he'd fix himself.

Now he couldn't even sit up, and his coughing fits sometimes made him pass out. Muzhduk wanted to take him upstairs, give him some sun and air, and his father agreed. But Fred didn't want to leave. He said he wanted to be comfortable. Muzhduk brought six flashlights to the basement to give Fred some light, but Fred said to turn five off. So Muzhduk spent his last week in Verkhoyansk in the basement, in near darkness, with a wall of grain squeezing him against Fred's death-cot.

"Thank you for moving the rug all these years." Fred pointed up to the irregular lines of light filtering through the axe-hewn wood-plank ceiling where the bearskin rug had been.

Muzhduk scratched wheat chaff out of his beard. He'd come to squeeze the last bits of information from Fred the Political Officer, who'd worked in America during his spy days. Instead, he kept thinking of the hours he'd spent down here with Fred. He'd talked more with Fred during his life than with anyone else in the six villages, including women. Finally, he said, "You want to play a game of chess?"

Fred said no. "I want to tell you what I know about America. Before you go."

He'd watched the Uglis for twenty years from under the floor, keeping the name *Everest* secret out of bitterness. It was what remained of his loyalty to Mother Russia. But Fred had heard the talk with John the Attorney and between father and son, and he knew that America would be difficult for Muzhduk. In the six villages even the chief can't tell another Slovak what to do—if half the village wants to fight Reds and half wants to finish the harvest, each does their own thing and doesn't question the other. The chief's opinion carries weight, but if he ever tried to force someone, the way the generals did before the Great March East, his own family would beat him to death out of shame.

Fred told Muzhduk that in America there's no single chief, but everyone tells each other what to do. They have fifty million laws, all written down. In Verkhoyansk nobody writes down anything important because human memory is faulty. In America they write everything, for the same reason. There are rules about what kind of plants you can smoke, when and where you can have a drink, and what you must wear on your head when you ride a motorcycle. They have rules against standing around and not doing anything. If you break a rule, they write it down so nobody will ever forget. And there is nobody to fight if the rule is wrong.

Fred tried to sit up, but only managed to turn onto his side. "That's a rule you must remember: men can't fight, even if they both want to. If your honor demands a fight, you must remember that honor is different there—"

"But—" Muzhduk started.

Fred gripped Muzhduk's wrist. "You absolutely can't hurt anyone physically, not even a dog, because in America pets are people too, and they have an internal army like the Reds, but they're Blue, and everybody helps them catch someone who breaks a rule. Don't trust anyone, not even friends, they all collaborate. If you kill someone, your own friend will call the Blues."

Fred told him things that would help. "The fastest way to learn the laws is to learn about the men who make them. For example: they are rich, unfit, and afraid, so their laws protect property, forbid nudity, and give the Blues a monopoly on violence. But it's complicated, because hypocrisy is important there. They consider it the first step to virtue."

"If you ever get in trouble," he said, coughing with nearly every word, "say that what you're doing is to increase safety. 'Safety' is almost like honor there. Another way is to become famous, or the *most* at something. My handler and I used to laugh . . ." Fred coughed at the thought of laughing. "That if we ever defected we'd call ourselves the world's tallest midget and the world's shortest giant and try to become rich on American television."

On the last day, Fred still tried to talk, but what came out was a ramble of fragments. About looking at the part of the swan beneath the water, how it paddles frantically, about bureaucrats who will insist Muzhduk have a number, and about his own life in the Uglis' basement. "In places like that," Fred said at the end, staring at the grain, "if a wall falls on a man and people want to know why, they study the wall. In this basement I've learned you have to know why the man sat beside it."

Fred died. Muzhduk sat with him for a while, then pulled his hand off his wrist. They burned his body as if he were one of the family, and since the smoke was in the shape of a deer, they threw his ashes into the air. Then Muzhduk the Ugli the Fourth left for his long walk to America.

CHAPTER 1

Bureaucracy

I stood in the back of a pickup truck. It was a 32, distinguished from a 13 or a 17, although some large minivans are also 32s.

Thirty-two people arranged with precision into the back of a Toyota pickup, we were on our way from one sandy part of the Sahara to another. The Sahara desert contains things other than sand, but the part where we started, the part we traversed, and the part where we hoped to arrive were all sand—a beige, nondescript sort of sand that did not always stay on the ground.

A mother sat on my feet nursing her daughter as we bounced over soft dunes and exposed rock. Using her weight as ballast, and pressed against the sharp metal bar corralling the truck's edge, I could sleep while standing.

Harmattan wind blew the top layer of desert into dust, washing-out colors and edges and leaving only an intense white dome above, a faint daytime smell of burnt flint, and the flat drone of the Toyota engine. We passed an endless blur of acacia trees, though calling them trees seemed sad compared to the mountain oak and beech I'd grown up with. Most were little more than short, insect-like bushes covered in a thick film of grey dust. We bounced, Mother landed, and I was again safe, pinned to the bed of the pickup.

My boots were steel-toed, steel-shanked, size-15 Kodiaks that took up the space of five Africans. I had paid only four times the price—the third person to board in Tillabéri, paying double because of size, double again because of skin color. I'd waited through the hottest part of the day for the bush-taxi to fill, tugging at my large ears and rough beard while the blistering sun sucked and boiled all life until it sizzled.

Mother was not all that heavy on my feet now, though the hours had made them numb. She did not talk through her nose or in any other manner except for the occasional "tisk" when I tried to shove my feet back under her whenever a bounce shifted our positions. As everything faded into the blowing sand, she became simply my anchor. Other details disappeared into the dust, along with my own reasons for being here. After meeting Peggy, and with my quest only half complete, it had made sense to come to Africa rather than return to Verkhoyansk. But after washed-out days of dust and desert bouncing in this bush taxi, what propelled me forward was the mother's ass, pinning me to the truck while I struggled with my lungs to relax and stop clenching asthmatically from the returning dust—a million tiny boulders thrown at my lungs.

Nighttime was better. Whenever we climbed a peak in the sand, I saw the moon growing over the Niger River, violently bright above the round African heads that bobbed and waved a foot below my own like loose springs in a mattress. My height advantage saved me from the occasional CLUNK of skull against skull, but it disassociated me further from the people and my surroundings. Losing feeling, I shifted weight from one leg to the other, hypnotized by the hours as I flew above an unconcerned mother and baby with a drinking problem; it never stopped sucking Mother's breast. That baby was the only one of us who still cared about anything, or maybe it just drank out of a mechanical compulsion, moving on an endless loop.

Sometimes the wind calmed suddenly and the dust let some light in. The world cracked and Mother tisked and I rolled my ankle around, searching for pins and needles, wishing I could lie down in my patchwork shorts. The tattered fool shorts had survived the long walk from Siberia to Boston, ripped and repaired three dozen times. They'd survived Montreal, a year at Harvard, and then the trip here, through sand and dust and half-delirium. Along with my goatskin backpack, it was the only trace I still had of the six villages in Verkhoyansk on the river Lena. I missed real trees and lying on the ground with my legs lifted up to the sky, eating watermelon. I would have liked nothing better than to get off that truck, lie on the desert floor, with or without the melon, and stick my legs up to the moon in delight, happy to be attached to a world so round.

A world that had shaken its collective head at the Czechoslovak Legion after World War I, when news spread that they'd marched around the globe rather than retreat. But Ugli the First hadn't cared that the world was round. He'd stopped walking, refused to keep going even if that meant never getting home. The thought worried me a little. I didn't want to get stuck here.

Introspection was permitted, this was still part of my climb, but I pushed the thought away. There's no point in trying to tell the shape of a box from the inside. Much better to focus on the roundness.

• • •

The truck was in the lowest gear, but it wouldn't move. We had crossed the border into Mali, but now we were stuck in the sand again. No one moved. We all waited. The moon was two-thirds full, but already bright enough to read by.

The first time the truck got stuck, I jumped down right away, eager to stretch my legs. I pushed, together with a Congolese, a Ghanaian, and several prescient Nigeriens and Malians. They jumped back into the truck a full second before it started moving. I barely made it back in, and then only with the help of an outstretched arm.

The Congolese man who helped me up had been staring at me almost without pause since Tillabéri, until I'd finally asked him his name. Amadou. His arm was thin, but remarkably long and strong, and he wore a little digital radio dangling off his wrist by a leather strap. He gave me a smile that split his round face, which he shook at my lack of foresight, though he didn't stop staring. I thanked him, but my spot was already gone. Words were useless. Only the pressure of my feet forced out a little space.

After several repetitions of this, nobody wanted to push. This time the driver came out. He was an Arab, a merchant. He shouted in Arabic and Bambara and Hausa, then grabbed Amadou and tried to pull him off the truck. At him he yelled in French. Thirty other people looked away. I understood, and felt guilty.

The two of us pushed. We failed. An additional person climbed down grudgingly and we pushed, failed, two more came down, failed, one more, and eventually we pushed the truck out of the sand. I was always the slowest to jump back in, lacking the sixth sense of when the truck was about to be freed. The nursing mother tisked at me as I tried to shove my feet back under her, gaining a few millimeters each bounce. Within fifteen minutes I was back to the position where I'd started. The truck continued on, a bouncing human porcupine, until the untuned engine whined, the exhaust from the tailpipe turned sour, and the truck bed under my feet softened for a second. Then the metal floor turned hard and we were stuck again.

Each time we got stuck, the driver picked Amadou first, maybe because he had seated himself on the back corner of the pickup, listening to music from the Congo on his little radio, or maybe because his round features stood out in this part of Africa. Amadou climbed down, always smiling, like he knew some secret nobody else knew. His hair began unnaturally far back on his head, leaving the impression that he was all forehead—Humpty Dumpty with noodle arms. He was headed to Europe, he said, on an underground railway of illegal immigrants traveling through Algeria, Morocco, and into Spain. He couldn't afford to lose his ride, and I didn't want to stay in the unclaimed gash of no-man's-land Sahara between Niger and Mali, so we pushed.

"And you. You come here for the sand," Amadou said, kicking the ground. The lighter bits were so fine they took a few seconds to settle back down.

I laughed. "No, definitely not for the sand."

"For a woman, then."

Why else would anyone come here, but for the sand or a woman? Another man climbed down, a man from Ghana, maybe a hundred pounds. He pushed too, but the truck didn't move and the rest looked away, nudged left and then right, and tisk, tisk as the driver yelled. So we stopped and waited, patient within African time. Another man finally came down, a scarred-up man who didn't stop staring at the spot he'd left as we pushed, the wheels spun, and we didn't move. The scarred-up man jumped back in to rebuild his space, so we gave up for the night.

I settled in beside the truck's rear wheel, tucked my goatskin pack under my head, and slept poorly. I woke in the middle of the night to nodding bodies hanging above, round heads falling onto shoulders. Amadou slept off to the side, unconcerned, and the Ghanaian lay leaning against another man on the roof of the cab. The rest all slept on their feet in the bed of the pickup, propped against one another, nodding and nudging in passive irritation.

I woke up again shortly before dawn to the sounds of pushing and yelling, a fight. I'd slept through most of it. The truck had separated into two halves—half the people had taken one person's side, half the other's. There was no room for a true line between them, but the angles of the elbowing bodies made a V shape like parted hair.

By mid-morning people were coming down from the truck in pairs and threes, doing their best to hide from the sun. I had two cans of mackerel, bought in Niamey, Niger—red cans with bold black writing stating that they were a *Donation from the Government of Japan. Not for Sale.* They had been cheap. I ate one and offered one to Amadou, but he declined, and we waited and hid from the sun along with everyone else.

By late afternoon we decided to walk. Well after dark, we climbed over a dune into a village of square red mud-and-thatch houses that Amadou said was named Ansongo. Men slept in front of their houses on little mats, hoping to cool off with what little breeze there was. But the Sahara is never cool—it's either hot or cold. Mid-summer it's always hot. I found a sandy spot to curl around my goatpack again, until morning.

"You will sleep there? On the ground?" Amadou asked.

I mumbled, and tried to get comfortable.

"I will go to the hotel."

This woke me up. "There's a hotel here?" It seemed odd in a village of thirty squares.

"Of course." He waved at me to follow.

We walked up to a row of people sleeping in front of their houses, and Amadou kicked one. The sleeping man grunted and rolled to the side. Amadou lay down beside him.

"Is that okay?" I asked, surprised.

"The hotel is…not so good. So I asked him if we could share his mat. No problem. Sleep." He turned his radio off, wrapped it in a shirt, and slid it under his head for a pillow.

"Do you know him, at least?" We hadn't checked anywhere for a hotel. I was hungry. The moon had set and the stars were so thick there was no space between them, just fainter stars. A few people were still dragging themselves in from the truck. Mostly the village was quiet. Something small and crawly landed on the back of my neck. I slapped it and cursed myself as its faintly acidic blood burned my skin. Amadou was already asleep beside the mat owner. I lay my head on my hollowed-out goatskin. My knife rested on my chest, and I hoped in drifting off that I wouldn't stab myself.

I dreamt that I had insomnia. Twisting left, right, left again, swearing, tired but unable to fall asleep. I cursed so violently that I woke myself up, face stuffed into my goatpack and confused. I rolled over, shifted the knife to my chest, and fell back into a deep sleep, only to begin dreaming that I couldn't sleep again.

My knife was gone. This thought woke me up. But there it was, digging into my ribs. Amadou stood a few meters away. The owner of the mat stared at me.

"Twobob," the mat-man said at me.

"Two Bob?"

"Twobob!" The man pointed, accusing.

I wasn't fully awake yet, and confused. Two shillings? Two knots of worms and rags on a string? "What?"

"He is saying that you are a *blanc*," Amadou offered.

Two Bob. Better than being only one Bob, I guess. And it gave the little kids a name to call out as if they knew me while they yelled for gifts and money as we drove by, running after us—those who had not been paralyzed by polio. The paralyzed ones ran too, but with their hands. Sometimes they ran with flip-flops on their callused little palms, sometimes they pushed themselves along on rollers, sometimes they used one stiff leg as a sort of pole vault, their tail bones sticking in the air, heads cranked uncomfortably from the triangles of their bodies as they loped forward, their speed matching that of the children on legs. Seeing them, I silently thanked Harvard. However much of a disaster my year there had been, at least they'd vaccinated me against these crazy diseases that had never crossed anyone's mind in Verkhoyansk but could wipe us out as easily as tanks or tourists.

I was the tourist here, and the only thing that changed in this landscape was my name: Ansara, Mzungu, Poo'mui, a dozen others, and now, Twobob. Another word for the collection—whatever I did, from the most mundane to the most outrageous, I was the same in their eyes. In Verkhoyansk, the difference between myself and a Russian was the biggest difference imaginable, beyond night and day. But seen from here, Siberian, American, and Italian were all the same. I wished I could share the thought with Buck, the one friend I'd made at Harvard. He had once told me that the concept of "white" as a race hadn't existed until the start of the slave trade.

I never found out what Twobob really meant—"stranger" or "whitey" or "burnt pink"—but the mat-owner was amazed that one had just spent the night next to him. Ansongo was a small village in the middle of the desert, with no true roads and no tourists.

"Good morning," I said, because the man continued to stare. "Thank you for sharing your mat." The oblique rays of the sun made this the most pleasant time of day. I put my knife away. After sneaking into someone's bed in the middle of the night, it seemed improper to wave a knife about in the morning.

The mat-man pointed to my boots. "Cadeau?" Then pointed at himself.

"Sorry, they're the only boots I have." This was the cost of being strange. I walked the surface of Africa and repeated the same conversations, often about giving away my boots.

I let Amadou decide the proper payment etiquette, but he ignored the mat-man and walked back to the truck. I followed. A large group of people waved their arms and said the truck wouldn't start yet, but they'd fix it *tout de suite.* We returned to Ansongo for breakfast, lunch, dinner, and endless hot Corpa-Colas while the sun consumed the sky. Selling near-boiling Colas seemed to be the mat-man's real business, and he sold a lot of them. They were glass, 250 ml bottles, and seemed to be what everyone drank in the desert.

Amadou tapped the bottle he was drinking against the plastic lawn chair he was sitting on. "This is the king of Africa. This is the power of the white man. Only when Africa is united, one magic, can we defeat Corpa-Cola."

We sat in front of the mat-man's house while people kept updating us on how the truck was fixed but still "needed to be checked." Something had gone wrong with the watered-down fuel. I drank hot Colas while Amadou searched in vain for hashish or women or some other form of entertainment to go with the hummingbird-quick soukous in his ceaseless radio.

The next day the mat-man asked for his "rent," which I paid in Central African francs, not boots. A short while later a van arrived on its way to Gao. It was full already, but those of us who could afford to buy a new ticket pushed in. The van was an overstuffed 17, almost a mini-bus, with people sitting on each other's knees. As I squeezed beside a Tuareg father and son, both wearing indigo robes, I saw the first non-African I'd seen in weeks: buried in the far back, a skinny Japanese mime sat with a white towel around his head and another around his mouth. Only his eyes were showing, and they stared expressionlessly out the window as the van drove on through the desert.

The shocks grated at every bump, and seventeen different ghettoblasters played seventeen different tapes: hypnotic kora, xylophone, and balafon mixed with high-pitched guitars and pile-driving bass from Mali, wailing vocals from South Libya, the river-blues of Ali Farka Touré, the metal bells of Yoruba agogô, Liberian highlife, apala, fuji, panko and sakara music from Nigeria, Hausa three-string lutes, Andalusian milhûn singers from Morocco, and at least six tapes playing the long caterwauls of Islamic ajisari religious music. Amadou threw his own into the mix and I ripped some cloth from my shorts to plug my ears.

Later that morning we were stopped by an army Jeep. Two men climbed out: one wore khakis and flip-flops and a French-modified German G-3 machine gun; the other, dressed in a bright Hawaiian shirt, pointed at the Jeep's white-on-green logo, which read, "Mobile Customs Brigade."

Amadou began to tell me something about logos, but was interrupted by the Khaki-man telling us to all get out, asking who had a radio. I didn't have one, so I stood in the shade of the van and hummed a Tom Waits song that I'd first heard two years earlier at a different border crossing: *Po-lice at the station and they don't look friendly, they don't look friendly, well they don't.*

But there was no station. There was the Jeep and a folding table the man in the Hawaiian shirt opened and pushed into the sand one leg at a time until it was level. Then he worked to ram a four-foot stick with a windless little flag into the ground next to the table. The flag didn't promote a country, just the same logo as the Jeep. The ground was the same nondescript sand as everywhere else, above was the same delirium-white sun.

When he finished with the flag, Hawaii noticed me leaning against the van. His belly button protruded where the shirt wasn't buttoned. Like Mr. Khaki he wore flip-flops, but carried a duct-taped old Kalashnikov. He smiled, shook my hand, and didn't let go. After a few seconds like this, he squeezed deeper and pulled me toward him, away from the van. I stopped humming. He pointed up with his left hand, into the sky, faced me and yelled, then pointed into the sky again. His voice sounded hollow in the heat. I squinted up to see what I was supposed to, but it hurt. I spoke no Bambara, except one word.

"Twobob," I said.

He frowned, then shook his head, squeezed, and yelled again. Mr. Khaki looked up from a radio he was examining and asked whether I understood.

"No."

"He said you like the sun, so stand in the sun."

But I didn't really like the sun. That sun was the Devil. Over 50 degrees Celsius in the shade, far too hot in the sun. My digital thermometer had changed from Celsius to Fahrenheit, hit 160, then broke. Now it read only "HH," whatever that meant. Maybe hell-hole.

Mr. Khaki continued to translate, though he was clearly Hawaii's superior. "You came to Mali to get a sun-tan, right? So now you must stand in the sun and tan."

They had machine guns and a funny sense of humor, so I stayed in the sun until they ignored me, and hoped they were joking. As they occupied themselves with gathering radios together on the ground, I slowly walked back into the shade of the van. For a few minutes no one noticed, then Hawaii remembered and pulled me back into the sun. I didn't resist, I'd learned Fred's lesson in America that fighting police can cause things to go wrong, but when Hawaii returned to the radios I went back to the shade. We repeated this many times, for hours, while the light grew heavier and more poisonous and the shade became a skinny shadow that had retreated to my feet. Sun exposure is punishment in Africa for unpaid debts.

When I was sun-hammered and delirious, Hawaii took my hand, as though he were shaking it, but again didn't let go. He asked,

"Are you a radio?"

"No, I'm not a radio."

"Looking," he pointed to my goatpack. Then he laughed and lifted the bag up above his head, staring at the dangling desiccated goat testicles that were part of the hollowed-out skin. He flicked them with a finger, then pointed at me. "You."

I took the bag from him, said, "No radio," and lifted the flap that had once been the top of the goat's neck and was now the cover for my travel pack. To show that I had no radio. My head was spinning, stupid from the sun, because sitting on my clothes, clearly visible, was Amadou's little radio with its brown leather wrist-strap. I hadn't seen him put it there. And I didn't see him anywhere now.

"Just a small one," I added, trying to think through my daze. "Because this is Mali." I thought this was funny, because *mali* means *small* in Slovak.

Hawaii turned to Mr. Khaki and pointed to me. "He is a radio."

"Later," Mr. Khaki said, and turned to the complaining Africans whose radios were grouped together in a circle. "You must have receipts from the place of purchase and one from the customs office." He spoke French, because the van-people came from a dozen different language groups.

Hawaii wasn't ready to wait. "You radio. Only? Are you a camera?"

"No camera."

Hawaii groped inside my goat, squeezed it from outside and flicked the testicles again. When he didn't find anything bulky enough to be a camera, his face became red from the sun and from his personality. He said, "Radio receipt?"

I put the radio back into my bag while pretending I was searching. "I don't have a receipt. I bought it somewhere else, not Mali."

"Are you a receipt somewhere else and a receipt Malian customs stamping that you entered in it?"

There wasn't a real border between Niger and Mali, just a guy with a pocket and a rubber stamp moving like a dune in a shifting no-man's land of pea sand, pebble sand, dust sand, rocks, and acacia trees ten desert-miles thick. The whole landscape was pale yellow, sometimes rust-red, with an occasional bleached grass tuft, but it all looked blown-out grey in the midday sun. And the constant dry smell of flint. Most people who crossed that border did it on silent asses carrying cantaloupes to sell in the next village, and that remained the only reasonable way to cross: thinking in terms of towns, not countries. "I bought it a long time ago," I said.

"When long?"

I shrugged. "Three years."

"Are you a passport?"

"Yes." I pulled it out.

"I asked not to see it. Also yes or no."

"Yes."

"*Quel age?*"

"Twenty-three."

"Twenty-three, but you are your papers. In order. *Oui?*"

"I am my papers in order, yes." Though I wasn't. Not in this sun.

"There is a radio, it is only three. It needs to be papers in order. *Oui?*"

"Where I come from we aren't papers for radios."

He smiled to show off his tooth and watched the sweat evaporate off my nose before it could drop. "Here is not where I come from. Here is Mali, and Mali is the Law. Give me radio."

"I'm sorry, I don't understand."

"You radio!"

"Yes."

"Give me."

"Yes. It is small."

His eyes bulged, despite drawn-down eyebrows, and he squeezed his Kalashnikov.

"Yes, my French is not so good." I nodded. "I don't understand."

"Small small stupid," Hawaii shouted, then switched to Bambara, or Hausa or Djerma or Bozo or any one of a dozen other tribal languages used here. He yanked me back to scorch and walked away. I repeated "*oui*," and nearly fell over, dizzy. *Oui* that I didn't understand; this time it was the truth. I went back to the van but the metal was too hot to touch now. I was sunstruck and Mr. Khaki walked up. He yelled at the old Tuareg who'd sat two seats from me in the van.

The Tuareg pulled out his radio and grudgingly gave it to Mr. Khaki.

"Why did you hide it from me?" Khaki yelled. "To insult my intelligence?"

The Tuareg didn't answer. Mr. Khaki hit him in the face, hard. The Tuareg staggered back, but didn't fall or otherwise react in any way. When Khaki left, the Tuareg's son walked over to check his father's face. His veil was down, and his face was lined and craggy, with a long hooked nose. And it really did have a dark bluish tinge, a stain from a lifetime of wearing cloth into which the indigo was pounded with a stone. *National Geographic* called them "the Blue People," and I liked that name. It fit better than *Tuareg* with why I'd come all the way here. Peggy had tried to turn me blue on our first date by putting cupric sulfate in my tea. She'd referred to them either as *Kel Tamasheq* or the Blue People, rather than *Tuareg*, which is the Bedouin word for "abandoned by God."

The punch had split the father's lip, but had done no real damage.

Peggy had told me a lot about them during my last month at Harvard, including that the indigo helped keep moisture in. I waited another hour in the sun, faintly wishing I were blue. The heat made me dumb and the machine guns took away my initiative.

Eventually I was called to Mr. Khaki. He sat behind a folded-out TV dinner table. "*Monsieur*, you have a radio."

"Yes, a little one."

"You have a passport."

I handed it to him, uncertain.

He flipped through it. "You are a Canadian."

"My passport is Canadian," I said, grateful that African borders didn't include computers. I liked Canada, but unfortunately, Canada didn't have much sway in Mali. "But when I am in Bamako, I stay at the French embassy. I am the land-surveyor sent for by my brother, the consular deputy."

Mr. Khaki flipped through my passport, without looking up. Finally, he asked, "So you have friends?"

It was his first sentence phrased as a question, so I stayed silent.

"What do you think of Mali?" he asked.

"I like it. Especially the people. And the weather."

"Where is your visa for Mali?"

"Is this a border?"

"It is a mobile border. We are the Mobile Customs Brigade."

He waved generally to the Jeep, and specifically to the heavy-caliber machine gun mounted on its bed. "You must have a visa for Mali, or," he hesitated, "or a visa for somewhere else, with an entry stamp."

I pointed at the open passport, at the entry stamp into Niger.

"OK. That's the proof I need by Law. You may enter. Now you must pay me one thousand francs, and I will stamp your passport."

"One thousand?" At 480 francs to the dollar, it wasn't much. But it was after being baked by these two in the sun all day. "Okay, I will pay you one thousand. But I will ask you for a favor."

"I am already doing you a favor."

"Yes, but you see, I have this argument with my brother, the consular deputy. And you can help me win this argument. I would be very grateful. My brother, the consular deputy, is a very stubborn man. He's family, of course, but he's very stubborn. Hard head, you understand?" I said, and knocked my own skull for emphasis.

Mr. Khaki smiled. "Yes, many Twobobs have hard heads. I know it."

"Yes, especially my brother. He always claims that such stamps," I said and pointed to his stamp and pad, "are free. I say they cost one thousand Central African francs. He does not believe me. He says they are free on arrival. Now I see that you also agree with me, against my brother. And you can prove me right. I will pay you the thousand francs, of course, because it is correct. And you can give me a receipt, and you can sign it to prove to him that it's real. And maybe put your military ID number there. I will show him this receipt, and then I will prove to him once and for all that I am right and he is wrong."

Khaki stared through me with pinpoint eyes, then smiled broadly. A friendly smile, eyes and everything, that didn't fit with the way he gripped his G3. He motioned with his finger for me to lean in closer. I wondered if he'd test how hard my head truly was. Instead, he nodded as though suddenly understanding me. "You are not from Mali. It is clear now. But I will explain you to Mali. Like a tourist guide, yes? Maybe you'll pay me extra for this information. The capital of Mali is Bamako. That is the truth. But Bamako is far away. Bamako is at the wrong end of Mali. We are here. At the correct end. And Mali is a very big country. In Bamako they are in charge, yes, but they cannot know things about the Mobile Customs Brigade. They are far. We are mobile, we must move. The Jeep drinks gas. Bamako does not know how much it drinks. We must buy the rubber stamps. Bamako does not know how much ink. Everything costs money, and Bamako does not know, you understand? Yes, I can see that you are a smart man. So while technically Bamako is correct, and your brother is correct, these stamps are free only technically. In reality, they cost one thousand francs. And as you can see," he pointed towards Hawaii, "we are in reality. You are, of course, free to go without this stamp. But at the next Mobile Customs Brigade, if they find you without it, they will send you back here. Where the sun is hot. And maybe there will be another Twobob, and I will have to spend hours talking to him so Mali understands him and he doesn't get hurt. And you'll have to wait in the sun until I finish. It is your choice."

Mr. Khaki leaned forward and put his elbows on the folding table, the two front legs sinking gradually into the soft sand as his voice took on a harder edge. "Just one more thing, and I will tell you this for free though you could pay me extra for the tourist information, and this you should not forget: your brother is in Bamako, and Bamako is not here."

I paid Mr. Khaki. He placed the left edge of the rubber stamp against an empty page of my passport, rolled it slowly to the right, then lifted it off with a sudden snap of his wrist. As he handed the passport back to me, he nodded gravely and said, "The loneliness of bureaucracy."

We shook hands warmly, filled with mutual understanding.

When we finally reboarded the van, it was night again and there was only one radio in the van. I handed it to Amadou. He grinned, but thankfully didn't turn it on. I was about to ask him to warn me the next time he hid things in my bag, but the young Tuareg beside me tapped me on the shoulder excitedly. "See that?" he asked, and pointed out the skeletal shell of a burned-out oil tanker we were passing. "I did that."

We made it to Gao in the late afternoon the next day.

CHAPTER 2

Pisuqtooq

From Verkhoyansk, Muzhduk took the northern route. It was a long walk through mazes of monotonous bogs, swarms of mosquitoes and blackflies, mirror-still lakes, a slippery pipeline slumping across a river, sudden blizzards, and months of lice. He crossed tilting Soviet towns built on permafrost, concrete apartment blocks sinking at odd angles, half-abandoned except for sporadic statues of Lenin that canted sideways as if explaining the crazy street lines, occasional Chukchi whalebone-roofed houses on crofts or forest-swaddled cabins, endless scrawls of lichen-covered rock, and even an Evenk riding a reindeer with a full bridle-and-saddle who mistook Muzhduk for a bear and almost shot him.

From the tip of Chukotka, Muzhduk floated on an iceberg across the fifty-mile Bering Strait that was only two miles wide because of winter, crossed Alaska, Yukon—where the permafrost houses were level and built on stilts—past giant lakes, the Canadian prairies, Manitoba, Ontario, and Montreal. He arrived at the border thirty miles south of the city late in the evening, on foot, less than a two-week walk from Boston and his goal.

There'd been no border along the Bering Strait or in the mountains between Alaska and Yukon, but here, far south and hot, heavy lights and highways gave everything a sharp edge without the humor of their toppling Soviet counterparts. The American border police had a computer, and the computer insisted on numbers: license plate, bus ticket, passport.

Muzhduk didn't have numbers, so he stood in the polite pose of a visitor—erect, motionless, and with his head tilted upwards to stare at the white bondstoned ceiling. The border police stood with legs spread wide and arms floating near guns and radios and handcuffs and flashlights and a belt full of black metal objects. They invited him into a small room, where they inspected him under fluorescent lamps while others typed into computers. A computer beeped, the police widened their stances, inhaled, and let their hands drift towards their belts. The season was late, the weather cold, and the probability of pedestrian border crossings at such a time was low. When the computer beeped again, the police thumbed their guns and looked as though they expected Muzhduk to charge past them, at which point they would make a tackle.

These were the Blues. A Blue with hair less than an inch long, a moustache, and a forward-jutting jaw searched Muzhduk and his two goatpacks: one held water, with just a touch of vodka, and the other was full of clothes. Other Blues moved in and out of the little room, swaggering around their belts, and looked over Muzhduk with expressions that said they were busy and uninterested and tense. When Muzhduk sat, they became less annoyed. They rotated, and a different person asked him the same questions—why did he have a bottle of reindeer pee, why was he walking, why was he dressed that way—until they had come full circle. They'd never before seen a man in a bearskin carrying two hollowed-out goats.

"He fits the profile," said the Blue with the jutting jaw to the fat one. "He's well outside the bell curve."

"Well, he's on our radar now," answered the fat one.

They discussed which file to put him in. They had a "generally suspicious" file and they could put him in that. And he had a beard, and there was a file for that. But his bearskin confused things, so they decided to talk to him.

Muzhduk explained that he needed to go to Harvard, and asked to meet with their chief, whose picture hung on their wall. The chief's name was W. The jut-jawed Blue—who from the side looked like an L—ignored everything Muzhduk said and asked for his visa.

"It's the Law," he said. "B, H(1)(b), J-1, F-1, TN, L, E." Or a green card, which he described as actually blue. He doubted that Muzhduk had a blue green card, he said, since he was wearing horsehide boots with upturned toes strapped to his legs with thongs.

"The burden of proof that you qualify is on you," the L-Blue said. "You have not met your burden of proof. The Immigration and Naturalization Services Act and the Patriot Act give me complete discretion to determine the eligibility of an applicant. I wish I could help you but I can't. It's outta my hands. It's the Law."

Outside the door, Muzhduk could hear someone yelling, "Move out the way, all you fine bitches. I got shit comin' through."

L-Blue flexed his jaw, then looked back at Muzhduk. He had a gun, and told Muzhduk to wait. The door stayed open and Muzhduk could hear music, a deep raspy voice singing: "*Woke up this morning with the cold water, with the cold water, with the cold. Well the po-lice at the station and they don't look friendly, well they don't look friendly, well they don't look friendly.*" The radio said that Tom waits.

Muzhduk waited too. After over a year of walking, there was a certain pleasure to waiting. *Maybe I'll wait a long time*, he thought.

Three hours later, the prognathous man came back in. "We are finished with you."

Muzhduk continued to wait, enjoying his new thought.

"You have to leave now, son, back to Canada, or you'll be deported."

Muzhduk told the man he wasn't his son, and walked out. He didn't have a Canadian identity to get back into that country either, but the nice lady at the border spoke French to him, so he replied in French, and the lady waved him through without asking for any documents. He walked the short distance to Montreal, to figure out a way to be accepted.

In Montreal, Muzhduk read books. In Siberia he had read every book his tribe owned, whole sheds filled with books stolen from Russian officers and gulag intellectuals and small town libraries to which some Central Committee had sent ten-thousand copies of the same treatise on economic history. Boronuk got all the blue tractors, Mooy-Bystybyt received only pool tables, while the absurdly cold town of Oymyakon received seventeen copies per resident of Wassily Leontief's Ph.D. thesis on circular-flow economics. One had to raid a few dozen town libraries in order to get any variety in reading material.

In Montreal the books were unlimited. One book told him he should have claimed he was a land surveyor. Other books taught him America was a land of boundaries, and each boundary had a series of tolls that had to be satisfied. The toll for law school was a test that didn't test strength or courage or wisdom. It tested game playing, and he could take a class that would teach him how to pass that test. *What's the point of a test*, he wondered, *if anyone can just pay to learn the answers?* But he was in a strange land, and knew it would take time to understand it.

He got a job with Cirque du Soleil catching cannon balls, because everything in Montreal cost money. For fun he joined the McGill rugby team. The game was similar to one he'd played in Verkhoyansk—an unmounted variant of buzkashi that his father had brought back from Afghanistan—except that in Canada they tossed a lopsided pigskin ball instead of captured Russians. He played well, and since the team had long ago been disowned by the university for being too drunk and naked, everyone assumed he was a student.

Through Cirque he met people from all over the world, including a Lebanese unicyclist who told him about a basement on Rue Berri where he could buy a Canadian passport for $3000. Through the rugby team he met girls who pulled him into a semblance of a life based on everyday events, helped him buy clothes that cut down the amount of staring, took him to the cinema, and left him, complaining that he bragged too much, either about the Dull-Boulder Throw, or later, his perfect LSAT score. Or they became annoyed with the way he walked because they couldn't keep up with his long, hulking strides, one saying it showed that he'd never spent any length of time walking on a flat surface.

Muzhduk paid for a class on the LSAT, but only went to the first lesson, which was about seven capital letters riding a roller coaster —A, B, C, D, E, F, and G.

"The first three cars have only one seat," the teacher read from the prep book. "Cars 4, 5, and 6 have two seats each." They read the rules together:

1. A, B, and C cannot ride in any of the last three cars.
2. G will not ride in a car immediately behind A.
3. B will not ride in the front car and will not ride in a car immediately in front of D.
4. E must ride in a car immediately behind D.
5. F and D ride in the same car.

In Verkhoyansk he'd laughed at the Yakuts and Evenks, the Chukchi and Koryaks, and all the other Siberian tribes that thought every mouse, rock, and leaf was a person with its own personality, that human shit was really an arrogant old braggart in an expensive brown jacket, quietly scared of getting eaten by a dog. But now he found himself wishing that the teacher would call the "A" Alice or anything other than just A. An A doesn't have an ass. But Alice was too much of a stretch for that classroom, so in his head he settled on Authority. Authority, Bureaucracy, Compromise, Deference, Equality, Frigidity, and Goodness.

"If C is seated in the second car," continued the teacher, "which of the following can be false? 1. F rides in the fifth car. 2. D rides in the fifth car. 3. E rides in the sixth car. 4. A rides in the first car. 5. G rides in the fourth car?" He started to draw letters and numbers on a blackboard.

Muzhduk mumbled, "What's good for the butterflies is bad for us. Goodness can be false."

The teacher looked up, distracted. "What *goodness*?"

Muzhduk ignored this. "The question is stupid, but the answer is #5, because it can be false."

The teacher thought for a second before answering. "Your answer happens to be correct, Mr. Ugli, but your methodology is faulty. Correct answers with faulty methodology suggest that you're guessing, or that you cheated somehow, and guessing or cheating on a practice test is not reasonable. Since the unreasonable action was yours, it means that you are being unreasonable. If you are not reasonable, you will never succeed in Logic Games. Now, if C is second and B cannot be first and A, B, and C cannot be in 4, 5, or 6, it must follow that—"

"Well, your methodology is ugly," Muzhduk growled. A girl off to the side in a floating white linen blouse asked him to please be quiet or leave. The teacher concurred, and so Muzhduk thought of glaciers, which have to be climbed early in the morning, before the sun thaws the snow too much.

Outside the classroom, Montreal was cold; it froze his eyelids together and left everything clear and solid again. He decided not to go to the prep class any more.

It didn't matter. Muzhduk scored a perfect 180 on the LSAT and was accepted into Harvard Law upon applying. He had spent almost a year in Montreal studying for the test, reading books, playing rugby, catching cannon balls, and learning about the culture from parties and other people's televisions. He now blended in perfectly.

But Muzhduk had a new problem. His LSAT score had guaranteed him admission into Harvard and full financial aid, but that morning he'd received word that the registrar would only send along his final admission package upon receipt of an undergraduate transcript. Which he didn't have. And he couldn't get a student visa without the admission package, and the Lebanese unicyclist's friends didn't sell student visas or Harvard admission packages.

That night he went to see *The Revolt of the Flesh* by Hijikata, a butoh performance at the Place des Arts. There was something soothing about seeing the Japanese mimes moving in slow, hyper-controlled movements, their ghost-white bodies like Arctic ice floes. After the show, he wandered the streets, frustrated that his mountain was turning into a maze.

The nights were beginning to lengthen. Walking from Siberia, he'd gone months without night and hadn't missed it. He liked the sun, circling the horizon in a crazy tilted orbit, tinting clouds with surreal purples, pinks, and crimsons. He missed gales that blew from all directions, but especially the north-west and south-west winds, who had once been in love but now screamed curses at each other as they passed, voices hard as axes, bringing rain, hail, and snow all at once—or arriving dry and cold, drier than any desert. He missed the polar bears that stretched out on the rocky ridges beneath glaciers before cooling off in the ocean, who floated with him on the ice floes, hunting for seals in breathing holes and savssats, making little snow-walls and covering their black nose with one white paw to better hide themselves from prey. Some people called them the great wanderers, *pisuqtooq*, and that was a name Muzhduk would have liked for himself.

He felt trapped in Montreal, claustrophobic on the poorly lit corner of St. Laurent and Maisonneuve, empty of people and cars, except for a parked Greyhound bus.

The Inuit had another word: *quinuituq*, deep patience. The great wanderers had patience, and Muzhduk missed the cold slow logic of the north. Arctic time, weather and solitude. But only during the daytime. When night began to alternate with day, everything changed. *Quinuituq* dissolved in his fingers. Everything became fast, clocks started to run, and suddenly it was the first weekend of September, one day before he was supposed to arrive at Harvard.

He considered walking across a forested part of the border, or swimming across Lake Champlain, but he'd seen the fences and guns and border patrol. He found himself staring at the Greyhound bus.

He checked the door on the Greyhound. Locked. Then walked around to the other side, pushed back the driver's window and pulled himself up. He sat in the driver's seat and heard a shout. The bus driver had been sleeping on the back seat. He reached the front before Muzhduk could open the door. Muzhduk hit him with a backhand, then bound and gagged the unconscious man, tied him to a tree behind a hedge, and stuffed two hundred dollars in his pocket in exchange for the keys. He had no idea what a bus driver made per trip, but two hundred seemed fair.

Muzhduk drove the bus—air brakes snorting, gears jumping—to the nearby bus station. As soon as he parked, a fat man began yelling at him. He had pulled into the Voyageur port instead of the Greyhound port. With some difficulty, he reversed the bus and parked in the right spot. A thin bored man came by to remind Muzhduk that his departure was scheduled for midnight, handing him papers and map, which he studied, waiting for the real driver to get loose and ruin everything.

Two hours later, Muzhduk helped the passengers load up.

At the American border, a female guard with hair like an 80s bank manager asked if he was new. Muzhduk nodded. Except for the goatpack with dangling testicles, he was dressed normally: jeans, a white shirt, a new pair of Kodiak work boots, and the too-small driver's jacket slung over one shoulder, as though he'd taken it off because of the heat. He had showered, his hair was cut, his blond beard trimmed.

The border guard said everyone had to go inside. Everyone

went, but that didn't seem to apply to the driver. Muzhduk waited by the bus, sweat beading on his sloped forehead as he imagined what it would be like to walk across the longest undefended border in the world, running past guard dogs, fences, lights, and men with guns, through forests and cornfields and highways.

After thirty minutes, the passengers re-boarded. Six hours later they were in Boston.

He stopped at a restaurant just after dawn, told the passengers the bus had a flat tire and asked them to go wait in the restaurant. "For safety," he said, trusting Fred the Political Officer's advice. They all went, single file and sleepy. Muzhduk put their luggage on the sidewalk, honked so they'd see their bags, and drove on to Cambridge.

In Cambridge, he got lost. Every road was a one-way and every post plastered with signs as convoluted as the LSAT, but more poorly drafted: No Parking on Tuesday, Thursday, and every third Sunday of months that have the letter "R" in their name, unless an avenue-abluter is scheduled to clean the street on a Wednesday. Signs everywhere, but no street names. He finally parked the bus under a mysterious sign that said "Blind Adult" and asked the first person he met for directions to Harvard Square. As he walked, he remembered Fred telling him about Egyptian hieroglyphs, where the square signifies achievement. Muzhduk couldn't think of a less inspiring shape, except that this square was balanced on one corner, and he had spent two and a half years trying to reach it.

It was smaller than he'd expected. And dirtier. And it was a triangle, filled with pierced teenagers painted harsh, unnatural colors, who were skateboarding, sitting, or sprawled out upon the stairs and banisters of a subway station entrance. Everything was covered with paper, garbage, wrappers, bottles, and cans. But looming above the triangle, the red and white façade of a Harvard building looked as it should, as he'd expected it to. He followed the red brick walls to a black iron fence and through a trellised gate. Months later, overhearing a group of tourists being guided around the campus, Muzhduk learned that the perimeter fence is named the Memorial Fence, and is considered one of Harvard's architectural marvels. He also learned that the gate is closed on 183 randomly chosen days per year in an ever-shifting game between Harvard and the Law to prevent a public right-of-way through the campus. By then he even knew that such a right-of-way is properly called an “easement.”

• • •

My legs were asleep as we climbed out of the cramped van into a bursting chaos of colors and people. Yellow, red, green, bright clothes, harlequin-patched *kente* cloth, turbans, and long flowing dresses, indigo-robed Tuareg men with white veils and thick turbans, the city a swarm of shifting color as a crowd of men squeezed in to ask if I needed a place to stay, a guide, a special travel assistant, a porter. There was even an official from the government with identification to prove that he was responsible for guiding all newly arrived whites in Gao. While pins and needles hobbled my movement, the men slapped curious urchins out of our way. *Monsieur, venez ici! Mister, I find you cheap-cheap. Kommen sie mit mir, Herr Twobob. Schones Hotel. Hotel Twobob. Señor, vamanos. Monsieur? Hello Mister? Boss? Twobob! Hotel Atlantide.* Yelling out different hotel names in various languages while elbowing each other.

Amadou had disappeared in the crowd. So had the Japanese mime.

I began to walk as though with purpose, at first in any direction, and then towards the center of the city. We had driven over a small hill just before arriving, and I’d seen a long town of brown-mud cubes, miles of flat-topped terraces that sprawled out from a curve in the Niger River, so I headed that way.

An enormous starfish-shaped red dune the size of the entire city towered over Gao upriver to the north. The government official with the identification to prove it followed me, metamorphosing in the late afternoon ambient heat from tourism official to porter, translator, attempted mugger, and finally back to tourism official, in several languages. “Vous parlez français?”

“No français.”

“English?”

“No English.”

“Deutsch. Ja, sie sind Deutschlander.”

“No Deutschlander.”

“Español, Italiano, pa Russki?”

I answered in Verkhoyansk Slovak.

Now the man became angry. "What's that? That's not a language, that's shit you're speaking. You make up language. You German. Only German Twobob makes up language." He spoke rapidly in what seemed like several different tribal languages, then switched back to French. "See?"

"See what?"

"You have words, but I have more words. You have power," he gestured to my arms, "but I have more power." As he said this, he drew his finger across his throat. "You careful in the dark, German Twobob who smuggles GPS radios. I slit your throat side to side. Give you second smile, *here*, under your chin. You don't talk shit language so slippery past the border when I cut your throat at night. You only make gurgle sound and smile with two smiles. With *two* smiles." Then he smiled to himself like Jack Nicholson from *The Shining*.

The threat felt rude, so I growled and he left.

I walked on—past block after block of identical brown mud houses, flat, featureless. Once I was alone the silence truly closed in and the city felt deserted and endless. My street seemed like the only street in the world.

After a while, dusty and yellowing palm trees appeared, lining the avenue with shade, and the city began to wake again. Throngs of people walked busily in one direction or the other, ignoring me after a long glance, fresh palm-branch-and-garbage fires burned in the middle of the street, and I could hear a drum in the distance. I wondered whether it was space or time that had changed: the part of the city, or the time of day and its unbearable heat. I knew that cities in the Sahara didn't fully come to life until well after sunset.

I passed the colonial pile that was the Hotel Atlantide, then continued along the chicken-wire fence that blocked off the river port's loading platform. There was a man with a cart full of mangoes so I walked over and bought one. As I watched him peel it for me, I heard someone singing. I couldn't make out the words, but recognized the voice and turned. "Amadou. What are you doing here?"

"I came in the same bush-taxi as you." He picked up four mangoes and began to juggle.

The mango man seemed unconcerned with Amadou's juggling until a little monkey jumped from Amadou's feet onto the cart.

Mango-man tried to slap it away. The monkey sat and hissed but didn't steal any mangoes.

"When did you get the monkey?" I asked.

"When? That is a strange question." The monkey picked up two mangoes and threw them in the air, as if to illustrate how stupid my question was. One fell into the cart, the other on the ground. Mango-man mumbled while he cubed and skewered, so I could eat the mango like a popsicle.

"You didn't have a monkey before."

"But Hanuman is a part of the family. I have family in Gao."

"I didn't know."

"Of course. There are many things you don't know. Why should you know everything? Sometimes I have lived here in Gao. And you, what do you do here?"

"Buying a mango," I said, and bit off a sweet sinewy yellow cube. The odd thought crossed my mind that the texture of mango was like love.

"Then we are the same."

"If you know Gao, maybe you can tell me where the Getaway Guesthouse is?"

"You stay at the Getaway?"

"I was thinking of it."

"Why the Getaway?" His expression didn't change, but something in his voice had.

"To get away. Do you know where it is?"

"Better that you do not stay there. It is run by a bad man. A French man. Better you stay with me."

"Thanks," I said. "I prefer the Getaway."

"Really, it is better that you stay with my family, here in Gao. This way, you will get the full tourist experience. Stay with a Malian family, eat Malian food. My family will feed you fufu and give you tea to drink. This will be better for you."

"Thanks. But I'm not so much a tourist."

"What are you, then, if you are not a tourist?"

"I am looking for someone."

"I knew it. A woman, yes? I can help you find this person." Seeing me hesitate, he added, "This is Africa, so you must tell me."

"Right now, just the Getaway."

"And other times?" Hanuman punctuated the questions with uncomfortable little jumps.

"Other times also the Getaway."

"Then I will show you. But you must tell me about this woman."

Hanuman led the way. We walked away from the wilting palm trees, past the police station and the Marché Washington, where a hundred tailors treadled away on hundred-year-old sewing machines, and on through the wide brown Gao avenues heading east. On either side rose mountains of garbage, some so tall they blocked out the houses behind. Goats sifted through the top, or simply looked down upon us speculatively like birds on tree branches. Aside from a clunking Peugeot taxi audible for a dozen blocks, and the occasional open sewer or animal carcass, there was no sound or stink, as though the oppressive heat clamped down on all the senses, leaving only unmoving air and the faint smell of flint again.

We left the wide avenues and meandered through winding alleys narrow enough to touch both scrobiculated walls at the same time, where the buildings reached two stories and the upper walls angled to within a foot of each other and the air took on a musty smell of dried mud and waste. I could make out an occasional human conversation or muffled barking dog. The sense of direction that had guided me across four continents and over the magnetic north pole, which could spin a compass like a gyroscope, quickly abandoned me in the narrow brown walls of mud.

There wasn't enough room for us to walk side by side, so I walked behind Amadou. I didn't trust him to walk behind me. There was something unnerving about the way he stared, the way he dug for information he already seemed to have. I'd have gone on alone, but my little map didn't include these winding alleys, just a blank area with squiggles—not a map for tourists or invading armies.

For all its complexity and convoluted logic, Harvard had been rational. Certain paths could be mapped out. Sure, there was some fuzziness at the edges, and Oedda had tried to make a philosophy out of alleys and curves, but even her postmodernist dismissal of logic was logical. There'd been nothing like this unmappable medina, nothing like the changing colors of the shifting sand, and no people like Amadou. The Verkhoyansk Slovak in me was annoyed with my own thoughts. Amadou had been nothing but friendly and helpful, but I didn't want to tell him anything about Peggy or why I was here. I didn't trust him, though I wasn't sure why.

When I didn't answer his question of why I was in Gao, he repeated that I should not stay at the Getaway, that I should instead stay at the home of his brother's wife's sister. Then, in the middle of one brown alley identical to all the other brown alleys, Amadou said, "Wait here," and walked through a narrow doorway. A studded door stood open, but my view was blocked by a thick purple cloth on which were embroidered eight swords, two vertical and six horizontal. The monkey ran after Amadou, and following its tail I caught a glimpse of a small, gloomy room.

After ten minutes, Amadou came out. "My brother's wife's sister says the Getaway has closed down, maybe. But you are lucky, you can stay here with her. They have made tea."

"It'll be dark soon."

"Yes. You are lucky. There is a curfew. The government shoots on sight after dark."

"I thought that was only outside the city limits. In Tuareg areas."

In Niamey and Tillabéri and every other Saharan city I'd been to, people slept through the middle of the day and didn't go out until well past dark.

"Yes, but the government decides the limits."

"I want to find the Getaway. Why did you take me here when I asked to go there?"

"Here is on the way to there. But there is closed."

The walls were too close and I couldn't tell where the sun was, though I knew it was setting.

"Just tell me which way is north. I'll go on my own."

CHAPTER 3

Before the Law (A Rebuttal)

Muzhduk walked to the center of the Quad. Everything was stately, Romanesque, the buildings buttressed, cloistered, but varied: three hundred years of red brick architecture around one long rectangle of green grass crisscrossed with narrow asphalt paths spotted with American Elms. Someone had sat and calculated the optimal location of each tree, though many were now suffering the yellow wilt of Dutch Elm fungus. The whole Yard felt carefully spaced and defined, even the sky above marked and divided by branches.

He walked north, past dormitories, libraries, halls, and chapels, past a statue of a man sitting in a large chair ("John Harvard, Founder, 1638"), past an old wooden water pump shaped like the hunched Russian babushkas he'd seen in Anadyr, Yakutsk, and Oymyakon. Sweating in the Boston heat of September, Muzhduk pumped and drank some water. A passing student in a pinstripe suit told him, with a perfectly modulated enunciation, that the water was not for drinking.

"I have been admitted."

"Congratulations," the student said over his shoulder without pausing.

Muzhduk pumped again, took a final mouthful, shook out his beard, and left the Quad by another iron gate on the north end. He continued past a boxy wall he decided must be the Science Centre, because it had a five-foot magnifying glass sticking out of it at eye-level, and rounded the corner to the Law School proper: more hectic, more organized, and more serious than Harvard Yard. It felt as though the barometric pressure had changed.

Campus maps told him that the registrar's office was in the basement of the Griswold building (he thought of it as Grizzwald, a forest of grizzlies, and smiled). He followed a path that curved into the ground. Landscapers were improving the path, adding decorative basalt pillar stones to the granite retaining wall as it sunk towards the half-basement black steel door of the registrar's office.

A gentle-looking, leathery old lady and old man sat at a collapsible metal table in front of the open door. Somebody's grandma and grandpa. Muzhduk approached and said, "Hello. I'm a new student. I would like to register."

"Please wait a moment," said Grandpa as he shuffled papers into a neat stack, licked his wide, flat thumb, and used it to move a bead on an abacus. Then he pointed out a small stool on which Muzhduk could sit. Grandpa's hands were enormous, out of proportion with his old crumpled body, and his fingers never ceased moving. Grandma was the same. Their eyes, however, remained nearly motionless, held low in their sockets by a watery gravity.

Muzhduk wondered how long they had been here, doing their duty. He sat, but after ten minutes stood again and approached. "Can I go in?"

"Not right now."

"Then how can I see the registrar?"

"You can wait, please."

He sat back down and waited. With nothing better to do, he could think loosely, and his mind wandered to the water pump that looked like a babushka again, and from babushkas to Oymyakon. He'd traveled the Road of Bones with his uncle to steal a Red baby, in order to pay a life-debt after his uncle killed a man from a different family in an argument over reindeer. His uncle had seen a pretty blonde whom he decided to steal instead, and the pretty blonde turned out to be a KGB colonel traveling with a full company of Internal Ministry soldiers. Soldiers were rare in Oymyakon, but they'd come to stop a small war after the Chief of Tomtor tried to take Oymyakon's "Pole of Cold," a monument marking it as the coldest town in the world. Because Muzhduk had been only twelve years old, his uncle had forced him to hide in a friendly babushka's bunker-like tobacco stand. He'd forced Muzhduk to promise he'd stay hidden, then fought the soldiers outside a Chinese restaurant. His uncle died in that fight while Muzhduk kept his promise.

A half-hour passed. Muzhduk patted his significant belly. He hadn't eaten, and it made a hollow sound.

Lazy grey turtle heads.

Muzhduk wasn't twelve anymore. "You said to wait a moment, right?"

The turtles looked up.

"A moment has passed. I have successfully waited it out."

"It is a figure of ex*press*ion," sloughed the old man, his spine curving even further, as though only his little belly held up his chest. Then he sighed, smacking his slow dry mouth several times. "Very well. It cannot be denied that a moment has indeed passed. What can we do for you?"

"I'm looking for—"

"What is your name?"

"Negro."

They peered back to the list on their table.

"Wait," Muzhduk interrupted. "I was just…it's from a book I read in Montreal about America. By Franz Kafka. You reminded me of—"

"When we have time to read," the old woman said, taking time for each word, "we use it to read the lists. As often as we have read the lists, they can never be read often enough. We recommend you do the same."

He'd talked to bureaucrats before, there were stacks of them all over Siberia's small towns, but these two were different. They had an almost philosophical quality. Maybe Harvard gave them special training. "My name is Muzhduk the Ugli the Fourth."

"Is that under U?" She looked up. Her eyes seemed unfocused. "As in Unattractive?"

"Yes. But ends in an *I*."

They looked at their list, carefully, and whispered back and forth. They nodded and shook their heads. Finally, the old woman said, "You're not here."

The old man moved the abacus bead back.

Muzhduk patted his belly again, but they ignored this evidence so he pulled his admission letter from his goatpack. "I have my letter. I had a perfect score."

"We don't examine outside documents."

"It's from you. From the Admissions Committee. The registrar."

"Outside the list."

"Then how do you know whether I'm supposed to be here or not?"

She looked at him like he was stupid. "We look at the list."

"But the list is wrong. See, I've been accepted." Muzhduk waved his paper.

The man pointed to his abacus. "Please return when you're on the list."

Muzhduk sat back on the stool. Lazy grey turtle heads. He stood up again. Battle and words and logic games. "What's this list for?"

"It's the long Longlist," answered the old woman, and reached into her purse. She took out a tomato pop-a-can soup and the old man pulled out two spoons from somewhere and suddenly they weren't interested in Muzhduk anymore.

When they finished their soup, the old lady sucked on her spoon, then held it two inches in front of her mouth and sighed, as if gathering strength. "This is the long Longlist," she repeated in the tone of the polite people who sometimes came to Muzhduk's door in Montreal with little pamphlets about Jesus. "And if you're not on this list, then you can't see the registrar. We are, after all, only the *first* list, the *long* Longlist. Beyond those doors," she nodded, "there are other tables, and more doors and tables, and on those tables other lists, each shorter than the one before. But of course we do not know this, not in any official capacity, because neither of us may enter. Our names are not even on the medium Longlist, let alone any of the Shortlists—if that is in fact what they are called. We extrapolate dangerously to even venture a guess. We have met *un*officially with *certain* inner-list proctors, by accident, but the further in you go, the more advanced and less accessible they are. By the third table, we can't make heads or tails of what they say, and trying to do so just makes it clear that we can at best be unclear as to what we actually know, or whether we ever knew anything at all."

She paused, out of breath. Then gestured weakly to the stool.

The old doorkeepers weren't your regular petty bureaucrats, but they also didn't have the thin black Tatar beards that he had expected from the guardians of the Law. He hadn't realized that's what he'd been expecting until now—Tatars, after Tartarus, the infernal abyss below Hell where Zeus had hurled the rebel Titans. The original Uglies, before the Great March East, had come from the Tatra Mountains in Slovakia. On the way east, Ugli the First had defeated the Tatar hordes. And before him his own father and grandfather and eight generations of Valibuk the Oak-Fellers had, at the very least, felled some oaks. Muzhduk the Ugli the Fourth was not about to prove himself less stubborn—even if these two were the Hinges of Hell themselves.

They cleaned their spoons with wet disposable serviettes from a box labeled "Wipies." When they put everything away, Muzhduk said, "Look, I don't want to sit on this stool like a little moon staring at manure while the world passes me by. I've read about this sort of thing."

He stomped the ground and tilted past their remonstrations, through the open door, under a sloping ceiling, into a hallway that was just a narrow corridor of metal doors arranged jamb-to-jamb on either side. He saw no one. No proctors, no tables, only another door at the end of the hallway. This one had an iron doorknob shaped like a bearded dwarf's head. Each strand of the beard was a tiny snake.

Muzhduk turned the head and pushed. The lightweight door swiftly banged into an inner wall.

He found an enormously fat man seated behind a large metal desk, smiling. The man wore a short-sleeved dress shirt, and the flab of his arms left two sweat stains, massive turkey-drumstick shadows, on the desk when he lifted them to shake Muzhduk's hand.

"Good morning, young sir," said the man, his droopy eyes settling on the testicles dangling from Muzhduk's goatpack. His own skin was covered in what looked like flakes of snow. The rest of the office was sparse. "What can we do for you?"

"I'd like an admission package, please."

"Excellent! Please send us a letter requesting an application for an admissions packet, care of the registrar's office, with your return address. Follow the instructions on the application and send the application to us. If you are admitted—"

"I did all that. I was admitted. But no package."

"Quite unlikely. Zero point one eight percent probability, in fact." Three chins jiggled. "What is your name?"

"Muzhduk the Ugli the Fourth."

"Oh!" The man scratched his neck, his tone changing in recognition. "The perfect LSAT score! I had a conversation about you just yesterday."

"You did?"

"Yes. With Professor Sclera, I'm sure you've heard of him." The registrar watched Muzhduk for a reaction.

"You haven't let me in yet. How could I know anybody?"

"Everybody's heard of Eugene Sclera. He's on Court TV all the time."

"I don't have a TV."

"Hmm. This is all so highly unusual. First time I've ever known Eugene to waive formality, all to try to get you in. If only you'd sent in a transcript. Any transcript. But you didn't, so you lost your spot. Quite a shame, really. So few perfects, these days. Two this year. Everywhere, imperfections abound. Like giant rabbits. Quite a shame. Next year I implore you to resubmit."

"My undergraduate school was studying rocks in Verkhoyansk, Siberia." When this didn't change his expression, he added, "I played rugby at McGill University."

"Rocks?"

"Yes, boulders. Geology. And metallurgy. My thesis was on how hard you needed to throw a rock of a given size to make it go through a given thickness of metal."

"McGill offered courses like that?"

"The Red Army."

"Oh good, military! Then they should have all the appropriate paperwork. Just have them send it to us."

"Why?"

"*Why?* Well, we can't just take your word for it, now can we?"

Muzhduk turned around, marched out of the room, through the doorway and corridor, past the list keepers, and back outside. He picked up a basalt boulder that the landscaping crew had just finished wiggling into position with the help of a small walk-behind backhoe, pushing past the renewed warnings of the old female proctor who insisted he should really return to the stool.

"Good morning, again, young sir," the registrar said, his eyes on the boulder. "What can we do for you now?"

"We can give me a test. Your table is made of aluminum alloy."

The registrar nodded encouragingly.

"The first question is what happens to an aluminum alloy table when smashed with—"

"Now wait just a minute!" the registrar interrupted, half rising from his seat, eyes wide. "As you were told, your admission was guaranteed by your LSAT score, so long as a certified undergraduate institution sends a transcript. We *need* to complete your file, even if the actual grades are irrelevant. Our ideal student, in fact, is one who has not been corrupted by unnecessary knowledge, has had no experience of any sort, but has a fully developed Logic Games faculty. So proving what you know about rocks and metals isn't going to help you."

Muzhduk didn't have a certified undergraduate institution. He was a man from the mountains looking for admittance to the Law. It was surprising enough that someone recognized his name. He stood before the registrar, slightly to the side, holding the boulder uncomfortably on one shoulder. If he wasn't going to smash the table, then he didn't want to risk scratching the floor either. "Logic," he finally said, "always comes to the same answer, regardless of who uses it. So students with perfect logic but zero experience are fungible."

"Fungible?"

The registrar repeated the word like it was a juicy plum, then shook his chins sadly. His voice softened as he turned introspective, letting Muzhduk know that seventeen years ago he had quit his job as Director of Test Design for the Department of City-Wide Administrative Services in New York, doing so *not* for the prestige of becoming the Harvard Registrar, nor for the salary, and certainly not because he wanted to move to Boston, but because the candidates here came closer to perfection than those taking the civil service exams he'd helped design. On the rare occasion he even got to meet a perfect score, perfectly distilled logic embodied within a human being, and it broke his heart that this year there were *two* students with perfect scores, and by a horrid act of fate, both would be denied.

"You cannot imagine how frustrating this is to me," he continued. "One perfect with an admissions packet issued but not attending, and one who wants to attend but has no admissions packet. It's terrible, unfair, depressing."

"So there's an extra admissions packet?"

"That's irrelevant. Different names, different files."

"Is the person coming or not?" This mountain was important, the six villages were counting on him, but theft was not honorable.

"No, it doesn't look like it."

"Then it's just paper. Change his name."

The Registrar's eyes widened. "*Her* name. And we cannot very well go and do *that*."

Muzhduk's heart skipped a beat. "Why not? Has Harvard has lost its power over names?"

"Of course not. But the file is the file."

Muzhduk frowned. "I do not believe there was another perfect score."

The registrar guffawed, then opened a filing cabinet and pulled out two manila envelopes. On the first page of each, in Second Coming font, was *LSAT 180*. "See?"

"I do see." Muzhduk rested the boulder awkwardly on a bent knee under his armpit. He picked up the papers within each file and placed each into the wrong folder. Instead of telling the registrar that in Verkhoyansk they avoided these sorts of problems by not writing important things down, he said, "You guarantee admission to a perfect score, which means that if the score is perfect, the relevance of experience is zero. And identity is only the sum of our experience. So two students with perfect scores are interchangeable."

The registrar was unsure. There were safeguards to prevent exactly this sort of vulnerability. The work was divided, parceled, and subdivided, and the registrar's job was to watch the movement of files from one door to the next. Only occasionally did he intervene to prevent an admissions proctor from accumulating too large a stack of files, which would elicit jealousy and grumbles from all the other proctors. When this happened, his job was just to lengthen the short stacks, shorten the long stacks, and smooth the ruffled feathers of any proctor who thought a file belonged to him. The registrar never opened these files, because they caused exhaustion and loss of faith. The proctors were bypassed only in the rare cases where the score was perfect, since no concerns about the registrar's continued health were necessary.

But Muzhduk's logic gave the registrar an opportunity to solve two problems at once: he could save at least one of the perfect scores, and he would appease Eugene. The registrar was still puzzled why the professor had walked down to Griswold personally to request that Muzhduk the Ugli the Fourth be sent a package despite his incomplete file. He had refused, of course, because he didn't play games with files, even if it meant standing up to Professor Eugene Sclera. But this was a perfect score, and every bit of him wanted to find a way to keep at least one. Eugene *was* on the Admissions Committee, and the single most powerful professor in the Law School, far more so than the dean—and this wasn't like asking for a nephew to be admitted despite substandard scores. This was a perfect.

"It *would* be such a waste." The registrar stared at the two open files. "And so rare."

"Fungible. A student with a perfect score is fungible."

The registrar flipped slowly through the papers. "The other score's mailing address is in Africa, so she'll probably never know what happened here. Though I imagine she'll be surprised when the State of Tennessee—that's her birth certificate—sends her a change-of-name confirmation." He sighed: "In one hour you can return to pick up Muzhduk the Ugli the Fourth's admissions packet."

After Muzhduk walked out the door, the registrar sat for a while, thinking. He picked up the phone and dialed Sclera's extension. To his relief, it went to voicemail. "Hi, Eugene, it's Robert in Griswold. Just calling to say that the student you'd asked about, the perfect. He's in. He's very, um, unusual. You mentioned you'd received a letter about him. You never told me what it said, but now, well, I have to admit I'm curious. Anyway, I'll put him in your section as you requested. Um, bye."

• • •

I walked in a random direction until I came upon a child. I offered him a coin.

He looked at it skeptically. "Women? Drugs? Whachya need, Dido get you whachya need."

"Getaway."

He shrugged, slipped the coin in his pocket and took my hand. His own was tiny but callused and stiff, and I felt awkward as he led me through narrow clustered alleys, turn after turn, past rows of women beating large, cracked, drumlike pots with pestles taller than themselves. Their shoulder sinews glistened in the small light playing off the cracked clay walls. The boy led me past walls and pots and burning oil barrels, maybe toward the evening part of town, as the women with pestles were replaced by half-naked ones, shoulder to shoulder, smiling, waving, and squeezing their breasts at me. The air was orange and turned the brown walls blood red.

"Hey, hey, where you going, Twobob, you come I do show you good-good time."

"You marry me, Twobob, and I be you good Twobob wifey. Every night good fuckee-suckee. Or one night, as you like it!"

The glare of a burning oil barrel blinded me. Suddenly a woman grabbed my elbow heavily and pulled, spinning me. I couldn't make out her features except for teeth reflecting the garbage fire. Another woman yanked me from the first and I twisted, tripped, lost my grip on the little boy, and was caught from falling into the barrel by yet another pair of hard female hands; female, so I couldn't fight, only push away as hands and arms and white teeth reflected the orange fire in the barrels, grabbed my crotch, unbuttoning my fly. The hands came from behind, from the sides, someone was on her knees in front of me and somehow I was in her mouth. I stumbled back, a voice shouting that I had to pay anyway. Dido's hands gripped me with his familiar tiny grip and pulled me back onto the street as I zipped up my pants.

"Do not go off the street, you do, end up all confused, Twobob. My sister better. I take you my sister."

"Just take me to the Getaway," I answered faintly.

"Good women, you like small, you like big, my sisters, better than those fire-barrel women there."

"Not today," I answered, still shaken.

He grumbled, pointed down the street for my destination, asked for a second coin. He walked away with a strut, his movements far too adult, and soon I was lost again. Though the sun had just set, the city was dark, unlike any darkness outside of Africa. There were no streetlights, no electricity, and I could no longer see the orange glow of burning barrels, the only lights in the city. Those weren't the colors I'd come here for and there were no signs on the streets here, nothing to tell you where to park or drive or where the Blind Adult was. The alleys were simply spaces between houses. Sometimes the houses connected, sometimes there was an alley. There were no clues about whether an alley would turn into a dead end—just the choice of the man who built his house further down the line.

I stopped and touched both cool walls, angry with myself. I had an urge to push the buildings apart, like Samson at the temple. Or pee on a clay wall to see if it would melt into warm liquid destruction. It never rained here. Instead, I sat and waited for the moon to rise.

Something hissed at me.

My eyes had adjusted enough to make out the form of a monkey. Amadou's monkey, though I couldn't be sure—I didn't know any other monkeys. "Hi, monkey."

Hanuman opened his lips to silently show clenched teeth. He raced away from me, then stopped. I stood and followed him. He looked over his shoulder periodically to make sure I was following.

• • •

Outside Grizzwald, Muzhduk returned the chunk of rock to its place, then wandered around the corner to a huge grey slab of a building, a granite version of arctic ice-islands that crushed anything floating in their path. Four-stories tall, rectangular, and long as a football field, it had been blocked from his view by buildings that were smaller but closer.

He could make out faint shadows in the wall, etched veins of darker grey where ivy had been ripped down and the walls scrubbed diligently. But centuries of sunlight had bleached the rock and so the ivy trace remained, like burned silhouettes in Hiroshima. Muzhduk followed the pattern with his fingers, losing perspective of the wall's height and breadth until he came to a single mushroom growing where the ivy had been strong and left behind a bit of earth for the mushroom to hang onto. The mushroom had taken on the color and spotting of the wall to make itself almost invisible. The wall had no cracks, unlike every modern building he'd ever seen in Siberia; no light, sound, or smell came through. It had no individual stones, just the fading spidery shadow of long-gone flora.

This was Langdell Law Library.

He banged a fist against the hard wall. "I insist."

Smiling, Muzhduk walked around the library and stopped in front of a tree, a beautiful oak with gnarled branches and roots that seemed to reach deep under the ground, deep and wide enough to hold up Langdell on one side and the Science Centre on the other. It was the first tree he'd seen here that hadn't felt planned, and it filled him with a sense of freedom, possibility, and nostalgia.

He pressed his palms against the tree, rubbed them against the pits of bark, wondering how his ancestors, the eight generations of Valibuk the Oak-Fellers, had knocked down such large trees. It seemed impossible.

Walking around, he spotted a little red door at the base of the trunk, hidden between two gently rounded ganglions of old roots. Above the door, in childish and wobbly block letters, a sign read, "POOH."

If he were a Koryak tribesman, he thought, this tree would definitely be a person, a woman jammed incongruously between the Law Library and the Science Center. He was tempted to open the little door—it barely reached the top of his boot—but he didn't want to find that there was nothing inside. He compromised and knocked.

"Th'hell you want?" someone yelled from inside the tree.

Muzhduk jumped back.

The door opened, and Pooh looked up at Muzhduk. He was a cross between a dwarf and a baby bear, with blue fur, standing on hind legs.

Muzhduk had drunk enough reindeer pee during long Siberian winters that a hallucination wasn't bothersome, though he didn't understand the mechanism here. And the mechanism was important. If you ate red-and-white *Amanita muscaria* mushrooms by themselves, you'd have visions, but you'd also die of toxic shock. If you dried them over the fireplace in a stocking and fed them to a reindeer, on the other hand, the pee that passed through had only the good bits and you could fly through the air until spring, if you wanted.

But he hadn't even had eggs this morning, let alone reindeer pee. And if he was going to have a hallucination, he was expecting a tree nymph, not a blue bear.

"So?" repeated the bear.

"You're not much of a dryad," Muzhduk said.

"This ain't much of a forest."

"What are you doing here?"

"I stay here."

"Aren't you a copyright violation?"

"I don't give legal advice," said Pooh, and slammed the door shut.

• • •

I followed the monkey for fifteen minutes before I lost track of him. Just as I was starting to feel completely lost again, I came upon a heavy, balding white man surrounded by dogs, closing a big iron gate. Unlike the pink, exposed dogs I'd seen so far in Africa, these were healthy, with fur. Inside the gates, I could hear a generator and see electric lights. "You're late," he said.

"I am?"

"I do not let people in after dark." He squinted at me. "Hurry and you can come in."

A small sign beside the gate read, "Claude's Getaway Guesthouse."

I walked into a courtyard with curved balustrades, partial mud walls with intricate filigree, complex patterns and coils, a picnic table and a variety of statues, all silhouetted and silvery in the weak light. There was no garbage anywhere, I noticed, and the place was big enough to fill a whole Gao block. The man introduced himself as Claude, and asked me whether I wanted a room or the roof. Both were cheap, so I said roof. It would be cooler.

• • •

The gatekeeper grandma had Muzhduk's admissions packet waiting for him. She checked again to ensure he was still Muzhduk the Ugli the Fourth, then told him that their lists had him listed in Ames building, in the Gropius Complex.

"That was fast."

"Yes," she answered with a genuine smile. "You're on the list." She handed him a map and pointed him in the right direction.

He followed the asphalt paths and flipped through the admissions packet. It included a photocopy of an official-looking State of Tennessee change of name form. The student he was replacing had been named Peggy Roundtree. Address: c/o Getaway Guesthouse, Gao, Mali, West Africa. Place of birth: Memphis, Tennessee.

He hadn't stolen her spot, he told himself. She wasn't coming anyway, though he wondered why not. He became distracted by all the squirrels running between trees and crossing the paths, and by his own thoughts of squirrel stew, squirrel dumplings, squirrel brains like soft hazelnuts. He'd skipped breakfast. The squirrels hurried past him toward a complex of monotonous yellow and grey buildings shaped like chicken coops, roughly assembled together—

Muzhduk stopped. After seeing the ivied undergraduate buildings in Harvard Yard, he assumed he'd be greeted by cobbled courts, gilded towers, heraldic beasts and shields, Gothic chapels, worn-out classical statues, gowns, absent-minded professors stumbling into students and each other, cathedral rooms looming above, dwarfing him and inspiring a feeling of existential inferiority. Instead, it was like many small towns throughout Siberia: a complex of faded-yellow, pre-stressed concrete buildings that formed a semicircle around a small field. In the middle of the field, slightly off center, an abstract statue of crisscrossed pipes reached for the sky. The only thing missing was a banner that read, "Glory to the Soviet People!"

In Montreal he had read about the architectural designs of Walter Gropius, subsuming all parts and details. He would be one of those parts now. This was his new home. It was ugly, but he was happy.

CHAPTER 4

Gropius

"Peggy Roundtree. American. Is she staying here?"

Claude caught the eye of the older of two white men playing chess at his picnic table, a thin bald man with bushy, Brezhnev eyebrows, anywhere between seventy and a hundred. Several Africans had also looked up when I said the name—a Tuareg, two Bambara, a Peul, and three Bella in black clothing marking them as slaves. I'd heard about the Bella before, had read that nearly a tenth of the population here was still enslaved. Africans stared at me all the time—this time the roles were reversed. Slavery had been used so often as a rhetorical device at Harvard that it felt odd to actually see them, not bound, not being beaten, simply wrapping up some tourist trinkets in a blanket, acting no different from anyone else in Gao. The trinkets included at least two curved Tuareg knives that I could see. I tried to imagine their life, their childhood, what sort of sad education they must have gone through in order not to use those knives, but it was all too far away. If they'd fight, I would help. But as it was, all I managed was a sense of wrongness, like I was staring at someone sick or in a state of shame.

"I must respect the privacy of my guests," Claude said.

"Peggy's my friend."

"If she comes, you'll know she's staying here."

"If shit were sweet, we'd be shitting in our coffee."

He lifted his arms defensively. "Relax. She stays here, but I don't know where she is at the moment. Now, do you eat fufu or chicken?"

"Which room?"

Claude pointed toward one of four short doors in a long rectangle that formed one side of his courtyard. "Fufu or chicken?"

I thought of wandering about town, asking random people for information—this works surprisingly well in African cities—but then Claude added that she might have gone into the desert. She often did, on day trips, he said, but when I asked which village, he shrugged a French shrug, all nose and lower lip.

After such a long trip, I could wait a few more hours. "Fufu?"

"Fufu," Claude repeated. "If you don't know it, you don't eat it. But you can try."

After tough chicken and greasy fries in every town on the way here, I was happy to try something different. I'd seen fufu once before, but hadn't tasted it. Claude brought out a cube of bone-white conglutination, slightly jiggly, like tough Jell-O, and placed it on the picnic table. I carved out a spoonful and bit in. As if there were something there. My teeth clanked on the metal of the spoon. It was like a fourth state of matter, with elements of air and milk, in the shape of a solid.

Claude smiled. "One is supposed to swallow it whole, like a pill. Biting is considered rude."

"What's it made of?"

"Bones, souls, the void." He laughed. "And a little bitter cassava."

He went to cook the chicken.

On the edge of the courtyard roof, I spotted the Japanese mime from the van. He sat holding his knees in his arms, looking out into space with a slow smile forming on his face. He still had a white towel on his head, but he'd removed the other towel from his nose and mouth. I wondered if crossing paths with him twice in one day was random.

• • •

Minivans lined the street outside Gropius, with mothers overseeing the transportation of microwaves, fridges, and couches. A lot of furniture was moving the wrong way, from the dormitory into the vans. "Why is everyone moving out?" Muzhduk asked a mother.

"Moving out?" the mother looked at him with a puzzled smile. "Oh, no, Lena isn't moving out. It's just that the rooms are so small. We didn't expect them to be so small." She picked her glossy fingernails.

Muzhduk watched as the scene repeated itself every thirty feet. Fathers, brothers, and boyfriends carried heavy objects, families huddled close, and a black man carried a Persian rug under his armpit, looking confused, searching for his van-mom-dad anchor. Muzhduk rubbed his shin, then took his shoe off and shook the sand out. He always got shin splints from standing on flat sidewalks. He imagined this was what his great-grandfather, Muzhduk the Ugli the First, must have felt as his tribe reached the river Lena.

The mother had called her daughter Lena. Maybe this was a good omen.

Or a bad one. His grandfather, Ugli the Second, had drowned in that river. People said that he had seen a beautiful woman on the other side. She waved and sang him a song about how much she missed him, which confused Muzhduk the Second, because he had never seen her before. But she sang and danced and undressed, and he threw off his clothes and swam across. The river was wide, and by the time he'd made it to the other side, she'd disappeared, leaving only her laughter echoing through the forest. People said she was one of those naked ladies of the forest who are beautiful from the front, but hollowed out from behind like an old tree trunk. Ugli the Second tried to swim back for his clothes and drowned along the way. That's what people said, anyway, though no one had actually seen it happen.

Muzhduk decided he needed a bicycle.

• • •

It took three hours for Claude to cook the chicken. There was no clock anywhere, but if the sun had set at six, then I guessed it was around nine—and the Guesthouse was just coming to life. While I waited, Claude introduced me to the two men playing chess at the picnic table, then began to work on a filigreed clay wall closing off his kitchen. It was too hot for that kind of work during the day. Beyond the kitchen I could make out a little café, five or six tables low to the ground and surrounded by pillows, all empty. Everybody sat outside in the courtyard, which had dissipated the daytime heat faster than the café. The older man with the eyebrows was named Mr. Rogers, French, and the other was Jean-Carlos, from Italy.

"Padania," Jean-Carlos corrected. "But I live in Libya until Padania is its own again." He said he was writing a book about Claude and Mr. Rogers.

"Are they that interesting?"

By way of answer, Jean-Carlos' mouth curved down, almost a smirk.

"And the mime on the roof? Is he interesting?"

"What mime?" Claude asked, mortaring toward an old wall that had a washed-out Air France poster of the *Tour Eiffel* on it, advertising the wonders of Paris circa 1974.

How many mimes could there be wandering the Sahara? I pointed. "The Japanese."

"Oh, he's retarded."

"So you know him?"

Claude gently pulled a metal cast off the clay, adding a new foot-square panel to the partition. "Don't trust Arabs or Africans. Not when you build a wall like this." He ran his fingers through the filigree. "You must do it yourself."

Jean-Carlos knocked down his king, and there was a loud clanging at the door, which set off a barrage of barking from Claude's dogs. It turned out to be Amadou and his monkey.

"I thought you didn't let anyone in after dark," I said, because the idea still made no sense to me.

"But this is Amadou," Claude said. "Hanuman's Amadou."

"You all know each other?"

"Everyone knows," Amadou said, as he walked in. "I told you the Getaway was run by a bad man, didn't I? A bad French man who helps the Bella." But he was grinning, and hopping foot to foot. "Do you want to know also? I will tell you everything. Jean-Carlos is a terrorist who cannot go back to Europe. Claude is addicted to girl-children, so he doesn't want to. He is a bad man, but does good things sometimes. Not so often, but sometimes. And Mr. Rogers here, he is the distributor of Corpa-Cola for Western Sahara and the Sahel region."

"Pah," Rogers said without looking up. "I do not *drink* it."

"The king of Africa?" I asked, making a joke out of our

Corpa-Cola conversation in Ansongo.

"Yes," Amadou said, still smiling. "He's here because he thinks the French still own it."

"Not true. I am here for the same reason every white man has ever come to Africa."

"To make money and fund civil wars?" Amadou asked.

"The whites have always come to Africa to be tied by no rules, because at home they have created too many."

Jean-Carlos pushed the chessboard between us. "Join the game."

He moved his white king's pawn out two steps. He didn't seem at all disturbed at the fact that Amadou had just called him a terrorist. Claude also didn't seem concerned. Either Amadou was lying, or these three white men felt absolutely secure in their positions here. And now that I thought about it, they seemed to be missing even that soft sourceless layer of fear underlying all of North America like suburban background radiation. There was none of the Harvard caution with words or a hyper-vigilance with regards to reputation. They threw their words at will, as though they weighed nothing. And they caught them just as effortlessly. "Claude, how about some tea."

Rogers looked up as though this was the first thing said that really interested him. "Tuareg."

I ignored the chessboard and asked Amadou, "So do you know my friend Peggy?"

"She is also a terrorist, no?" Amadou answered, grinning at me.

"What?"

"I'll make the tea," he said, still smiling. On the ground under the Air France poster was a hot plate and an Arabian Nights metal teapot, thin, tall, and blue. He turned the plate on, filled the pot and began rinsing three glasses, all without taking his eyes off me. I knew from my bush-taxi rides that Africans find impatience hilarious. So I waited.

Amadou finally said, "I knew her even before."

"Why didn't you tell me?" I didn't like the coincidence.

"I asked why you came to Gao. Everyone has a reason for here. This isn't Timbuktu. But you are now playing the game, so you should move your piece." He pointed at the board.

"What do you mean she's a terrorist? Where is she?" He kept pointing. I really wasn't very good at patience anymore. After Harvard, it was hard to consider it a virtue. "Hurry the fuck up" would have been a better virtue. But I bit my tongue and moved the black king's pawn out.

Water started boiling and drops sparged out of the teapot's long, curved spout. Squatting, Amadou filled a glass and dumped it back into the teapot. He did this three times and waited for the water to boil again. Claude had stopped mortaring and watched, together with Rogers. I moved chess pieces to avoid being hilarious. Eventually Amadou said, "She was here before, and then she left. Then she came back."

I put 10,000 CFA on the table. He smiled as he took the two steps to the table. "She's my friend, so this is the same as nothing." But he took the money, dividing the ten notes into a half-dozen different pockets and hiding places on his body. "She first came two, three years ago. To paint the desert, which is very strange already. Don't you think so?"

The water was boiling again. Amadou filled a shot glass with sugar, then poured hot water into it, stretching his arm to lift the teapot as far from the glass as he could. Then he dumped the sugared tea back into the teapot, filled the glass with sugar again, poured high again, and again flicked the full jigger back into the teapot. He repeated this process over and over. "I took her to the places she liked, dunes of different colors, lava, cave paintings, things that tourists like. With the Tuareg Wars, it's important to have a guide. They do not like strange travelers from a distance. They think it changes people's character and makes them steal, behave badly. The Hausa and everyone, they just found it strange that she traveled without a man, but the Tuaregs don't care about that so much as the distance. And the worst for them is people who travel without a reason. It was lucky for her that I explained she was traveling to paint. They've seen tourists offer money for the old cave paintings they chipped off, and so thought she was here to paint her own, to sell at home. She learned Tamasheq. I helped her but she's smart." He tapped his head twice with an index finger. "And sometimes when we stopped at wells, the Tuareg women complained about how they were poisoned with a chemical—"

"Dieldrin," I said. Peggy had told me about the locust-control program that had poured a half-million liters of Dieldrin into local water sources. I knew the rest of her pre-Harvard story: she'd come to Africa to paint, but had been pulled into the tragedy of aid agencies that tried to help and ended by poisoning people. It was the irony that hooked her, I think, as she had no family link or honor-bond obligating her to care.

She'd come to paint, found a dirty well, and tried to clean it like another painter might clean her studio before starting. But unlike a dirty studio, her problems didn't have walls or edges. She'd convinced some NGO to dig an entirely new well. But the new well was also poisoned—because the aquifer was poisoned. They'd had to fill it back in with rocks. The locals removed the rocks as soon as the agency left, because cancer kills slower than thirst. The result of that particular well was that the Mali government banned toxicology kits, and aid agencies stopped digging for fear of foreign lawyers claiming they were creating poison wells.

The wells gradually turned Peggy from artist to activist, a voice of the Blue People who lived in the High Sahara. But she'd picked a difficult people. The twelve Tuareg tribes were nomads who didn't recognize Niger, Mali, Algeria, Mauritania, Libya, or Chad—only the Tibesti Mountains, the Atlas Mountains, the Aïr Mountains and Ténéré Desert, the Niger River and the Atlantic Ocean. Not that different from the river Lena and the Verkhoyansk Range, except instead of one attorney in a helicopter it was an endless tide of farmers and vegetable eaters with countries who took over the rivers, put up fences and armies, and blocked off the clean water holes and the fertile land. Of course, the Blue People fought back, declaring war on the governments. The nomads knew the deserts, they were better fighters and the governments submitted—by making a deal with the ten small Tuareg tribes—then used these to fight the two larger tribes. This new war had no end, and the type of help that western governments and NGOs offered was schools, churches, farming, and fences. Government stuff. Sedentarist stuff.

We weren't nomads, of course, not since the Great March East. We didn't move our villages and houses and fields, and I didn't see the world in terms of sedentarist vs nomad, the way the Tuaregs did. But there wasn't a single fence in Verkhoyansk, let alone a school or a church. Not yet. And all the things Peggy described as international help sounded just as much a threat to us as it was to the Tuaregs. I worried that whatever would follow John the Attorney to Verkhoyansk, whether it be farmers or soldiers or butterfly lovers, what Peggy had described happening here was the future of my own people.

Eventually, she had decided grassroots activism was hopeless in a country with no grass, one that still had "slave tribes" and where giving someone a voice usually meant shooting someone else. She decided to get a degree in international environmental law, to try helping from the top down. But her passport had been stolen, she had never received her admissions packet, and by the time she made it to Cambridge her name had been changed to Muzhduk the Ugli.

I wondered how different my year at Harvard would have been if I'd gotten to know her in September rather than in the cold April rain with a head stuffed full of rational discourse. My entire childhood I'd been taught that my grandfather, Ugli the Second, had been a fool to swim across the river for the sake of a woman. Or a song. But maybe there's a timing to these things. Maybe nobody else had heard the song because only he'd been ready. Maybe he'd only died because he'd tried to swim back for his clothes. Or maybe the whole story had been made up to give meaning to a meaningless death.

Meanwhile, Amadou had poured the tea thirty times, each time adding a jigger full of sugar.

• • •

Muzhduk found his room, #324. It had a tiny closet, a single bed, a foot of space, and a writing desk. He opened the closet to see if there was another room hidden behind it. There wasn't. Bookshelves ran along the walls and above the tiny windows. Muzhduk stared at the white walls for a while—his palimpsest for a year—then nailed his new bicycle to the wall, upside down. It fit the Gropius "form follows function" motif. Its handlebars stuck out awkwardly and the pedals, gears and brakes gave the room a jagged, disjointed feel. He felt small. He had to, otherwise he wouldn't fit either.

He needed to buy some books. He decided they would make the room bigger. Also, the bed was too short; his feet dangled from the end. He tried to nap, but even in his tossing and turning he had to be careful—in his sleep he dreamt he had cut the top off the mattress and sewed it onto the bottom. It made the bed longer, but then the handlebars of his bike kept hitting him in the head, over and over, until he realized someone was knocking on the door.

It was his next-door neighbor saying "hello" with a Hong Kong British accent. He looked a little like a Chukchi tribesman, which was a happy thought. Muzhduk had liked all the Chukchi he'd met in Siberia. "Hello," he said, still blinking himself awake as they exchanged names.

"Since I've seen your room now, would you care to see mine?"

Muzhduk walked over and peered around the door jamb, into Clive's open room. It was military clean, with tucked-in sheets. Muzhduk said, "Smallish."

Clive frowned—the rooms were the same size. He was actually much softer and paler than the Chukchi. He wasn't fat, but everything about him looked soft, except his eyes. Those were in constant motion. He picked up a thin book on his desk and asked, "Have you been studying?"

"Studying what?"

"The facebook," Clive said and flipped its pages. "It was in the admissions packet. The photos and biographies of all incoming students. There is the orientation boat cruise tonight. It wouldn't do to forget somebody's name."

"No." After a pause, Muzhduk went on. "But you're right about names helping. To orient. Like when I was looking for Harvard Square, I just said the name and people pointed me to it."

Clive stared at Muzhduk.

"Clive," Muzhduk said. "Is that from the Latin *clivus*, meaning hill?"

"It has several meanings, including to cleave or parse, as one does to a legal argument."

"Or to climb. It's a funny name."

"You are Muzhduk the Ugli, correct?" Clive recovered, and smiled in relief that Muzhduk had overextended himself. "Your picture is not in the facebook."

"I was late. I barely made it."

"Oh." Clive wondered why anyone would admit such a thing. "From the waiting list?"

Muzhduk shook his head. "I didn't wait. Well, not long, anyway."

"Of course." Clive nodded. He couldn't tell whether Muzhduk

was a fool or a jerk, toying with him and his obvious nervousness about initial contact with his fellow Harvardites. He'd said nothing improper, he was sure of it, and yet this large man was clearly not responding in kind, had even laughed offensively at his name. Maybe even made a surreptitious ethnic slur with the "orient" thing. And he looked as though he smelled. Clive had always thought that big people were stupid, and he reminded himself that he had to be careful not to be caught off guard by his own prejudice. This was Harvard, after all. *First you are like a maiden, so the enemy opens his door.*

"You know, the facebook thing, it's just casual," Clive finally added, screwing up his facial muscles to mirror the expressions of Muzhduk. He found this difficult, his own face was so different from Muzhduk's bearded mug, but it was important that he understand his neighbor. "Flipping through, seeing what kinds of faces there are to see. You know."

"I know," Muzhduk answered, because it looked like Clive was expecting a response. "But I'm not sure whether we know the same thing."

And Clive didn't know where to go from there. The conversation fizzled out, although neither stopped staring at the other. Finally, Clive took a deep breath, lifted his eyebrows, and as he exhaled smiled, tilted his head, and said, "O-kay."

• • •

"Yes, Dieldrin," Amadou nodded, and finally brought Rogers, Jean-Carlos, and me a jigger of dark orange Tuareg tea. It was so strong I shuddered. "The Dieldrin made her upset and so she went back to America. A few weeks ago she came back. And now you're here."

"Where is she now?"

Amadou shrugged. Jean-Carlos and Rogers took shallow sips of their tea in silence. I did the same—it wasn't too hot, but too bitter to gulp—wondering how many meadows of mint it took to beat out thirty ounces of sugar. And how Amadou had fit it all into the little Ali Baba teapot.

"All very boring," Rogers said suddenly. "Westerner does bad with good intentions. This is the day-to-day of Africa. There are only two things that are interesting about this woman."

"Oh, and what are they?" I asked coldly, resisting the urge to argue about what she had "done bad."

"Amadou told you already, but you did not listen."

"What, that she's a terrorist? That's nonsense."

"The government decides who is a terrorist, no? Nonsense or no, what does it matter? If you don't want to be a terrorist, change the government."

Jean Carlos interrupted, "It is not the time to talk about women."

Rogers mouth and lips went down and he let out a small pout of air. In Montreal, I'd once heard an Anglo refer to this very French expression as a face fart. But then he shrugged and turned back to me. "Tell me, what is your opinion on Tuareg tea?"

"Bitter."

Jean-Carlos nodded. "Bitter as life."

Amadou collected our empty jiggers. "The first glass is bitter as life. The second is mild as death. And the third is sweet as love. Or some people say that the first is for the power of a wild animal, the second for the reason of man, and the third for the sweetness of woman." He began to repeat the tea-making process. His movements were slow but efficient, except for the overdramatic high-pour.

"So are lies life or reason? Because you lied to me, Amadou," I said, trying to turn the topic. "If you knew Peggy, then you also knew who I was in the bush-taxi. That's why you kept staring at me."

Jean-Carlos moved his queen. "That is why the first glass is bitter. When Amadou lies, it is by squeezing truths together, like mint and sugar."

"What does that mean?"

"You are a very large white man in Africa," Amadou laughed. "To look is normal."

"And what is your opinion on the Blue People?" Rogers asked. It was clearly his decision where the conversation in this courtyard went. "What do you think of Ibrahim, here?" He nodded at the lone Tuareg in the Getaway. Ibrahim wore a darker shade of indigo than the Tuaregs I'd seen, and his veil of the same color was loose, showing most of his face. He was young, wiry, and blue. Like many Tuaregs, he had an almost Roman nose. His eyes were a pale hazelnut, shiny and intense, and right now he seemed to be staring right through me.

"I want to finish this first." I pointed at Amadou. "Tell me about Peggy."

"Each pot makes three glasses," Claude said, his voice vaguely threatening. "All three must be drunk. And each person must drink from the three pots. The correct order is inevitable, because they are all made with the same leaves."

"So what?"

"So you're jumping ahead."

CHAPTER 5

Orientation

The boat pushed off from Boston harbor to the rhythm of engines and low-volume dance music. The walls were covered with Cowboy Art, setting suns, broad mountain landscapes. There was no moon, the electric lights were too bright, and no students danced. They rotated around the bar in two lines, picking up plastic cups and transparent beer while contorting their faces to mirror those of the students in front and behind. Muzhduk understood that people here were different from his little group of Slovaks in Siberia, but this boat-full of students was by far the most alien he'd ever met. He had the impression that people's body parts weren't fitting, as though they'd been re-assembled too many times. The line took a half-step forward, and the person behind Muzhduk said, "Hi, my name is Charles."

"I'm Muzhduk the Ugli."

"Moosh-duke?"

"Muzhduk the Ugli the Fourth."

"Muzhduk the—? Where did you go to school, Muzhduk?"

"This is my first time."

"I'm sorry, the music is loud. This is your first time doing what?"

"Being schooled."

Charles' pale eyebrows climbed his pink forehead. Then he laughed. "Yes, we all feel that way, I guess. It's the first day of the rest of our lives. The first day that matters, right?"

"I think this morning was important," Muzhduk said, thinking of the registrar and how close he'd come to failing his quest. "But not this afternoon. And definitely not this evening."

Charles watched Muzhduk, then looked away, put his hands in his pockets and shifted his weight. He looked up, as though he were in an elevator. The thin woman behind him was in the middle of a conversation, so he persevered. "By this morning, you mean, I take it, metaphorically, the, um, effort required to get here. So which school *did* you go to?"

"I have never been to school. I wouldn't lie to you about it."

"And the Admissions Committee didn't mind?"

"I lied to them." Seeing Charles' expression, he added, "They're a collective, an institution, not a person. A collective is a lie, so it's okay to lie to them. I said I went to McGill."

"McGill?" Charles seemed relieved. "That's a good school, I hear."

This time Muzhduk recognized what he was supposed to say: "And you?"

"Oh, Princeton." Charles nodded.

"Is that a good school?"

"Oh well, you know, it depends on what you're studying. What did you do at McGill?"

"Rugby."

"Oh, a sports scholarship. I didn't think we offered those."

"You know how it is."

"Yes." But Charles didn't know how it was. He always wore a helmet.

Or maybe I don't know how it is? Muzhduk thought. "I told the registrar I studied rocks. And you?"

"Oh, political science, with a minor in economics." Charles rubbed his lower lip. "Tell me, I've heard that McGill's economics program is quite fragmented, but that they have some strong names. I am particularly interested in the work of Professor Charles Taylor. You must have heard of him, even if you studied other things."

"You mean the mercenary running Liberia?"

"No, no, no. The political economist slash political philosopher," Charles continued, earnest and relieved, flooding his sentences with words like *legitimacy*, *democracy*, and *development*—but nothing about himself or his family or moments from which he'd gained honor, nothing Muzhduk could draw a picture of in his mind. He could follow Charles' sentences if they were a Logic Game, but this was a party.

"Do you feel like something's been smeared on our eyes?" Muzhduk interrupted.

Charles looked around again, starting to resent Muzhduk for wasting his time.

They arrived at the front of the line, where they were handed Budweisers. Muzhduk drank his, but it was not good beer. Charles moved away quickly, walked up to someone at random, and affably introduced himself. Everyone was interested in everyone, like a clothed version of a Verkhoyansk mid-summer's eve party.

Muzhduk stared at his beer. He imagined the party waiting for him when he returned to Verkhoyansk. After the broken step and the plum brandy and the women, everyone would gather to hear the stories of Mount Harvard. They'd expect to hear about the whimpering of smashed enemies, the roundness of conquered bosoms, and the blistering battle that came after endless years of eyelash-freezing and beard-cracking ice. So far it hadn't exactly been that way.

Maybe he was wrong, maybe this evening was important. *Maybe this is not really a party.* Maybe these people didn't differentiate between competition and celebration, and mixed the fight and the climb—though those who mix objective and subjective become cross-eyed. *It's a competition to make allies, a sneaky start to the blistering battle. It's a competition and I'm losing, because my words are alienating the people around me. And here it's all about words.*

The idea of *allies* made him uneasy. People should fight for themselves, their family, friends, and tribe, not dishonor themselves into groups. But he'd killed enough Russians to know they often fought alongside men they'd never met before they joined the Red Army. And this was the mountain he'd accepted. *Since this is Harvard, these people must be smart; if smart then interesting; therefore my words are alienating interesting people; interesting people like interesting things; ergo what I'm saying must not be interesting.* It was a Logic Game.

He understood the problem, now he'd find a solution. He stood alone in the middle of the room and listened to the conversations around him:

"...yes, Yale was *worthwhile* but I wanted to experience some variety, and I was tired of New Haven..."

"...and we had this fascinating case where we sued the military, you must have read about it in the papers, about the female Marine cadet who..."

"...do you think majoring in English constitutes a credible preparation for law school?"

"...Hi, my name is Charles..."

"...I really liked the Reading Comprehension and Logical Reasoning portions of the LSATs, but the unpredictability of the Logic Games makes them ill-suited for standardized..."

"...living in New Haven, surrounded by projects and what *some* people label 'slums' was very good for giving one a *real* picture of the suffering and inequality, and thus the democratic legitimacy-gap, in our system. Despite the *poverty* and *crime* the people there really do have a sense of *community*. It is very good for the spoiled Ivy League kids to see how some people..."

"...I like Cambridge, my father teaches here and I became familiar with the quality of professors, so I didn't see any reason to attend a law school elsewhere..."

"...but as a statement regarding the role of women we still felt that we had accomplished a significant if belated..."

Between everyone else, these conversations flowed smoothly. Smooth and flat as the pickle on a hamburger the one time he'd tried the famous McDonald's. Though the talkers talked about poverty, justice, suffering, family, the listeners had no way to discriminate between what had been drawn from a mountain swamp with a struggle and what was just market gossip.

He decided to introspect. It was okay, this was his mountain and it was necessary. To understand these people he had to understand the distance between himself and them. *What do I find interesting?* he asked himself. The answer was easy: *Battle and bosoms, like anyone. They're here, but like the man who hides turnips under the wheel.*

Enough. He turned to a pretty brunette in a black dress that showed off her sinewy shoulders and tight, perky breasts. "Hi, my name is Muzhduk the Ugli." It was time to flirt. "Back home, I won the Dull-Boulder Throw."

"Hi, Muzhduk. That's an interesting name. My name is Elizabeth Silverstein."

No, that was clumsy. They think it's bragging even if it's true. Talk about the girl, be funny and use the correct sentences. "Do you come here often?"

"What?"

"I'm joking. Where are you from?"

"Oh, Iowa."

"Is that the place with potatoes?"

"I guess. Maybe you're thinking of Idaho." She smiled weakly.

"But you're not from Idaho. I can tell you're not from Idaho."

She stared up at him, uncomfortable.

He didn't want that. "So where did you go to college?"

"Duke." She was not asking the obligatory "and you," he noticed.

"What did you study?"

"General humanities."

"So, then, what do you think of humanity?"

"It was a good preparation for law school, I think." Elizabeth Silverstein looked off into the crowd, searching. The conversation was broken. Maybe he should have gone with something physical after all—clapping her ass or dancing. It was so much easier in Verkhoyansk, where he just had to defeat other men to get the women, or find a nice meadow where they were already lying in convenient positions. He hesitated, annoyed with his own clumsiness. "I'm sorry we talked. We both know it was an accident."

"What? No, no. I'm just...I see a friend over there. It was very nice to meet you, Muzhduk. I hope we see each other around campus." And she ran off.

"Hi, my name is David," someone beside him said, a short guy who shifted his head sideways but without tilting it, as though it were sliding off his shoulders.

"Muzhduk the Ugli. I'm a clumsy mountain man from Siberia. I see that you're short, shifty, and prematurely balding."

David turned away, as though he hadn't heard. The other conversations continued pleasantly around him, the same words on his left, right, in front, behind, and probably on the decks above and below as well, hundreds of conversations until there wasn't enough air. He wondered whether there was an outdoor deck. Why were they all crammed inside, tight and overlapping, with all the windows shut? *McGill. Rugby. Yes, I'm on a sports scholarship. No, Harvard doesn't give sports scholarships*. The air made him dizzy. Professor Charles Taylor?

"Is your name also Charles?" The same questions, though a different face. *I'm the only one who hasn't read the facebook. I robbed myself.*

"No, not me. Professor Charles Taylor. I hear that he's good."

The pressure in Muzhduk's ears was off balance, his own voice sounded strange to him, and his blood pumped harder on one side than the other. He held his nose and tried to pop his ears out. Not-Charles looked at him wide-eyed, as if he thought this was Muzhduk's response to his question and he didn't quite understand.

Voices flew around the boat like five hundred north-west and south-west winds, but controlled, burrowing little slivers of raw meat under the skin that would later bring ulcers and sores. The sounds clumped together to make syllables, words, sentences, slogans, political statements, arguments to die for. No doctor would be able to convince them not to bunch up, the way you had to talk to kidney stones and tell them to spread out into small pieces so you could pee them out.

Mouths circled, yielded and deflected, but the ears were as tough as the sounds and soon the conversations changed. People began to dispense with Charles Taylor and injustice and environmental law. Personal details slowed them down, others were meeting more: name, place of origin, school, degree, and move on, next—don't monopolize my time, don't make me feel rude by hanging on to the conversation. They made friends in four to six questions. More than six was rude, less than four and the other person wouldn't remember.

But Muzhduk was a fast learner, slowed only by his own stubbornness, and within hours he could answer correctly his name, section number, and which professor he had for Civil Procedure. And an occasional sesquipedalian word that wound its way up off the vibrating floor.

Something's wrong, Muzhduk thought, but wasn't sure what it was, until he realized he wasn't breathing. *Inhale, count to five, exhale.* Here and there someone still tagged on an adjective, a description, but it was always the same, efficient flourish. Too many people to think of new words for each. The boat had found its harmony, as someone beside him talked about eliminating transactions costs and another repeated that New Haven was still great for opening one's eyes to others' ears, no, to inequality, fairness, administrability, and justice in the individual case. *My ears are not ambiguous, they are my ears, give them back. You cannot have them, but something's wrong again! What is it? Same thing as last time. What was it? Breathe! Inhale. Exhale. Slower. Don't forget, breathing is important.*

The nose. That's what he would go by. The nose knows. It can smell fresh air. He sniffed. It was an effort to think, almost unbearable in the face of the squirming words and chemicals—deodorant, antiperspirant, Osco waterless antiseptic soap, artificial perfumes subtly applied. Smells are never funny or sad. Smells are about survival. A drop of moisture fell off the tip of his nose, sweat dribbled down from his sloping forehead through thick brows and into his eyes. *Think! Reason. Ratio. At least in Montreal people played rugby and broke their noses. Anybody who has played rugby has had a broken nose and nobody who's played rugby would steal my nose. They tape them back against their head—we did. If nose, then no ears. It was this sort of logical deduction that got me here, to this party without body odor. Ridiculous, how can I forget to breathe?*

Muzhduk searched the milling crowd of swaying people holding pale beer that never waned in two-thirds-full glasses. They shifted continuously. A dust cloud of Law Students, wall to wall, shifting and increasingly interconnected by an accumulating quantity of words.

There was one. A black man drinking the same pale beer—there was no choice—but with a crooked nose. A broken nose, he'd seen him before: the man with the Persian rug and no van outside Gropius. Muzhduk pushed his way purposefully towards the man, moving like a 300-pound Siberian icebreaker, smashing conversations as he stumbled forward.

"Hi, my name is Buck," the man said, unsurprised, when Muzhduk reached him.

"You've had your nose broken, haven't you?" Muzhduk asked.

"Where—" he began.

"I went to McGill," Muzhduk preemptively answered with his little lie.

"What?"

"Me too, look." Muzhduk pointed in an exaggerated manner to his own massive, awkward nose, pinching the kink in the middle. Then he pointed to Buck's, accidentally touching it in his enthusiasm. "Your nose was broken too, right?"

There was a long pause while the boat danced and the people

talked. Muzhduk wasn't sure whether Buck didn't answer the question because he thought Muzhduk was kidding, or in a fit of offence at his touching his nose, or whether he merely said, "No."

• • •

"I don't have an opinion on the Blue People," I repeated. "I came here to find my friend."

"Your friend speaks Tamasheq," Claude said. "And she knows that there is a war here."

"What does that mean? That I should care through her?"

"A war means life or death." Claude pointed at Amadou, who handed me a new jigger full of tea, as well as one each for Jean-Carlos and Rogers. This was the second cup, death, and it did taste milder than the first, despite Amadou's repeated pouring. I drank it quickly, knowing I wouldn't get any answers about Peggy until I reached the third glass, and Amadou wouldn't even start making it until the other two had finished sipping theirs.

Meanwhile Jean-Carlos was pointing at me to move my chess piece. Too many things were going on, and the two jiggers of tea were making me dizzy. The mime had come down from the balustrade to join the rest of the Africans in the courtyard all gathered around a game I didn't want to be playing, yelling advice to us both. They leaned over our table, gesticulated and calculated, their advice based on the point values of the pieces. Jean-Carlos preferred to move pawns and knights. I stared at Jean-Carlos' half-full glass, then moved a bishop to threaten his queen: "En garde."

The audience exploded. Everyone spoke at once. Ibrahim took a step closer, almost menacingly. Amadou grinned. Men pounded the picnic table from all sides, until the chess pieces danced. Claude said, "You only need to warn if you are threatening the king, not the queen."

"I prefer to give fair warning."

"You are a difficult person." The crowd, listening tightly, repeated *difficult* in unison. Many shook their heads, some slapped their knees. "There, in the night, you were the outsider, here you have been welcomed in. Now it is your choice."

"'En garde' is just a courtesy. It's polite chess. So you win by skill, not luck."

"Your stubbornness is a strange one," Claude said. More knees were slapped, as *strange one* echoed through the crowd. "You say 'en garde' for the queen, in America?"

"I come from Verkhoyansk, and there we say it."

"But that makes you lose the game," said Claude.

"The pawn wants nobility," Jean-Carlos sneered.

"Only a woman has a chance," Amadou said with a grin.

Claude pointed at the chess board. "There is no polite chess. Not for a man. You are black, or you are white. You choose a side and then you have no more choices."

"I've had enough black and white," I said. "Or even shades of grey."

"Ah," Rogers smiled. "Another tourist here for the red and yellow of the desert and the blue of the Blue People. Your friend also came here for colors but learned that she had to choose a side. This is one lesson of the first two cups."

"So then let's start the third." I said this calmly, but then slammed the picnic table so hard that my king fell over. Everyone insisted this meant I forfeited the game.

Jean-Carlos finished his jigger. Amadou collected all three, and started the process for the third time. Ibrahim and Rogers talked in a low voice to each other. I bit my tongue.

Amadou brought the third cup of tea. Sweet as love. Somebody else's love: like drinking *baklava*. The thirty new jiggers of sugar were too much now for the thrice-used mint.

"Okay." I put the glass down. "You said Peggy chose a side."

"You're not drinking."

"It's too sweet." But I took a sip. "This is the time to speak about women, right?"

"Yes," Ibrahim said suddenly, with another hostile look, almost like a rival. "A woman can change. But she was a great help to us in the past, and will be again, so we would not allow her any harm. She went to a Kel Adagh *eghiwan*, a camp in the highlands with many sick children. She will be back tonight." Claude stepped into his kitchen for a few seconds, then came back out with a beer for himself. Jean-Carlos and Rogers were sipping their tea, and the others didn't seem to count. "Now, it's your turn. What is it you want with her?"

"She's my friend."

"And? What will you do with her? Take her back to America?"

"That's up to her."

Rogers looked up from his tea. "For now, I think, intention is more interesting than will."

"My intentions for Peggy?"

Claude answered for him: "Yes."

"That's not your business."

"Anything to do with Peggy Roundtree is our business."

"How's that?"

"You should have paid attention during the first two glasses. Now you've made it clear your business is not our business, and ours is not yours."

"It is too late for that," Rogers cut in. "He is already in."

Claude nodded. "You helped Amadou get his radio across, and for that we are grateful enough to forgive certain other things. You can stay because you are Peggy's friend, but maybe you should eat your chicken and go to sleep." He waved and one of the Bella brought a leg of chicken and some greasy fries. Everything became uncomfortable, but it didn't matter. As long as I didn't lose my temper, I would see Peggy tonight.

I bit into the chicken and my teeth bounced off. I tried again, and my hand slid off. I grabbed the drumstick with both hands, placed the meat of the thigh firmly into my mouth, and bit again. This time, the leg couldn't escape, but I still couldn't bite through. I bit down hard and pulled on the leg with all my strength. Everyone around the table stared at me as I pulled, unable to rip off a chunk. I grabbed the thigh with my left hand and the drumstick with my right and twisted. After one full turn I could hear the bone crack inside, but the meat wouldn't give. It stretched with each turn, more bones cracked, and finally after seven full turns the meat ripped. Now I had two pieces, but couldn't bite a chunk off either. "What is this, Claude?"

"It's a chicken."

"What do you mean by chicken?"

"A chicken. What does that mean, 'what do I mean by chicken?' It's a chicken."

"Is it a stewing chicken? A boiling chicken? A fryer, a capon, a stag, a hen, a fowl? An old rooster? Is it cooked?"

"This is Africa. A chicken is a chicken."

I went to bed hungry and knowing little more than I had before the self-important tea riddles. I wanted to wait in Peggy's room, to make sure that we wouldn't miss each other, but didn't want to feel like a stalker. She'd have no idea I was in Africa, and might be with somebody. I had no claims on her by any objective measure, we'd only known each other a short time at the very end of my year at Harvard, and as far as she knew I'd just disappeared. But I changed from the roof to the room next to hers, so I'd hear when she came in. It was a square of adobe mud, with a window, a tatami mat placed on a two-foot-high mud ledge raised along one wall, and a tough, grimy pillow at one end. There was no furniture, no blanket, nothing else. The room sweltered without the breeze that had made the roof bearable.

I lay down on the mat and listened. And waited. It was uncanny how Rogers seemed to see through me. He was right, this giant Africa detour was as much about understanding how she could see the color in a word as it was about Peggy herself. I needed him to be right so that I could justify this as part of my crazy Verkhoyansk quest. But at the moment I had a hard time thinking about anything other than seeing her again.

For the next few hours I eavesdropped on the muffled voices of Rogers, Claude, and Jean-Carlos talking on the other side of the mud wall. I hoped they'd say something that would give me a clue as to where Peggy was, why they called her a terrorist, whether she was in trouble. At the very least, I hoped to learn something about the Tuareg Wars and the positions of the tribes, governments, and various ex-pats. Instead, the first topic of conversation was the Geography of God, followed by the Watering of Meaning, Interaction between Nouns and Verbs, and finally Whether Genius Is Still Possible. As the evening wore on, Rogers talked more and the rest talked less, until only he was talking. About the Flatters Expedition, and how absurd it was that Niger, Mali, and Algeria had ever become countries, how much better off they'd been under the French, but if anyone deserved to be independent it was the Blue People, who had at least put up a good fight. These nomads had stymied the French army for fifty years, while the great city of Gao fell to ten Frenchmen in a day.

Rogers then moved on to rationality and its relationship to the golden mean, the most beautiful number in the world, a line divided such that the ratio of the small part to the large part equals the ratio of the large part to the whole. This is the ratio of nature, the spiral of a hurricane, the grooves in a pineapple, the perfect tones on a stringed instrument and of every line in a pentagram. The length relative to the width of each full cycle of a DNA molecule's double helix is golden, as is the depth divided by the width of a woman's uterus when she is most fertile. The British Inns of Court had revived the fascination with the golden mean from the Pythagorean Brotherhood of over two thousand years earlier, Rogers said, and Hippasus of Metapontum was killed for betraying the Brotherhood by revealing that the number, roughly 1.618, was irrational. It could not be expressed as a ratio of any two whole numbers. "The universe is rational," Rogers' voice punched through the mud wall and the glassless window, "although it is built of irrationality. As below, so above. That is the principle of the pentagram, the pineapple, and the revolutionary. Positions shift, people change sides, but the ratio endures."

The hypnotizing drone reminded me of Professor Sclera and his Procedure. I closed my eyes. Time after time I jerked back awake, thinking I heard Peggy, but no, there weren't any sounds coming from her room. Why was she out so late in the desert, with a shoot-on-sight curfew beyond the city limits? She'll come when she comes, and I waited, listening as Rogers' quiet, constant, self-satisfied voice lulled me to sleep, talking nonsense. It was easier to wait with closed eyes. When she comes, I dreamt, she'll know I'm here and knock, smiling. I should have a blanket, so she can slide under the blanket with me. My stomach rumbled.

• • •

Morning. Muzhduk stood up. He'd been dreaming of Fred the Political Officer's story about the capsule hotels in Japan, where your body touches all six walls at the same time. Muzhduk opened the window. "Grr," he said, stretching, then took two fingers of vodka.

He walked through the narrow hallway towards the toilet. Halfway down, someone in track pants, a dress shirt, and glasses stopped and stared at him, lowered his eyes to the carpet, then ran back into the bathroom. The carpet was somewhere between beige, grey, and yellow. Muzhduk couldn't hear himself walking.

The bathroom was all mirrors and sinks and urinals, with

showers in another room behind the urinals. It was all male, no women on this floor. At the porcelain sinks, men brushed and groomed themselves like women. More chemical deodorant, more cologne, slightly aggressive in a subdued way, reminding Muzhduk of frogs that change gender when the gender ratio is off. "Morning," Muzhduk said to the two people he recognized: Clive and Buck. There were tiles everywhere.

Everybody looked at him through the mirrors, and stopped brushing their teeth. Clive slowly spat out his toothpaste, looked at the seven other students in the bathroom, only then at Muzhduk directly. Finally, he said, "You didn't walk down the hall that way, did you?"

"Yes." Then he asked, "You mean naked?" His morning erection was long gone.

"Umm-Yah," Clive answered, using an intonation that was exactly similar to one used by a character on a popular TV show. It added a matter-of-fact propriety and humor that softened any appearance of overreaction; it focused attention on Muzhduk's transgression, not Clive's attack. But Muzhduk didn't watch television. He turned toward the urinal.

Several of the students in the bathroom chuckled, but still didn't look at him directly.

"Well?" Clive pushed.

"Well, what?"

"Why did you walk down the hall naked?"

"Because there's carpet on the ground."

"That makes no sense."

"It's not cold. There's no reason for clothes." He looked around, starting to realize that he'd missed something. "Why are you all staring through the mirrors?"

No one answered or moved, but Clive's glare was magnified by all the eyes looking down or away. "Nobody's staring at you," he said, using each word carefully, conscious that it was the first day of the rest of his life, soon with a diploma that proved it, a Harvard class ring—more people owned yachts than Harvard rings—a clerkship in a Federal Court, maybe even the Supreme Court, then associate at Cravath, Swaine & Moore, partner within seven years, then politics maybe, a judgeship, then maybe a governorship, the Senate…at the very worst he would retire stinking rich to some island. He hadn't chosen where yet. But he had an opportunity to take a leadership role here. Five of the nine Supreme Court Justices are Harvard graduates; in forty years it could be any one of these seven teethbrushers. Reputation begins with one quality, a quality which would set him apart and get others talking about him in a way that didn't make him look like he was seeking attention. The story that would come out of this morning would be about the big naked man named Ugli, but attached to it, almost as an afterthought, seven future powerbrokers would remember Clive as a decisive man on whom they could count to uphold the rules. David to Muzhduk's Goliath. Some doubt remained, because nobody admitted to Harvard could really be this dense, and there was a risk that Muzhduk was playing dumb to put him off his guard—*masquerading as a swine to catch a tiger*, as the Chinese say. Possible, but unlikely. Based on descriptions, Goliath himself had suffered from acromegaly, with significant visual impairment that made him see double. David had killed a lumbering, mentally handicapped, half-blind giant using the contemporary equivalent of a gun in a swordfight, and yet it was David who went down in history as the hero. So long as the opponent is monstrous enough, nobody would remember the details.

The seven other people in the bathroom clearly felt as Clive did; Muzhduk had even addressed them as a group. There was an objective wrong being committed here, and thus an opportunity. What is unseen counts for nothing—Clive knew and made up his mind. It was time to be David.

"Nobody really wants to see your naked…ness," Clive said. "Perhaps you are trying to make a point of reputation for yourself, or are simply looking for attention, but we would all appreciate if you would dress yourself."

"You've discussed this?" Muzhduk asked.

Buck, standing by one of the sinks, flinched and looked up. Tension clearly made him uncomfortable. "The possibility that the *casus belli* here is rooted in a cultural dissimilitude ought to be maintained in the realm of, um, possibilities."

He got no response and looked back down.

"Consideration is universal," declared Clive.

"I've always walked—"

Clive cut him off with a wave. "That's more information than we want to know."

"Why is that?" He could easily crush Clive's bones, but Clive was too small, smaller even than women in Verkhoyansk. A fight with anything other than words would be dishonorable. Muzhduk didn't want to fight at all—this was supposed to be the objective eye, not the subjective, competitive one. "Would you be more comfortable if I only talk about my name, undergraduate, and who's my professor for Civil Procedure? If nothing ever touches anyone, nothing reaches past their undergarments?"

"You can reach in past your own 'undergarments' whenever you like in the privacy of your own room. Just place a small sign on the door warning that 'you are now entering the State of Nature,' a separate jurisdiction just for Mr. Ugli. In your room, with proper notice, you may engage in any auto-erotic activities you like. But don't involve us in it. All we're asking for is a little consideration for the people around you."

"That's just a way of saying 'don't touch me.'"

"Well?" Clive snickered. "Is that too much to ask of a naked man?"

"How does it harm you?" Clothes were for weather, or battle, or to not make furniture sweaty. And nobody, no matter how shallow, went to the toilet with his clothes on.

"We don't want to see it."

"Maybe I should get breast implants then."

"What?"

"If it's all about your viewing pleasure, then some breasts would be nice, no? What if I were fat or deformed and you didn't want to see *that*? Would you demand I go on a diet, get surgery? Or you could just look the other way?"

No one answered. Finally, after waiting the appropriate length of time, and using an optimized intonation, Clive said, "What are you talking about—breast implants?"

Muzhduk saw the carpet-gazer peeking out from the shower room, and this time it was Muzhduk who looked away in embarrassment. He had lost. He wasn't sure how, but it was clear from the reaction of everyone in the room that he'd lost. "*Fas est et ab hoste doceri*," he said, and walked out of the bathroom. It's right to be taught even by the enemy.

I should be happy about losing, he told himself in the hallway. Clive was the type of opponent he could learn from. He dug in his goatpack for his towel, but the goat seemed longer than usual; the towel was at the very end, far down. As he wrapped his body, he grew annoyed with himself. Words he could have thrown back at Clive came to him one after another, too late. *This is my home for the next three years. I'm not a guest, having to observe someone else's etiquette.* But how had Clive convinced the seven others in the room to take his side? And how had he left Muzhduk speechless, without an answer and willing to wrap himself in a towel like some twelve-year-old girl leaking for the first time?

This is why I came here.

When he arrived back in the bathroom, Clive and the carpet-gazer were gone. The rest still looked at him sideways, but he could no longer trust whether he was imagining it or not. He finally peed, then sat on the shower bench and waited for a stall. All four were full, but only two were running water. He hoped a shower would wash away the poor start.

Finally, one of the shower curtains moved, and a fully clothed short guy walked out—black dress pants and a pinstriped button-down shirt. It was the sarcastic guy from the water pump, Pinstripe Bob. *He kept me waiting while he dressed,* thought Muzhduk, *with a shortage of stalls.*

Pinstripe Bob looked down as Muzhduk hung his towel and walked into the shower. When Muzhduk pulled the curtain shut, Pinstripe shouted from the other side, "I thought you had consented to not be naked."

"I'm in the shower!"

"You should change *inside* the shower."

Muzhduk stuck his head out, startling Pinstripe Bob. "Are you excited?"

Pinstripe disappeared around the corner. His voice didn't come back, but Muzhduk heard Buck laugh, and he could hear other voices in the main part of the bathroom. Everyone had heard the exchange, they would see that he was not completely wordless.

• • •

In my dream I could remember my father saying to me, "If you want to eat well, stick to one woman." I walked into our home at the high end of the village, near the stream, and could smell the roast Peggy had cooked almost ready in the oven. She included vegetables with the meat. To most people that wasn't a good thing, but I'd grown to like vegetables as a small side dish, and I liked her cooking.

While I was peeking into the stove, she came into the room from the back door. She looked beautiful as she threw off her bearskin coat. Underneath, she was wearing her American purple sundress that flowed around her, light and airy and always on the verge of revealing, her breasts swollen with milk for our six-month-old son. She'd always had a great behind, and with the swollen breasts she looked almost unreal, a cartoon rendering of a barbarian mountain goddess. She said, "That's not for you."

"It smells good."

"Too bad. I slept with Gorzol last night, so it's for him."

"What?"

"You were off with someone else, so I did the same—"

"It's not the same!"

"Why not?"

"It's worse to get shit on the inside of your boot than on the outside!"

"—and this dinner is for Gorzol. Go get fed by whoever you fucked last night. Barbora, wasn't it?"

"I brought you flowers."

"It's your culture, not mine."

I put the yellow clover-flowers on the table and walked out the door, down along the stream path with its stunted willows, to Barbora's house. I didn't want to go to her house, I wanted to be with Peggy. I only went to Barbora when the baby was screaming and I needed a little break. I knocked on the door. "Open the door, Barbie!"

Barbora stuck her head out the window, her small, round face peeking through the little amaryllis garden she had growing on her windowsill. "Hi."

"Can I come in? Peggy won't feed me."

Barbora scrunched up her nose. "I would, but I've got someone else in here now." Then in a whisper, she added, "I'd rather it were you, but I can't change now. People would talk."

It wouldn't be honorable. She'd chosen her partner for the night. "That's okay."

"Maybe Hana?" Barbora offered, helpfully. "She really liked you before."

"Thanks. Have fun." I didn't mind *her* getting shit in her boot.

I walked away from the stream, through a field, to Hana's house. Hana opened the door, but turned angry as soon as she saw me. "What happened to that American wife that you're so worried about all the time?"

"I hate frozen reindeer heads."

"You should've thought of that earlier." She slammed the door.

I'd hardly slept with anyone else since bringing Peggy here, and in the process offended most of my female friends. Barbora was the exception. Always happy and light and didn't bear a grudge.

I walked back across the field, past the schoolhouse, the beer vats, and the barley silos, to the bachelor house. Except that it wasn't really for bachelors, it was for men who couldn't stay anywhere for the night. The men built the family houses, but once they chose a wife, the wife ran it, and if they left and someone took their place, well, then this was where the pathetic ones ended. Tomorrow the whole village would mock the five of us who slept here tonight; there are more women than men among the six villages (the men tend to die), so it's mock-worthy to end up with no place to sleep. But it happened to everyone at some point, so we all donated reindeer heads and occasional upkeep to the bachelor house.

We pulled a frozen reindeer head from the cold cellar, skinned it, and ate the cold meat around the jaw and face, then the ears, eyes, and brain. While the other four "bachelors" complained about their women, or gave each other advice, I lay down in one of the straw beds and imagined Peggy sleeping with Gorzol the Tree-Trunk.

She was unhappy here, after coming with me all the way to Verkhoyansk. *Maybe we should really only have sex with each other*, I thought as I drifted into sleep, *and if any man says we're acting like old people, I'll crack him. We tried it half-and-half, and it didn't work, and all the way my way would make her leave. So we'll try it her way*, I thought in my sleep, and heard Peggy banging on the door of the longhouse, her and all the other women I'd ever slept with, not just Hana and Barbora and Oedda and Lena, but all the women I'd come across in meadows and after parties and through life. They were banging so hard they seemed to be knocking the walls down. Peggy was screaming.

I jumped awake, and instead of a straw bed in an longhouse covered with animal skins, tusks, and antlers, I was in an empty mud room in Gao, and Peggy was screaming next door.

• • •

Breakfast before orientation: six coffees and six chocolate-chip muffins. There was no swan stuffed by permission of the king, nor widgeon, roast ox tongues, or any of the other flatulent fare Muzhduk had read about. Decadence at Harvard stopped at the chocolate chip muffin, but he was nevertheless happy and hummed a song about a chocolate Jesus. He could've had a doughnut, but those were for cops. So he drank coffee, stronger than any caffeine since Verkhoyansk, ate muffins, and read a case in his admissions packet about someone infringing upon Johnny Carson's trademark expression by selling toilets named "Here's Johnny." It said there was an important policy issue of whether taking a standard expression out of the cultural lexicon impoverishes society or gives incentives to greater linguistic innovation. An analysis of the case was due at orientation.

At the table next to Muzhduk, Clive calculated Markov chains, 8x8 matrices, eigenvalues, Leontief input-output models, regressions and second derivatives, calculating the expected amount of mental activity that would be required of him on the first day, plus an error term.

"It's a hobby of mine, playing with numbers," Clive said when Muzhduk stared.

Muzhduk was surprised that Clive was talking to him. He said, "Wassily."

"What's silly?"

"Wassily Leontief's input-output." Muzhduk pointed at Clive's page. "Your puzzles."

"They're not puzzles." Clive used math puzzles as though they were real. He smiled coldly and stared back at Muzhduk's own homework, clearly annoyed that Muzhduk was doing it at the last minute. Muzhduk was annoyed that the coffee had no brandy. The word "coffee" meant "wine of the bean." It should be drunk with alcohol.

• • •

I jumped off my bed-ledge, disoriented between sleep and dream, and saw dust floating through the window on flickering lights. Outside, dozens of torches passed by. People shouted, it sounded like hundreds, and I opened the door in time to see an earless dog fly over the Getaway gate. It landed dead in the courtyard and lay there in a quiet, eye-of-the-storm moment. A few seconds later, a mob of Bella came streaming in from the street.

Claude stood on the picnic table in the flowing white robes of a desert djellaba, and waved his arms. The Bella yelled, "Le Diable Blanc," and left an empty circle around him. The Japanese mime stood on the stairs—his white towels reflecting the flickering torches. The wind slammed my door shut behind me and blew gusts of dust-sand into my eyes and teeth.

A few Bella stood around Peggy's door. Three Tuareg men came out of her room, almost invisible in their indigo robes and veils.

Then Peggy, in her purple sundress. A fourth Tuareg had his hand on her mouth, too strong for her, though she was struggling.

I ran toward her, yelling her name. The surprise at seeing a screaming naked white man charging got me halfway through the mob. Then a stick smashed down on my left shoulder and someone grabbed my hair. I pulled him along, then another, and another, until I was dragging ten people. Fists came from everywhere, and more sticks. They made dull thuds on my head and shoulders. Peggy saw me as she was being pulled away, looking surprised and worried. Someone jumped on my head as I charged forward. I couldn't see anything, and the man on my head punched the side of my nose. It broke with a small explosion of white. I grabbed his ear and pulled as hard as I could. He screamed and I could see again. His ear was dangling half off.

Three Tuaregs had guns pointed at me. I saw red, swung people left and right trying to get to her, bent spines backwards, ripped arms out of their sockets, stomped kneecaps, growled, shouted, but there were always more, and now the Tuaregs and Peggy were slipping away. I saw the mime beside me in flashes, moving inhumanly slow, like a bag of water suspended on a string; with lead weights for feet and fists, he attacked my attackers. He knew where the people would be seconds before they arrived. I had the urge to slam my fists into him—it made no sense, fighting together should make us friends, but the urge to hit the mime was nearly overwhelming. There were twenty Bella on the ground and a hundred more coming and I'd lost Peggy.

• • •

Orientation was a disaster. Muzhduk was the last to enter and told to sit in accordance with his packet number, between Buck and a girl with very long dark red hair, cold blue eyes, and a knife-ridged nose.

A skinny guy in glasses welcomed everyone by saying they were all now members of the student body of Harvard Law School, and this was orientation. He leaned against a desk in the center of a room in Pound Hall. His pants were too short at his ankles.

"My name is Muzhduk the Ugli," Muzhduk whispered to the girl.

She looked at him suspiciously. "I'm Lena."

The girl with too much furniture. "My grandfather drowned in a river named Lena."

"What do you mean by that?" she asked.

"I like your name."

"So?"

"It's a compliment. It means *big river*."

"No thank you." Her eyes seemed dry.

"Hi, I'm Skip," the welcomer in front broke in. "Skip Enkelphin, 2-L, BSA. Are you in orientation A-group EE? This is A-group EE. Advising group number EE." The packet had explained that Skip was a member of the Board of Student Advisors—second-year student volunteers who hadn't made Law Review but wanted to do something official.

Like drunk donkeys. AA-group EE. But Muzhduk was determined not to repeat the boat cruise.

Skip advised everyone on rules, told them about their "pigeonholes," and gave them a copy of their homework assignments for the first day of each class. He gave them baskets of goodies, shaving cream, razors, packs of NoDoz caffeine pills, deodorant, hand-sterilizer ("although there are sterilizing stations in every bathroom and in key locations throughout campus, with which you will familiarize yourselves naturally over the course of the semester," he added), and a bumper sticker that read, "Real estate agents are lower than lawyers." Muzhduk opened a package of Osco hand-sterilizer. It smelled like Lena. He sniffed Lena, discretely. Yes.

"No condoms," Muzhduk said, remembering September at McGill, where the whole campus, every rugby game, every party seemed awash in free condoms.

Everyone looked at him.

"That's correct." Skip nodded. He had a way of looking slightly to your left as he talked, so Muzhduk wasn't certain whether he was addressing him or the whole class. "Fifteen years ago, fornication—that's sex outside of marriage—was still illegal in Massachusetts, and the Harvard University Corporation lawyers determined that handing out condoms could cause the Corporation to be found guilty of 'conspiracy to fornicate.'" He mimed quotation marks at both ends. "Now, the anti-fornication law has been expunged, but what if a condom handed out by the Corporation were used in a rape? Or in a sexual harassment situation? Could Harvard be liable? But I'm glad that you mentioned this, because we do have to talk about this very important subject." And then, to Muzhduk's amazement, he went on for twenty minutes about rules that Harvard had created for sex. Silence does not constitute consent, it must be affirmative. Consent is not valid if the consenting party has consumed alcohol. Consent for a particular sexual act does not constitute consent for other acts.

"Is the division temporal or spatial, or both?" someone asked.

"Aren't single people supposed to sexually harass each other?" Muzhduk asked.

"Go on," replied Skip to the first person.

"I mean, if a hypothetical defendant has received permission to, uh, affirmative consent with respect to a particular...I mean, does the policy classify particular areas collectively as one, uh, jurisdiction, and that consent is valid for the entire jurisdiction?"

Skip was not oblivious to these fine issues. "Read the fourth paragraph of the definition of 'consent.' In fact, let's all read it. Mr. Ugli, perhaps you could read it out loud for us."

"Me?" Muzhduk looked to his left, just to be sure.

"Yes, page eight."

All Muzhduk could think about was that until fifteen years ago fornication had been illegal here. Compared to the simplicity of Verkhoyansk: drink plum brandy, have sex. And if someone got jealous, you fought, and fighting was fun too. For the same effort, you got sex in a meadow in Verkhoyansk, a friendly kiss in Montreal, a cold hello in Boston, and criminal charges at Harvard. Floating alone on an iceberg over the Bering Strait, he had resigned himself to masturbation, but this was a sweltering city of two million people in the Deep South.

All at once he doubted his quest. A year-and-a-half of walking through cold nothingness and a year waiting in Montreal hadn't dented his determination, but suddenly it seemed a crazy idea that he would stay in a place like this. This was serious, a flash of introspection that made him understand why introspection was taboo in the valley. He could fight anyone, climb anything, but to spend three years living like a priest? It would make him sick, turn him into a pervert. It could destroy anyone without even a true fight. Like fighting an illness.

He wasn't going to accept this path to climbing Mt. Harvard. There had to be another way. People were looking up at him again, and he remembered he was supposed to read something.

"Do cats eat bats? Or do bats eat cats?" he said out loud. "Whereat, for the purposes of this ziggurat, a cat meets a bat, they shall not engage in all *that*, except under the fiat of a technocrat and a diplomat, who shall negotiate all appropriate thereats, whereats, caveats, and jurats..."

"That's not—" Skip cut him off. "Your behavior is childish, mister, mister...what *is* your last name?" He didn't believe "Ugli" could be a real name.

"Kiss-Lena."

"Muzhduk Kisslena," Skip almost yelled as he searched his list. "Okay."

Muzhduk tried, but Lena blocked him with an elbow to his Adam's apple.

"Good God!" Skip shouted. "Are you insane?"

Muzhduk coughed.

"Do you want to press charges?" Skip asked Lena.

She shook her head, not now, maybe later, but their only contact had been his throat with her elbow. It didn't violate the Policy, except maybe the part of creating a hostile environment. She opened her Osco hand-sterilizer—from her pocket, not from the basket—and ignored Muzhduk as he handed her his own Osco. Skip looked at Muzhduk as though he were potentially dangerous and told Lena he'd talk to her after orientation, then continued to read the Policy himself. His voice shook as he explained that for the purposes of the Policy, consent shall mean affirmative permission granted by the female student for engaging in each of the following three stages of sexual activity: *kissing*, petting, and copulation (hereinafter "stage" individually and "stages" collectively). "Consent for an activity that falls in one of the stages of sexual activity shall not constitute, infer, or imply consent for activities falling within the other stages—"

What have I done?

"If the sexual comments of one party make another party feel uncomfortable, this constitutes 'hostile environment' sexual harassment."

What if they're your enemy? Can't you make them feel uncomfortable then? Or are there no enemies here?

From sex to toilets. The Λ-group discussed "Here's Johnny," and with the tension dissolved, conversation flowed smoothly again. Lena and Buck had neatly typed pages, with headings for "Facts, Statement of the Law, Rule, Holding, and Dicta/um." *Who has told them to do this, and how to do this?* Everyone had the same headings, down to the backslash between dicta and um, even as Skip was explaining for the first time how to "outline." Since most exams were open book, these schematic summaries of the laws, cases, and professor opinions covered in a class would be their greatest resource, Skip said. People would struggle for the best outline and dream about the Outline of the Covenant—the perfect outline, created by twelve *summa cum laudes* long ago and now buried within secret vaults deep in a place called Gannett House.

Skip told them how lucky they were to be admitted. He praised the diversity of the Law School, repeated percentages of various minorities admitted, praised the variety of nationalities and backgrounds, and said that the admissions committee, in their wisdom, even admitted one *asshole* every year, just for the sake of diversity. Then he blushed.

Skip passed out the classroom schedules. They were lucky to be in an experimental section, he said, with all the best professors: Sclera, Dershowitz, and the other Greats.

The whole room murmured with the repetition of these names. Lena glanced at Muzhduk, who glanced back. "What's an O.J. Team?" he asked. "And how do people know the professors' names already?"

"Please do not talk to me."

Muzhduk asked her what's one kiss, more or less, in life? Lena said it was both wrong and illegal. She said men have for far too long seen women as objects and that it was telling that he didn't kiss a man. Muzhduk said that if he liked men he would have kissed a man. She challenged him to kiss a man, so Muzhduk tried. Buck sputtered and swore, pushing Muzhduk away. Lena scoffed, declaring that the dominant culture treats minorities within a similar paradigm to the way it treats women. She quoted Catharine MacKinnon, who once wrote that the definition of "woman" is to be rape-able, a position that is social and not biological, so Muzhduk had just turned Buck into a woman. Buck objected, pointing out that MacKinnon's argument makes all men inherently rapists, and, if he remembered correctly, she'd once claimed at a conference to have been raped 596 times, and that Lena's argument was contumelious and disparaging to both minorities and to women. Muzhduk stopped talking and just listened, stunned.

"Our sizable friend here doesn't appear to be steeped in the dominant cultural paradigm," Buck said. Then he turned to Muzhduk, as though the degree of difference was just now sinking in. "Where *is* this place you're from, that you haven't heard of anything?"

"I fell off a strawberry and bumped my head. And here I am."

But by then Buck was listening to Skip describe the *Get to Know Your Library Scavenger Hunt*. It was five pages of questions and a list of teams. Muzhduk was happy to learn he was with Lena and Buck, though Lena had already changed seats.

Skip read the first question: "What is the first word on page 2961 of 580 F.2nd 2680?"

A fragile-looking student in the bottom left of the room raised his hand. Skip pointed, as much with his torso as with his arm. "Yes?"

"Will we be graded on this?"

"No, but it's mandatory."

"What happens if we don't do it?" Muzhduk asked.

Skip looked puzzled. "It's good for you—" His voice trailed off as he noticed someone standing in the back, by one of the doors. It was an old man in a three-piece suit, and he was looking at Muzhduk. "Oh, Professor Sclera, um, thank you for your surprise visit." But the old man had walked out by the time Skip finished his sentence.

• • •

The mime and I fought our way together up the stairs, through a door on top of the balustrade, through a small room to a second-story door that opened ten feet above the street, but only two feet above the top of the garbage heap, as though the builders had assumed the ramp of garbage. I half jumped, half fell onto the garbage, sliding down on slime and rotting things and cutting my cheek on a sharp fish can that read, *Donation from the Government of Japan, Not for Sale.*

We ran into the street. The mime went right and I went left, toward the entrance, hoping Peggy and the Tuaregs would come that way. The avenue was filled with Bella, hundreds of men with sticks. They pressed north, cramming into the Getaway, so I ran along the south edge of the street. Two men tried to stop me and I knocked both down and continued past the Getaway, searching for Peggy.

Three blocks later, Gao ended. It was suddenly just open desert, complete with the wreckages of cars and cows. At any other time I would have said there's something pleasant about a town that ends on a line, but now it was like falling off a cliff. The moon was bright but I couldn't see any special tracks in the sand. Nothing said, "Peggy came this way."

I walked into the empty desert to a lopsided Jeep chassis, stripped of everything except metal too warped to be useful. A small trace of the Tuareg Wars that would soon be buried by the shifting ground it stood on. I didn't know what to do. The wind whistled faintly on the twisted metal and tickled my nose with invisible dust. The rocky desert turned into waves of mounded dunes just at the edge of sight. I stood and stared, out of ideas, until eventually I felt a burning sensation in my bladder. Maybe the metal had a current that would flow up the stream and zap me, or a fast swimming bug, or something nasty. I pissed on it anyway, wondering if my bloody urine was disturbing life or feeding it, and why the night time desert seemed to be pulsing.

My knee was swollen, and my back was starting to spasm. Someone had hit me in the spine as well as the kidneys. I couldn't stand here, letting the adrenaline wear off. So I limped, then ran, back across the city line, avoiding the main avenue and pushing into wavy claustrophobic alleys barely the width of a man, around dark corners where the heat reminded me it was still there, still dulling the body into a numbness unbreacheable by sticks and stones. Not a straight angle anywhere, just curves and intersections. Every ten meters a separate alley world cut into another, opening and dissolving for miles in every direction.

I gasped when inhaling, shallow and fast so the dust wouldn't set off a coughing fit. My ribs hurt. I ran in ever-wider circles. The mob must have dispersed. Whenever I came across a man I grabbed him by the armpits, picked him up off the ground sometimes, and shouted. The Bella didn't understand French, I didn't speak Bella. Nobody knew anything, and I was still naked.

When the night became grey, and there were no more people to shake, and the barrel fires were out, I tried to find my way back to the Getaway, exhausted and guided poorly by a vague sense that I'd spun in too many circles. I finally collapsed against a tall, studded doorway. I was covered in blood and stink, and couldn't walk without all the muscles in my back twitching and spasming. A stick had ruptured a blood vessel in my head, and my face was sticky with blood. I punched a mud wall across from the doorway as hard as I could. It hurt my fist, but at least I made a hole.

• • •

Muzhduk picked up his assignments, bought his books, arranged them first alphabetically, then by substance, changed his mind again and arranged them by size. Then he knocked on dormitory doors to see if anyone wanted to go out drinking. It was Saturday night, classes hadn't started yet, but everyone else had already made plans to stay at home to study.

So he walked alone to the Ratio Pub. During the day the Pub was a Chinese restaurant named The Hong Kong, but at night it was

Harvard Law School's campus bar. There was a baseball game on television. He'd heard of baseball in Montreal but had never watched. He found it strange—one guy throws the ball to his friend, who hits it to another friend, who throws it back. He kept waiting for ten other guys to come onto the fields with their own sticks. Instead, they played nine on one. It seemed unfair.

By the end of the night he learned that Massachusetts law required a minimum of two people to order a pitcher of beer, that Harvard was worth more than every major league baseball team put together, that there were 177 ABA-accredited law schools in America, and growing, and that Harvard was consistently ranked last in quality of life, #177 out of 177, which was the number of days the Roman games lasted in the 4th Century and the same as someone's batting average during the Atlanta-Toronto World Series. He forgot who. And he saw a pretty girl asking for a job at the bar. But he stumbled home alone.

• • •

Light shot through the new hole in the adobe. Then the doorway beside it opened. A veiled woman gestured for me to enter—the first veiled woman I'd seen in Gao; otherwise only the Tuareg men wore veils here—I stood up from the floor of the alley and stepped into a dim room filled with smoke and covered in hung fabric. Her eyes had an energy like sexual organs. Despite her veil, she ignored my nakedness.

"The White Devil is out tonight," she said, and I was unsure whether she was talking about Claude or me.

I went in through the door and realized I'd been here before. This was the little café attached to the kitchen of the Getaway.

"Hubbly bubbly?"

I just wanted to cross the café and courtyard to the rooms and get my clothing. Everything hurt. But when I reached the first table I collapsed on the pillows, annoyed at myself, at the weakness that a year at Harvard had allowed. It was just small undernourished people with sticks. No tanks, no Red Army, no helicopters. All the engraved chessboard tables with heavy wood pieces showed games in progress. Teak versus ebony. And large glass hookahs; mine was embroidered with a glass mosaic of orange and green Xs.

"Tobacco or hashish?" the girl asked. Her contours had an eerie haze to them, as did all the furniture in the café, as did the walls and the whole town of Gao. I found myself looking for lines, but there were none. Even the normal angles where walls met other walls were hidden by pillows or billowing fabric that covered the ceiling in bellies of cloth. A bird was singing somewhere and dust motes shone in the new morning light coming through the hole I'd punched in the wall.

I wanted to shower, to wash off the blood. I was tired, and freezing, until I became suddenly hot, waiting for the sweat to freeze again. The girl watched, and I could feel a twinge from the clash of my nudity in front of her eyes and her too-much clothing, until I noticed that Amadou was standing beside me, and Rogers was eating eggs at the next table.

Three hundred hairy ones, what's wrong with me?

Amadou put his hand on my forehead. "Twobob, you are hot and cold?"

I nodded.

"You have malaria."

"From sticks?"

"From the female anopheles mosquito," Rogers said, without looking up from his breakfast. "More precisely, from the sporozoan parasites of the genus Plasmodium of the phylum Apicomplexa with which the anopheles injected you, bringing about ague, delirium, and sometimes death."

All of it? Such things are smeared out. Someone once told you that.

Rogers was still talking. "All your activity last night probably accelerated it. I would guess you were bitten on the way here, three to seven days ago."

My activity last night.

I forced myself off the pillows to Rogers' table and sat across from him. As I did, he glanced up at my crotch, then wiped the last of his runny egg with a piece of bread.

"One wonderful thing about Africa," he said, putting the bread in his mouth. It made him mumble. "Is the eggs. In Europe they'd rather eat tasteless eggs than see the little chicken fetus. But there's no comparison, really."

CHAPTER 6

Mt. Harvard

Tuesday, 9 AM, Civil Procedure with Professor Sclera: Langdell North, seat #129. Everyone had prepared, read, outlined, and discussed the necessary materials from their packet all Labor Day weekend. Especially graduates of Duke, because Sclera started with someone from Duke every second year, and this was a Duke year. Muzhduk remembered everything that Fred the Political Officer had taught him and memorized almost everything he'd read, but where did everyone get this information about the professors? Was there a facebook for this too? Tradable Harvard baseball cards?

Muzhduk arrived at Langdell North at 8:45, determined to be early, but everyone else was inside already, seated. The room was an amphitheater but felt like a big pit. Two sets of stairs trisected a long staggered semi-circle of desks, leading to two exits, one of which was perpetually locked. In the center of the pit sat a large desk, the focal point of all the seats. Behind it was a blackboard, and above that, high in the air, were twelve large paintings of stern and slightly startled judges wearing grey wigs, red robes, and a dislocated gold-leaf background that made them float and vibrate without dimension. They stared squarely out of their frames like Byzantine Virgin Marys.

Muzhduk pushed through the 120s and said "Hi" to Lena and Buck, in seats #128 and #130. He sat on a creaky wooden chair with a finger-sized hole in the center. Lena groaned.

The class waited, a few whispered, most arranged papers with Skip Enkelphin's headings in front of them. 9:00, nothing. 9:05, still no professor. Buck read his outlines, his face awkwardly close to his notes, while Lena whispered with the girl next to her.

"You think he forgot?" Muzhduk asked Buck.

Buck didn't answer. Around the room the whispering died out and the air thickened. Everyone looked around uncertainly. He must have been there for a while, standing in the back of the room like he'd done at the A-group orientation. But this time, he stood behind a woman seated in the last row whose pale face brought to Muzhduk memories of ice. She was older than any of the students by at least a decade, and dressed like a German schoolmistress. He guessed she wasn't a student. He would talk to her at the end of class, he decided, while everyone else stared at the apparently famous and frightening Eugene Sclera. Students had been talking about him in the hallways and bathrooms all weekend. Muzhduk didn't respect the gossip, but couldn't help but be made curious by all the wounds Sclera purportedly inflicted on students with his words. And the registrar had mentioned that Sclera tried to secure Muzhduk's admission, though Muzhduk had never met the man.

Sclera seemed almost unhappy that he'd been noticed, descending the stairs with deliberate steps, neck erect, eyes fixed on the floating judges. He wore a three-piece pinstriped suit, pinched a white slab of poster board under an armpit, and held a large coffee mug in the other hand while pressing his shoulders as far back as they would go—it pushed his vested torso out and made his arms look unnaturally short. His hair sat upon him like a grey geisha wig.

He arrived in the pit and placed the white poster board on the desk. It was a diagram of the classroom, with passport-sized photographs attached to every seat location and names underneath. He examined his diagram for a full minute, while Muzhduk, Lena, Buck, and a cloud of a hundred and fifty-seven similars floated above, waiting for the great Sclera to speak.

• • •

Rogers leaned on his elbows and absently pinched the loose skin of his forearms, staring at me with his careless old-man eyes. I stared back.

Thinking was hard in that room with no edges, tilting occasionally with waves of heat, cold, and delirium. Claude walked up and asked if I wanted breakfast. I said yes, eggs, the kind with the fetus in them, the tasty kind, and my clothes, if he wouldn't mind getting them. Rogers sipped his coffee and I steadied myself until the girl brought me my goat. I dug inside for my shorts and a shirt, happy to be finally dressed, and Claude came with the eggs. As he put the plate down, I asked, "What happened last night, Claude?"

Claude looked at Rogers. Rogers sipped his coffee with a bland almost-smile. I grabbed his collar and pulled him across the table. We met halfway. The hubbly bubbly on the edge wobbled but didn't fall. Claude and Amadou didn't move. "I don't like to hit old men," I growled.

Rogers looked down at my arm, then tapped my wrist. This close, I could hear the rattle in his breathing. I let go of his collar, and he sat back on his pillows. He cleared his throat, then stared at me with the same look he'd given the coffee. "Have you ever considered the passivity of the West?"

"Into God's cunt!" I swore quietly in Verkhoyansk Slovak. I wanted to repeat, over and over, *Where is she?*

"Africa's lethargic," he went on. "Like a feral dog in heat, with no shade, it comes to life in the dark. The West is passive, energetic sheep all running forward together in bright daylight." I rubbed my temples trying to think of a better way. He raised his shoulders, face, and hands, unmistakably French. "And so, what are you looking for? Besides your friend, of course."

"Sahara yellow," I finally said, going along. "Like you said. And the shadows cast by words and the number zero and whoever it was that took Peggy, so I can snap his ribs. What else? Nothing else, I'm not looking for anything else."

"In Timbuktu there is a library. When the Scholastics began burning books in Europe, the Gnostics smuggled thousands to the library at Alexandria. Before the Church burned Alexandria, these books were evacuated again, to the library in Timbuktu by the trans-Saharan salt caravans. Salt traded for gold at parity in Timbuktu, Gao, Agadez. They could afford books. From Alexandria, and from the House of Wisdom in Baghdad, rescued when the Mongol sacked the city. But it is very hard to reach." Mr. Rogers paused. "That should be interesting to you."

"You're saying I can find her in the library?" Memories of the one time Peggy and I'd made love—in the Harvard library, the late spring night we destroyed it—rushed in. It would be fitting.

"The question is, which book. For example, if you really want to find the cipher, the number zero, the library has the original *Kitab al-Jabr wa'l-Muqabala*, by Al-Khwarizmi—"

"I don't care about books anymore. And certainly not algebra."

"They contain the Law."

"I've had enough of the Law."

"I suspect we don't mean the same thing by that word. You are a tourist here, in search of some sort of anxiety. I can help you become part of Africa. Or you will have to leave. It's up to you." He didn't remind me of Sclera anymore, he reminded me of Oedda. And maybe if I hadn't tried to prove something to Oedda, then I wouldn't have ended up a tree. Or maybe Peggy would've waited for me to get out of jail.

"I'm running out of time," I said, suddenly angry. "What happened last night?"

"You saw what happened. Your friend was here, then she left."

I slammed my palm down on the table. The hookah fell as the table cracked off-center from Rogers to me but didn't collapse. "May your mother recognize you in kebab meat and your father fuck her in the center of her eye!" I swore. "She didn't *leave*. Your friends *took* her. Now you're going to tell me where! And who and why!"

Claude picked up the hookah and put it on another table.

"It would be very difficult for you to understand," Rogers said. "If a wall falls on a man—"

"I know," I cut him off. It would demean Fred the Political Officer to hear his words in Roger's mouth. "You have to know why the man sat beside it."

Rogers raised his short eyebrows. "You have to know both: what was wrong with the wall *and* why he sat beside it. But at least you know which of the two can be answered in Africa."

"Why did they take her?"

"She is not the man. You are the man. This was generously explained to you by Amadou during the chess game yesterday. The wall fell on you. So why are you here?"

"To find Peggy."

"You found her yesterday. Success. You can leave now." He held up his hands in front of him as he saw me start to rage. "Okay, so you not only want to find her, you want to keep her?"

"I want to talk to her."

"You think she can teach you something? You think it's something she can hand over to you like a sword or a gun or a chicken egg?" He poked his empty plate with a fork.

"Listen, you seven-polka-dotted prick," I growled, losing control. My blurry malarial eyes didn't help. "None of this is your business. Tell me what happened or I'll rip your arms off!"

"I thought you didn't hit old men."

"I won't hit. I'll pull."

"Ah, a lawyer." He looked sad.

I slammed the table again, and this time it broke, caving in its middle, spilling Rogers' coffee and making him yell in pain. Claude and Amadou still didn't react. Claude stood a few feet away, hovering. Amadou was in his favorite position, shifting from leg to leg while grinning. The girl in the veil sat at the furthest table, near the kitchen, watching us.

I grabbed Rogers' wrist. Like bird bone. "They looked like Bella and Tuareg."

He nodded. "This is a place where friends are just as likely to kidnap you as enemies. You will never understand Africa. Even if I explain for days, even if you go to Timbuktu and read all the books there, you will still never understand."

"Amadou," I said, still holding Rogers' wrist, "last night you said that Claude is 'a bad French man who helps the Bella.' How does he help them? Why do they call him White Devil?"

"He's their guardian devil. When he's not having sex with girls who don't menstruate."

"Shut up," Claude snapped. He sounded hoarse, as though he'd shouted all through the chaos the night before. Then to me: "I wore my white djellaba the day I finally got sick of their complaining that they should get paid 1700 CFA instead of 1500 per month. The government set a wage for all Bella, 1500 CFA, $3 US per month, so they can tell the Americans that Mali has ended slavery. The Bella wanted $3.25 instead of $3, but they wouldn't fight for the right to quit a job or to not be beaten or raped. So I organized them. They got their 25 cents a month, and I got a year in a Mali prison. But when I broke my leg, two blocks away," he pointed west, toward the center of town, "they were the only ones who didn't laugh. Everyone else thought it was funny, me crawling back here. The rest of Mali calls them a subrace, but *putain de calice*, they're the best of the bunch." He waved an arm as though dismissing it all. "You haven't been to prison until you've been to one in Mali."

I didn't understand. "So why would they attack your guesthouse?"

• • •

When Sclera finally did speak, his voice was surprisingly high. "Is Ms. Silverstein here?"

A small hand raised itself hesitatingly off to the far left and a few rows above Muzhduk. The girl to whom it belonged looked up at the hand in horror. "Here."

"Ms. Silverstein. You went to Duke, I believe?"

"Ahm."

"I take it you have read *Tickle v. Barton* and prepared it thoroughly."

"Well, I—"

"Good. Please tell the class about it."

"Well, um, there is, ahm, the plaintiff, Richard Tickle, an infant, who sued Raymond Barton, an old man, for personal injuries inflicted upon him," Ms. Silverstein said. "By a motor vehicle, operated by the defendant Barton. In a heedless and negligent manner...the defendant Barton was inveigled into West Virginia for a factitious banquet... in order to obtain personal jurisdiction...before long-arm statutes... the court held that the amended plea in abatement was sufficient on demurrer..." She continued, fast and clunky, while Muzhduk imagined a shapeless metal entity with pipes, pulleys, and levers sticking out at odd angles, running down an infant.

When she stopped, a long pause followed. Sclera stared at her until she wished she had gone to Yale. "Well, um," he finally said, imitating, "you got the word 'sued' right."

Muzhduk looked up, interested for the first time. It was difficult to take Sclera seriously, with his peacock walk, or the class, with such senseless fear. But now he saw that Sclera had crushed Ms. Silverstein with a sentence. She sat in her seat dazed, temporarily useless, as if she'd received a boulder to the head. He didn't like the image, only brain-damaged people threw boulders at women. But these were just words, so it was a struggle not to dismiss Silverstein as a wimp, or a child. If someone attacks a child, you don't analyze the method as a great example of military ambush. You protect the child.

But perhaps it wasn't just her. If all lawyers were oversensitive, then he should learn. He was here to learn how to fight lawyers, after all. It was like fighting Russians: you could use tools and tactics and whatever else it took to win. He wished Sclera would pick on him.

"I do not accept unpreparedness in this class," Sclera said when the correct amount of time had elapsed. "I do not accept the word 'pass,' I accept only the correct answer. If you cannot be prepared, you shall bring me, in person and before 8:30 AM, a note with one word written on it. That word shall be quote *unprepared* unquote. You shall not explain why, and I will not call on you that day. Are you or are you not aware of the fact, Ms. Silverstein, that you attended Duke?"

"Y-yes. I mean, I am."

"And did you or did you not know that every second year, for the past thirty-eight years, I have first called upon a Duke student?"

"Yes." Her voice sounded squeezed.

"I can't hear you, Ms. Silverstein. Did you or did you not know I would call upon a Duke student today?"

"Leave her alone," Muzhduk said to himself, but not in a whisper. "She's already down."

"I heard that you might," she stammered.

"I keep thinking I am becoming too obvious, but students somehow never get it. Or perhaps it is the other members of the Admissions Committee who do not get it. Schools like Duke should stick to basketball." He raised his eyebrows. "I quite enjoy watching basketball."

He returned to his poster board. Everybody tightened until Sclera picked a name.

"Mr. Hale. Do you think you can do better than Ms. Silverstein?" Sclera asked, still looking down at the cardboard. When he didn't get an answer he looked up. "Mr. Hale?"

A student in the second row swallowed hard and said, "I can try."

"Good. Why don't you 'try.' And I suggest that you illustrate why Ms. Silverstein doesn't belong here, or I will do so to you. When I rip a student to shreds, it is a divine task, done for the benefit of the class as a whole. Now, you will please do more than try."

Mr. Hale swallowed once more, and again explained the case. Periodically, Sclera said, "Uh-hmm," ending the word each time in a dramatically high-pitched hook.

"And what is this *demurrer*?"

"It's an objection...an objection of Law, rather than a dispute of fact, saying that even if the other side's case is true, the defendant can't be in trouble."

"In *trouble*? Like a little boy?"

"I mean, that the court could not find for the plaintiff, even if what he says is true."

"*True?* Is this a church, Mr. Hale?"

"Yes. Say 'yes,' Mr. Hale," Muzhduk half shouted, disgusted by Mr. Hale.

"I mean undisputed, stipulated, or determined by the fact-finder to be a finding of fact."

"No!" Muzhduk yelled, at the booming top of his voice. "Don't back down, Mr. Hale. Don't let him shit on your head like that. Open your mouth, Mr. Hale, open wide!"

The class froze.

Sclera turned slowly to face Muzhduk, his mug held high in front. "What did you say?"

"I said Mr. Hale is a coward who has wasted his opportunity."

"What is your name?"

"Muzhduk the Ugli the Fourth."

"There were three others?"

"Yes."

"Equally ugly?"

"Uglier."

"You do realize that this is only the first day of class, *hmmm*?" He shook his head. "Amazing. You will be in Mr. Hale's position soon enough. Until then, you will sit still, be quiet, and learn. I will overlook your outrageous and ungrateful outburst on account of the fact that it *is* the first day. But such a thing will not happen again.

"Now, back to Mr. Hale, the coward. By the way, do you believe, Mr. Hale," Sclera paused to take a sip from his coffee; he glanced back at Muzhduk, then turned back to Mr. Hale, "do you believe the court?"

Sclera returned to the law school variant of the Socratic method. Mr. Hale's Adam's apple bobbed and Sclera *hmmm-ed* and pushed his chest out in between attacks. Sclera badgered Mr. Hale, accused him of being just as useful as Ms. Silverstein, and insisted on knowing where he had read that insurance is the key to every tort case. Finally the lopsided debate focused on the issue of the defendant having been enticed into the court's jurisdiction.

"—and the court doesn't want to see itself as condoning the inveigling of defendants."

"Why not? Is the Law in the business of preening?"

"It has to maintain its legitimacy?" Mr. Hale answered. "It, it has to use means that are consistent with accepted norms, and inveiglement is seen as egregious?"

"So it can use police, bounty hunters, the electric chair, long-arm statutes, but not seduction, is that the holding of the case? Seduction is beneath Lady Justice?"

"I think...yes?"

"*I think.* Are you certain?"

"I think, I mean—"

"You think, I know. I don't want your deep thoughts. I expect correct answers, and the correct answer is, 'Yes, that is exactly the reason.' Or was in 1924. Which comes before when Mr. Hale?" Sclera took a satisfied sip from his coffee mug.

"Before," his hesitation turned him a pale green, "before 1938."

"Before 1938. This is the first day of class, as has already been pointed out, Mr. Hale. How do you know that 1924 comes before 1938? Are you trying to show Ms. Silverstein that Princeton is better than Duke? Maybe it is. Or maybe you are just a bookworm, Mr. Hale, and have no life other than to study Hornbooks all summer? So you can show up your classmates to compensate for the fact that you are losing your hair already at the tender age of twenty-two. Nevertheless, it is gratifying to see that some students still take Harvard Law seriously. And you happen to be correct this time; 1938 was a great year. I remember it fondly. It was the year Equity was assimilated by Law and the great Federal Rules of Civil Procedure were carved into our social fabric. This case came from a Court of Equity, which had jurisdiction here but declined to use it because jurisdiction was obtained in a manner that reflected poorly on the court. Equity cared about such tender things, which is why it is extinct. So too bad for little baby Tickle that his skull was crushed, the court was not going to allow this case to go to the jury."

Sclera returned to the poster board. Everyone waited in silence for Sclera's sudden shrill "*Hmmm?*" Muzhduk could see that his colleagues were sweating, terrified, their ass muscles clenched and exhausted.

Halfway through, at precisely 9:45, a large hunched man entered the class carrying a big mug of coffee. Everyone watched him except Sclera, who continued talking, and a student in cowboy boots whom Sclera was questioning about how someone from Alabama had learned to read, let alone get into Harvard Law School. Without a break in his sentence, Sclera exchanged his old, now empty, coffee mug for the new one. When he sipped from the mug at one of his carefully chosen moments, a form of punctuation, Muzhduk could make out the bold black lettering on its side: YOU KNOW WHAT THEY SAY ABOUT THE SIZE OF A MAN'S MUG.

"That's not such a big mug," Muzhduk whispered.

"I understand he has a Ph.D.," Buck answered in a voice that was barely audible.

"Who?"

"Corey. Sclera's secretary." He made a small gesture at the retreating hunchback.

"In what?"

"Literature, I believe." Then Buck placed a shushing finger on his lips.

Five minutes before the end of class, Sclera let go of a girl from Minnesota and walked back to his desk. Students began to put their papers away. Sclera looked up, flapped his arms like small wings, and said, "The class finishes at 10:30. *Not* 10:25."

Everyone stopped.

"There was a time when such things were too obvious to be spoken." Sclera paused to take a sip from the bottom, steeling himself for an unpleasant chore. "By way of your acceptance here at Harvard Law School, both you," he gestured with his coffee to include the class, "and I, undertake certain obligations. On my part, I will teach you Civil Procedure. I will also teach you how to think like a lawyer, for that is also a Procedure of the Law. By virtue of an almost alchemical process, the males among you shall be thoroughly refined into the delicate modern-built frame of pap-nerved softlings—diplomats pale and pretty, nearly as masculine as your sisters. The females shall be hardened, taught to think in terms linear and logical, as simple, as grossly rational and almost as feminine as your brothers. *Ars totum requirit hominem.* You are now vessels, empty, to be filled by me, but before you leave these hallowed halls, you *will* breathe, think, and act like lawyers."

Sclera was throwing uphill, crushing everyone. His arguments begged to be thrown back, but the class just said thank you and stacked the boulders that bounced off their heads into neat little piles, careful to not let them roll back into the pit where they might hit Sclera and trigger another throw. There was no real test, no elimination of weakness. It was clear to Muzhduk that Sclera's real teaching was in the method, not in the nonsense he said, and the method begged someone to recognize it and fight back. Muzhduk raised his hand. Sclera must have noticed the hand, because his voice faltered, though it wasn't clear whether it faltered out of surprise, or whether out of happiness, or whether it wasn't really his voice, but only his eyes, which moved elsewhere as he continued to talk. After a few seconds, Muzhduk put his hand back down.

"There was once a time when I also said, 'Look around you: of any four, only one will graduate,'" Sclera continued. "Those days are unfortunately gone. I do not understand how my colleagues hope to make passable lawyers out of you by pampering you, but that does not mean that we will *all* treat you in such a manner. If you cannot handle me, you will not be able to handle a real judge, one who lacks my compassion." At this, his empty left hand did a sort of queen's wave, pointing above and behind him at the Byzantine paintings. "Needless to say, I strictly enforce the compulsory attendance policy. I expect, however, that you will attend every class fully prepared not out of compulsion, but out of gratitude."

It was ten-thirty. Sclera placed his white poster board under his armpit and slowly, methodically, head still at an awkwardly high angle, began to walk up and out of the amphitheater.

Muzhduk raised his hand again.

Sclera tried ignore the hand. But he couldn't. He had carefully planned the ending, as he did every year. His speech was the sort of Truth that would last beyond his death, and his exit served a key function. But that function was at risk of being blunted by Mr. Ugli's tree-branch-sized arm jutting up from the middle of the classroom, seat number #129, Sclera knew without looking at his cardboard. He had gone out of his way to ensure Muzhduk was in his class, but even if he hadn't, he had the seating plan memorized, along with the undergraduate institution of each student, and only brought it to class for that moment of tension that his contemplation always caused. Tension was important in any performance, whether on Court TV or in class.

He didn't want to engage just yet. He knew that Muzhduk was not really a girl from Tennessee. One of his former students, John Ashcroft, had sent him a short email some time ago about a local tribe squatting on his newly purchased property in Siberia. He'd described the mountain men as naïve to the point of stupidity, arrogant, anarchic, and extremely violent, then concluded, "On the off chance that the chief's son actually makes it to Cambridge (he started on foot!) you should know that he's determined to attend HLS. If seen, I'd advise contacting the police immediately. They are completely lawless, take offence unpredictably, and have developed no mechanism other than violence for resolving disagreements."

Sclera was delighted. He had been waiting years for a Kaspar Hauser, a Franz Biberkopf, an Idiot—a student exactly like the one John's email had described—but he had considered the problem of admission tactically impossible. To get someone like that admitted would be such an obvious overreach of his position on the Admissions Committee that there'd be no point in it. But then Mr. Ugli arrived with a perfect 180. It was almost too good to be true, which made Sclera extra cautious. But now he had the immediate school year to think of, the risk of losing authority over 150 students—the cost of inaction outweighed the benefit of full preparedness.

"Oh, what is it?" he skirled without stopping. His one failing, he recognized it himself, was that he'd never learned to control his intonation. Each word came out at a different pitch. The students nearest him flinched, but didn't dare cover their ears.

Muzhduk said, "I have a question."

"*Non licet quod dispendio licet.*" That which may be done only at a loss is not allowed.

"Whose loss?"

"Yours, you block!" Sclera continued up the long stairs, slightly shaken by the incongruity of the mountain man understanding Latin. But there were ways to trip up an idiot savant. "I have answered your question, now you explain the reason for it!" He didn't slow his movement; he wanted to suggest the explanation could not be very important. Again, only his intonation was wrong.

"I can see you think I don't have words," Muzhduk said. "I have many, though not as many as Clive, and I won't fall over if you tell me that one of them is right, like Ms. Silverstein." Sclera continued to walk, almost ignoring Muzhduk. "If that were to happen, if you were to throw words at me, I'd throw this one back at you: *education*. From ēdūcere. It means 'guiding or drawing out,' not the perverse pouring-in of yourself that you demonstrated today."

Now Sclera did stop, three steps above Muzhduk's level on his slow journey up to the doors, out of the pit, his eyes wide in genuine amazement. The class was completely still. "So the word and its meaning are misaligned. Form and substance are at odds. I can think of a few other words that are misaligned, including the name of this school and certain members of its student body. Will you realign them for us, you oversized oaf, by lecturing *me* in *my* own room? On the first day? *Hmmm?*"

"*Contrariorum contraria ratio est.*" The reason of contrary things is contrary.

Sclera focused his entire attention on Muzhduk. Students had challenged him from time to time, but never personally, never so early in the semester, and never in Latin. The boy was perfect, exactly what Sclera had hoped for. He needed more time to study him, but for now he had to crush him publicly or lose control of the class.

Ugli knew Latin, so he probably knew the three other respectable languages: Greek, German, and Sanskrit. Sclera had decades of Socratic method behind him, but he also knew other ways to tie students into knots, including pre-Socratic methods, tropical loops that would stump an arctic square. Always. And Ugli's strength was his perfect LSAT score. Sclera thought back on what John had written about the boulder-throwing rituals. There was a linear logic to boulders that fit well with the LSAT. Maybe the mountain man was a square.

"Mr. Ugli," Sclera finally said. "I have been teaching here since the Law was dictated to me by an old woman, a hermeneutic. The study of those passages demanded supreme scholarship to interpret, years of intense application, and it has still not been wholly worked out. In order to help me, the old woman gave birth to my grandmother, who bore my mother. When my mother gave birth to me, there I was, deciphering the dictations of the old woman. And you dare tell me how to teach this Law? You show no gratitude, that this is being passed on to you? *Hmmm*?"

Muzhduk paused thoughtfully under Sclera's glare. One hundred and fifty people who had waited for this day since they were each elected president of their kindergarten class sat on the edges of their seats, listening to an argument that suddenly made no sense and for which they had not prepared, wondering how this might affect their grades.

"I understand," Muzhduk said, absorbing the impact of Sclera's words. His brain tingled like muscles on the mountain ridge when he faced Hulagu the Stupid. "As for me, when I study Law in my little Gropius room, I have some books on a shelf, and when the ones from the top shelf are cited in a case, I connect twenty-two long poles, but even then I can't quite reach them. So I lie on my back, naked as my first day here, and am able to use my cock to pluck them, open them, and process all the relevant information within."

Sclera's eyes glittered. "Good. One day soon I will come and see." He walked out. A few seconds passed before anyone moved.

Finally, Buck turned to Muzhduk in delayed astonishment. "Holy shit."

Muzhduk noticed that a gaunt student from the aisle directly in front was staring at him. "Look," the student said in a cold, threatening voice. "Just don't attract attention this way, okay?"

Muzhduk nodded absently and fingered the small hole in his chair while everyone packed up their outlines and headed out the door. Only when the room was nearly empty did he remember that he'd wanted to talk to the pale German schoolmistress in the back. But it was too late.

• • •

It was hard to concentrate without hard edges, with the glazing on all the tables, pillows, and people, like a painting by a neurotic—hundreds of coats of glaze on everything. But the picture was slowly coming together. One: the Bella loved Claude because he was one of the rare few who ever helped them, though many of the Bella were owned by Tuaregs. Two: Rogers admired the Tuaregs, who were at war with the government, though it was a weird shifting war with tribes and people changing sides. Three: he'd kept pulling the conversation back to the Tuaregs the day before, to see what I thought of them. Maybe to see what side I would take. But the only thing that mattered to me was Peggy, whom the Bella and Tuareg had taken away.

"I want to talk to the Tuareg who was here yesterday. Ibrahim," I told Rogers. Ibrahim had mentioned that Peggy had gone to a camp in the highlands, and he'd known she'd return last night. He had looked almost jealous.

"You've already talked to him." Now Rogers was acting like Sclera again. The Law here was *do what you will*, so long as you followed the rules of Rogers' riddles. The bastard was having fun. I twisted his wrist. "The people who took her are not her enemies. Fine? Yes? But you, you are dangerous to her. You are dangerous to everyone. You don't know what side you're on. You allowed a man to follow you from the bush-taxi—"

"What man?"

"A government man."

"The tout who spoke languages?"

"Everybody here speaks languages. Except for you."

"He wasn't a cop, just some guy trying to make a franc. He tried to convince me he was from the government. Even showed me identification to prove it. Which means he wasn't. Right?"

Rogers shook his head. "He even told you, and still you did not understand? You are stupid, and that makes you dangerous. Go home. Be happy to know she is safe."

He stood up from the table with an audible pop in both his knees. I pulled him back down, grabbed his shoulders, collarbones like matchsticks, and pushed him onto the pillows until his body buckled and he was on his back. I picked up a pillow. "Where did they take her?"

Claude left the room. Rogers glared back at me, trying to look dignified in his awkward position, lying on his back, half sliding into the broken table.

I pressed the pillow into his face with my weight. He didn't struggle. I counted to twenty, then lifted. He breathed sharp and heavy, his eyes directly under mine, only inches away—it was a weirdly intimate moment, killing an old man. His eyes were washed-out green with sagging lids, blue veins on yellow-grey, with no fat on his cheeks. I put the pillow on again.

Amadou tapped me on the shoulder. "Twobob, don't do this."

I looked at him, still holding the pillow down. "I don't believe she's safe."

"There's a better way. I'll help you. I can find her for you. We'll go together."

I hesitated, mentally exhausted from trying to muster the will to suffocate an old man who wasn't fighting back, violating every rule. I lifted the pillow off, disgusted, seconds before Claude ran into the room with Jean-Carlos and five Bella. Jean-Carlos had a machete and the Bella had their sticks from last night. One of the Bella had a big bruise on his cheek.

"Meet me at the Port Authority," Amadou whispered quickly. "At the ticket office."

I was still holding the pillow. "Jean-Carlos, you look like a violent man."

"I am," he said, and came at me with the machete.

"Good." I jumped back from the machete and tripped on a bolster. Jean-Carlos and the five Bella came at me, all striking down. I grabbed a table leg and swung the half-table as hard as I could into Jean-Carlos' knee and he crumpled in mid-swing. Sticks hit me, I don't know how many, but when they saw Jean-Carlos fall, they backed off.

I rolled up, then grabbed Jean-Carlos' neck. "Do you know?"

"*Porco Dio!*"

New men ran into the café, a dozen, all but one in military uniforms, all pointing machine guns at me. Their black skin had an inky-blue tinge. The only one in full Tuareg robes and veil was Ibrahim. He didn't have a gun, just the traditional sword at his side, its hilt sticking out from his robes. "Twobob," he said. "You must leave now."

• • •

On the fourth floor of Langdell, Muzhduk, Buck, and Lena walked into an enormous titan-buff-colored domed room. Where they met the ceiling, the thick marble walls were engraved with slogans. *LEX EST SVMMA RATIO INSITA IN NATVRA.* All were in Latin except three: *OF LAW THERE CAN BE NO LESSE ACKNOWLEDGED THAN THAT HER SEATE IS THE BOSOME OF GOD* and *IN THE BEGINNING WAS THE LOGOS, AND THE LOGOS WAS WITH GOD, AND THE LOGOS WAS GOD* and *THE RAM IS BEFORE THE FISH, AND THEY ARE ONE.*

"I heard a song about a chocolate Jesus once," Muzhduk said to Lena, staring at the library walls in awe. These were mountains on their own.

"What's a chocolate Jesus?"

"Same as a chocolate fish." Muzhduk shrugged. "A slogan on the wall."

"Those are maxims," Buck said. "Rules of conduct that make one great—*maximus*. Usually about the greatness of God. *Slogan,* on the other hand, comes from the Celtic *sluagh-ghairm,* which means 'battle cry of the dead.'" Buck was smiling.

"One day I should tell you about Fred the Political Officer." Muzhduk pointed to *IN THE BEGINNING WAS THE LOGOS.* "How about that one, *slogan* or *maxim*? John 1:1, right?"

"No," said Buck. "John 1:1 says that in the beginning there was the *word*, not logic."

Muzhduk thought about the idea of the word being first. It seemed like bad logic. But even logic being first was bad logic. Unless chaos comes out of order, rather than the other way around. The whole train of thought was silly—how could there be a *first* anything?

The domed Reading Room extended far to the left and right, aisle upon aisle of large antique bookshelves, followed by rows of old desks, thirty feet long, each with tall modern lights. Then more rows of bookshelves, individual cubicles, and thick columns. In the center of the room sat soft chairs, sofas, loveseats, all in colors ranging from N8 neutral grey through N3 neutral grey, interspersed with ficus trees. On the other side, past the grey elevators, was the reference desk and another complex: the subciting room, more grey shelves, and computers reserved for persons checking the accuracy of footnotes.

As Muzhduk watched students crisscross the room with books, papers, and distorted faces, Buck wanted to make sure they all appreciated the *moment* of the moment. "Here Holmes, Story, Learned Hand, Friendly, all the great jurists of America found their answers and resolved their problems."

"Those are all real judge names?" asked Muzhduk.

"Absolutely. Learned Hand was a second circuit judge and judicial philosopher, a pioneer of statutory interpretation. Here perfect function and symmetry are embedded in classical stone. Here, the word was invented and stripped of its shadow."

Buck went on, but Muzhduk didn't listen, remembering a box he'd once opened in the medical morgue of a Soviet labor camp he'd raided with his grandfather. It was a very large box engraved with curlicues and hand painted with bright swirly happy shapes. He was eleven or twelve. When he'd flipped the lid open, he found it full of human parts—surgically quartered bits of people thrown in at random. The thing he remembered most clearly was wondering, *What is that?*, because his mind had been slow in bringing two parts of a head together to see it was a human face. The delay had been the worst thing. He grabbed the lid to close it and found, written on the underside, the words: *I'm devoid o' my humanoid.*

"We'll split up," said Lena, handing Muzhduk two sheets of treasure hunt questions. She hadn't been thrilled with the grouping, but wasn't going to oppose the numbers dictated by their packets. And between Buck's cultural argument and Muzhduk's behavior in class, she'd accepted that he was just different. But that didn't mean she wanted to work with him. "Your half, my half."

Your half, my half. He tried to shake off the memory of the split faces. Both Lena and Buck cared about the hunt, and the three of them were a team, so Muzhduk focused. The first question: a particular word on a particular page of a particular *Federal Reporter.* He walked towards *SCIRE LEGES NON HOC VERBA*...the sentence continued around a corner. He didn't know where to look. The walls here were covered with *Federal Reporters*, all the same yellow and red oxide, each thousands of pages thick. Somehow he found the correct *Federal Reporter* and wrote down the word. Next: an *Atlantic Reporter.*

"Fuck, is this 257?" he heard Clive erupt behind him. In a tangle, three people were pulling on a single book, one covering up her answer sheet with a free hand as she noticed Muzhduk behind her. He briefly remembered Fred the Political Officer's comment about looking at the part of the swan that is beneath the surface, paddling furiously, then pulled on a corner as well. It seemed the thing to do. Clive slipped, cursed, and fell over backwards. Various objects fell out of his open backpack. Things that Clive didn't want anyone to see, as he struggled to stuff them back in.

There followed a long interval of pursuit and mutual hostility. Muzhduk's head rang. He wondered what had happened to all the caution and unjustified friendliness. They—books, students—accumulated on the tables, like goats chinning through garbage, squirrels hiding stacks. A few wandered around, dazed. A few were reshelved incorrectly, flipped through, passed. Then Lena materialized, saying that she had found most of her answers but a few books were missing. "How about you?" she asked impatiently.

"Somewhere missing. Some were missing," Muzhduk enunciated each word carefully, as the air smelled funny. "Do you smell something?"

"We have to finish," Lena replied.

"Maybe we should get organized," Buck added, laughing. He seemed drunk, almost wild. "Or go query a librarian, they're the authorities. Hey Muzhduk the Ugli, you coming? I appreciate that name. *Muzhduk the Ugli*. You don't mind if I call you Ugli, do you. It's your name, after all. Lena can keep searching while we seek guidance from the authorities."

Lena was already off, not even annoyed that Buck had told her what to do.

"I don't like authorities," Muzhduk said, feeling irritated.

They found the librarian behind a bookshelf helping some students. Buck said, "Excuse me, ma'am?"

"Yes, just a second."

Muzhduk finally recognized the smell. He walked out of the aisle to the central runway of the library. "Does anybody smell smoke?"

• • •

I picked up my goat and walked out the front door of the Getaway. The street was wide and empty, still in the shade. There was no place to hide and wait, except the garbage, the talus of trash on either side of the road, a full story tall against the two-story houses. There wasn't a single source of cover, not a single doorway with a deep enough entrance. I could stand at the corner of the long block and wait, but everyone would know that a Twobob was standing there. The market would already be active, and it wasn't long until everyone started their day. If I hurried, I could climb into the garbage.

It was an awful prospect, but I was out of ideas. If I could hide, and if they left by the main gate, then maybe I could follow Ibrahim and Rogers. Too many ifs, but I started to dig into the pile, gingerly moving rusted cans, twisted nails, bleached animal corpses, dried goat droppings, unraveled cloth, fish skeletons, dead thistle plants, and hardened solid goo. Every time I moved something, a thick throat-tickling fungal smell stirred up, or a death smell, or others that just made me gag and shudder, and several times I came close to vomiting. There weren't enough large objects for cover, and the one natural valley in the garbage was covered in what looked like human feces that I couldn't bring myself to touch. I gradually made an indentation against which I could half-sit, half-lie. Hulagu would have a good laugh if he could see me hiding in garbage, but when we fought the Russians we didn't stand in front of their tanks like idiots. Charging Tuaregs with machine guns wouldn't have helped me find Peggy. I began to carefully place garbage onto myself.

There was a dog body, bones and skin, but when I pulled on its leg the skin ripped and the leg started to come off and smelled awful and after that I couldn't bring myself to put it on top of me. A little boy ran down the street, about four or five years old, pushing a rusted bicycle rim with a long stiff wire. He saw me, half-covered, holding the dog leg, at the same time that I saw him. He stared for a few seconds, then ran off, frightened. I liked the rusty cans the best, they seemed the safest, without maggots, the least liquid, and after I accidentally squeezed against something that went in my ear and down my shirt, I wanted to stay away from liquids.

The little boy came back with a dozen other half-naked, finger-sucking children. They made a circle, watching silently, deciding whether I was a monster that their grandparents had forgotten to tell them about or just another Twobob doing strange Twobob things. One yelled "Gift, gift, gift," and the others took up the cry. Some of the older ones carried pots on their heads, and some their younger siblings on their backs. I pleaded with them to be quiet, I threatened them. The Getaway door opened, and one of the armed men who'd come in with Ibrahim poked his head out.

• • •

The library was on fire. The thought finally sunk in like an early morning sleep-wrapped realization that you're late for something important. Muzhduk ran back to Buck and the librarian. He could hear a distant crackling of old hardcover volumes that sucked the air out of the room as they burned. "There's a fire!"

"—although we have perused all the proper venues." Buck showed her the numbers.

"Well, today they could be anywhere," the librarian explained with a childlike shrug.

"There's a fire!" Muzhduk repeated.

"Could you venture a conjecture?" asked Buck, ignoring Muzhduk as though this were just another one of Muzhduk's odd behaviors, or simply too caught up in his own hunt.

"Every year somebody tries to prevent the other students from getting the answers by taking a black marker to the relevant portions of the books, or by ripping out pages. I have to order new copies of everything, which only arrive in time for the beginning of the next year. They really should have these things at the end of the year, so that we might at least have the books during the semester. But the professor insists." She seemed resigned.

"The library's on fire."

The librarian nodded, "There's no predicting it."

Muzhduk felt her nonchalance start to pull him back under. It was almost hypnotic. In Verkhoyansk people fought fires with the strength of the whole village. If it became certain that the fire would win, then the owner of the house declared a loss and threw in some of the objects he'd saved to show that he wasn't a bad sport. The more clear his judgment of when the fire crossed the point of no return, the wiser he was; the more valuable and sentimental the objects he threw in, the better a man he was. From the moment of the owner's declaration, everyone enjoyed the burning house as a rare spectacle and the night turned into a party that could rival the Dull-Boulder Throw and the I Know Nothing Festival. Both as an enemy and as a friend, fire was intense, and nonchalance seemed a wholly inappropriate reaction—but listening to Buck and the librarian, he absorbed their mood, and Buck kept asking for help in their treasure hunt.

"Sorry," the librarian said. "I can't suggest anything because that might imply leaving out something else, which could make me liable for your incomplete work. But I can say good luck."

A film of smoke obscured the other end of the library. Muzhduk could still make out *IN THE BEGINNING WAS THE LOGOS*, but now it glowed with orange reflected light.

"Ma'am? Is that from John 1:1?" Muzhduk asked. He had been thinking about the quote since Buck had disagreed. He was here for a word, after all, and nobody else seemed to care about the fire.

"Why, yes," she answered. "Yes, it is."

"Shouldn't it say *word*, instead of *logos?* In the beginning there was the *word?*"

"Why, it depends on your source, of course. Most English bibles say *word*, but in the Septuagint the word is *logos—kai Theós* ēn *ho Lógos*—which in English can be translated as either *word*, *ratio*, or *logic*. Martin Luther nearly translated it as *verb*, before settling on *word*. At its roots, *logos* is a sort of ordering of reality through pressing out one's self onto it. Rationality perhaps. The Chinese might call it *yang*. Old Testament stories were originally Aramaic, Canaanite, Mesopotamian, and Egyptian, with some Hebrew. These were all translated into Hebrew, and from Hebrew into low Greek. Most books of the New Testament, including John, were written in low Greek. This was later translated into Old Latin and then into the Vulgate in the 4th century by St. Jerome, and from the Vulgate came a number of English translations, including the King James. But Greek is definitely the most appropriate for St. John, and *logos* is too semantically distinct from *word* to permit such a simple translation."

A fire klaxon began to sound, finally. The siren was alone and very old, a half-choked moan, but it was enough to shake a number of students out of their daze, including Buck. The librarian looked up with the annoyed body language of an office worker who has been putting up with weekly fire drills for years, but started to walk towards the exit.

"Perhaps it would behoove us to hasten our egress," Buck said, then yelled at a girl in the distance with a sleeve on fire: "Stop, drop, and circum*vo*late!"

He ran toward the burning end, away from the exit.

"Where're you going now?" Muzhduk asked.

"To find Lena."

They ran to the table where they'd left Lena and found her among the mob that had earlier been pulling at books and who were now panicking but not leaving—students elbowed each other out of the way, giving and receiving jabs and scratches. There were no rules, despite all the maxims surrounding them. Everything was flammable, but still the students ran for books, not doors. They couldn't tolerate a blank answer. Fire had consumed all the judgments of *non-liquet*, all the places once labeled "here there be dragons." Muzhduk wondered if this was the dark side of every quest for Mt. Baldhead.

"We found the books," Lena snapped. "Someone hid them under a sofa."

As Lena spoke, a towering wall of *Federal Reporters* behind her tottered, on fire. Muzhduk grabbed the shelf and tried to keep it upright. Burning law books fell from the sky, hit his shoulders, two-thousand-page flaming hardcovers.

"Is there anyone on the other side of this shelf?" he yelled as loud as he could, unable to see. "Hello? I'm pushing!" He pushed the shelf over. It landed against the marble wall, leaning away from the other bookshelves.

Brushing his hands, Muzhduk looked Lena up and down. "You should put your hair up, Lena. How'd you find the books under a sofa?"

"We looked everywhere else. Where were you?"

"Watching the person who started this fire, I think."

"Who?" asked Buck.

Instead of answering, Muzhduk lifted his beard to his nose. It smelled burnt, nasty. "Let's get out of here before the fire reaches the exit."

There were still enough students searching through stacks that the archway exit wasn't clogged, despite the bewildered firemen in large hats and dark yellow coats running into the room, howling as they ran amok, smashing windows. They ushered students out of the building, threatening some, carrying others. An army of red trucks, packed in like toys around the huge granite building, doused the north side of the library with streams of water. A Channel 7 camera crew drove across Holmes Field, tearing up the manicured grass. A wind blew the smoke heavily.

As the three of them watched, Lena handed over the missing answers. Muzhduk imagined her running through the burning library, the largest law library in the world, overturning sofas, desks, bookshelves, whatever stood between her and the answers.

CHAPTER 7

Ratios

I climbed out of the garbage, knowing my self-burial had been for nothing. So many wrong turns and failed climbs and wrong mountains. I walked around to the back, toward the café entrance, out of ideas. The children followed me, growing in confidence. Little hands reached into my pockets and came out with pieces of paper, American coins, a pencil, a Canadian penny, a twig from the toothbrush tree—*salvadora persica*—that I had been using to brush my teeth, some uneaten peanuts, a Dictionary of Legal Latin maxims, even a few Central African francs. They milled around and fought each other. Then adults noticed the commotion and yelled at the kids, and pushed them away, slapped them, asked me questions. One middle-aged man who held his arm straight out as if his elbow couldn't bend asked if I was the big Twobob staying at the Getaway. He offered to take me there, said I wasn't far, then went to the café and waved at me, "*Venez, monsieur. Ici. Toute de suite.*"

I tried to tell him I wasn't lost, just going in circles, but he banged on the café door. The children made a crowd and fought each other for room to bang on the door with him, to help. The veiled girl opened the door and made a sound of disgust at my smell. The café was empty, with no sign of Amadou. Everyone was gone.

In the kitchen I found the Japanese mime cutting a tomato. He placed it on a piece of bread with cheese, then wrote on a page tacked to the wall, with a pencil on a string, in English: "1 bread, 1 cheese, 1 tomato," and then a Japanese character.

I wanted to thank him for his help the night before, but again found myself oddly muted. Even last night, in the middle of the fight, there had been a discharge of contagious silence around the mime. And not just in terms of sound. The silence he radiated reached into my head and interfered with my thoughts. Squeezed together in the kitchen like this, it was all I could manage to ask, "Where did they all go?"

Timbuktu, he mimed.

• • •

The Friday following the library fire, Muzhduk, Lena, and Buck sat together in Lincoln's Inn, the last of the great law fraternities. The original Lincoln's Inn in London was older than Chaucer. It had outlasted Grey's Inn, the Middle Temple, and the Inner Temple of the Order of the Knights Templar. Its purpose had changed over time, from discussions, moots, and bolts to baseball watching; Hieronymus Bosch's depictions of Hell had been replaced with abstracted sailboats, setting suns, and the Progress of America. There were no humans on the walls, and all the real power had shifted away to a whispered-about place called Gannett House.

Lincoln's Inn was looking for new members. Every first-year student gathered and signed his name: some for the free alcohol, most for the networking opportunities. But it was off-campus, and subject to the Boston Police Department's noise regulations, so at eleven they were all herded into the Ratio Pub, where a line of Harvard students waited to stumble first into a tiny foyer and then up the steep stairs inside. At the top, a heavy iron sign read, "R=1/R".

"Tea-totaling architect," Buck muttered. "Stairs constructed without a full appreciation of the uses of ferment." Upstairs, the pub was a swelling of people pressed against people. A rock beat pounded a repeated melody as each person moved alone and with the whole room. After a week of appropriate conversation, people who had spent their lives sipping politely without ever finishing a glass found themselves drunk. There were no dancing couples.

Muzhduk realized that he didn't like crowds. It was a sudden thing, something he'd never thought about before. Of course, if the only place where such thinking was allowed was a mountain top, it wasn't a realization he ever would have had in Siberia. But it was more than just a dislike. Crowds unbalanced him. He pushed through, past a pale older woman who didn't fit with all the jabbing elbows and bouncing and feet. She saw him knocking people out of the way and stared. He remembered her from the back of Sclera's classroom—the German schoolmistress—then the crowd separated them and he was at the bar with Lena and Buck and Clive. *How had they made it through without shoving and pushing?*

He turned to the bar to pick a drink, and saw a beautiful barmaid. He'd seen her before—she'd been applying for a job here on the evening of the baseball game. Her bra-free breasts had a perfect shape, the curve from her armpit clearly visible in a white tank-top that didn't fit with the Pub at all. Though the line of her breasts did. They were the spiral of a shell or a hurricane. And long nipples, like August raspberries in Verkhoyansk. And soft peach hair, when she lifted her arms, the first armpit hair he'd seen in a long time. He wanted to smell her. Instead, he waved drunkenly.

"Y'all want to drink something?"

"Beer," Muzhduk said, trying to figure out the appropriate ritual.

"No beer tonight," she said. "Nothing fermented, only distilled."

Hah, Buck had been right. "*Slivovica*? Plum brandy?"

She shook her head. Her pony tail waved.

He tried to think of an American drink. He'd had two dozen gin martinis at Lincoln's Inn, and they were good, so he asked for one of those.

"No martinis." She spoke in soft, rounded tones. Even when she yelled.

"No martinis? It's easy. Take some gin, let it look at a vermouth—"

"We don't make martinis."

Muzhduk wondered whether this was odd. He only liked vodka in the morning and he couldn't think of anything else, so he asked for directions to the toilet.

"It's that way," the barmaid pointed. "But I have to tell you that although the bathroom feels that it is part of the bar, the bar does not consider the bathroom to be in the same establishment."

Muzhduk shook his head. He walked where she had pointed,

down a corridor that he could reach without having to cross the dance floor. The men's room sign read: "Rawls' Stalls and Urinals—please do not enter if you are intoxicated." *Ha! Ha!* he thought.

He opened the door and an attendant in a starched white outfit pointed Muzhduk to the end of a long queue of waiting men. "Your starting position, sir."

The room was all mirrors and shiny multi-surfaces, reflecting Muzhduk endlessly. All the people in line were discussing each other, bobbing like teeth. Muzhduk couldn't understand them. The air was stuffy and hot.

"Water, alcohol, or other?" The attendant was again standing beside him.

"What?"

"Water, alcohol, or other? Which will you be micturating today, sir?"

"All of the above."

"Comprehensive." The attendant jotted something on his notepad, then looked back up. "Unfortunately, the comprehensive urinal is not set at a reasonable height today."

"How high is unreasonably high?" In Verkhoyansk, distance-peeing contests were common when drunk. It was the only thing about the toilet rules here that made any sense.

"Unreasonably. In fact, the only one at a reasonable height today is the water urinal."

After an interminable interval had passed, Muzhduk was at the urinal. On the wall above, like on the walls of all Harvard toilets, a small plaque said: "Veni, Vidi, Wiwi." And the air, like the air of all Harvard Law School toilets, smelled of coffee. The porcelain was an old diarylide yellow, and in clear black lettering proclaimed itself to be "American Standard."

When Muzhduk returned to the bar, Clive and Buck held drinks. Lena was just picking olives and candied cherries from the barmaid's box.

"What are you drinking?"

"Gin," said Buck.

"Martini Rossi," volunteered Clive.

"Marti...that's a brand of vermouth, isn't it? What? Hey Barmaid!"

She looked up at Muzhduk, neither more friendly nor more irritated than before. She had bright, calm brown, and long eyelashes. Her face startled him and made him feel dumb.

"You told me you can't make a martini," he finally said.

"We can't." She almost smiled. Juicy lips.

"Well, he's drinking gin, he's got vermouth, and she just ate an olive." He pointed to each of his companions in turn. "What's missing?"

"This pub does not make martinis."

"Why not?"

She shrugged. "We decided not to serve martinis."

"I don't understand anything in this place." He scratched his head and leaned over the bar to speak over the thumping music. The barmaid touched his hand gently with the tips of her fingers. They were warm and surprisingly calloused.

"Is your name Muzhduk thc Ugli?"

"How do you know?" He was surprised she knew his name, but then the whole pub was odd.

"You have a sweet face," she said. "But the Pub won't make exceptions. You can try to convince me, of course, but you should also think about why you insist on limiting your drink selection to something we don't offer."

"What's your name?"

"No personal details. Sorry."

"A name's not personal."

She laughed, nodding. "My name is also Muzhduk the Ugli."

"That's weird."

"I thought so too."

He could have a vodka, but that would be giving up. There was something crazy about the barmaid. Telling him to think about *why* he wanted a martini. That was just stupid. Beautiful, but stupid. "Okay. I'd like to order a glass of gin, a glass of vermouth, and an olive. Two olives."

She smiled again. "It seems likely that you would try to mix them. In the traditional way."

"They're for my friends," he gestured vaguely behind him. "A round of drinks. The second olive for me. Like Popeye."

The barmaid gave him a measured look, then poured a gin, a

vermouth, and placed two olives on a napkin. Muzhduk paid, watched her take the money and put it in the cash register. As soon as she turned the other way, he dumped the vermouth out, poured the gin into the vermouthed glass, and plopped the olives in. As he placed the glass to his lips, someone grabbed his other wrist and twisted it behind his back. Muzhduk spilled martini on his white T-shirt.

"Hey!" He wanted to spin around and punch, but he didn't want to let go of his drink.

"You're out of here," a voice said above his left ear. *Must be a big man.*

Muzhduk gulped his martini as the bouncer pushed him through the crowd. He twisted hard enough that Muzhduk was forced onto his toes. But he was happy. This was the first proper physical activity he'd had since he'd left Verkhoyansk. Catching cannonballs for the Cirque didn't count, that was man against cannon, not man against man.

Muzhduk's happiness irritated the bouncer, who jerked harder and higher until Muzhduk had to bend forward to compensate. He looked for a recognizable face in the tilted crowd to share the good news that he was going to have a little fight outside, but found only the pale German schoolmistress squeezing through the crowd towards him, telling him something about the beauty of violence as the bouncer kept pushing all the way to the indoor stairs and off.

Muzhduk flew through the air and landed on his face. He stood, brushed himself off, and walked out the front door. He waited thirty minutes for the bouncer to come for their fight, but he didn't. As Muzhduk waited and breathed the fresh outside air he became angry—the coward had taken the free shove off the stairs and then made him wait like an idiot—and walked back through the door.

"You can't come in," said another bouncer. He was as big as the one who had thrown Muzhduk down. Harvard seemed to import Maori giants to guard the Ratio. Or perhaps Muzhduk was shrinking.

"I just want to find your friend who threw me down the stairs and finish properly."

"I can't let you in for that."

"Okay." Muzhduk hesitated. *Words.* "You've got your job, I understand. But when I was thrown down the stairs, I didn't have a chance to tell my girlfriend I was kicked out. The new barmaid. She'll be looking all night. Can I just go in for a second to tell her?"

The bouncer called in on his ear-and-chin radio, but nobody answered. Muzhduk continued. "Look, I understand you don't have the authority to let me in, but if she thinks I just—"

"I have the authority. But you gotta come straight back."

Muzhduk broke his way back through the crowd, en route to the bar. The first bouncer was gone, and so were Lena, Buck, and Clive. The barmaid was leaning over the far side of the bar, handing a drink to someone. Tight jeans and white tank top and pony tail that danced lightly as she spun from customer to customer.

"So what's really your name?" he asked.

"I told you. Ratio Pub rules."

"I saw you apply for the job last week."

Her face turned a shade darker. "I wasn't expecting to need a job here."

"What were you expecting?"

A hand grabbed his shoulder again. The bouncer.

"Whoa, wait," Muzhduk held his hands up. "They said I could come back in, so I want to buy you a drink. To apologize. See, straight vodka, shared among friends."

"Thcy said so?"

"Yes, but weren't sure whether you have the authority to accept."

"Sure, I have the authority to accept."

Muzhduk took the vodka glass from the barmaid. "Since I promised you both a drink, we must be careful. The vodka belonging to me is on top. That for you, Ms. Barmaid, is in the middle. And the vodka for you, Mr. Bouncer, is on the bottom. If we're not careful, it will cause a dispute."

"That's silly," said the barmaid, but her tone and smile made the sentence an affirmation.

"If R equals one over R, like the sign says, and it takes three to make one drink, then each drink has three. And vice versa. This is the Ratio Pub."

"You're drunk," said the bouncer. "Your logic is suboptimal, and you're using the wrong meaning of the word Ratio. It's Latin, dummy."

"*Veni, Vidi, Wiwi*," Muzhduk said, standing up. "I'm going to hit you now and throw you down the stairs. Please get ready." The bouncer stood and shouted into his headset. Other bouncers poured in from all sides. *Finally,* Muzhduk thought and threw himself on the retreating bouncer. His fist connected with the man's chin, throat, and earpiece. The bouncer's spine bounced off the bar, returning him to Muzhduk. Muzhduk hit him again and his nose exploded.

Everybody sucked in at the sight of blood. Despite the abundance of bouncers, this much violence had never been seen in the Ratio Pub before. Bouncers threw people and, in an acknowledgment of the arbitrariness of life, people stayed thrown. Fists were swung occasionally, but none had ever connected. The music stopped and for a second the only sound was the raspy breathing of the unconscious, bleeding bouncer. Then another dove at Muzhduk with a high football tackle. Muzhduk got an arm under and lifted the bouncer in a fireman's carry. He ran, giddy with joy and relief, far lighter with the bouncer on his shoulders than he'd been at any point since crossing the border into America. Three bouncers appeared at the bottom of the first-level stairs near the front door. Five approached him from behind. It was glorious.

Muzhduk ran down the stairs and dove, using the flailing bouncer on his shoulders as a flying bumper, bowling the bottom bouncers. Everyone said "Huahhh," and lost the air in their lungs. Two stayed unconscious, one was dazed, one got up, and the five from behind grabbed Muzhduk and pushed his face through the entrance door.

Outside, someone kicked him in the forehead, over and over, with cowboy boots. Sharp and steel toed. Then they rammed Muzhduk's head into the brick wall of the building. It was the color of a desert sunset, pretty.

Muzhduk struggled to hold on to consciousness. The gradual fading—with little jumps toward darkness every time his head hit the wall—was a feeling he'd experienced only a handful of times in his life. Usually he preferred a dangerous world over a dull one, but the moments of losing consciousness like this he didn't enjoy. But these moments were necessary, he told himself as his head went into the brick. Danger must be frightening—make aware, enliven, and unite. But there was no one here to unite, except maybe the bouncers, who kept ramming him into the wall until flashing blue lights appeared in his blurred peripheral vision.

No more banging. He dragged himself back up to a sitting position against the wall. His nose was broken and his head was bleeding, his face a sheet of red. His eyes stung from the blood, but he didn't feel damaged. He moved his nose left and right, through the explosive whiteness of the grating cartilage—nose break number seventeen, if his count was right—then aligned it properly in the center of his face. It felt like an old pear. "Does anyone have a mirror?" Muzhduk mumbled at the crowd of Law Students that had gathered a safe distance away.

The older pale woman was there, in back. She stepped forward and offered Muzhduk an oval vanity mirror. She said, "I think you look rather handsome."

Maybe she was a ghost. Muzhduk wiped new blood from his eyes and saw an imperfect reflection of his nose already swelling. When had everyone gathered? Had they all just watched the ten-on-one fight? Maybe they didn't want to interrupt his fun. He systematically pressed the ridge of his nose to make sure it was as straight as possible. A few students asked whether he was all right, and an old cop had come out of a patrol car and was now looking down at him. Muzhduk noticed everything as if it had already happened. He couldn't see well, like someone had smeared Vaseline on the edges of his eyeballs. Concussion. He wiped his face, but he was smiling in the mirror.

"You better be going home, son."

"I understand that, officer. But those bouncers in there who bent my nose. They should come out and finish. One at a time. Honorably."

"You don't want me to arrest you now, do you?"

"I think you will have to arrest me, sir. Because I intend to wait."

The cop sighed. "If you wake up in jail tomorrow, you'll be unhappy with yourself."

"I'm already very happy, sir. For the first time here. Being arrested won't ruin it."

"That's the wrong choice, son."

"I know. Sometimes a man has to make the wrong choice."

Before the cop could say anything else, Buck came through the crowd. "Our apologies, officer! We'll ensure that he gets home in a safe, peaceable manner." Lena was with him. Buck helped Muzhduk to his feet, but Lena seemed disgusted by the blood. She opened her little bottle of waterless antiseptic soap and squeezed a dollop of foam out.

"Come on." Buck pulled. He was uncomfortable, but his urge to help was stronger. "Notice all these people observing. They're going to think we did something egregious. Let's *go!*"

The cop walked back to his patrol car, its lights still silently flashing blue. Muzhduk could see Harvard's crimson *VE-RI-TAS* logo and the words *Harvard University Police Department*. "You make sure he gets home and sleeps it off. The BPD would collar him without a thought, you know."

"Thank you officer," Buck called back as he pulled Muzhduk along Massachusetts Avenue as Lena continued to sterilize.

• • •

Most of the houses in Gao were square mud bricks—the French Colonials thought them more "cultured" than grass and straw huts—but the port authority was an old French building, with a faded wood-plank sign that read, "Comanav." It looked transported from a New Orleans ghetto.

Inside, I asked for a ticket to Timbuktu, paid my money, and received a slip of paper with one sentence written on it, in English: "*I know that I have been hanging from the stormy tree for nine consecutive nights, wounded by the spear, as an offering to Odin: myself offered to myself.*"

"This is a boat ticket?" I asked the clerk, a knobby-jointed man who kept touching his hairless chest through an unbuttoned shirt.

"Yes."

"What does it mean?"

"You bought the ticket. You must ride the boat."

"There's no date, no time."

The man picked it up, looked at it, and slapped it on the counter. "Wednesday, of course," he said, then picked it up again and walked into the back. Wednesday, Odin's day, of course, except we were speaking French and what he'd actually said was *Mercredi* and I'd never have made that leap unless we'd been speaking English. Language changes how you think. Maybe I should try thinking in Slovak again, I thought, just to remember.

I waited for a while, with no sign of the clerk. The port authority was hot and decrepit, with veneer flaking off buckling walls under a high broken ceiling. There was no breeze, and more than the usual buzz of flies. I climbed over the knife-scarred counter. Before I touched the ground on the other side, the clerk, two other men, and a very fat woman ran in from the back room. The clerk yelled, "You cannot be on this side, Twobob!"

"I'd like my ticket back."

"You know when the boat comes," the fat woman said. Each of her breasts was the size of a turkey and together they gave her words authority. Except for her flat nose, she looked like a dark Slovak mother. "Now go back into the public space."

"I need my ticket."

"It's only paper."

"So how do I get on the boat?"

"That is up to you." They all laughed.

"Then what did I pay for?"

"Knowing."

"Of when the boat comes?"

"Yes."

"But everyone knows that."

"Now you know."

"Then I paid for the paper. If it's useless, I'll use it on the toilet."

The fat woman took the paper from the reluctant clerk and slapped it down on the counter, just as the clerk had done. Her whole arm jiggled, and a breast as well.

I took the paper. "So what does it mean?"

The fat woman looked annoyed. "How should we tell you?"

"But why is it in English? Nobody here speaks English except me."

"Well?" She looked at me like I was an idiot.

"And that doesn't seem odd to you," I asked, "that there is a special ticket just for me?"

"The only thing that seems odd to us is a Twobob, mister," she answered and shook her head. The three men all laughed and slapped their knees.

Wednesday. Woden. Odin, the wanderer. The god of war and poetry. Sometimes he wore a bearskin and went berserk. He degenerated into a hunter eternally in pursuit of...I couldn't remember what for certain. A woman? Seeing the Wild Hunt—a ghostly group of men led by Odin—presaged catastrophe, war, plague, or an abduction to the underworld. That was all I remembered about Odin. And that at the end of eternity he sacrificed himself to himself, by hanging in a tree. And in French? *Mercredi*, Mercury, the Roman version of Hermes, god of messages, roads, potential, and intellectual energy. The god of hermeneutics. Mercury scattered his words throughout the universe, by way of his sperm. I remembered that much from a book my uncle, the one killed in Oymyakon, had given me, probably stolen from a Soviet gulag, titled *Logos Spermatikos*.

The boat would leave in two days. I stopped on my way out. "Did anyone else buy a ticket for Timbuktu on Wednesday?"

"Your Japanese brother," the fat woman said. "He said you are coming."

How did he know? I wondered as they laughed. "When did he buy it?"

"This morning, very early."

"Did he speak English?"

They all laughed again. "No. He can't speak anything."

"But you're sure his ticket was also for Timbuktu, leaving Wednesday?"

"It is the only ticket we sell. To him and your other brothers."

In Africa everything breaks down.

• • •

Outside Gropius, Buck gave up trying to make Muzhduk promise not to go back to the bar, and left Lena to sterilize his forehead. She hated blood, but Muzhduk had kept the burning books off her and she didn't like owing anyone a favor. She felt stretched and ragged, needing to rest, but didn't want to go to her little room and be alone.

Lena knew she should not keep company with a man like Muzhduk. Other men were more dangerous for hiding it, for always maintaining plausible deniability, but he was obnoxious on many levels and association with him would harm her reputation. There were only two things at Harvard that mattered: socialization and networking. Learning the crisp, analytic way of thinking like a lawyer in order to beat them at their own game, that was the second most important thing. *Most* important were the connections that would last a lifetime. Not connections with people such as Muzhduk. He could, perhaps, end up president of some little country, god forbid, but it would be a very little country.

And then there was the danger of infection. Human emotions and thought patterns transmit from person to person, she'd read, and brainwaves are like a woman's period. They synchronize with those of the people near you. She should spend time with successful people whose character traits she sought to absorb, not someone named Ugli.

She was surprised at how barren Muzhduk's room was. A bicycle hanging above the bed and four books. It made him less alien, a little pitiful. Her own room was just as small, but stuffed full. He must be poor.

He sat on the bed as she swabbed his forehead with a vodka-soaked T-shirt, conscious of his breath at her chest. He was an oaf. Surely she couldn't find any mystery in a brute.

She could use him for a night, perhaps. She didn't date men for their looks, and certainly not for their muscles, but he did have those enormous crazy blue eyes, like Klaus Kinski in *Aguirre*, and at least with him there was no risk she'd become attached. An attachment could only interfere. She could use him, but could she accept knowing that he'd also be using her?

She talked. She swabbed his forehead and told him he was disgusting and childish and arrogant and self-centered, obnoxious, and her breasts were in his face as she swabbed his forehead. She normally would never have played such a game, such a stereotype, but she was a touch offended—Muzhduk the Ugli, who couldn't control himself about anything, why wasn't he even trying now? Perhaps it was all a show.

As these thoughts ran through her mind, Lena began to sweat. A tiny amount, but it fought past the chemical antiperspirant, past the hand sterilizer, and the subtle industrial perfume. Despite her chest, the roundness two inches from his face, Muzhduk had been cut off by Lena's absence of human scent. The trickle of angry sweat was enough. It wove through the stitches of cashmere surrounding her breasts dangling roundly in front of him. Muzhduk gently bit the left nipple, through the sweater, and said, "That's soft."

She froze, two contradictory emotions jamming her voice.

Early the next morning, Lena lay on Muzhduk's bed, wishing for a pillow—she didn't want to use his arm—but otherwise satisfied.

She'd needed the sex, and he was not nearly as selfish in bed as she'd expected. And, though she'd never admit it to him, she'd really enjoyed the feel of his weight on top of her. She remembered something and turned to him. "In the library, you said that you saw who started the fire."

Muzhduk lay on his side so there'd be room for both of them. He noticed again that Lena's aureoles were enormous and very pink. They covered most of her breasts. She dropped her red hair over them, hesitated self-consciously, then pulled the sheet up over everything. Muzhduk sighed, "I thought I saw Clive under a cubicle trying to light a small stack of books. But I was in a daze, and it was difficult to make out where one person ended and the next began. Everything feels so unreal here sometimes."

"That doesn't make any sense. Why would Clive take a risk like that?" She chewed on her bottom lip, while Muzhduk tried to gently pull the sheet back down, so he'd have more to look at. She yanked it back up, irritated. "You have to inform the authorities."

"I would never do that."

"But Clive's not even your friend. He refers to you as the barbarian with the oppositional defiant disorder. And he says your head looks like a buffalo. Or he calls you Lenny, which I find especially annoying."

"They have names for such things?"

"What?"

"Oppositional defiant disorder."

"It means you're a rebellious freak. So are you going to tell someone or not?"

"No."

"Well, then I'll do it myself. Besides, expelling Clive will help the bell curve. I heard he graduated with a 4.0 from—"

"I told you in bed. Post-coital confidences are sacred. If you reveal them, you destroy the bed."

Lena sat up, still clutching the sheet with both hands at her collarbones. "That's nonsense. No privilege attaches to drunken one-night stands. We'd have to be married for such a privilege to attach, and Massachusetts doesn't even have spousal privilege, I think. We have no relation except one single, drunken evening together. You're large, muscular, and...and outside the Harvard social fabric, more or less. No offence. But the thing I wanted I got last night.... That's all." She was red and annoyed.

"I really don't care what Massachusetts thinks about it."

"Well, I really don't care what your male code thinks."

"*Please* drop this."

"No." She had regained her edge. "It's a good lesson for you too."

Muzhduk stood, hesitated, wrapped a towel around his waist, picked up an empty glass, and went to the bathroom. He returned with water and he looked out the window at the blocks of other Gropius dormitories. It was early morning, just before sunrise, and the faint light made them look grey and blockish, and at the same time insubstantial. The buildings seemed far away and threatened to become further still. Muzhduk sighed, knowing that he was about to make himself even more celibate. He hated being celibate, but if you couldn't let your guard down even in your own bed, then where?

Lena sat on his bed, wedging herself back into her Control Top Pantyhose. Her skirt was still on the chair. He threw her skirt on the bed and emptied the glass on top. A few drops splashed Lena.

She jumped, almost bouncing, and shouted in a self-possessed whisper, "Are you insane?"

"You tell about the library, and I'll tell everyone that we had to wash out the stains."

She stared at Muzhduk for a full three seconds. "What planet are you from?" The skin on her face looked very tight. Then her shoulders lifted and in a much quieter voice, she said, "You contemptuous bastard!"

"Contemptuous?" He didn't understand. "I just want to make a deal and this is your only weakness that I can see right now."

"Why do you want to protect Clive so much, that you'd rather destroy my reputation?"

"I'm protecting my bed, not Clive. I couldn't care less about Clive."

"Or anyone else."

• • •

I wandered with hordes of children through the Gao bazaar, past young women in bright dresses who yelled out from their shops for me to stop and talk, shaded from the poisonous sky by cloth hung above stalls filled with carefully stacked pyramids of tropical fruits, tiny tomatoes, spices, onions, and even lettuce, as well as buckets of sour milk, baskets of eggs, dollops of hand-ground peanut butter spaced like about-to-be-baked cookies on newspaper, various juices in transparent goldfish bags, raw chickens, split goats, fresh and dried river fish, and all the brands of Corpa-Cola. There was no sign of Peggy or Rogers or Amadou.

Food turned to crafts, jewelry and desert wares. "Twobob, come talk to me," a girl called from her stool. Her hair was plaited in a spiral off to one side of her perfectly round head, with green beads woven in; the same beads were her merchandise. One cheek was engraved with a tattoo of a ladle, the other with seemingly random checkers. Her teeth, when she smiled, were small and filed into points. "Come. Sit and talk. I am not so bad to talk to."

I hesitated, tired, more interested in sitting than conversation.

"Or to look. Maybe we just look and talk small-small. No good for men to talk much."

"That's the truth."

She reached out and took my hand, caressing the skin as if testing it. "You like to look at me, Twobob?"

I smiled. "Sure, you're nice to look at."

"And you like to touch a little?" She smiled. "What's your name, Twobob?"

"Muzhduk the Ugli. But no, thank you, not today."

"Little One. You be married, Ugli Twobob?" She smiled. "Just Twobob, okay. Name doesn't matter for you, Twobob. Who gave you this name? Your father? It's not such a good name. Maybe you pick a new one. So, you must tell me. You be married?"

"Not married."

"You lie to me. Why you lie to me?" she asked, becoming angry as I stood and walked away. "You be married. Everybody knows. But you divorce your Tuareg Twobob terrorist and marry me. No problem."

I wandered through more alleys, over the Red Dune, an enormous red star-dune as tall as a small mountain and as sprawling as a suburb, to the Askia tomb, and back to the bazaar. Everything was fluid, malarial, and I was still walking in circles. Or maybe they were spirals.

I found myself back at Little One's kiosk.

• • •

After the Ratio Pub, school started in earnest. Muzhduk spent weeks drinking coffee in the Hark Box, casebooks in front, yellow highlighter in one hand, chocolate muffin in the other, shutting people up like telescopes, reading, occasionally thinking about the barmaid from the Ratio Pub. He saw her from time to time on campus, at the Au Bon Pain in Harvard Square, at the bookstore, and wondered whether she was a student. She was always too far away to ask, and when he did try to walk over she slipped out before he could make his way through all the other students buying their coffee or their *pain* or their books.

And there were a lot of books. One day Alan Dershowitz assigned 574 pages for the next class. At that speed, the words were everywhere. Letters appeared in select students' pigeonholes inviting them to try out for study groups. One letter from a student named Ted Cruz went out to everyone, announcing that Ted was accepting resumes to put together a study group, but that no one from the "minor Ivies" need apply—only graduates of Harvard, Yale, or Princeton were welcome. Ted was instantly mocked for his clumsiness.

Muzhduk didn't join a study group. He could tell how much he'd read by how much he'd highlighted. The information went straight from the page to the highlighter, the archive of all knowledge. It didn't really pass through Muzhduk. Later, when he tried to study from these books, he only learned the unimportant things, as the few resilient words that had managed to stay white stood out in sharp contrast to the highlighted yellow book. Yellow as old bacon, which Muzhduk hadn't seen since leaving Siberia. He missed old bacon and thick barnyard eggs.

Buck used multiple colors—along with the neon yellow, he had green, pink, blue, and purple—as he sat with Muzhduk and wove legal doctrines together with snippets from Derrida, Foucault, Wittgenstein, Nietzsche, Leibnitz, Kierkegaard, Goethe, debating the relevant merits of both sides in the Gadamer–Habermas letters, and so on. At least once every thirty minutes, something in a case would trigger him to look up and say, "Hey, Muzhduk, how about this?" followed by a poem by Bashō or feminist critical theory by Luce

Irigaray, subaltern theory by Gayatri Spivak, or a principle of war from Clausewitz, always tied into the readings in some convoluted hypothetical way. He was the most well-read person Muzhduk had ever met, and while everyone else turned grey from lack of sleep, he remained perpetually cheerful at the idea of actually being at Harvard Law School.

He was friends with everyone, provided regular updates about Sclera's appearances on Court TV, and asked Muzhduk at least twice a day to tell him "another crazy story" from Verkhoyansk. Lena avoided Muzhduk for a week after their night together, then acted as though nothing had happened. Buck was his only real friend.

Then Buck disappeared. He stopped going to the Hark Box for coffee and didn't come to class. Since the three of them sat next to each other in every class with assigned seating, his absence forced an unnatural level of conversation between Muzhduk and Lena. At the end of the week, Muzhduk went to find Buck. He phoned, knocked on Buck's door in Somerville—he'd moved off campus at the end of September, the only first-year student Muzhduk knew who didn't live in Gropius—and kept knocking until Buck cracked the door open. He said he'd been sick but was feeling better and promised to come to school tomorrow.

True to his word, Buck showed up at the Hark Box the next day. Muzhduk asked him what had been wrong. Buck shrugged, said "nothing," fidgeted and finally asked whether Muzhduk had read the letter from Ted Cruz.

"About the study groups?"

"Yes."

"What exactly do they do?" Muzhduk asked. "I always thought studying was solitary."

"They discuss cases, prepare outlines, engage in legal discourse," Buck answered. "I need another coffee. You want another coffee?"

Buck brought two more coffees, sat hunched forward, looked around, then explained in a whisper that he'd attended a state school. Sure, he'd graduated first in his class, but it wasn't even Berkley, the one acceptable state school.

"Ah, so you think your 'first in class' was like a one-eyed man beating out the blind?"

"Yes. No. I mean, that's how it will be perceived. Perhaps I don't really belong here."

"You're wrong. And whoever perceives it that way is also wrong."

Buck held up his hand to stop Muzhduk from interrupting. "I know it's not true, that undergrad shouldn't matter, but I can't help it. It does matter. Outside, I can always say I attended Harvard Law. So long as I don't fail out, of course. But *here,*" he poked the table with one finger, "people can tell if I'm a fraud. Am I a fraud? Sometimes I can't tell myself."

"You know more than Fred the Political Officer."

"You, you're so sure of yourself, Muzhduk the Ugli the Fourth. But I can never be that sure. I *was* admitted, after all. But it's obvious you're immune, that's what's so beautiful about you. But on the rest of us, our schools are like serial numbers—no matter how much we read or study. Because we care. It's all in the facebook: name, school, major. And now it's interfering with my chances of getting into the best study groups, the groups that will create outlines to prepare for any possible exam questions. One of the groups might even find the Outline of the Covenant. But I won't be part of any of that."

Muzhduk had never heard of this Outline of the Covenant. As they sat at the Hark Box Café eating muffins, Buck confided in Muzhduk that he'd been admitted a year earlier, but had dropped out after two months. Harvard had allowed him to come back based on a medical certificate of a nervous breakdown. No one was supposed to know, but the registrar knew, the professors might remember his face, and the facebook showed that he had graduated with his Bachelor of Arts a year before he officially started. Buck worried that people would find out that one year ago he had locked himself in his room without food, and hadn't dared leave. At the end of three weeks he'd been taken to a hospital where nutrients were pumped into his veins.

Harvard allowed him into this year's class, and surely if even the doctor had signed off after his breakdown, then it was not fraudulent. But he wouldn't get a third chance. So now he paid extra to live off campus and kept enough canned goods there to last out a small war.

"I'm honored that you told me," Muzhduk said when Buck finished.

"You won't tell anyone, will you? I thought, you know, since you're kind of prehistoric-level old school."

"My word," Muzhduk said, and stopped talking because Lena walked in.

"Are you discussing *Rush v. Commercial Realty*?" She looked angry.

"Yes."

"I was uncertain," Buck said, "as to my concord with the court. I mean, on the one hand, the plaintiff knew that the floor was defective and he could have used the other outhouse, but on the other hand, the defendant was negligent in having a defective floor in his outhouse."

"Whereas I thought," Muzhduk said, "that the correct standard is *gross* negligence, rather than just negligence."

"Ah, but I cite Judge Baron, 'gross negligence is nothing but negligence with a vituperative epithet,'" Buck quoted with a grin. "In any event, defendant should have kept his outbuilding floor safe."

Lena gestured at Muzhduk for Buck's benefit. "He was trying to be funny. Do we know whether there was a statute or a state law mandating adequate outhouse flooring?"

"The doctrine of *negligence per se*," suggested Buck. "Or perhaps *res ipsa loquitur*, the thing speaks for itself, attributing strict liability?"

"The outhouse speaks for itself?" asked Muzhduk.

"It speaks as it breaks. It says 'Negligence!'"

"Was there privity of obligation? One of those outdoor privities?" It was all privities and negligence, thought Muzhduk. And efficiency, fairness, administrability. Or "justice in the individual case," as law professors called what elsewhere was simply referred to as "justice." Not just at their table, but at all the other tables where people did something other than color their books quietly with highlighters, the humorless conversations were about defective outhouses. Everybody recognized the structure of their society within the outhouse. Everyone said it was "egregious." Somehow, nobody found it funny that a man had fallen into shit.

"Outdoor privities of obligation," Buck said, nodding. "Very funny."

"I have a joke too," Lena said and smiled sourly. "You want to hear it?"

Buck and Muzhduk both nodded.

She turned to Muzhduk. "I just found out that we're partners for Moot Court. Your letter's in your pigeonhole."

Buck and Muzhduk both started laughing hysterically.

• • •

I let Little One choose the restaurant. I wasn't hungry, but ordered a beer. She ate with her right hand and rubbed my erection with her left—like it was her own leg or a handle that gave her absentminded comfort—while she told me what she knew about the Getaway Guesthouse. She was linked into the web of hidden information conduits that tied an African town into a living whole, though I had no way of knowing what was true and what was not. She made the Getaway sound like a secret power center that controlled half the country. Rogers was a powerful Twobob who could buy anyone and, people said, a Twobob babalawo as well, so it was better not to say his name out loud. Claude bought fourteen-year-old girls and helped the Bella rise up against their masters (Little One was Bozo, not Bella, so helping Bella was an additional indictment). Jean-Carlos was a new Twobob but people said he was crazy and a cannibal. And Peggy was a strange Twobob woman who traveled without her man and helped smuggle things for the Tuaregs, but nobody knew what because the government was biased and always helped the Blue People even though they were fighting them. And now people wondered whether Muzhduk was Peggy's man, here to take her back home.

"I think what people say is wrong," I said when she finished. "I think the Getaway is just three sad old expats who sit around talking."

"No," she shook her head. "Is you be wrong. Getaway is dangerous."

When the rumors were exhausted, there was nothing else to talk about.

"It's hot in Gao during the day."

"Yes."

"There's a lot of sand."

"Yes."

"It's cold at night, though."

"Yes, mostly now."

I put my jacket around her. It really was freezing—the middle of the Sahara, and it felt like Siberia or Montreal, or Boston at its best—but the cold here was deeper, like at high altitude where the body can't produce heat and even the warmest blanket only holds in coldness. I wondered how Little One could handle it.

"You have the shiverings," she said. "I thought cold be good for Twobobs."

"It is."

"Your lips be blue, and you have the shiverings. Maybe you needs your jacket."

"I'm fine," I stuttered. "It wasn't this cold yesterday."

"It was same-same." She pointed out, toward the desert. "Every day is hot and every night is cold. Here is a little more cold, because we talk about so many Twobobs today. They makes it colder." She touched my forehead. "You burned to death. You got there fever and there blue lips, with the pale white face. I don't wanna kiss them lips all blue. You takes your jacket. I don't want catch no death from you. Take the jacket and we go jiggy-jiggy in my room. Warms you up." The thought made me a little nauseous, even as the friction warmed my middle.

"What do you do during the day?" I tried to change the topic.

"Sell there jewels," she said, and touched the green beads in her hair. Then she shrugged. "Many things. Sometime sleep. Maybe I sew you a sweater, and you buys from me. You be Mr. Rich-rich? The plane ticket from Twobobland, how much money you pays it? You takes your jacket for now. Maybe gives it to me after you not cold, buys another in Twobobland. How much CFA for this jacket cost, in there Twobobland? Okay, you tell me in dollars, no problem."

"No problem," I repeated.

• • •

Classes continued whenever they weren't canceled in favor of Court TV, and Sclera continued to rip through students. He didn't call on Muzhduk, didn't visit him in Gropius as promised, and Muzhduk didn't raise his hand anymore. Sclera focused on proving that *procedure* is more important than *substance* in all law. "Even criminal," he said, and read a name from his poster board: "Mr. Wang Clivus." Clive.

The class was *Civil* Procedure, not criminal; no one had prepared the Texas case that Sclera wanted. It was an appeal of a death penalty conviction of two people for the same crime. A man had confessed to a crime he didn't commit, but upon receiving the death penalty got scared, recanted, and proved beyond a doubt that the murder had been committed by his sister, not him. The same prosecutor who had obtained the death penalty for the brother used this new evidence to get a conviction, and death, for the sister. But he refused to release the brother, because it would have lowered his conviction ratio, and prosecutor careers depend on batting averages. The brother appealed, and the Texas Supreme Court ruled that "in the absence of procedural error, innocence is not a valid stance for appeal."

But somehow Clive knew the case, and was prepared. He gave the facts, the holding, and the dicta. When he finished, Sclera ripped him apart anyway. He administered justice in a way not seen at Harvard since the quartering of Campion, and Clive didn't get any more words in. "You are a disgrace," Sclera concluded. "You pretend that you know procedure trumps substance, but you do not. You have not internalized it. You may think that students cannot be expelled for sheer incompetence. I will even give you the right not to be expelled for incompetence. Here," Sclera gestured with open hands. "Do you want any others?"

In Verkhoyansk, a person who shamed himself had to give five public blowjobs to the chief, while the whole village watched and jeered. Clive didn't answer, just stared wide-eyed.

"I asked you whether you want any other rights? Answer me or get out!"

"N-no, sir."

"N-no, sir," Sclera mocked. "I will give you all the substantive rights you can think of. If I keep the rules of procedure, you will always lose. And I run the Administrative Board, which expels students."

It was weeks before Clive recovered. He wandered the hallways in a daze. People whispered about him in any room he entered, told colleagues in the other three sections about "Clive's Correction," and generally avoided him out of a vague fear that his shame could be contagious. Muzhduk, who had experienced a similar ambient buzzing the first few weeks of school, felt sympathetic and tried to start conversations with Clive. Each time Clive simply apologized and walked away.

• • •

I woke up on a wooden bench at the port as the sun was setting. *A wooden bench, Woden's bench, they were right*, I laughed, waiting for the boat, then fell back asleep. I didn't know how I'd arrived there. After leaving Little One at the restaurant, my night was lost to rolling waves of colors and cold and malaria. The orange barrel fires were burning, making skin glow and the port shimmer with sweat and freezing. The bench was everything, any light irritating. Sometimes I was on the bench, and sometimes I was far away and couldn't get back. Even then, I felt the bench against my back, a solid piece of wood, something to hold on to, not words. I was heavy, aching, the cold piercing like electricity. The night went on forever and the longer it went on the more I was on the bench. When I was on the bench, I could see the air. It was glazed, thick, and it bent the lights from the little wood-and-thatch kiosk next to the bench and the people milling everywhere.

Someone told me to stand, so I stood. They told me to walk, so I walked. Everyone walked. I had always walked. Into a small hazy room, empty except for the glazed air and sweaty walls peeling whitewash, a faintly angry crowd, a desk and a man behind it with a rubber stamp. A ten-watt bulb glowed with shallow light through the thick air. The man moved with complicated care. He assured himself that the left side of the stamp touched the proper location on the paper in front of him, yelled at the crowd to move back and give proper room to the government, then rolled the stamp slowly from left to right and, with a snap, lifted the stamp off the paper. He verified that the stamp had fully connected at all points, without blurring, and finally handed the paper to the waiting-man without making eye contact, without looking up from the papers or changing the expression on his face in any way. "Next."

I was jostled by the crowd and too weak to push back, until I was last in line. I could barely stand. I endured the rubbing crowd and even the deliberateness of the placement of the stamp. But under that flickering ten-watt bulb, the important snap-and-flick of the wrist at the end was too much. I decided to kill the stamp man. I was sick enough, so it would be fair.

I gave him Odin's words and he began to stamp. I placed

an arm on his desk to steady myself, gathering my strength. He stopped moving mid-stamp. "Is this how you would treat the desk of a government official in your own country? With such disrespect?" I nodded. "You come to Mali and mock us, wearing such tattered dirty clothing." He pointed at me. I seemed to be glowing brighter: the tassels of my ripped shorts each formed a strand of beautiful light, aurora malarialis. "You are trying to imitate our poverty in mockery? Purchase some proper clothing, and remove your hand from my desk immediately."

Still bracing myself against his desk, I took his stamp, pressed it into its pad—he sat frozen by this audacity—and slammed it into his forehead. "Gao-Kabara, 3ème classe."

• • •

Lena wanted to get a head start on their moot court preparations. It was an obscenity case, so Muzhduk suggested going to see a pornographic movie, a Swedish porn documentary from the 1970s that had made it to the Supreme Court and created a new legal test for obscenity. The Court had given it five thumbs up, and it was playing at the Brattle arthouse theater, off Harvard Square. *I Am Curious (Yellow).* Lena refused.

Buck had told them that for years before the *Curious (Yellow)* decision the Supreme Court held secret movie nights where they showed all the films they'd outlawed as obscene. "Nine old white *men*," said Lena, wondering whether the movie was racist as well as sexist. Buck understood her question. "No, there was also an *I Am Curious (Blue)*, and an *I Am Curious (Orange).*"

So instead of the Brattle, Muzhduk and Lena went to the library, which had reopened. It was a sunny late October morning with a cold, crisp wind. Muzhduk lifted his face to the sun, moved his eyes around under the lids, letting the sun heat as much surface as possible. He had taken to doing this lately, burning off a sort of fatigue stored in his eyeballs.

"What are you doing?" Lena asked, annoyed that she had to wait.

"Photosynthesis." He waited a few more seconds before opening his eyes, then blinked at the harsh reflection from the bleached library steps. A woman was walking down, dressed all in black with a black scarf waving behind. Her face was the same color as the stairs.

She was the ghost from the Ratio Pub who'd given him the mirror, the woman in the back of Sclera's class, and she walked as though she held every stray cell of skin from wandering off. If Buck were here, he'd say she was rejecting a sentence Italo Calvino had written, about how it is in the process of throwing away, of shedding dead skin, that we discover what parts of us remain. If there is anything left after taking out the trash, Calvino said, we are still alive. Closer up, her skin looked like porcelain, flawless. The contrasts made her look as if she weren't really there, or at least intended to walk right past Lena and him.

"Hi," Muzhduk called out when they were both on the first step.

"Oh, hello," she answered with a start.

"Want to go see a movie?"

"A movie?" She glanced at Lena. "When is it?"

"Tomorrow," Muzhduk said and hesitated. Her eyes were green, almond shaped. "We met at the Ratio Pub."

"Yes, I remember. What are you asking now?"

"Whether you want to go see a movie."

"If I give you my number, this time will you lose it?"

"No." Muzhduk said, momentarily confused. Had he asked her at the bar too? He didn't think so, but he'd been very drunk.

"Because it is rather offensive to have one's number lost."

He was almost certain that she'd never given him a number. There was an uncomfortable silence before she took out a pen and paper and wrote down her number and name in long, almost calligraphic script: "Oedda."

"I'm Muzhduk the Ugli."

"Yes, I know."

"I mean, do you want my number too?"

"No. You will call me."

"I'll call you. Tonight."

"Very good."

He suddenly felt that he should have made more small talk before asking her on a date. She didn't blink. Since he'd said "hi," she hadn't blinked. "Do you live around here?"

"At the library?" she asked without laughing. "Good-bye." She included Lena in the valediction and walked on down the asphalt squirrel paths. She didn't turn back to look.

Lena and Muzhduk walked into the library, found a table and began to read through obscenity cases. After a while Lena asked, "So?"

"So what?"

"Who was she?"

"I don't know."

"You don't?" Lena looked up from her *Federal Reporter*. "Then, this is a first date?"

"It's two people going to a movie."

"To that movie you were asking me about? The porn?"

"It's research. Does it bother you that I asked both you and her to the same movie?"

"I was just amazed at how awkward your conversation was. And I guess I'm still surprised that you're taking a woman to watch porn on a first date, though I probably shouldn't be." Lena touched her pocket, hesitating. "She's not in our class."

"I think she's a visiting professor. She was in Civ Pro on the first day, but not since."

Lena returned to her book. "Does she know what kind of movie it is?"

"Probably not. You think I should tell her?"

"I'd be pretty scared if some creep took me to see porn on the first date."

"But I'm not a creep."

• • •

"Pick a pill," Amadou said. "Cotecxin or Halfan?"

Which to take depended on what had caused the malaria and why I had come to Africa. And it depended on them, the sporozoan parasites of the genus plasmodium, etc., bringing about ague, delirium and sometimes death. I was on a bunk with dozens of people watching. New mosquitoes were eating me. The pillows and bellied-out fabric had been replaced by flaky yellow metal walls and droopy bunk springs just above my face. I ate a pill at random, dreaming of a boat.

"Good choice," Amadou answered, after I'd swallowed the pill. "Mixed with mefloquine, Halfan causes blindness. Twenty dollars. You can pay me back later." One eye, two eyes, no eyes. I'd been eating mefloquine for a month.

CHAPTER 8

The Blistering Battle

That afternoon, immediately before Torts class, Clive wrote, "Word of the day: Bangkok," on the blackboard. Under it he wrote, "Contest: $5 to whoever uses it most frequently during class," then erased everything before Synovia walked in. Muzhduk was happy that all the careful calculation was over and now it was time to throw words back and forth for fun.

Synovia was a short, mostly bald man with a slight tremor and too much energy, which he focused on turning Law into Math. His formula for all Law was *Burden equals Probability times Liability*, and today's manifestation was the McDonald's hot coffee case—the plaintiff, Stella Liebeck, was awarded three million dollars for her coffee being too hot.

"The estimated aggregate market value of all the body parts in an adult human is $46 million, not including intangibles," Synovia said, explaining why the verdict was correct, even though the damages awarded were too small. "Now, let's say the chance of coffee burn causing death, including risks of car accidents, etc., is one in a hundred million. A minimal risk, right? But McDonald's serves 1 billion cups of coffee per year. So, even leaving out non-fatal burns, the proper societal burden for McDonald's to carry is 0.00000001 times 1 billion, probability, times 46 million, liability. Equals $460 million." He wrote the numbers on the board quickly, annoyed with his own delay.

"Statistically, the annual cost to society of fatal burns from McDonald's coffee is $460 million. If it costs less than $460 million per year for McDonald's to regulate the heat of its coffee, then in the interests of societal efficiency the burden should rest with McDonald's, not with the drinkers of the coffee. Does anyone wish to argue against the court?"

Muzhduk raised his hand for the first time since Sclera's class.

"Yes, Mr. Ugli."

"In a less legalistic place, like say Bangkok, McDonald's would be guilty just by virtue of being McDonald's. But if we focus on the legal argument—"

"This is a law school, Mr. Ugli, so yes, please let us focus on the legal argument."

"Then we could analogize this issue to the case of the contaminated sheep from Bangkok…were they from Bangkok? I don't remember, but I think they were from Bangkok, that's why I had Bangkok in my head. Anyway," he noticed Synovia's round old face wrinkling up at his dissipative manner of speaking, "I don't remember the case name, the one where the sheep had to be thrown overboard because they were contaminated. That court said the sheep shipper put his sheep in the hands of the captain and had to accept the consequences."

He was in the lead with five *Bangkoks*, and the class took on the fish-eye glow that adrenaline gives to the world, the way the audience had always receded during Dull-Boulder.

"Yes, the purchase of the coffee constitutes a contract with an implied waiver of liability, as in the contaminated sheep case," Synovia nodded, busy with his own agenda. The origin of the sheep was not a *relevant characteristic* of the case, but *relevant characteristics* and the structures of analogies were the pet intellectual interest of the contracts professor, not Synovia. Synovia cared about an efficient restructuring of society through the courts, because Congress was too emotional to do it properly. "So what is the policy argument for upholding such a contract? Let's say it's explicit, written on the coffee cup."

Muzhduk half-swiveled away from the contest for Bangkoks. "Reasons why it should be okay to accept the risk of hot coffee?"

"Yes, yes."

"Well, respect for the coffee."

"You mean for the person drinking it?"

"No, I meant the coffee. But it's close enough."

"So you're basing your view on the policy of consent and autonomy of decision?"

"If you want to put what I just said into little legal boxes, then yes, we can use those."

"I'm clarifying, not boxing. Do you think people should be able to contract themselves into slavery?"

What? Muzhduk suddenly realized he was in a word-throwing battle. *This is what I came to learn.* He squared himself against Synovia: he wanted to talk about coffee, not slavery, but if he said no, then Synovia would eat away the distinction between one type of consent and the other until Muzhduk proved himself wrong. He decided to open up the gap, hoping it wasn't the verbal version of ducking. "When you buy a coffee, you're not making a decision with an impact for the rest of your life. Unlike slavery."

"The plaintiff had permanent damage to her thighs and groin. But fine, we make the slavery contract for a short period; there are no issues of capacity to consent, these are all well-educated adults and so on. Should people be allowed to contract into slavery?" Synovia pressed his attack: blurring the difference by focusing on the dividing line.

Muzhduk knew he was in trouble. Two days ago he'd had a conversation with Buck about the relationship between quantum mechanics and legal reasoning. Buck's theory was that legal reasoning focuses on an issue with the pinpoint accuracy of quantum mechanics, slicing the baloney so thin it's transparent—"it draws data from the quantum foam of uncertainty below h-bar, where anything can happen, where an electron can be in two places simultaneously." But then, he argued, legal reasoning tries to extrapolate this select datum back up to the macro scale, and asserts that it understands nothing other than Newtonian physics, that quantum whatever is just a theory with no practical application.

"Mr. Ugli, I asked you whether or not people should be allowed to contract into slavery?"

"Yes. Make the time periods short enough, say eight hours, say nine-to-five, and you are in the quantum foam. During those hours, you can contract into slavery."

A menacing rumble erupted throughout the classroom. Buck,

sitting beside Muzhduk, groaned and put his head down on his arms, as Lena shook her head. Though no one could hear over the rumble, Muzhduk continued, "It's called a job. S&M types also do this sometimes. And they are not always either submitting or dominating. There is such a thing as a dominant submissive. The coffee drinker, choosing to submit to the taste of McDonald's coffee, forces the minimum-wage employee to bring her a cup."

The wrinkles on Synovia's face all climbed to the top of his forehead. He'd assumed that the taboo in his question would work as a solid wall against which to squeeze. Muzhduk had crashed through the wall, but the wall was there as a sort of social protection; it still existed for the rest of the class. Synovia felt a tinge of pity that the big boy was too blind to see the damage. He could be molded so much more thoroughly than the cynical ones, if he only had a little more instinct for self-preservation. Synovia had been at Harvard a very long time. All the professors fought to teach the first semester of the first year, where the students still had energy, still could be shaped, still had something to their selves beyond the quest for the perfect outline. The cynical ones could be shaped as well, but the energy had to come from outside. Every class needed an Ugli, someone to sacrifice for the learning of the class as a whole. It was efficient.

Synovia let the rumbling continue, silently measuring the beats. At the appropriate moment, a gesture of his hand quieted the class and he concluded, softly and definitively, "*Contra negantem principia non est disputandum.*" There is no disputing against one who denies first principles. "If you believe in slavery, or think so lightly of it that you'd compare it to a 9-to-5 job, then you may also believe in assumption of risk and liability waivers."

"What I believe in is hot coffee."

"A circular argument."

"Not if you care about the taste of coffee."

"Based on whose palate?"

"Well, mine for one."

"If your argument is only about you, it has no social value and is a waste of the class's time."

"Who else can I talk about? Human—?"

"A humanist! A self-centered humanist who believes in slavery, no less!" Synovia dismissed him. The crescendo had peaked, further discussion would only weaken the impact. Like Sclera, like all the professors at Harvard Law School, he was an artist. Having made a strong association, he now generalized his conclusion: "Such is the paradox of contract. People contract in order to gamble on the unknown future, but courts shouldn't enforce contracts if the people are not well informed. The way out of this dilemma is to evaluate which groups in society are the most efficient avoiders of costs. This is the CCA—the *Cheapest Cost Avoider*—principle of Law. By not permitting risk acceptance, the Law will force McDonald's to take the best decisions in the aggregate. Other examples of such CCA groups include doctors, dangerous sports organizers, owners of slippery sidewalks, and so on. Society as a whole will be better off, safer, more efficient, more fair, and Law will finally become a science."

Muzhduk had somehow helped steer the class to this sterile conclusion. In Verkhoyansk they had a saying left over from the bad old days when Slovaks still had rules and crimes that "nothing is as evil as justice," but that was because they'd never heard of the "cheapest cost avoider," "efficiency," or "insurance." Muzhduk suddenly understood that it was possible to have an enemy who is not a person, but a way of thinking.

"So is that all Law is?" he asked loudly. "Social engineering? Economics? What about 'justice in the individual case?' Maybe coffee drinkers as a collective group don't know what they're doing, but groups don't have a co—" he caught himself, knowing if he said cock it would distract from his own argument, "don't have a tongue or lips or a soul. People as a category have 9.97 fingers. But unlike a group, I exist, and when I have my morning coffee I like it hot enough to sweat, and I know it might burn if I am greedy about it."

"Justice in the individual case?" Synovia looked at Muzhduk incredulously. "Go live in Montana if you want justice in the individual case."

• • •

I spent days on the boat. The mime was there from time to time, and Amadou. They stood over me, smiling, silent. They fed me papayas. I didn't know where they got papayas. I could eat only small quantities, though they helped against the malaria. I wanted fufu, of all things.

I only climbed out of bed to go to the row of sour holes smeared with human feces at the back of the boat. Shit was on the walls, on the floor, in piles without space for feet in between. No wonder people shat off the side of the boat decks rather than trying to negotiate the minefield around the toilets. And either I was hallucinating or a crocodile blocked the way to the toilet, anyway, tied to the railing just past the room I shared with eleven others. CLANG. The chain around its neck hit the railing every time it lunged. CLANG, it tried again, its jaws snapping shut. People laughed as I went around instead, down a flight of steep rusted stairs. Down below, sleeping, squatting, standing, or card-playing people blocked the passage ways—snapping cards, cracking knuckles, hissing urine, dangling assholes and a clanging crocodile—in my malarial delirium it was all one wavy obstacle course.

When I staggered back to my room, I found a woman in my bunk and wondered how long I'd sat leaning against the shit-smeared walls. She reminded me of Little One, but older.

I sighed. "All right, but I want the side with the wall. I'm scared of falling."

"Eh? Big Twobob scared of falling from the bed." All the room laughed, repeated that the big Twobob was scared, slapping their knees. *From the bed*, SLAP, *ha-ha!* Why did I have a top bunk? The woman reached for me. "Please go." *First fuckee-suckee.* "No fuckee-suckee." I pushed. She landed on her feet. The room laughed. *No fuckee-suckee!* SLAP. *The Twobob is not so stupid. So stupid,* SLAP. The prostitute yelled. The crocodile clanged. The reek of the toilet blew in on the wind and from my boots, where I'd leaned against the walls. *You lay in bed with me, you give me five dollar or I come back in.* The room pondered, serious now. The men nodded their heads. They would decide. Economic decisions were a matter for men. The woman looked nervous. Anything could happen. The men split into two factions, pro and con. It took a while. Those in favor of my paying were in the majority, but I had to finish fuckee-fuckee. They were serious. I gave the woman five dollars and went to sleep. Ten men woke me, saying she had to finish fuckee-fuckee. It was the only just thing to do. She waited, sneering. *Maybe Twobob can't do fuckee-fuckee.* The room repeated, *Can't do fuckee-fuckee*, SLAP, *ha-ha!* "It's my choice what I do with the five dollars." This confused the room, because it was not justice for her to get the money without fuckee-fuckee, or at least suckee-suckee. It proved that all Twobobs, even sick Twobobs who stay in third class, are given too much money by the CIA so that they would vote for continued oppression of the people of Mali.

"Then give everyone money, Twobob, and you can sleep," said the first man to complete the proof. Everyone laughed. *Sleep*, SLAP, *ha-ha!*

After that I couldn't leave my bunk without finding someone in it. Belatedly, I realized that I should've agreed I can't do fuckee-fuckee. The prostitute had been kind despite my rudeness. She had offered me a way out, which I'd been too stupid to see.

• • •

Frankfurter Synovia, the Richard A. Posner Professor of Law and Economic Analysis, was annoyed with Muzhduk the Ugli the Fourth. He resented being pulled to the point of insult, where he told Muzhduk to go live in Montana. Despite the laughter of the class, insulting a student could only weaken the professor in the long run. Such was the nature of the power imbalance between professor and student. Unless the insult was clearly justified. He needed to make it justified. "Let's move on to our next topic, related to assumption of risk and whether consent is a meaningful concept or just a means for tortfeasors to protect themselves. Sexual harassment. Would you argue in favor of assumption of risk, Mr. Ugli?"

"Professor Synovia, the Ugli family does not duck." Muzhduk knew that this was an ambush and that he was throwing uphill, but he also knew it was the only rematch he would get.

Synovia shook his head a little. "Your argument please."

"Don't do it," Buck whispered. "He's using you."

"Statistically," Muzhduk started with Synovia's favorite word. He still didn't know the rules fully, but if someone throws sandstone at you, then it must be within the rules to throw sandstone back. Well, except in baseball, but Muzhduk didn't have time to think about the asymmetries of baseball. "Pretty women get paid higher salaries than ugly women, correct?"

"Yes. Biddle and Hamermesh have regressed out a 'beauty premium' of an additional 5% per hour in wage income, as well as a 'plainness penalty' of 9%. *Ceteris paribus*, of course. Judge and Cable later concluded an annual $789 salary gain per extra inch of height, as well. Your point, Mr. Ugli?"

"Except for jobs where looks affect performance, like entertainment, that 14% wage difference could be an implicit compensation for assuming the risk of being sexually harassed." Another rumble shook the class, this time accompanied by hissing.

"Quiet!" Synovia cut off the hissing. "So which is the true market wage, Mr. Ugli?"

"In terms of the economy, each gets paid the market wage for the services he or she provides. Why shouldn't good looks be considered part of the whole? It lowers transaction costs, increases overall social utility, makes co-workers come to work early and stay late."

"From the perspective of a male," Synovia said, too quickly, all his wrinkles lifted in a bunch. He was a little stunned that Muzhduk was taking it so far.

Muzhduk picked up the biggest boulder he could lift: "Now you're making assumptions about sexual orientation and power roles. It could be a good looking guy who's worth more because of his looks too. How much do companies spend on corporate culture, communication networks, company parties, all to generate enthusiasm about work? Maybe plastic surgery is cheaper, more efficient. We need to do the numbers, see whether the law should require surgery. In the economic analysis, an omission is no different than an act, right? Cheapest cost avoider would be at childhood probably—correct crooked teeth, improve bone structures, stretch the femurs, Botox the wrinkle-zones, pump up the tits and ass, change the gender if the numbers require it—"

Muzhduk stopped, empty. The rest of the class was a cohesive hissing unit now. Hissing through their teeth, so no one could see movement. But everyone was hissing, so why hide it?

The moment passed, the class ran out of air, and with a frown Synovia told everyone to settle down. He stared at Muzhduk and rubbed his forehead, perplexed. Finally, he decided that Muzhduk the Ugli was a show-off. He'd successfully mocked his method, but failed to understand that every argument has a jury. The more Synovia thought about this, however, the more he rubbed his head. He normally didn't like juries. They tended to inject irrationality into what should be a scientific process. The whole thing bothered him, but there was no time to examine it all while the class waited. He moved on to the technical mechanics of *hostile environment* law.

On the way out of the classroom, Clive handed Muzhduk $5 with a smile. "Best five dollars I ever spent." No one else had used the word Bangkok. Clive stopped for a moment to chat with Buck, who sat on a bench outside the building. When Muzhduk approached, Clive walked away as Buck sat uncomfortably, scratching the back of his hand. "You upset a lot of people."

"This is a law school."

"I understand your point. 'He is no lawyer who cannot take two sides.' Charles Lamb. But that's different. Pro-life vs. pro-choice, that sort of thing. Even pro-slavery, if you really want, though I know that wasn't your point. But there's no second side to rational discourse. You can say whatever you like, but should put it into a more considerate form. Don't use feminist arguments to present chauvinist ideas, or mock things that people find important."

"Synovia's 'rational discourse' would turn us all into ants, not men. Not even mammals. It's not the substance of what he says that's wrong, it's the method. Like Sclera always says. And so the only real counter-attack must be methodological. Call it the only real diversity."

Buck looked away, toward the planters filled with marigolds beginning to turn in on themselves in the Boston fall. Then he shrugged. "Clive was upset you associated Bangkok with contamination. The rest was in a debate about legal standards, however mocking, but that one you threw in gratuitously. And he'll use it against you."

"He's the one who chose the word. And the game!"

"Yes, of course. Because he knew you would say something obnoxious that would change the conversation from him getting humiliated by Sclera back to you. You could try to be more aware of people. Of their character, not just what they put up on the board for everyone to see."

"Why?" Muzhduk asked, more emphatically than he'd intended. "There's only 550 of us here. It's not like we can choose who's in our class. If I can't separate myself from Clive no matter what brilliant insights I have about his character and motivation, then there's no benefit in knowing who he *truly* is or what he's thinking when he puts a word on the blackboard. But there is definitely a cost in replacing life with endless calculation. It's a sickness. A sickness of big cities, cowards, cops, and novel writers, always trying to 'figure' people out, as though people were jigsaw puzzles. I'd rather face what people say and do, not what I imagine that they might be thinking. If everyone here accepted each other at face value, this would be a far happier place." He walked down the three steps lining the patio of Pound Hall.

"Muzhduk," Buck called out, and Muzhduk turned. "People ask me all the time why I'm friends with you. They think you're a crazy person. And together with your size, it makes them nervous."

Muzhduk thought for a moment before answering. "Back in Verkhoyansk I had a rival named Hulagu the Stupid. One day Hulagu and twenty of his friends decided they wanted a fight, to build up some honor. So they raided a Red Army barracks in the town of Kharaulakh and left a clear trail of Soviet uniforms leading back to one of our villages. The one with the best ambush cliffs. But the village was in the middle of its harvest, and didn't have time for tanks rolling through its fields. The village picked up all the uniforms before the Reds found them, so Hulagu stole more and put them on the path again. Four women from the village spent all their time searching the paths for uniforms, instead of reaping, and Hulagu kept putting more uniforms on the path and they kept collecting them, and this continued until the village finished its harvest and was ready to fight. Only then was my father, the chief, called in to act as a general for the fight. But the village would never have asked Hulagu to stop putting the uniforms there, and even someone as stupid as Hulagu would never have asked the village to stop picking up the uniforms. And nobody would ever, ever, have tried calling my father to decide between them."

"That sounds like a bit of a crazy system."

Muzhduk laughed. "To you. To me it's the Law that's crazy. And when people study it, or obey it, they lose their minds too. I *am* sorry that it's spilling over onto you though."

That was the day Muzhduk began to receive hate mail in his pigeonhole. It was anonymous, so there was no one he could challenge to single combat.

• • •

The top four levels—deluxe through third—received meals with their ticket. The only difference between first, second, and third was the number of people crammed into the rooms and how high up in the boat tiers they slept. Height was important because the garbage was swept off the decks, peeing was off the decks and sometimes so was the other. Deluxe had air conditioning and gourmet meals that added a course of ramen Cup Noodle instant soup. Supposedly, they even had private toilets, though at least sometimes they used the decks as well. Store High In Transit, the mime mimed when I asked, because shit explodes when its fumes can't rise.

Fourth class, which was actually fifth, was the open deck, and the ticket didn't include meals. Further down, deep in the bowels of the enormous riverboat, were bars, a dance club, kitchen, television room, gambling lanes, cock fights, and nearly as many prostitutes as passengers. In between it all was sixth class, unofficial, filled with people from every tribe, many of them with paired animals, aware that they still lived under an Old Testament God who could at any moment decide on mass-murder. The animals reeked of jail and soiled themselves every time someone kicked them to move.

The deck crocodile disappeared a few days after I began to recover. It ended up in our food, two or three little cubes each, on top of rice. I received the smallest pieces because I was slowest to grab my plastic plate. The meat was surprisingly white and dry, like a paler version of pork, but tasty.

Both the mime and Amadou disappeared at random, and I didn't know anyone else. A man stood beside me with an open mouth. When I took a drink of water, he grabbed my fork from my plate and scooped from his own plate. He put my fork back. He didn't eat my food, but used my fork for a single bite, though he had his own fork. I stared at him. He ignored me, looking at his bowl while he finished his food, using his own fork. I took a forkful of my own crocodile and rice and little yellow moths. Little yellow moths were in my crocodile, everywhere. Hundreds began to fly into the room, spin around the ten-watt glow that hung from a wire in the center.

The fork-borrower opened the door of the cabin. A wall of yellow flew in. They were shoulder to shoulder, beating each other's wings, one silent solid block of bug that pushed the fork-borrower back into the room.

The other men ran to close the door, but there were already too many moths inside. Someone shut off the light and fluttering wings flew into my mouth, nose, ears. I stumbled out of the door coughing, not healthy enough to run. In the dark, a swamp rustled quietly, illuminated by the boat lights. Streams of yellow filled the air like an extension of the swamp, of the whole river, like a giant yellow fist slamming into the riverboat, big enough to tip it easily, had it been made of something other than moths. And then we were inside the fist and I couldn't see. I covered my nose, coughed out wing dust and breathed more in. My neck and face and arms were covered in broken wings and little pecking feet and living air. We pushed toward the TV room. It was air conditioned, hopefully airtight. The people already inside were not opening the door. The crowd outside banged on the windows and the door, together with a million beating bugs.

• • •

Muzhduk was tired after Torts. But he'd promised to call, so he dialed the number.

"Oedda Hecaten on the apparatus."

"On the apparatus?"

Dead air.

"This is Muzhduk calling."

Still dead air.

"Hello?"

"I have not disconnected." The phone lowered the pitch of her voice.

"You didn't say anything."

"To the mockery? Or to your stating the obvious?"

"I asked you to the movie earlier today."

"Yes. I remember."

"It's tomorrow at 7. I could come pick you up."

"Very good. I shall wait for you in the lobby of North Hall at 18:30."

"Great. Wait," he thought of Lena's comment, "there is one other thing, I guess. The way I learned of this movie was in doing research on obscenity."

"Even better. I shall see you at 18:45."

"Didn't you just say six thirty?"

"And then I changed it to 18:45. Think about it." Click.

Think about it? And he hadn't even told her the Supreme Court ruled 5 to 4 that the movie had some scientific, literary, and/or artistic value.

• • •

The moths died quickly once all the lights on the boat were turned off—I had no idea why—leaving a three-foot cushion of fuzzy yellow on the floor. I wished Peggy were there. *An experience, to make love in a three-foot cushion of dead moths.* But the way I'd phrased the thought made me think of Oedda instead, about bugs dying and settling to the floor, breathing moth dust, broken wings and crunching legs. I sneezed just as the boat struck something. Everyone slid forward. A man fell in the bugs beside me. He had a long face and caved-in cheeks. He said I had to pay 500 francs. "Why?" I asked. He stared at me. He didn't have an answer. So I didn't pay.

• • •

After hanging up the phone, Muzhduk opened his yellowing casebook. He stared at it, then out the window. It was dark outside. He saw lights in all the other matchbox rooms. *Sameness, that's what the Law is about.* The only difference was that his curtains were open. And that he was sipping reindeer pee.

Mt. Baldhead was clear. You can see its outline, you can mark your steps. Here the only steps are minutes, hours, days, passing at the earnest rate of one second per second.

Muzhduk closed the window and turned the light back on. He saw his reflection. Who was that guy who sold his shadow? With this huge effort to get it back. All Muzhduk had to do was turn the switch. Peter Schlemihl. A fool, tricked by the devil. The devil saw Peter would never sell his soul for simple wealth, so he made the deal for Peter's shadow instead. The devil knew human society couldn't accept a man with no shadow, even warned Peter that there is no sun without a shadow. When Peter had suffered long enough to understand, the devil offered to return the shadow in exchange for Peter's soul. Peter rejected the offer, but was forced to live in the wilderness. Siberia, perhaps. Only when he became sick, a shadow of sorts, was society willing to accept him again.

With the lights off Muzhduk could see out into other people's drawn curtains. On, he was here and that was it. He hadn't come here to be a lawyer. Not just to be chief either, nor duty.

At home I didn't stop eating polar bears just because the bears ate seals and seals ate fish and fish ate the pollution from all the Red factories. I ate the bear, though the next day my liver hurt and my eyebrows fell out. It's something to kill a polar bear with a knife, and if you kill it you eat it. I came here for fighting words, Law—not to be a lawyer but to defeat one. My mountain, where introspection is proper.

He saw himself drowning in paper, scarred by thousands of little paper cuts, pathetic war wounds of the men who fight with words. Buck had called them paper samurai one night after a few drinks, and then gone on in a long breathless string about "lawyers who believe there really are right answers in the Law and they are defined by the width of the margins and by whether you concisely state your core issue; who get a narcotic thrill out of channeling abstract power into an eviction notice to a welfare mother; who feel the Law as a constant poking, like the poisoned barbs the matador uses on the bull to induce a tired death; men who were born lawyers, or who became lawyers on the first day of law school; who are narrators in a cardboard packing plant, providing roles and identities to increase the efficiency of narration; who don't care whether the Law is a transcendental entity or just a bunch of upwardly mobile Black's Law Dictionary definitions so long as when someone asks them they can answer; men who jog; who justify first-strike nuclear attacks but say that if I punch you in the nose I'm a menace to society; who can discuss the killing of two million people in the same language as an overdue phone bill; who vulgarize what they once knew by virtue of being human by backing it up with legal reasoning; who snort coke from the grotesquely bloated bosom of blind Justice, though some of them don't inhale and others just don't breathe very deeply; who honestly insist that just another couple of years and they'll get out of the Law; who say that *determination is negation* or who believe that it's all just a bunch of *ipse dixits*, and so what; who hope weakly that meaning will emerge as a by-product of their manipulations, not daring to ask what it means to live off by-products; lawyers who scream, become outlaws, determine to live without society and eat dog food in an alley—sated, they look at the bag of Alpo for some after-dinner reading and see that the dog food is FDA-approved—"

There was a knock on the door. Muzhduk flipped the lights and his sweating, chiral reflection disappeared. Another knock, more insistent. Muzhduk opened the door.

It was Sclera, wearing a burgundy cardigan emblazoned with the letter H. He was short this close up, but his pressed-back shoulders made him look like he would topple into the room. With the tilt of his head, he looked like Benito Mussolini. "Good evening, Mr. Ugli."

Muzhduk stared. The timing was bad. He'd been drinking and thinking and his own sweat had a smell he couldn't respect. *It's not introspection that's dangerous,* he thought. *It's self-indulgence. It's not just a Rule.*

"Professor," he finally said. "What do you want?"

"To watch you open the books on your top shelf with your penis."

• • •

The shore was spinning somewhere between Bamba and Bourem, like one of Oedda's hermeneutic circles, each loop just a tiny bit tighter than the one before it. Amadou brought fufu. And then we were stuck in a swamp. Malarial mosquitoes ate us, and I wondered whether I was immune now as I listened to the rest of the room talk about how the captain had knocked a screw loose, against the bottom of the riverbed. Then about whether AIDS was a French tactic to sell more condoms or American propaganda to limit African fertility and tilt the ratio of black to white people in the world. One man, fat with status and respect, did believe in AIDS, to everyone's surprise. But he believed only white people died of it. What did an African have to worry about a disease that took twenty years to kill?

He was a religious man, with peg teeth, taking six Bella with him to Mecca. Pretty ones, to sell at the end. He made the pilgrimage every year, earning his title of Hajji many times over.

"That's ugly," I said.

"You Twobobs, you are all liars. You own slaves for hundreds of years, but when the African man owns them, you cry. Yet you have a Bella yourself. I noticed him, he's arrogant."

"Are you talking about Amadou?"

"It is better to be careful, Twobob. You might find yourself waking with a slit throat."

A slit throat, SLAP! the other men laughed. My foreignness and the Hajji's status made our conversation interesting to the whole room.

"With your throat slit, it will be hard for you to speak," he continued. "And if you can't speak, how will you explain to Rogers what you're doing with his Bella?"

Apparently everyone knew Rogers. But Amadou wasn't a Bella, as far as I knew. He certainly didn't belong to Rogers, or anyone else, and I had thought the Tuaregs owned the Bellas at the Getaway, not Rogers, though Rogers seemed to control everything there. I'd given up on following the convoluted politics of the Getaway Guesthouse. They seemed built on sand, shifting too quickly on currents I was too blind to see, let alone understand. What I could understand was a threat, and the slave-trader put the idea of throats in my mind. So I grabbed his.

I was still too weak to lift a fat man off the ground. His neck blubber worked its way out around my fingers. Everyone threatened. No one hit. One man plugged an iron into the wall socket, shaking it inches from my face. With one hand I squeezed El-Hajji's throat, and with the other yanked the ironing cord out of the socket. The man plugged it back in. He waited for it to warm up. I remembered that the power was off.

I loosened my grip, and El-Hajj told me that everyone hates the Blue People, because, like the whites, they took slaves from the wrong tribes. They are raiders and killers, but most of all they are arrogant. Foreigners love to help Tuaregs, he said, but the Tuaregs are too stupid. They wander off, no matter how good a well or school anyone builds for them. The foreigners build contour mounds and plant trees, they teach them how to grow millet and sorghum and how to read and write, not just in Tamasheq, but also Arabic and French. But the Tuaregs don't value it. They want to raid and steal and ride around like animals. They don't respect borders and don't understand paperwork. So they get kicked from country to country. When the droughts come, they have to sell their animals cheap, and when smart businessmen from the cities buy the cattle, the Blue People act like they're too proud to be herders for other people's animals.

The iron man continued to wait. I wondered why he didn't just hit me with it—cold or hot, what did it matter?—then saw the mime sitting peacefully at the other end of the room, unworried.

El Hajj didn't know anything about Peggy except that she was one of those countless foreigners who always help the Blue People. He said Rogers was a Tuareg-lover who had supported France's failed attempt to create an independent Saharan state for them. Everyone knew that. But he was also a babalawo and nobody was willing to fight him. He said Rogers was on the boat, in Deluxe.

I went to leave but a man was blocking the door. He threatened to cut my throat, until I took a step towards him, then he ran around the corner. He followed me at a safe distance, threatening to cut my throat, over and over.

• • •

Sclera waited in the doorway. "I'm here to see how high the shelf is."

"I just threw back what you threw at me."

"But you were right." Sclera gestured into Muzhduk's room. When Muzhduk didn't respond, he continued. "Words have meaning, they are legal acts. Speaking is a procedure of civil society. In the case of your twenty-two-pole penis, it is an uncivil procedure."

"I don't understand what that means, but come in." It was proper to be polite to enemies. Muzhduk offered Sclera a beer and some cake. Sometimes he baked cakes in the common kitchen. He didn't have plates, so he served it in a Frisbee. He didn't have cutlery, so he gave Sclera chopsticks. He felt a little guilty for not sharing his drink, but he had so very little reindeer pee left. Sclera sat on Muzhduk's bed eating a five-layer flourless chocolate cake with chopsticks from a Frisbee, while Muzhduk did the same at his desk, less than two feet away. The scene reflected in the window, repeating perhaps in every other room in the Gropius complex.

• • •

I searched for Rogers, passing snake charmers, plotters, thieves, liars, surgeons, carpetbaggers, mountebanks, whoremasters, mechanics, acrobats, fallen women, preachers of religions, political rallies, illnesses, crying babies, huddled families starving because they had not planned on the boat becoming stuck, and every human activity performed by every type of human being. But I couldn't find a way into deluxe. Everyone said there was one, but no one knew where the entrance was.

I stood on the quarterdeck and watched the crew disassemble our bent starboard propeller. Each time they reassembled it, only the port screw turned, and the boat spun in circles. It was a three-screw boat but the middle one had fallen off years ago and no one had replaced it. And they were scared of moving the port screw to the middle, because it was the only one working. Two days passed like this, with me on the quarterdeck, watching the disassembling and reassembling. Occasionally I shouted from frustration to stop disassembling and just use the one screw to get us out of there. However slowly, at least we'd be moving.

On the third day I found two young soldiers waiting for me on the quarterdeck. One had squeezed, triangular features, the other a face like a cylinder. They asked for money. I told them I didn't have any. They didn't believe me. "How much your plane ticket cost, Twobob?"

"Do you know Mr. Rogers? I'm looking for Rogers—"

"Shh." The shy thin one greyed a little. "He will follow his name."

The squeezed soldier's lips twitched and he rubbed his shaved head with both his hands. "You know my dream?" he said. "My dream be to go to Washington and be a taximan. If I can only go there, I be rich-rich. My cousin be there in Washington. A taximan. He be so rich. So difficult to get there, so expensive, but once I am there, BAM, I will be a taximan."

"How do I get into deluxe class? To find Rogers." It was a weapon to say his name out loud.

"You don't know deluxe? You be in which class on this boat, Twobob?"

"Does it matter?"

"Does it matter?" He shook his head dramatically, once to each side without taking his eyes off me. "You strange, Twobob. You ask questions but don't even know what be the matter."

Both young men laughed, but stopped when I said, "Third."

"Eh? Now you lying, Twobob. People lying who says you stay there third class."

"I am in third class."

The taximan placed his arm next to mine, then pointed at each in turn. "Second class, third class." He laughed again. His shy friend laughed also. Then, suddenly, the taximan gave me a look that was all concern and sympathy. "Why you be poor, if you white?"

"I'm a student. Or I was." It was the simplest answer.

"Eh? They make white people study too?" the thin shy one jumped in.

"But you be a student over there? If you be *poor*, why don't you be there taximan? You already there, in America. I don't understand. Maybe you not in Washington. Really, you need go to Washington. If I be there, nothing stops me. BAM."

"White man don't be taximan," the thin one told his friend.

"Why not?" the taxi-dreamer asked, then shrugged off the paradox as irreconcilable and thus unimportant. "And you be poor, Twobob? Then I tell you for free, because you stay in there third class. I tell you so you can go to Washington. I tell you that you better leave there this boat soon, or some people gonna be come get you."

• • •

Sclera finished the cake and asked, "Why do you have chopsticks but not a fork?"

"If I had a fork, I'd have to get a knife, and then I couldn't hold my plate. I'd have to eat at my desk facing the wall, which is depressing. And technically, I'm from Asia."

"Hmm. Yes, I heard about your Torts. Have you read Confucius?"

"Only in a cookie. It said, 'To eat is sex.'"

"I could use a different mythology. West Africa, like your trickster comment—"

"Confucius is fine."

Sclera straightened his back to make himself taller while still sitting on Muzhduk's bed. "In your opinion, then, is Harvard a trade school? Or an ivory tower of intellect? *Hmm?*" He skirled the end of his question, like misplayed bagpipes. In the tiny room it was awful.

"Trade school, mostly."

"Mostly. Except the undergrad, which is about coming from the right prep school, which, in turn, is about wealth. But then…how far did you walk, Mr. Ugli, to get here?"

Sclera waited a few beats to let his question sink in, then answered it himself: "It's all in the name, Mr. Ugli. Absurdly obvious, trite even, but important. A name like Harvard is not a label for the Truth. Nobody comes here for the buildings or the professors or the books or the other students or any other reason except the name that sits on top of all this." He gestured around at the concrete-slab walls, the hanging bicycle, the mini-fridge. "Truths are the illusions that we have forgotten are illusions. Harvard, the word, is a Truth. Isn't that why you came? So much energy devoted to getting here. For one word."

"So what?" Muzhduk said, then yawned, irritated. He covered his mouth with a vague feeling that Sclera was contagious. "I don't know what you know, or how you know it. Maybe everybody walks here. My father and grandfather climbed mountains instead. Nobody cared how steep or how many ridges the mountain had. The only thing that mattered was how many meters. We all agree on one goal and we all compete for it. The rest doesn't matter. Procedure over substance, as you remind us every day."

"Is that how you see it, Mr. Ugli? But didn't you say your penis was longer than twenty-two hooked poles? That it could master even Law?"

"That was a reaction. I was fighting on your terms."

"Yes, it was pure reaction. Pure opposition. Like an immune system response, without thought, but correct in every way. Though you realize, don't you, that in your mountain analogy, it took you downwards? I could expel you for talking about your penis in class. Or for not being Muzhduk the Ugli. The *real* Muzhduk the Ugli, the female painter from Tennessee. As far as I can tell, the other Ugli, the chief wannabe from Siberia, never sent in his transcript."

Muzhduk frowned and pulled on his beard with a fisted hand. Sclera knew an awful lot, from the registrar, from John the Attorney, from someone. For the first time, Muzhduk understood why everyone was scared of Sclera. But the professor was right. *The two eyes—the objective and subjective components—are blurred here. Sclera is both Hulagu and the mountain.*

"My comment didn't take me downwards," Muzhduk said, wary. "It was just a different path. Or are you challenging me?"

Suddenly Sclera smiled. It was a very odd thing on his face, a lipless cracking and crinkling all over that showed him to be far older than he looked. "No challenge, though it has been an unexpected pleasure. No, this is just a proposition. For you and your twenty-two-pole penis that recognizes no truths, not even your own goals. Think of me as your guide, here to tell you where your path lays." He paused, because he knew he had Muzhduk's attention. "I want you to destroy the library."

Sclera had sent Clive to burn down the library. Probably in exchange for an easy grade, which was all Clive was really after. "Why?"

"'To eat is sex.' Confucius had a prescription for repairing a corrupt empire. The first and most important step was the Rectification of Names. As empires rot, the names stay the same while the ground shifts until the reality of a thing stands in opposition to its name. The Ministry of Education slowly shifts from educating children—as you said, pulling out what's special within each—to ensuring that they don't have a single creative thought. Hospitals save the man with the heart attack and give a deadly virus to two who came in with sprained ankles. The FBI has organized more terrorist plots in the U.S. than any terrorist organization, and the police kill around a thousand people a year in the name of public safety. For every hundred thousand people, there are fewer than two hundred violent crimes, but more than 3,200 people under some form of correctional control. Even something as simple as a car—the polymath Ivan Illich calculated that if you add up not just the time spent in a car but also the time working to buy, fuel, and care for the car and its infrastructure, and divide that by the number of miles driven per person, you get an average speed of 3.7 miles per hour. This sort of counterproductivity affects every institution over time.

"Confucius assumed that Substance was real and Name an illusion, a simple label that's easy to re-align. He would have renamed the Ministry of Education the Ministry of Stupidity, believing that 'truth in advertising' would create the pressure for a new Ministry of Education, and so on. The old one would die out and the cycle continue. Perhaps that worked in China 2500 years ago, but not here, now. Harvard as an establishment of books and buildings doesn't actually matter. Only the Name matters. Oh, we tried changing the motto from *Veritas* to *In Christi Gloriam in 1650. Veritas returned in 1843.*

We tried again in 1847, changing it to Christo et Ecclesiae. But Veritas returned again, revived by a poem by Oliver Wendell Holmes. Truth. We can't get away from it. How much worse if we tried to change Harvard? No, we can't change the Name, but we *are* out of alignment. And the corruption of the best is the worst. *Corruptio optimi pessima.* So the Substance must be rectified, to conform to the Name."

"So re-align it. Hire better professors, admit different students, write better books and dissertations, tear down Gropius and put up a dormitory where humans can live."

"The professors have tenure, the shelves in the library are full and new acquisitions controlled by complex contracts, all the dissertation topics have been used up except for ridiculous minutiae, and Gropius is protected as a heritage landmark. And it's not the professors or books that are the problem. It's the students. Those admitted here are in such awe of actually being here that they offer no resistance at all. There is no tension, nothing to keep us honest. Only someone immune to the Truth can re-align it."

Muzhduk nodded, finally understanding at least part of what Sclera was talking about. But he was wrong about Muzhduk. "I wear a towel when I walk to the bathroom now."

"I have been teaching here for longer than the school has existed, and not a single student has ever been so irreverent on the first day of class. They all knew that such tricks are *ignis fatuus* before logic, authority, and procedure, leading only to an F. You weren't concerned with this, nor my name and reputation. You trusted absolutely in your foolishness, in your ability to find a way, and so it worked.

"I realized long ago," Sclera continued, "that logic itself is an institution vulnerable to counterproductivity, so I developed a more powerful weapon: listening. Or, rather, hearkening. When you interrupted, I controlled you through your own words. You didn't hear my listening, you thought I was speaking and that you alone could resist it. In the end, you did escape, but only for that one class. So you really did not escape at all, you see. Unless, of course, you understood that I was listening, and put up your foolishness as a mask and a shield. But that seems unlikely."

Muzhduk pulled on his beard.

Sclera nodded. "As refreshing as it is to have a student who fights back, you clearly stand no chance of making it through HLS.

You are a throwback, with an admissions file that is, shall we say, 'name-rectified.' And yet, you are the embodiment of precisely the sort of disorder," here he smiled, "precisely the sort of ugliness that can bring back a new order, a Rectification of Substance such that it conforms to the Name. Movement away from order is the only way to create greater order. In exchange, you'll get your degree."

"And if I refuse?"

"Have you heard of the old German Whitsuntide rite, the Expulsion of the Wild Man?" He smiled. "You have until Pentecost. Think of this as an exchange. One might even call it friendship." Sclera rose and walked to the door. "I have waited many years for someone like you, Muzhduk the Ugli the Fourth. Goodnight."

With Sclera's words running through his head long after he'd left, Muzhduk needed to get out of his room, to breathe some fresh air. He walked out of Gropius. The grass in Holmes' Field was covered in autumn leaves, but the asphalt paths were clear even in the windy moonless night. One or two stray leaves. He stopped in the middle of the field, at the Statue of Protrusion and Contraption, the jagged pipes at odd angles sculpted to go with the Gropius dormitory. Its official name was "World Tree," by Richard Lippold, but it felt like the antithesis of a tree. It made Muzhduk think of a machine, the motor vehicle that had run down baby Tickle in Sclera's first class. He climbed the sculpture, wrapped the crook of his knees over a pipe and hung upside-down. There were no mountains in Boston, and tall buildings were the opposite of mountains. But hanging upside down made him feel better.

After a time, he began to bend the pipes. It took all his strength, and felt good. As he worked, he sank into a trance. He didn't notice how much time had passed, until he heard a voice behind him. It said, "Are we there yet?"

• • •

"Who's gonna come get me? Rogers?" I asked the soldiers.

"Why do you think there boat be spinning? It spinning for you, Twobob. The spinning be for forgetting, for forgetting that I need go to Washington. Some forget, but I not forget so quickly. Some people gonna come get you, but not your man. The other of your man."

"Who other?"

"The people who sit. In Bamako."

That night I slept poorly. If the rebels took Peggy and the government was against the rebels, maybe I should help the government come get me. But then I remembered the Mobile Customs Brigade. They didn't sit, but they worked for the people who sat. Everything was always attenuated in the real world. When I did finally sleep, I dreamt of circles, a spiral with an opening in the center, through which I could jump or fall. I dreamt of Peggy in the library, the tea cups, and of Oedda. Without lights, the river looked like it had no shore.

In the morning the mime suggested leaving. He'd negotiated a pinasse to Bamba from one of the chicken sellers, a Bozo tribesman who sold chickens to the people in fourth class. There were unsold chickens in his boat, along with Amadou, the mime, the two soldiers, and me, all in a row. The pinasse was a hollowed-out tree trunk, with no keel. Water reached within an inch of the gunwales, and the boat wobbled every time the driver leaned on his long pole to push us along. The rest of us watched our loose-screw riverboat as it shrank in the distance. A group from fourth and fifth classes climbed on the outside of the decks. Each held a long stick, and as a huddled group looked sharp, bristly. There was no crocodile to hinder their passage, it had been eaten by first, second and third classes as the boat spun and the deeper classes ran out of food and money. And finally turned into a mutiny of sticks, tiny in the distance.

It was Bamba's market day: over the water we could already see the bright colors—bundles, boxes, sacks, camels, sheep, goats, and people.

As we approached, the pinasse driver started to push manically on his pole, using his entire body, his eyes wide and panicked. I looked around for what scared him, trying not to stand and tip the boat, but saw only water filled with bilharzia, river-blindness, and murk. If he pushed any harder, he'd flip us.

He managed six or seven more pushes before a hippopotamus head rose out of the water directly in front of us. It was long and bumpy, no more than six inches above the surface, with thick white stubs in its mouth. The boat rose as we slid off the hippo's face, and we almost tipped over. The boatman fell, but landed in the boat. The chickens squawked. The hippo could easily snap the boat in two—crocodiles were afraid of hippopotamuses, every animal was afraid of them, and the two soldiers had no guns. The hippo struck again and launched us forward. The boat rocked, spun, and took water. A soldier fell against me. I caught him and heard a splash behind me. Amadou was in the water, to be killed by the aggressive vegetarian monster.

The six of us stared dumbly for a few seconds, at the hippo and at Amadou. His head looked tiny next to the hippopotamus as he tried to swim backwards. *Things don't stay, people don't stay, everything changes, people come and go based on who they are, not on who they were.* I jumped into the water, pushing off hard to land between Amadou and the monster. I kept my eyes closed underwater, remembering that the tiny Onchocerca worm liked to burrow in through the pupils. I broke through the water less than a foot from the absurd hippopotamus head.

It stared at me, its big eyeballs lined up like gun sights two feet behind its volcano-crater nostrils. It was a different view from this close. The taximen soldiers screamed. The boatman yelled. Amadou splashed behind me. I heard them all in a faint distance, barely audible, as I stared back. The whole world was in those two hippopotamus eyes, now only implying an enormous mouth underneath, the dull gaze of peace and classical beauty wrapped in thick red-brown and yellow lids. Those soft eyes dampened all the screams, staring back without differentiation between me, the boat, the water. After all the darting eyes I'd seen—Harvard eyes, African eyes—here in the water were the eyes the ancient Greeks admired, the calm enlightened gaze of a cow, not at all frightening. They looked one last time and disappeared underwater.

The soldiers pulled Amadou back into the pinasse, then me, and we quickly toweled off with shirts to get rid of as many invisible filarial worms as possible, while the driver recovered his pole. Unlike river blindness, bilharzia could get through skin, but that took minutes, not seconds.

When we were as dry as our clothes would allow, Amadou said, "Thank you."

I hadn't really helped. "It swam away by itself."

Fifteen minutes later we were at the market in Bamba. The yellow, red, green, and orange of the Bozos' boubous met with the indigo Tuaregs on camels bringing in rectangular white slabs of salt from the other end of the Sahara, as they had done for a thousand years. Like this, they seemed ancient, hard to imagine as a threat, if for no other reason than how slowly they moved. It made no more sense to think these Tuaregs knew anything about Peggy than it would to think a Slovak in Europe would know anything about our villages in Siberia.

It might have been worthwhile to travel with them, if they hadn't moved at such a slow pace. Instead, we searched for their competition, finding a motorized pinasse on the way to Kabara. One was headed there, but it would only take Amadou and the two soldiers, not the Japanese mime or me. The taximen-soldier became angry with the boatman, and in a show of solidarity, came with us instead aboard an empty Arab salt truck we found going directly to Timbuktu.

The truck had a name, PARMENIDES, written on its side like a ship. With no road, we drove over endless waves of sand dunes again.

• • •

Muzhduk dropped from sculpture to face the little blue bear who called himself Pooh.

"Are we there yet?" Muzhduk repeated Pooh's question, as though that would help it make sense.

"That's what *I* asked."

"Not what am I doing?"

"I see *what*. I wanna know *why*."

"Honestly, I don't know."

"So you don't understand our Wonderland, yet," the bear continued. "I'd give you fifty-fifty odds, if you at least understood yourself. But if you go silly, don't know who you are or when you've arrived, someone'll tell you. And your village with you."

"I know who I am. A little reindeer pee won't make me forget who I am." Why hadn't he climbed Everest instead? From what he'd learned since Verkhoyansk, Everest was a high-altitude hike. The forty-foot Hillary Step is the only place your hands have to touch rock. The rest of the climb is really just a hike. Children could do it, if they could stand the thin air. Everyone back home would have accepted it as a worthy challenge, and he would be a chief with two eyes. Except not really. He wouldn't have seen the world that was coming towards the six villages on the river Lena. This world of the statue of protrusion and contraption, and torts and civil procedure.

"What do I do *here*? You called it Wonderland. If I'm Alice, hallucinating little bears, do I grow? Do I shrink? Do I choose between the March Hare and the Mad Hatter?"

Others become logical in law school; I'm becoming associational.

"I'm plain bonkers," said the bear. "You got screws loose. We're all gone silly." He turned to walk away. "Wonderland is the last stop. On the blue line. And don't get caught vandalizing school property. Even that poor Bauhaus thing."

"Wait, Pooh!"

Pooh stopped, his short back slumped. "What?"

"Why am I, uh, talking to you?"

Pooh cleared his throat. "A long time ago, Justice Oliver Wendell Holmes wrote to John C.H. Wu that life having thrown him into the Law, he must try to put his feelings of the infinite into that, into a comma if necessary, to exhibit in the detail a hint of vista, to show it in the great line of the universal. Some time before, I taught that same Law here, along with your Professor Sclera. These years have not favored me as well as they have Eugene. They can't completely remove me—I have a special sort of tenure inextricably rooted to the substance of this place—but if they let me teach again, the whole school would shake with voices. That's what Holmes told Wu in 1936."

Pooh walked into the darkness. Muzhduk stayed with his mangled pipes and wondered if things like this repeated at Harvard year after year.

CHAPTER 9

Justice

The salt truck drove on enormous wheels over mounds and dunes and an endless ocean of blowing sand that smelled of burnt flint, through villages bombed out in the Tuareg civil war that still raged as life went on. A war with no end and no road, only truck skeletons. We rolled past these remainders day and night. It's the constant movement of sand, more than its dryness, that makes it so inhospitable to life. My malaria was never quite gone—hallucinations at the edges of my vision trying to creep towards the center, the dust covering us all—and the wheels of the salt truck revolved but the center point of the axle never moved: not in the heat of the sun or the cold of the night. The horses under the hood pulled mightily, escorted by the daughters of the sun.

At dusk we drove through the mud-walled gates of a ghost town. Small adobe buildings, ruined and roofless, were spread among makeshift wells blocked up with twisted metal and sticks of warped acacia wood. Sand slowly drifted in. Beside one of these deteriorating wells stood a woman, beautiful, proud, erect, like a saint on a bridge. Like her nipples. She was completely nude. Our driver stopped the truck and we stared.

The Japanese mime ripped off his clothes and the towels on his head. He jumped off the back of the truck, stark naked. The rest of us continued to stare, dumbfounded, as he ran and tackled her. There was mud where she stood beside the well, and they wrestled in the mud and sand and sticks and well-rounded truth.

When they finished, the mime yelled to us, "It is necessary to say and to think Being!" Then he turned and walked off into the desert.

We all understood what he had meant. The shy soldier said he would build a temple for the girl, right there beside the well. He was smitten. He would tell her story authoritatively, asserting that the spokes of night and day really were different. The taximan soldier yelled that no, her temple should be in Washington, they are the same, see how they rotate. They began to argue. By the time we thought of the mime again, he was gone. But it wasn't important. We had watched him wrestle, and we understood. We made it our own.

The woman watched as the soldiers argued, indifferent. Amadou offered her some cloth and I tried to pull some muddy water from the well. Like coffee. We could discuss her over coffee. As I watched, Amadou taught her to dance. It was a technical dance and I was surprised he knew it, with this veil held just so, using three fingers, and that veil thus, using four. He reminded her often that she could not let the veils fall. But the woman dropped the veils as soon as she understood the dance. Maybe she was bored. Upon seeing this, Amadou picked up one of the seven cloths and blindfolded her. The shy soldier walked up to her blindfolded face. The taximan soldier yelled about how they would all go to Washington. The shy soldier slapped the woman hard with the back of his hand. She buckled, then picked up the veils and began to dance again. She clutched the veils, her knuckles pale. But there were six veils and she had only two hands, and in order to hide her nakedness, she had to dance as she'd been taught, three fingers here, four there—shift, flow, blend, and separate—her hands too busy to tear off the blindfold. I wanted to interfere, to help the woman. Amadou stopped me silently, shaking his head no. The soldiers had guns now: a French-adapted G3 and a Kalashnikov. It was not clear when they had acquired the guns. As the woman danced, the two soldiers nodded approvingly and said that they would go off to build that temple for her. They would take her to Washington. As she danced, she wiggled and gestured confidently, as Amadou had taught her, gesturing for me to come to her, for those of us in the back of the truck to come down to her.

We drove on without the two soldiers, over long dunes that were braided and folded and angled against the wind. Amadou drove, for the driver had gone off with the soldiers.

CHAPTER 10

Timbuktu

"What did you think of the movie?" Muzhduk asked as they waited for nachos and beer at John Harvard's Brewery & Ale House, underground, surrounded by dark oak and thick brass pipes.

"The Swedes are so funny," Oedda said without smiling, picking out a stray leaf in her hair blown there by the windy October night. "They are very stupid people, but they are funny."

"You don't like Swedes?"

"Of course not." The nachos arrived. "Please ask the waiter to kindly bring silverware."

The goateed waiter was still placing the plate on the table, his face was two feet from Oedda. He'd heard her request, and gave them a look Muzhduk had sometimes seen when he worked for the circus.

• • •

Over a sand dune, sun-struck and malarial, and suddenly we crossed a paved road: the cracked asphalt of the Kabara-Timbuktu highway. The first asphalt in weeks. Then buildings appeared: Andorran Initiative for Development, Hungarian Operation for Organic Kitchens, Yemeni Outstanding Kindness for the Empty-handed, Russian Energy Liaison for Internet Advancement and Nurturing in Timbuktu—aid agencies filling both sides of the street in neat little buildings with white siding and green lawns, perpetually watered in the heat. No adobe houses. We passed the Danish Engineers for Progress in Education, Nutrition, and Dentistry and then the U.S. Peace Corps, distinguished only by the loud caterwaul of a generator. Except for the avenue of foreign agencies, Timbuktu looked like any other French-African city. Brown adobe, square, filled with children laughing and screaming. "Cadeau, gift, argent, geld, money, dinero, okane, soldi, peniaze, uang, penger, raha, pénz, akçe, pecunia, sinten, mynt…"

When we stopped, little hands reached into my pockets. They were empty. Amadou laughed and pointed towards a building with minarets, stone latticework, and towers, like out of *One Thousand and One Arabian Nights*. The sign in front read: *White Shoe Hotel*. A near-naked man squatted to the right, under a fence. He rubbed his belly, then pinched the loose skin there and turned it ferociously, as if attempting to turn his stomach upside down.

"If you hit them, they will leave," Amadou said. One older child threw a rock at me. He missed, but others got the idea. There was something sweet and nostalgic in the idea of children throwing rocks, but also disturbing—you can't catch a hundred little stones and you can't throw back. I thought about the naked woman and the mime in the desert. Whatever he had said, it made no sense anymore. Had he really spoken, and in English?

I turned to the hotel. Something sharp jabbed into the back of my leg, above the knee. I yelled, spun, and almost hit a skinny grinning ten-year-old. He held a small knife.

As the boy and I stared at each other a very tall, very thin man in a black suit and white bow-tie approached from behind and smashed him in the side of the head with a large stick. The boy ran off howling and holding his head, tilting to the left as though trying to steer away from the pain. The man in the white bow-tie bowed and welcomed us to the *White Shoe Hotel*.

We entered the zone of air-conditioning. White and Asian couples sat at café-style tables sipping Corpa-Colas, Budweisers, cocktails. Puffy from too much liquid. Many were listening to young, nervously twitching locals, thieves, rapists, and murderers speaking all the languages of the rich countries, while upstairs prostitutes assumed the position with puffy pink men.

• • •

Between nachos Muzhduk said, "Your pupils are dilated."

Oedda raised her eyebrows. "Do not flatter yourself."

"You're quick."

"You look like a Swedish hockey player."

"And I take it that's a bad thing?"

"Swedish hockey players have their uses."

"Are you flirting with me or insulting me?"

"Is there a difference?" she asked.

"Of course."

"Do you think so? Well then, I have already answered your question."

"I didn't understand."

"So much the worse for you."

"Now you're flattering yourself."

"I need to, since you do not."

"It's only our first date."

"Is that what this is?" she asked, and pursed her lips. "Well then, if you do not even flatter me on our 'first date,' as you call this, how can I expect any flattery later on?"

"So there's going to be a later on?"

"That is what I am trying to determine."

"And for that, you require flattery?"

"I am a woman."

"Well, I did compliment you on your quickness."

"Pfft. The very fact that you consider that a compliment is insulting."

"Why?"

"That, you should figure out yourself. It will be useful for you in life."

Another "think about it." Maybe everyone here read body language and shifts in pupil dilation as a matter of course, so it was like complimenting her for knowing the alphabet. But he didn't want to think about it. He wanted to tell her about his night meeting with Pooh. He wanted to ask if she thought everyone at Harvard was accumulating a grey cloud, and if she had a need to use her body for more than strangling pipes. If she also hadn't had sex since getting to this awful place. Except one night with Lena. But he had learned from Lena. "I would've complimented your appearance," he said. "But I figured that you hear it too often."

"It would sound more convincing if you did not use such a tone." She stopped herself and shook her head slowly. "Actually, no, it wouldn't. It's like you learned to play this game yesterday."

"Give or take a few days." In Verkhoyansk men and women gave compliments through sex, smiling, a wild boar—not words. He felt like he'd been on the verge of understanding the complicated North American steps required to get a girl into bed. But Oedda was turning what he'd learned upside down.

"It doesn't suit you. Still, I do require flattery, so I will have to settle for what you can muster up."

"All right. You look as though you never age."

"Better." She nodded. "But only because I won't ask what that means."

"You know, I've been learning—"

"Probably a bad idea," she interrupted.

"And most women here want to be complimented on their intelligence, not looks."

"Then you have surrounded yourself with women who fear they are stupid."

"You're pretty but you still want to be flattered on looks."

"Pretty?" She gave him a cold smile and raised eyebrows. "Great. Am I 'nice' too?"

"I was the one trying to be nice."

"So I am not pretty?"

Muzhduk started to laugh.

"Please don't laugh in public. It's yet another sign of stupidity."

"You seem very concerned about the subject."

"What I am concerned about is that you do not know how to flatter a woman. Flattery has to come out naturally, even when it is a lie. And I do prefer lies. But clearly you do not understand this part of the game, so let us stop it. You can go back to your Swedish hockey player role."

The date continued, more like combat than dance, but close enough to both. Muzhduk realized he was enjoying himself immensely.

• • •

"Bienvenue, welcome, willkommen," a man at the front said with a toothy smile, enough teeth for several mouths. Unable to peg the right language, he continued in French. "Are you here for the restaurant, bar, hotel, guide, tour, girls, boys, hashish, shopping—?"

I walked into the restaurant still thinking about the kid with the knife. Not a nice kid, but still a little kid. The toothy man showed us to our table, next to a white couple, and explained that if I wished to stay at the White Shoe Hotel, I'd have to use the White Shoe guides.

"Two beers and a shot of vodka," I said. The waiter brought two imported Bière Niger and a nameless vodka, then whispered in my ear that the man I was with was a bad man.

I poured the vodka on my leg. The cut was very small, but a bit of antiseptic couldn't hurt. I didn't respond to the waiter but did wonder about Amadou. He said he was from Congo but had family in Gao. El-Hajj had called him a Bella, but Bella lived mostly in the Sahel area. I'd met him by seeming coincidence, but he'd been Peggy's guide, and had known all along who I was. He was clearly a liar, but he was also my only friend here.

"You're not taking a cut on these beers, are you, Amadou?"

"Like this scum? You offend me, Twobob. I may cut, but not on a few francs of beer."

"Excuse me," said the middle-aged man from the next table over. He and the woman with him wore unprovoked smiles. Bob and Julie from Sleepy Eye, Minnesota, though Julie was from Brainerd originally, Bob explained. Just married, in Timbuktu. Isn't that wonderful? Both of them had been married before. They were so happy.

"Well then," I said, stumbling. Despite all the time I'd spent in Montreal and Boston, I was still clumsy at this sort of talk.

Bob chuckled, a laugh that had nothing to do with humor. "The ceremony was back home, but we wanted to perform the legal part here. Some people fly in just to get their passports stamped 'Timbuktu,' but we thought wouldn't it be great to have it on our wedding papers?" They'd flown in, charter flight. There was an airport just outside of town. Next to the Cola plant. A private airfield, but they lease out landing rights. "Don't you have a *Lonely Planet*?"

I groaned, not at the mention of a tourist guidebook, at least not initially, but at the fact that I could have flown directly into Timbuktu, had I known I'd be coming here.

"People do it with all kinds of documentation," Bob continued, "but we thought the wedding papers would be the most romantic. Do all the legalities here. I'm a lawyer myself and there's a whole special marriage law for foreigners. In the rest of Mali you have to prove you're the same religion, but not here." He looked around the restaurant, suddenly self-conscious. "I specialize in mortgages, real estate, that sort of thing."

The *Lonely Planet* part sunk in. I imagined Verkhoyansk in twenty years, with Minnesotans flying in to have *Siberia* stamped on their documents. "Can I help you with something? Or were you just being friendly?"

"Well, actually, yes," said the man. "Mahmoud, our guide, has gone to the police to pay. 10,000 CFA. Mahmoud said it was required, but we already paid once, 25,000, at the airport. He says this is a different department, but I was just curious if everyone had to pay, and, well, you look like you came in over land. But, I mean," he was flustered somewhat with the possibility that he had been rude, "I was just curious. And you seem friendly with the locals."

His wife smiled across the restaurant to a young man approaching in a Mickey Mouse T-shirt and pleated dress pants. She reached for her cigarettes and handed him one. "My husband is very suspicious," she said as Mahmoud sat down. His eyes jumped back and forth between the two tables, trying quickly to absorb what was happening.

"Do you speak any language he doesn't?" I asked, but my question was stupid. Mahmoud would speak every tourist language and a dozen tribal ones. English was for lawyers and businessmen. The small-scale cheaters, thieves, and murderers still had to learn the nighttime languages.

"No, no," the Minnesotan said with a self-deprecating grin. "Only American."

"You, Twobob," Mahmoud said in French. "You talk to your own table. Don't talk here."

"Mahmoud just told me I'm not allowed to talk to you."

"What? But that's silly, Mahmoud. This is our friend."

"These are my tourists. You cost me money, I cut you up," he said in French, but unable to hide his rising anger. "I know about you. You the new crazy Twobob, you roll in garbage and eat people. But I'm crazy too, and I cut you up if you lose my money. I don't care who owns you."

"Mahmoud just told me he would cut me up—" I began to explain.

Mahmoud jumped up and yelled in English, pointing at me. "You cannot talk to this man. He is a bad man. He eats people." Then he calmed down, reconsidered. "He is wanted by the police. I just came from the police, they will tell you about this man. Come, we go together."

"Let him finish his sentence, please, Mahmoud," said the man as his wife fidgeted with her cigarette. "Everybody will have a turn."

"*Honey*," the word wasn't sweet, "if he is wanted by the police—"

"What's this nonsense about eating people, anyway?" said the wife. "White people don't eat people."

Mahmoud looked frustrated. "He smuggles for terrorists. Everybody knows this."

Amadou was smiling.

"Amadou, can I see your radio?" I asked.

"Get out of here, Twobob," Mahmoud said to me in French. "This is not your hotel. Not just me, Twobob. All these people here. We all make money, we all cut you up."

"What are you going to do to me, Mahmoud?" I asked in English. "Tell me in English."

"*Tais-toi, Twobob. Je vais te couper la gorge*," he answered. "*D'un coté à l'autre, une coupe parfaite. Attends-moi ce soir. Tu verras.*"

"I don't understand in French."

"Tonight when you sleep!" he shouted in English. All the guides and tourists at all the tables turned to look at us.

"Now, Mahmoud," said the husband. "You can't be threatening our friend. I want to get to the bottom of this."

"Your friend," I said, shaking my head. "No offence, but in the States we'd never even say hello. Mahmoud doesn't want me to tell you there is no 10,000 CFA fee. At most he may have paid 1000 for the stamps, although even that's not 'legal,' as you would conceive of it."

Not legal. What did I mean by not legal? The wife asked if this was true. Mahmoud denied it. The man had been ready to distrust him from some residual instinct. He was desperate, and relative to others in Timbuktu, I was like him. His wife was saying that I was rude and they don't even know me. Mahmoud ran his finger under his neck. The two tables separated.

"Why did you do that?" Amadou asked.

"To help them."

"You just ruined their honeymoon. The francs are a cheap price for them to go home feeling good. Now they'll feel bad. And Mahmoud, if he cannot cheat them, maybe robs them in a way they will understand. And if he doesn't cheat them, someone else will. The fat man is a lawyer. He will understand that this is also a law."

Mahmoud and the Minnesotans left for the door, the husband a step behind, with a glance back at me. Amadou nodded toward them. "This is the place for finding information, but you made it difficult now. Mahmoud will go to the police. And that's never good for anybody."

• • •

"Show me a naked picture," Oedda said. "Of you."

It was a way to be invited to Muzhduk's little Gropius room, but it was confusing, both direct and not, sexual but at a distance, one layer removed.

He still had some cake in the fridge, but she didn't want cake. She grabbed his armpit without warning, through his shirt. He kissed her. She kissed back, open-mouthed but lips only, keeping her tongue to herself. He tried to find it, but it was nowhere and the whole procedure became awkward. The bed was against the back of her knees, so he pushed her down. She opened her eyes under the hanging bicycle, and stopped.

"Well," she said, limp. "Oedda is not going to subject herself to sex in this kind of a room. She wanted to touch your chest. She understood this means she might have to sleep with you. She does not mind that cost. But not here."

"You don't *mind that cost*?" Muzhduk ignored her use of the third person.

"But I do mind discussing it. Since you have no appreciation of the feminine, I am forced to explain that I like to be pursued, not interrogated. Vanity is a frequent characteristic. And leave your watch at home." Without waiting for a response she was already out the door.

He hesitated for a second. When he caught up to her on the way out of Gropius, passing the door of Clive's room closing, he was still confused, but smiling.

• • •

"Maybe we should go our own ways now," I said to Amadou.

"And where will you look?"

"Rogers mentioned the library." Or not. Rogers had answered my question about where I could find Peggy with a riddle about the Timbuktu library. Though he might just as well have been talking about what I'd been missing at Harvard. Maybe I was imagining things, maybe all the meanings I ascribed to his riddles were just my own projections, but I was out of other ideas.

"The great Timbuktu library. None of the books there are in French or English. And you don't speak Arabic, Bozo, Djerma, Bambara, Hausa, or anything else that matters."

I leaned over the table. "And you speak all those languages."

"I am African."

"And all the European languages."

"Sometimes I'm a guide."

"But you're not taking a cut on the beers. So why have you come all this way with me?"

"*Why*, Twobob," Amadou said. "It is your favorite question. Why? You should talk to Rogers, he speaks about the death of *because*. I don't know what it means for a word to die. If you kill a man, he shuts up. You are similar to those Americans from Minnesota."

"There is nothing similar."

He grinned his standard grin. "Have you ever wondered what distinguishes one grain of sand from another? One is just like a million of its brothers, but another enters the oyster."

"Is Timbuktu the oyster?"

"Timbuktu, the Sahara, the world. But I do not care about the world. If there is a pearl being created here, here is where my interest lies."

"So? Is there a pearl being created here?"

"I said 'if.' Beauty needs an ugliness around which to grow." He waved his hands widely.

"I've been told that. Over and over, it seems."

"Yes, those are malaria echoes. The Bozo call it the 'echo sickness.'"

"Are you suggesting my malaria changes what people say to me?"

"Of course. How can you not know this?"

"And you? Amadou-who-knows-so-much. What do you do?"

"I am a Malian Bella, a lowly slave. A sub-race. I am like a word."

"Not from Congo?"

"Congo? That was a different Amadou."

"I thought you reminded me of someone."

He nodded gravely. I had expected the grin.

"What does that mean, you are like a word?"

"I watch. I lie. I tell the truth. Sometimes I steal. Very occasionally I murder. I belong to Mali. Like that man in front of the Hotel, hoping if he could turn his belly a full circle, the witch inside would leave him. Is he not like a word? He too, belongs to Mali."

We finished our beer, checked into the hotel, and left for the great Timbuktu library.

• • •

Oedda's room was in North Hall, a former motel that Harvard had bought and now rented to visiting professors and wealthier students. The garbage cans were still labeled "Motel 6."

They took their shoes off at the entrance. Oedda wrinkled her nose and disappeared into her bathroom. He looked around the room. Its main feature was a queen bed with fluffy pillows, and a pale green quilt embroidered with red swords melting at their tips. A desk was buried in papers. Above it dangled a large white clock with no numbers and a sign that read "EVERYTHING IS FLIPPABLE," upside-down and mirror-reversed.

Muzhduk stared at the clock. It was also running counter-clockwise. "Your clock is off."

She tensed. "I asked you to leave your watch at home."

"It didn't make any sense."

"You could not respect that simple request?"

He put the watch in his pocket and went to look at her books. There was a whole shelf of thick leather-bound tomes with names like

Lex Malleus e Malus, *Lemegeton*, *Errores Gazariorum*, and *Postmodern Approaches to International Law*. The name Hecaten on their spines.

"Is your father a writer?"

She smiled. "Because of you, I don't have a father."

"Because of me?"

"Yes. You will be my father now."

Muzhduk didn't know what to say to that. "Is Hecaten a common name? It sounds like a witch."

"It is common to the books I wrote."

That stopped him again. Oedda's face turned intense, and she whispered, "To make someone ill, you concentrate while tying a knot in a string. Then you bury the string near the victim's home. If you have enough focus, you can even kill the person." She laughed.

The sarcasm left him nowhere to go, and he wanted to have sex. He kissed her. She kissed back, again with no tongue. He guided her toward the bed, but she slid out of his arms. She found several candles, lit them, then lit incense and placed it round the room.

He moved her hair to the side and bit the back of her neck. He pushed his erection against her ass, bending his knees, and cupped her breast in one hand and her throat in the other. She lit more candles, poured water into a bowl and dripped drops from little bottles that said "dwarf palmetto" and "civet cat musk" that gave the room a strong heavy resin smell. She placed objects near the bed, removed others, and finally began folding laundry while Muzhduk tongued the back of her skull and groped her from her throat to her crotch. She gave no reaction, not a pause or a hesitation except, maybe, a hardening of her nipples when he pinched them. He couldn't pull her shirt off because she wouldn't lift her arms. After the laundry, she prepared a drink.

"Do I not have a beautiful skull?" she asked suddenly, without stopping her movements.

"Yes."

"You did not notice? I have a particularly well-shaped skull. Drink this."

Muzhduk drank and almost spat it out. It tasted like condensed pine tree. "What is it?"

"It is a drink I made for you. That should be enough."

From under her shirt, he undid her bra. Her breast had a shifting density to it, one moment small and firm, then large and watery, as she wiggled out of his embrace yet again to begin watering the little garden of weeds and herbs that grew on her windowsill. He recognized one to be a mustard plant. "Is this less interesting than mustard?"

She turned around, as if only now fully noticing him. "Why are you still dressed?" She walked to her closet and pulled out a laundry basket. "Undress."

"I was hoping you could do it for me."

"I will play Mommy for you some other night."

Muzhduk dropped his clothes in a pile and lay on her bed. Her sheets had a hard cleanliness—in his waiting he imagined that they'd been dried on a hill in the arctic sun of some cold spring morning while a war raged on the other side.

"You do not fold your clothing?" she asked, eyebrows raised.

"No, I pile it up in piles," he said, frustrated. "Like Samson with the jawbone of the ass, piling Philistines in piles. Not in lumps. Lumping should be in lumps, but piling in piles."

• • •

The library had a faded hand-painted sign: *Bibliothèque du Tombouctou*. The building had once been yellow but now looked bleached, with rust-covered bars on the windows and two steel doors. It had a courtyard with one lacy tree. A thick man in a white djellaba sat under it on a two-piece folding wooden chair before another sign: "Great Library. 1000 CFA."

I paid the thousand and another thousand for the guided tour. Amadou did the same. Only then did the man stand up. After I filled out several forms in triplicate, he opened the door to a room lit by the sun filtered through windows covered in dirt, soot, and fly guts. Crowded flypaper coils hung everywhere. I hadn't seen flypaper coils since Verkhoyansk, but these were dry and drab, depressing in the heat. There were stacks of books on tables and on the floor, but most were locked in glass-fronted plastic and plywood cabinets. Each cabinet was slightly different, as though they'd been gathered up from a few dozen North American garage sales, but most seemed to have been made in the 1960s or 70s and were starting to fall apart, their sides bulging and warped. The librarian explained that their contents were old, with some of the scrolls dating back to the Crusades.

"But come, this is our newest greatest acquisition." He turned to a huge book, four feet by four feet, open atop a table. "A gift from President Muammar Gaddafi of Libya. It is a Koran, written in great style. And look here, the last word was written in by President Gaddafi himself. A gift from His Excellency to the people of Mali."

I looked at the last word: red and green ink, unsteady Arabic lines shaped vaguely like a Corpa-Cola logo. I didn't want to look at Gaddafi's Koran. Maybe the scrolls in the cabinets were from the Library of Alexandria, pre-Socratic books that predated Aristotle's proof of God by outlawing infinity and the void. I realized just how much time I'd spent in libraries since leaving Verkhoyansk, from the scavenger-hunt-turned-fire to endless hours studying, to that final night in the library making love with Peggy. I remembered looking up at the paintings on the ceilings, and that slogan: *In the beginning was the Ratio, and the Ratio was with God, and the Ratio was God.* Libraries made me think of her now.

The librarian explained how the four-foot size symbolized some important ratio in Mecca, and I stopped my mental drift. Drifting here was dangerous. We walked to the next room. It was filled with old-looking trinkets, green, worn-out copper, faded brass.

"Maybe you'd like to buy an artifact? Here." The fat librarian pulled out a bracelet. "From Kankan Musa himself."

"I'd like to buy information about Mr. Rogers. The Corpa-Cola Frenchman."

He nodded, sweating but not surprised. "Timbuktu has many books, a million books. We have only 25,000 here. The rest are in private libraries, around the city."

"He took my woman." I pulled out money.

"It's better to look somewhere else."

"You are a librarian." I pulled out more CFA bills.

"The private libraries have more money."

"But they are far away."

"Not so far." He looked at Amadou. "They've been here one thousand years."

"But they don't share their books with you."

He managed a smile. "They should."

"Yes, they should." I held out the wad of money towards him.

Amadou spoke quickly to the man in Arabic. They started to argue.

"Amadou," I interrupted. "Please speak French. I want to understand."

"Give careful," Amadou said in Russian. "You don't know information is any good."

"Don't speak to me in Russian," I said in English.

"So the man don't understand." Again in Russian.

"In the bush-taxi from Tillabéri, why didn't you tell me you knew who I was?"

"This is not the time to talk about this."

The librarian looked back and forth between my handful of money, Amadou, and me. "Please," he said. "The library is closed now."

"Amadou, can you wait outside?"

Amadou yelled at the man in Arabic again.

Still holding the money, I grabbed Amadou by the throat with my free hand. "French!"

In one fluid movement, he tucked his chin and punched my thumb where it met my hand, spraining it. "Be careful, Twobob." He walked out.

The librarian wouldn't take the money. He'd been on the verge before Amadou's Arabic outburst. I sat on a stack of books and forced myself to remember how I'd failed in beating information out of Rogers. When I was calm, I went outside.

Amadou was sitting in the librarian's lawn chair. There was a man at the courtyard gate. He looked at us. Amadou and I looked at him, and he disappeared into the library. And then I remembered: he was the tout from Gao, the persistent one who'd started off pretending he was a government official and who had, in fact, turned out to be a government official, an undercover cop of sorts, if I could believe Rogers. All of Gao seemed to be in Timbuktu. But I had to figure out what to do with Amadou first. I handed him the wad of money. He took it as if there was nothing odd about my paying him a second after choking him. "I need a guide."

"Where do you want to go?" he said, counting the money.

"You decide."

"Me?"

"Yes. What do you want?"

"No one has asked me that before." He showed bright round teeth, each with a space between it and its neighbors. "I want a Cola."

The Corpa-Cola factory. And their stupid riddles. It was obvious, but Rogers had talked so much about the Timbuktu library that I had libraries on the brain. I cursed myself as I walked into the street and right past the Mobile Customs Brigade Jeep parked in front.

"Twobob!" Hawaii yelled out the driver-side window.

• • •

Muzhduk watched Oedda finish her chores and undress, meticulously folding her underwear before placing it into a basket. For a moment she was naked—porcelain white skin, green eyes, red spoiled lips and long black hair—before she wrapped herself in a purple robe. Only her hair stayed loose, and it shimmered as she moved, catching a little on whatever other dimensions were curled up within space at every point around her.

She sneered, then smiled, then removed her robe.

• • •

Hawaii watched as I went to the passenger side.

"Now you are in Timbuktu," Khaki said. It wasn't a question.

"You too."

"We are mobile. Do you still have that radio?"

"I gave it to a friend."

"And where is your friend?"

I thought of how Amadou had disappeared during my last meeting with the Mobile Customs Brigade as well. "I don't know." I paused and made a decision. "I need your help."

"Help is a strong word."

• • •

"I'm cold." Oedda curled under the covers, facing away from Muzhduk.

Does she want to go to sleep? Muzhduk wondered. He bit into her shoulder, then again harder. She stayed asleep. He opened her legs, bit her pelvis. She pushed him off.

He lay on his back, breathing. An unacceptable condition. Surely everyone would understand if he explained that climbing Mount Harvard would have meant giving up on being a man. His father had mentioned that sex was complicated in Afghanistan as well, but based on the stories, not nearly as bad as Boston.

Oedda stood up on the bed, stepped over him, and grabbed his penis with both hands. "Why, it's just a little old thing," she said and pulled.

He shouted and arched his back.

She let him drop back to the bed and sat on his penis, holding it so it didn't bend.

"Ow! Maybe we should get you wet first."

"I knew a man once who had a broken dick," she answered, and smiled naturally for the first time since they'd met.

"Let me guess. Instead of coming he went?"

She just frowned at this. But thinking of other men's penises reminded him that this wasn't an isolated mountain valley and he didn't want to lean against the wall every time he tried to pee. "I'd prefer to use a condom."

"And I would prefer not to mediate my life-encounters with synthetic fabrics." She rolled her hips, just slightly too far forward for him to be comfortable.

He tried to push her toward his legs so his penis wouldn't be bent in an L shape, but she didn't let him. Apparently, she liked that spot. He pushed, she clamped down, and the struggle rocked them into a rhythm. "Are you on the pill, at least?" he asked.

"No." She continued to roll.

Muzhduk stopped moving with her. "We just met."

"Not true. There is never an unambiguous location in space or moment in time when people first meet. Encounters are always smeared out."

"I don't want a child," he said. "Especially not with you. With someone I just met, however smeared out."

"Maybe I do." She grabbed his armpits again, digging her thumbnails into his chest, deep enough to draw blood. Her lower belly grew rounded, rolling on him as if it were dancing. Not in and out, but in circles, ellipses, intricate patterns. "One night, and I never have to see you again. Sex is never as good as the first time, so why spoil the memory?"

"Most women think the other way. Even in Verkhoyansk."

"Then your women have sex in their heads."

"And you? Do you get pleasure out of fucking with me?"

"Are you so numb that you have to ask?" She grinned and squeezed. "You have your little foreplay, I have mine."

Despite her tone, there was no denying the advantages of being inside. Suddenly she stopped and stuck her tongue in and out rapidly, in caricature of cunnilingus. "Is that what your usual girlies like?"

"What?"

"Do they like it?"

"Is this talk turning you on? Because it's turning me off."

She looked down at their joined pelvises and squeezed her vaginal muscles with remarkable strength, shallow and deep in alternating succession, creating a soft sucking tugging inside. "It does not feel that way to me. You have some kind of taboo against talk during sex?"

"Mmm."

"Tell me what your taboos are." She arched her head back.

"I don't have any."

She stopped her internal massage. "I will find you some, if you like."

"Okay. But not now." He pressed a hand against the soft hair and belly just above her pubic bone. "Do that again."

For a second he thought she was going to spit on him. "You want me to pretend I'm your Mommy, to undress you? You can wear diapers next time. I had a son once, but he disappeared. Or I can wear the diapers. Sometimes I need a Daddy. I told you I don't have one of those either. But do not take my pleasure away from me."

"Okay. But squeeze again." He tried to focus on the smooth space where they connected.

She rolled for a few minutes, squeezing and sucking him inside. When he became fully immersed, she said, "You have not told me what you like."

"That." He touched her moving belly.

"You want to slap me a little? Go ahead. Here, slap my breasts." She slapped her own breast from underneath. It jumped and jiggled. "Do it!"

"I don't like that."

"Hah, your taboo reaches all the way to your penis." She waved her left arm in a visual imitation of flabbiness. "It's for me, so do it!"

So he slapped. Gently, so as not to hurt. Then a little harder. Then hard.

"Harder," she kept saying.

When he couldn't bring himself to hit any harder, when it was almost as hard as he'd hit a man in a fight, he was completely flaccid. His belly felt empty. It was *for her* and he didn't know what to say. What finally came out, like the chest-bursting creature in the movie *Alien*, was Torts: "I don't know if it's possible to consent—"

"Don't you *dare* bring Law into my bed!" Oedda hissed.

Her breasts bounced violently from one side to the other, distorted, fleshly mesmerizing—he almost bit them but it felt wrong. Not S&M, but something underneath it, some wrong mix of things.

"Forget it," she said, sad. "I'm playing. But there will be times when I want to be hit hard, and you will have to learn how to do it. One day you will throw me through the wall." Her breasts were still shaking. Muzhduk tore his eyes away from them and to her face.

"Why?"

"Because one feels guilt and wants it to be slapped away. So one turns it into a game. One is a realist, and realizes it is all a game anyway. But games have to be played *mit heiligem Ernst*, with holy earnestness. Which means you have to hit for real. Now it is your turn."

"What do you feel guilty about?"

"Guilt is a game too." Then she started to move again, silent for a few minutes. "For consuming you, perhaps. So many things."

And she continued, balancing the rolling and talking just enough to keep him hard, pulling his mind and body in opposite directions while learning his penis, honing in on that line between on and off. She asked about family members, Verkhoyansk, poking for a weakness as she squeezed internal muscles in counterpoint to her rolling, sucking him in. Then something changed, and suddenly Muzhduk needed to concentrate, not wanting a child. Nor to be defeated. *Don't think about monkeys.* He had never before considered an orgasm as defeat.

"Let go," she hissed through clenched teeth.

"No."

"Let go!" she insisted, nearly snarling. "It stops me, if you do not let go!" She scratched his chest with two handfuls of nails, gathering his skin under them. *If there is anything left after taking out the trash, we are still alive.* Calvino forgot to look under the nails. Oedda threw herself backwards and clawed at his balls and finally pulled him in through his penis, writhing on top, head arched, arms back, hair flying and alive—it seemed to change color, to a burnt orange. Thirty seconds later she was still coming, until he began to think she was playing a joke on him again, replaying the moment over and over, washing it out until she collapsed and rolled off Muzhduk and returned to the fetal position in which she had started.

"Should I thank you?" she whispered away from Muzhduk.

"You're a strange girl."

"If someone tells you that the fire is bright, don't pay any attention. When two thieves meet, no introductions are needed. They recognize each other."

"I don't recognize you. I've never met anyone like you."

This made her look. "I cannot be a strange girl, for I am twenty. You saw one tonight. She found you some taboos. Perhaps you should take your taboos home now so that Oedda might sleep. You can call her tomorrow. Leave the candles but do not turn on the lights on your way out."

Muzhduk gathered his clothes in the flickering light and walked out. It was nearly December, and the night was chilly as he walked towards his little room in Gropius. From behind, the moon struck him in the head.

• • •

I told Mr. Khaki that Peggy had been kidnapped by Tuaregs and might be at the Corpa-Cola factory. I was guessing, my guesses so unglued now that I was basing them on Amadou wanting a Cola. The thought was almost funny. Maybe he was just thirsty. But in the shadow logic of the Sahara that was about as close to cause and effect as I was going to find. I didn't explain and Khaki wasn't interested anyway. He just wanted to know about my relationship with "the rebels." I told him that if the rebels were the kidnappers then my relationship was hostile.

"So why did you smuggle the GPS in for them?"

"You mean the radio?"

"The radio was also a GPS."

"No it wasn't."

"Do not contradict me."

"You saw it. You approved it."

"So that we could see who you were helping."

Amadou, I noticed, was not behind me. "My friend. A woman."

"And she helps the rebels. So you are helping the rebels."

"I saw them kidnap her! One of the kidnappers hit her!"

"She has smuggled many illegal things."

"If she were helping them, why would they kidnap her?"

He shrugged. "Sometimes people kidnap their friends."

The tout from Gao came out of the library. He gave me a look like a curse, then climbed into the Jeep with Khaki and Hawaii. They talked in Bambara—I couldn't understand—then Khaki turned back to me. He said that it's easy to find me, then drove away.

Amadou came out of the library a few minutes later.

"Do you still have that radio?" I asked.

He shook his head. I followed him, somewhat sullenly, out of the labyrinthine medina into the northern outskirts of Timbuktu, then along a wide, modern road leading out of the city, past buildings that stopped on a line, like in Gao, and opened out to empty, seemingly endless sand dunes. After the city line there was no shade anywhere. We followed the road over a high dune and down through a pebbled valley until we arrived at a tangle of steel buildings and yellow curving pipes that led into a complex of silos, smokestacks, and what looked like a giant funnel-mushroom standing against the sky. It was a bright blue-white day. We came to a barbed-wire fence, where two large guards sat waiting in chairs under umbrellas. Next to them a tree branch was planted into the ground with a faded red plank nailed to it. It stated, in white letters, in English: "The Corpa-Cola Company. *The Stop that Stimulates*. Prepare to be searched."

The checkpoint guards lazily pointed guns in our direction without getting up. They told us to wait, but didn't otherwise move. They didn't call anyone on a radio or do anything except to lower their guns to their knees, seeming as tired of borders and fences and gates as I was. But Amadou spoke to them in Bozo, gesturing toward me, and they waved their muzzles that we could pass.

"I told him we were friends of Mr. Rogers."

I wondered how Khaki and Hawaii would take that news.

We entered the factory by the main door in the warehouse, where a tiny man with bushy eyebrows sat behind a desk in another reclining chair. He resembled the navel-turner in front of the White Shoe Hotel. Starting on the floor below us and extending up on escalator belts clanked empty bottles. They jittered forward in two symmetrical bins. They were pulled, sent through loops, filled from a giant vat far above, capped, hung by the neck and saddled off in rubber belts. But there was something not quite right.

"*Where there's Cola, there's happiness*," the tiny man said in English, without expression. I saw no one else in the factory. "*Thirst knows nothing*," he added.

"Are these real?" I asked him, looking closer at the machines.

"*It's the not-fake thing.*"

But it was a lie. The whole thing was a kinetic sculpture of independently moving parts with no connection to each other, a parody of a Cola factory sitting in the desert, a joke that no reasonable person could mistake for the real thing. The same empty bottles climbed and the full ones always descended. Half of each loop was hidden. If this was the rebel base, how had they ever fooled the government?

"*You can't beat the not-fake thing*," said the man.

"What's his problem?" I asked Amadou.

"*Often Corpa-Cola.*"

"He is doing his job. That is all."

"*The best friend you'll ever have.*"

"His job is to—?"

"*Corp is it.*"

I tried to ignore the man and look only at Amadou. "Where's Rogers?"

"*Around the bend from nowhere.*"

"Is that really a Corpa-Cola slogan?" I asked. "*Around the bend from nowhere*?"

Amadou shrugged.

"*Whoever I am, whatever I am, wherever I may be, when I think—*"

"This is the tourist area. The real factory is behind."

"*What you want—*"

"Shut—" I was cut off by shouting from behind.

With no warning, Amadou ran to a service ladder, slid down, crossed the floor, hurried up a ladder and bolted toward the vat where the fake bottles appeared to be filled. I looked around and spotted soldiers running through the front gate. I ran after Amadou, following the path he'd taken, eventually squeezing between the animatronic loops. I turned to find the slogan-turning man following us. There, the walkway opened to a mechanized jangle of unoiled machines, conveyor belts, and smaller vats, dirty and chaotic. Gusts of gas blew out of gaskets, liquid poured, and sweaty people moved heavy things.

"*Look up World.*"

More soldiers streamed in behind us. Below, men with guns wearing the same khaki as the soldiers sprinted between the machines as workers screamed and ran. Someone fired his gun—I could hear bullets bouncing off metal—and then everyone fired his gun.

• • •

The water in the bathroom was too hot, then too cold. When it was on the verge of being perfect, Clive confronted Muzhduk: "You had a woman in your room."

Muzhduk stared at Clive dumbly. He hadn't slept enough. "So?"

"I don't suppose you cleared it with the RA, as per the Gropius Regulations?"

"*Into-Snow-White's-seven-polka-dotted-cunt!*" I swore in Slovak. "Some of us will defend death penalty cases."

He began to walk away. If Clive had known Lena had spent a whole night in his room rather than Oedda's few minutes, he'd have blown a gasket in his hurry to snitch to someone. This school was for children.

Clive grabbed Muzhduk's wrist and started to say something about how he was going to speak with the RA. Muzhduk picked Clive up off the ground. But Clive was so much lighter than he'd expected that he stopped himself in mid-throw. Clive stared down at Muzhduk, in shock. Finally, Muzhduk put him down and walked out of the bathroom.

• • •

Bullets, glass, and syrup sprayed around the factory. I ran after Amadou. The flume turned into a flue, a tube the height of a man. I trudged through the stuff with big slow steps, getting sticky but not shot. We could still hear the gunfight but it was all muffled. The stuff stung my skin.

The flue went around a corner, where the liquid fell through a grate in the floor. We went up another ladder, to more grated floors and then a hallway. I could see Amadou's footsteps from the muck, each step fainter, leading through a door and into a corporate library.

The background noise of shooting stopped.

"*Where there's Corpa, there's happiness.*"

The small library had old-fashioned movable metal shelves on the right side and small cubicles for personal study on the left. Directly in front, at a wide table at the end of the room, sat Rogers. He was sipping tea and watching me. Amadou was standing beside him, sweating from the run, and there was a third man I didn't recognize sitting at the table. A double chin marked him as a lawyer.

I didn't see Peggy, or any men with guns. Each of the metal shelves had cranks on their sides, with walking room only between two shelves at a time. A person would have to pick the aisle they wanted to open and crank the crank corresponding to that crack. All the shelves would then move on their track, squeezing away the original space.

Rogers pointed to a ragged, browned book on his table. "This is what you're seeking."

I approached. The cover of the book he'd pointed to said *Secret Formula*. The first page had a big X, then a recipe for *Nerve and Brain* Tonic:

INGREDIENTS:
2 oz. citrate caffeine
2 quarts lime juice
6 oz. citric acid
60 lbs. sugar
2 oz. vanilla extract
10 oz. flavoring
8 oz. fluid extract coca plant
5 gallons water
caramel sufficient

FLAVORING:
10 coriander oil
20 nutmeg oil
20 cinnamon oil
20 neroli
40 orange oil
60 lemon oil
Half quart of alcohol

DIRECTIONS:

Boil water; add lime juice, caffeine, acid; cool; add flavoring and vanilla; let stand.

NOTES:

Mix syrup with carbonated water in a 1:6.5 ratio.

For fluid extract of coca plant, 10 pounds of coca leaf will flavor 36 gallons of syrup.

Use lower cocaine levels, as cola is too bitter if use high-cocaine coca leaf.

For citrate caffeine, use African kola nut.

"The original recipe," the lawyer said. "When Cana Sandler bought the company, he added glycerin for preservation, replaced cocaine with spent coca leaves, lime oil with lime juice, and sugar with corn syrup. We sweetened it again after the New Cola mistake, because in blind tests people preferred the taste of New Cola, but only if they couldn't see the label. If they could see the bottle, they preferred the original Corpa-Cola taste."

"Who are you?"

"The name is Babu Chirpy, Esq., I am a trademark attorney for Corpa-Cola."

I turned the book over to see whether there was anything on the back. There wasn't.

"And in Africa," he added, "the recipe is even sweeter."

I waved the book. "I don't care about this."

"You don't?"

"No. Why are you showing it to me?" I threw it back on the table. "What the hell does Corpa-Cola have to do with anything?"

Amadou began to laugh. Loud, holding his belly.

"What's so funny, Amadou," I asked, angry.

"A man once came to the Getaway Guesthouse," Amadou explained, still laughing. "Many years ago. The man bet Mr. Rogers that he could answer the most difficult question. The man was like you, Twobob. Mr. Rogers took the bet. So the man said that the most difficult question was the question of what is the most difficult question. And since he had just answered it, he felt that he had won the bet."

"And?" I remembered the way my father had once smashed a neighbor's oak table in two during dinner out of irritation. "Did he win?"

"That remains to be found out, Twobob," he continued to smile. "The man trying to turn his belly outside the White Shoe Hotel? He was that man, I think. It's hard to tell now. He has become African, and does not look as he did before." Amadou leaned forward. "This happens sometimes. A thing is offered to you, and you do not recognize it."

"That's the secret formula for a stupid drink. I'm here to find Peggy."

Rogers spoke for the first time. "I don't think you have understood correctly the situation. Peggy is our friend. We were protecting her from *you*."

"I saw—"

"She told us about your situation in Siberia. About the lawyers and the merchants and men who have no honor but now control the world. We have been fighting the same war here, for much longer. I am offering you the answer, and you don't recognize it. The secret of Corpa-Cola is that the formula is not secret. Its secret is that people prefer the taste of the old Cola only when they can see the label. Peggy Roundtree also told us about your year in America, how this is something you never understood."

Peggy hadn't known me for most of my year at Harvard. We'd gotten to know each other shortly before the end, but I'd told her much of what had happened. The information had probably come from her, but that didn't say anything about how they'd gotten it. And I didn't have any more patience for tangential conversations and riddles that I didn't know how to interpret, even if they were about Verkhoyansk. "I want to see Peggy. If she tells me to leave, then I'll leave. If you're telling the truth, then it's easy. I think I've waited long enough."

Rogers sighed and Amadou went to an old-fashioned Dewey

Decimal card catalogue, then to a shelf, and cranked. The right hand panel, along with dozens of others, squeezed down, making room for me to enter. The alley of books was surprisingly long, each shelf at least thirty feet. An opening appeared in the back. Amadou handed me the yellowing Dewey card.

I didn't know what this was supposed to mean. I looked at the number, followed the ordered books to a small moleskin notebook. I opened it at random, and realized I had no idea what Peggy's handwriting looked like, whether this was hers. It wasn't a diary, there were no dates, but it had individual entries, like Nietzsche's aphorisms.

The first was short, and read, "R=1/R."

The second read, "But it seems that this moment of recognition has less to do with power & sacrifice and more to do with mimesis and mimetic rivalry. Not that the two are so distinct. It seems Muzhduk thinks Oedda knows something, some secret of being. He wants to know how to get it and thinks she can teach him, or show him. So he tries to figure out what she 'wants,' in a general sense...because she is the mirror of Harvard, which is bad, and so he suspects that she is the kind of person who knows what's good. This is very convenient for him because he will know what to want too. And then he will know what she knows. Unfortunately for both of them, she feels the same way about him..."

• • •

Anonymous letters signed "Your §4 Friends" appeared in Muzhduk's pigeon-box two days after Torts class. The letters said that his admission diminished the value of the Harvard name for everyone. Muzhduk took the letters as a challenge, but he didn't know how to accept. He searched for a week, asking everyone in his classes, standing in the hallways before and after Torts, Property, Civil Procedure, Contracts, and Criminal Law, asking each person individually whether he or she had sent the letter. There were only 550 people in his class, only one-quarter of them in his section. Everyone denied it and expressed proper outrage that such an intolerant letter would be sent at a school like Harvard. The letters continued for a short time before stopping, with the last one accusing him of having made them up in order to get sympathy.

Buck told Muzhduk not to worry. He said the "section four friends" sent those letters to remind themselves that they truly were at Harvard Law School. Muzhduk appreciated Buck's support, and the way he dropped his own annoyance with Muzhduk as soon as he heard about the letters. But Buck's logic hurt his head—he had to decide how much he wanted to re-learn everything. He didn't want such calculative thinking, but he also hadn't thrown Sclera out the window.

Sclera was wrong to think Muzhduk was immune, so maybe he was also wrong about whether he could make it through. But did it even matter? He didn't really care about the "Rule Against Perpetuities," or whether policy considerations weighted in its favor or against. He was here to climb Mount Harvard and he was faced with a problem: he didn't know where the summit was. Was it getting in, or graduating, or making friends with all the other future-important people: skating fish who had determined generations ago that three comments every five classes was the correct number for optimizing reputation for intelligence without being seen as a "gunner," adjusted for comment type, length, quality, and external stress variables like barometric pressure, applying LSAT exam skills and second derivative calculus to social situations? Like in the Dull-Boulder Throw, there were no referees, no one to hand out grades based on these formulas. There was only "rational discourse," an arena where words warped. The juiciest words became the weakest. "Use" became "utilize," "want" became "desirous of," and "bad" was always "egregious." The word "I" was the most awkward. In rational discourse, any sort of personal anecdote, any real experience, became as unacceptable as "fuck."

There were advantages—communication, interaction, society, norms, propriety, Law, and the perpetual motion machines that were surmounting everything that was simultaneously surmounting them. The machine flew on, carrying with it Harvard, America, and eventually the rest of the world.

One day it will reach Verkhoyansk...

A law degree wouldn't help, but understanding what was coming would. And Sclera was right. Muzhduk could climb or fight, but not both. He went to see Oedda. Maybe she'd know what to do.

• • •

The bookshelves began to squeeze together. Amadou had stepped out of the aisle. I shouted, braced myself, trying to hold the shelves apart. Somebody was cranking the crank and the mechanism was strong. I was closer to the back of the shelves—I ran toward the room in back I'd glimpsed there, then stopped between shelves because I saw Peggy sitting on a sofa, one leg tucked under her the way she always sat, but she was wearing a Tuareg indigo robe, seated across from Ibrahim, her kidnapper, with her hand on his thigh.

At the last second, I jammed my feet in against the bottom shelves. I fought the gears as they squeezed the bookshelves together, trying to open a gorge, pushing apart the pillars of a Philistine temple, the parallel cliffs of Mount Baldhead, Oedda and Sclera, Harvard and Mali. But the mechanism was strong, the shelves already too close together. I was too late and too weak with the echo sickness, my malaria. The bookshelves groaned—I imagined thousands of small straining cogs, and thought, again too late, that I'd been warned by all the navel turning—I yelled out, and then I couldn't yell because my ribs were pressing into my lungs too hard, crushed by books and sentences and words.

CHAPTER 11

Nullius Filius

"It is unfortunate that you must advertise your visit," Oedda said as Muzhduk placed his boots neatly beside the door, guarding her apartment against the barbarians who lived in the mountains.

"I can bring them in. They don't smell that bad."

"They do. You carry your own scent with you wherever you go, and destroy my effort."

"Well, it's too cold to walk barefoot."

"It is not really the boots. It is you. Leave them outside." She closed the door, shook her head, and mumbled to herself: "Now you have me talking about inside and outside. Impossible."

"I came over to get your advice on something."

"My advice is that you wash your feet."

Muzhduk didn't think they smelled, but he washed both carefully between the toes, around the heels, all over. He walked sockless back into the bedroom.

Oedda was sitting on the bed in red underwear and bra. "Hey, baby."

He didn't know what to say, so he said, "Hello."

"Wanna fuck, baby?" She walked up to him, rubbed a breast against his belly. "I show you good-good time, fuckee-suckee, you and me. Cheap-cheap."

Muzhduk played along. At the end, curious how far she'd take it, he offered her $10.

"Is that what you think I am worth?" she asked, then took the money.

I have found my Mary Magdalene, Muzhduk thought. *If Harvard is the Madonna, with paintings of flat airy judges facing directly out, then Oedda is Magdalene, all profiles and reliefs.* He'd found an answer to the cold antiseptic functionality. In Oedda there was something dark, moist, and swampy. Almost bacterial. He felt like a physicist, who, bored by Newton, suddenly discovered quantum mechanics, relativity, and dark matter all at once.

• • •

I woke up with Peggy hitting me in the face.

My ribs hurt. I was on the sofa, where they'd been sitting. She was looking down into my face. She looked different, more tanned maybe. It was her, nothing had changed really, but her overall look, her glow, was foreign. Maybe it was the geometry-pattern earrings, shiny Thaler silver. She'd traded the *haik* for hiking pants and a white T-shirt, but she still had the earrings, her eyes were still dark with Tuareg-style antimony makeup and her fingernails tainted with henna. Her hands were also harder than I remembered, and her hair wilder.

My wrists chafed. I'd had rope on them, but it was gone. "Why are you hitting me?"

"So you're not faking."

Leaning heavily on the armrest, I stood up. "Why would I fake?"

"So I carry you." She smiled, kissed me on the lips too quickly, then pulled on my arm again. "We don't have much time."

"Where's Ibrahim? And Rogers?"

"They're talking cease-fire with the government. We have to go." She ran to the shelves.

"Peggy! Wait. You're here. I need to finish with Rogers." *And Ibrahim.*

"And what, punch him in the nose? If you're here to rescue me, rescue me first."

I followed her through the bookshelves. Soon we were running, and I was thinking that the baggy Tuareg cloth wouldn't have done her rear justice when a Tuareg opened the library door. A Kalashnikov hung off his shoulder and a Takoba sword from his waist. His eyes opened so wide they filled the whole slit in his veil, but he pulled out the sword in an impossible fluid motion that seemed like it was just a wave of his robes. I heard Peggy yell, "Duck!" She was already past him, twisting mid-run to see.

My last thought was, *I don't duck.*

• • •

As December progressed, Muzhduk went back and forth between Oedda and the Law. He read until his eyes hurt: Lex Aquilia, Lex Atilia, Lex barbara, through the alphabet to the jus. Jus aelienum, Jus belli, Jus civile, and on to the final Ius cogens which is spelled with an "I" and has no laws inside, only a statement that it is the highest international law there is, which nobody can agree on. Justice, squeezed from all this jus, is the title given to judges. According to Professor Synovia, it can still be found in Montana.

Muzhduk read laws while walking, eating, shitting, at every moment other than those he spent in North Hall. Everybody read. Everybody walked with a sideways stoop to balance their book bags. Once, in the Hark Box Café before class, Buck looked up from this Property textbook and said, "You know, it just occurred to me that all this mental energy might be digging unnecessary warps in the fabric of space-time, hurtling us forward chronometrically."

"What does that mean?"

"It means we're living toward exams, moot court, and retirement. You know the maxim *Lex non patitur absurdum?* The Law does not suffer an absurdity?"

"Yes."

"And the Chinese proverb says *it is later than you think.* But quantum mechanics says you can get large amounts of energy into a small volume if the time is short enough. That's why lawyers bill in six minute increments—and divide days into hours, hours into minutes, and minutes into seconds—so we can read, prepare, discuss, do it all and still drink like, like..."

"Like a cik. In Verkhoyansk we say 'drink like cik.' Though here we don't."

"What's a cheek?"

"It's a made up word. But everyone knows what it means."

"So what does it mean?"

"It doesn't mean anything, it's just a word used in that one expression. Forget it. Drunk like a rainbow. We also say 'drunk like a rainbow.'"

"That's an odd place you come from." Buck peered at his watch and returned to work.

Muzhduk had read a quantum mechanics textbook in Siberia, but all that he could think to say was a lame joke about balancing on the h-bar. He wanted to tell Buck about his visits to Oedda, which somehow left him more exhausted than his work, and his indecision about burning down the library, and all the other bits and pieces that were making him feel alien to himself. But Buck rarely had time now for more than a one-liner or a discussion of outlines as he struggled to stuff every obscure case and professorial opinion into a single document that he could carry into the quickly approaching exams. Rebuffed by Ted Cruz's resume-based group, he joined a study group he was unsure about, then another. Soon they discovered he belonged to two groups and he was forced to make a choice. He chose the new group, but soon began secretly having coffee with members of his old group, asking them how their outline was progressing, who in turn inquired about the new group's outline. They danced, vaguely and indirectly, but the new group caught on and began to have meetings without Buck, creating outline sections to which he was not privy. Ultimately everyone had an inner outline they shared with no one, surrounded by concentric rings of information that turned to disinformation as the rings moved further out. Grades were meted out on a bell curve and trades were always for inferior outlines. Second year students, 2-Ls, who had chosen to study Negotiation found themselves negotiating for outlines that would teach them how to negotiate. The rich got richer, the poor got poorer, and Buck's indecision pushed him gradually further out, as he himself admitted when he offered Muzhduk his own outline, filled with euphuistic and periphrastic catachreses, but no mistakes. He felt bound by his word not to share the one made by his study group, though nobody except Muzhduk believed him.

Muzhduk also made an outline for each class and freely asked people if they wanted to swap copies. Except for Buck's, he was given ones full of errors, along with a polite smile.

In the end, all outlines were measured against the almost-platonic Outline of the Covenant: an indexed set of twelve tablets or tomes (the rumors were unclear) with all the possible permutations of all the possible questions that a professor could ask on any exam. The sum knowledge of all *summa*s in Harvard history, this outline was the grail of the Gannett House cult. It was against this outline that the cult judged every citation and footnote in every law review article submitted by eminent professors from around the world. Buck had become obsessed with it.

Muzhduk wanted to go search for it. He and Buck spent too much time talking. This would be the closest thing available to fighting Russians together.

Buck refused. There was nothing more prestigious than being invited to join Gannett House, but it had to be done after an optional ten-day exam that began the day school ended. Nearly all One-Ls took it while their summer law firms waited.

Muzhduk shrugged. "Let's go to the Ratio Pub then. I like their barmaid."

"Aren't you still seeing that weird visiting professor?"

"I still like the barmaid. Though she's rarely there these days."

"It's Friday," Buck said, and so they stayed. Friday nights the Hark Box served free beer, so they could have a beer while discussing cases.

Much later, after the Hark Box closed, after he'd visited North Hall, Muzhduk went to the Ratio alone. But he'd waited too long and the bar was closed. The Memorial Fence was locked, so he had to walk through Harvard Square. It was windy, with the first snow of the winter falling. Wimpy snow that melted when it landed. He decided to stop at The Tasty, a four-stool diner that was the last holdout of an older Harvard Square. Inside, Buck was curled around a moleskin notebook at the counter, his back to the door. Surprised, Muzhduk nodded to The Tasty's owner-chef, Hussein, and silently sat beside Buck, who was too absorbed in his writing to notice.

I borrowed will from lies and my feet
Walked as long as I could
Kept up unspoiled—

"What's that?" Muzhduk asked.

Buck jumped and covered his notebook, going from startled grey to angry. "It's private."

"It's really good."

"It's private. It's just something I do when...for amusement."

"I bend the pipes in the statue outside Gropius. I watch the shapes change."

"That's you?"

"It balances out my brain. If Harvard insists on bending me, then I'm going to bend something back. But it's not really the same thing."

"Why not?" Buck stuffed his book into a pocket.

"Because your poetry is really good." He lifted his beard and let it drop several times. "If you can write like that, maybe you shouldn't be a lawyer."

"Maybe you should mind your own business." He rose and slunk out of the diner.

Muzhduk stood, wanting to explain that Buck had taken the comment wrong, just as Hussein slid a plate forward on the counter: low-grade beef with a fried egg, several slabs of bacon, all smeared with mayonnaise, sitting in a drip-pool of grease. He knew Muzhduk always ordered the "Heart Attack" after visiting Oedda.

Muzhduk ate his meal in silence, thinking about Buck and his poem. When he finished, he wiped melted fat and egg off his face, then walked through campus to the whitewashed wooden walls of Gannett House. If Buck was a neurotic on the outside and a poet inside who ate at The Tasty, then maybe he should be curious about Gannett House. He didn't try to pin the logic down, just walked to Gannett House and worked his thumbs to scrape the last bits of egg from his beard.

It was the only wooden building on campus. A perfect white square topped by a white triangle that seemed to float above thanks to a broad hidden fascia. A single window in the middle of the triangle made the whole thing look like the Masonic "new order" Eye of Providence on the U.S. dollar bill. He'd seen the Gannett House students a few times, usually off in the distance, always at the other end of campus. There was a cohesion to them, a cold synchronicity of movement in their skinny tensed legs when they walked in a group.

Now he stood on the Gannett porch, raised by four thin steps and framed by four simple columns. There was nobody around. *I borrowed will from lies and my feet.* The front door was unlocked. It opened to an empty hallway and a large windowless room where four people sat in desk-cubicles next to stacks of thick code books. They wore tight black hats, like old-fashioned football helmets, and overlong black shirts that covered them down to the thighs. They were wearing shorts, or nothing at all, he couldn't tell, but he could see their pale, almost reddish legs.

When he came in, all four arched their necks, turning towards him like time-lapse sunflowers turning to the sun.

Performance art? Muzhduk wondered. Then the four men, women?—he couldn't tell—stood up, unsteadily, as though walking on their ankles. They reminded him of a painting of Hippomenes he'd seen once, or of the Bhutto performers in Montreal. Except that the Bhutto players had been firmly attached to the ground, with every step.

He passed them quickly on the way down a hallway with doors on either side, past more misshapen members of the eighty-six winners who'd been sifted out from the general HLS population by that optional ten-day exam. The more obstacles, sleepless nights, and desperation placed before them, the more actively the hyper-rational students tried to get into the little house. Muzhduk remembered Buck telling him that structures repeat as he wandered down hallways and spiraling staircases until the ground was wet and smelled of iodine and rotting codebooks. Rats scurried about and sometimes screeched in outrage. In one corner, he found a bookshelf overflowing with thick glass jars with metal clasps and labels: "talent," "love," "humanity," "testosterone," "femininity," "curiosity," "ambiguity," among others. Each label had a name, a resume, and a few vignettes of integrated life-experience.

As Muzhduk stopped to examine a jar, a figure flew out at him from an unlit nook.

"*Lex est tutissima cassis!*" the skinny figure howled and ran head first into Muzhduk's chest. The figure had such speed that despite their weight difference, it knocked the air out of him. Or perhaps it was right, perhaps Law is the safest helmet.

• • •

I crashed into the Tuareg just before his sword struck my shoulder. I felt his spine bend backwards, a feeling of feather-lightness as he crumpled. The sword lost its connection to his feet and became empty, barely cutting in. I stumbled once on his robes, caught my balance, and kept running.

• • •

"Nullius filius!" The helmet-head charged again and Muzhduk swung his knuckles into its cheek. Helmut collapsed into a shelf, sending jars crashing.

Despite his irritation at being called the son of nobody, a man conceived in a barn, Muzhduk placed a jar of valor on Helmut's skinny chest before pulling the helmet off and squeezing his own head into the stretchy metallic leather, like Lena's Kevlar pantyhose—Control Top, she'd called it—that re-arranged flesh into fitting shapes. Then he took his pants off, placed them in a cubicle, and went to search for the center to the labyrinth.

He didn't find it. Instead, he found that Gannett House has twenty-two centers and stale air. Feeling like an invading army deflected by the contorted shapes of the suburbs, he sat at a cubicle to rest. Another Helmut approached and handed him an article titled *Giffen Goods, Cop Shows, and the Death Penalty*. It concluded that people commit murder if they see the benefit as greater than the cost times the perceived probability of getting caught. Society, it argued, can decrease murder rates by increasing the cost via the death penalty while increasing the perceived probability of getting caught via cop shows. *Non nasci, et natum mori, paria sunt*—not to be born and to be born dead are the same, and there is a war between those who thought legal maxims trumped economics and those who thought they didn't.

Muzhduk marveled at the sterile argument and when a Helmut came to take his article, Muzhduk said he wasn't finished. Helmut became agitated, yelling in Latin that Muzhduk was only supposed to check the footnotes. Other Helmuts poured in, like sand, distressed that Muzhduk had read the body of the text. They asked where his subciting Bluebook was. He didn't have any blue books, only yellow ones, he said. They hooked elbows and charged. A flying wedge. These had been outlawed in rugby.

• • •

Peggy and I ran out of the factory to a loading area surrounded by an adobe mud wall. The wall was left from a temple built in 1056 by the poet Abu Ishaq es-Sahéli, a sister temple to the Askia tomb in Gao. Now it was the back fence of the Cola factory. Wooden beams were mortared into the wall at two-foot intervals, jutting out at wild angles like quills on a sparse old porcupine. The oldest of the beams had been brought here from Mecca. Now, monkeys swung from them.

"They're here for the Cola," Peggy said when the monkeys bared their teeth at us. "We had a big baboon problem at the hospital too. A gang of about 150 would raid us and pull out the IVs from patients. City monkeys. The Sahel's too dry for them otherwise."

"Baboons raided the hospital?"

"Most IVs are just dextrose solution. Sweet. They pulled it from the patients and drank from the tubes. I don't know how they first learned it, but they did. Half my time there was fighting baboons. We have to climb, we can't go through the gate." With the decision to climb, we could stop thinking. I kissed her, finally. She kissed back. Soft, warm, but too rushed, as though we hadn't had time to recognize each other yet. Nobody was following us.

"I saw you with Ibrahim."

"It's a long story. We should go."

I touched her breast, then turned to face the wall of monkeys. We climbed from stick to stick, Mecca crossbeam to Mecca crossbeam, the temple went to the heavens and we couldn't understand each other anymore. Monkeys were everywhere, screeching and stealing minor possessions, a banana I had in my pocket, giving me scratches in return for my defense of it. They swung on their arms and attacked with their hind legs and we climbed and our palms became sweaty and the sweat on my back froze despite the late-afternoon sun. We climbed, the stars became visible as the atmosphere thinned and then we were at the top of the wall, huffing. It hadn't taken all that long.

The wall was made of mud, after all, low to the ground. Just high enough to be interesting for the monkeys.

• • •

The flying wedge knocked Muzhduk down, and the stale air prevented deep breaths. The Helmuts dragged him through endless underground passageways. Like the roots of a giant tree, Gannett House had spread far and wide under the Law School. To the west, north, and east, they'd expanded far beyond the surface confines of Harvard property and now owned most of the "mineral rights"—ownership of the ground beneath the surface—in Cambridge. It bothered no one, because people live on the surface. The east had been a two-hundred-year struggle, but the School of Divinity's foundations finally fell to Gannett House in 1966. Then they shifted their energy south. South of the Law School was Pooh's tree, and south of that was the Science Center. The tree was the final obstacle to unifying Law, Science, and God, creating the ultimate Trinity.

They arrived at a room with a real non-cubicle desk. The Helmut at the desk had legs as bare and skinny as all the other Helmuts, but, unlike them, he was fat in the upper body. He looked Muzhduk up and down with disapproval. "You are Muzhduk the Ugli."

"Yes. Who are you?"

"I will ask the questions," the man said, but answered anyway. "I am VP Subciting, a member of the Council of Gannett House. You are trespassing here, in violation of the Law."

"This building belongs to the school."

"It is customary that only members of the *Law Review* may enter Gannett House. Custom plus Time become Law."

"Has anyone from outside ever tried?"

"Never."

"So your custom speaks only to the fact that members of the *Law Review* may enter. It says nothing about whether others may or may not, since they have never tried."

A wary look came into the eyes of the VP Subciting. "Why are you trying?"

Muzhduk didn't have a good answer. "I'm looking for the Outline."

"The Outline of the Covenant?" the VP repeated, and visibly relaxed. "You don't even know what it is. When you know what it is, you will have found it. But you are missing a limb." He palmed his table as though working a smudge out. "The laws of Harvard are a full generation ahead of those of America, and America is a generation ahead of the world. America has 50 million laws in force right now. The laws of Harvard approach the infinite. And Gannet, well, Gannett is transcendent."

"Who was it that said, 'The more numerous the laws, the more corrupt the state'?"

"Tacitus," cited the VP. "Alexander Hamilton believed the exact opposite, directly overruling Tacitus. And given jurisdictional issues, Hamilton's is the more correct citation."

I remembered Fred on his deathbed. "Like smoking the wrong type of grass, or sitting on a milk crate, or climbing a tree within city limits—"

"Yes." The VP shrugged. "In his or her ignorance, the average American commits three felonies per day. There is no opposing the Law. Besides Gannett House, there is only Skull & Bones at Yale. Where else does a Justice come from? Or a president? The Outline of the Covenant is the living Law, it is the ancient Covenant between Harvard and Yale, but most of all it is the Law as a way of thinking, to be approached within yourself. There is no such thing as opposition to Law. Nor is there appeasement, except in the short term. If criminality increases, it justifies more laws, higher budgets. If criminality decreases, the Law simply outlaws additional—"

There was a commotion from the other Helmuts in the back. A Helmut whispered in the VP's ear. The VP straightened in his chair. "One of the Kind Ones is here," he said, in awe.

The Helmuts opened up, stepped aside with reverence. From between them came Pooh, his cheese-grater voice preceding him. "Woe unto you, Lawyers! For ye have taken away the key of knowledge; ye entered not in yourselves, and them that were entering in, ye hindered."

The Helmuts milled, disconnected from each other. Finally, the VP answered, "New Testament, Luke, 11:52," as though he had been asked a question. "The quotation is accurate."

Muzhduk shook his head, surprised that the Helmuts could see Pooh. Pooh ignored them. "The root of existence is fire. Better to know nothing than to turn your head into a dump."

"I know nothing," said Muzhduk, thinking of Socrates. He had become popular in Verkhoyansk after Fred the Political Officer explained one year that Socrates was the wisest man because he knew that he knew nothing. This came as a great relief to all six villages, and a week-long carnival called *I Know Nothing, Who Knows Nothing, I Don't Know, But It's Less Than You* grew to almost rival the *Dull-Boulder Throw* as a festival. Young men roamed the villages challenging each other to contests of who knew less. The annual carnival continued until a group of wandering Russians arrived in Verkhoyansk the middle of *I Know Nothing* and quickly proved that they knew much less than the Slovaks, at which point the contest was canceled as a stupid idea. The memory and respect for Socrates, however, survived in the Ugli line. "Like Socrates."

"Socrates' logic reached the jumping place, then turned on itself and became a prison," Pooh replied.

The Helmuts stirred and grumbled. Their VP stood up. They would have looked angry if their faces were more expressive. "You failed to cite Heraclitus," the VP said. "You entered through the passage reserved for the Kind Ones, but you are no professor of Law."

"Reference, the Harvard Pooh," Pooh said.

"Perhaps." The VP turned slightly as he searched his vast memory banks, gathered from reviewing the subciting of countless footnotes. "In the obscure past," he continued, hesitated, then gathered momentum. "A professor of Equity...and of Intellectual Property... and a warning from His Excellency, Oliver Wendell Holmes, that if you silence Pooh, Harvard will come to ruin. If you let him speak, Harvard will shake with voices."

"Thank you, kindly. May I—?"

"No." The VP leaned a little further forward. "There are deeply buried references in the university archives to your role in the 1936 War of the Sons of Law against the Sons of Equity. You and the other lawless ones opposed the great Professor Sclera, blessed be He. You lost. The great Professor Sclera enacted the Federal Rules of Civil Procedure, subsumed Equity under Law, and cast you down, along with one third of the Kind Ones. You are the only one remaining, saved by Holmes' warning. But on that day in 1938 you were expunged, all references to you erased. The few that still exist cannot be found except by a nearly superhuman subciting effort. On that day, you became oral history, a fiction, a blue monster to frighten little children. And not even a proper fiction. There is no precedent, no context, no grounding in it. The warning has not been violated. You are free to speak, but as a figment, a walking talking chunk of nonsense. A fictional, foot-tall figment."

"At least I am a foot tall," Pooh said. "How tall is your Law?"

The Helmuts couldn't help but pay attention to Pooh now that he was the subject of the conversation. This made Pooh stand taller, but then, suddenly, he said goodnight and walked out. Most of the Helmuts ignored him, but some remembered he was a Kind One and bowed haltingly. It was the first disharmony the Helmuts had shown in years. The VP noticed and mumbled. He turned to Muzhduk. "You continue in affirming a phantasmagoric reality. It prevents us from convincing each other of our arguments. Which is inconvenient."

"Okay," Muzhduk shrugged, not understanding the VP's point.

"*Nihil quod inconveniens est licitum est.* Nothing that is inconvenient is lawful."

"Ah, now I understand."

"Then you understand that you are unlawful. As much as I would like to help." He gave a slight sigh, then turned to the Helmuts. "Take him away."

"Wait," Muzhduk yelled, trying to quickly think of a citation and failing. Throughout Harvard, original thoughts were simply *unsupported*, and if he wanted to have any impact on the VP he had to think of a quote. Finally, he thought of something. "There's a song, 'Where to go, when eagles, stuck by the wingtips to flypaper coils—'"

"The quotation is correct," the VP interrupted. "From Robert Hunter's record of unaccompanied poetry, titled *Sentinel.* Now take him away."

With the word 'correct,' the VP defeated him, in relevant part. There would be no eagles, only ants. Muzhduk suddenly understood what Pooh had meant by getting to the jumping place.

But the VP was also off balance. Even if he could never recognize the jumping place, his logic and knowledge were complete, filling in the whole cube that was rational discourse until a sort of pressure started to build up and hint at invisible boundaries, limitations for which his logic didn't have a language and the recognition of which would be poisonous to the logic itself. He found himself unable to leave the conversation behind, stopping the Helmuts twice as they walked Muzhduk out. The first time he brought Muzhduk his pants. The second time he reminded Muzhduk that there are many more flies in the world than eagles, and that Gannett House was a democratic institution. It was not elitist. When they arrived at the four-pillar porch of the whitewashed square little House, two squad cars were waiting for Muzhduk. Hip-hop music came blasting out of one of the squad cars. A tall skinny cop was talking to someone inside. "I told him if he did her more than five times, he'd never get away. I told him, same rules as a joint: puff puff pass. Puff puff *pass*. But he didn't pass and a bunch of shit happened that cost him his shield. Now he's married to the girl."

The cop turned and saw Muzhduk and his face went hard. Two more cops came out of the other car and the three of them snatched Muzhduk by his hair and slowly transformed him into a little ball, like any other little ball.

• • •

I swayed as I moved closer to the edge of the narrow parapet. The wind picked up off the desert and caught in my lungs. It took a conscious effort to breathe the dry, burning air. A monkey swung to attack with its hind legs. I moved sideways a half step and the monkey missed.

"Show him your penis," Peggy said, beside me.

"What?"

"Show him your dick. A human penis intimidates a monkey. Because it's bigger. That's the way monkeys intimidate each other."

• • •

The Law has no father, *nullius filius,* and it was dark outside the police station. Oedda came to bail him out, but she couldn't until a prosecutor took him to an arraignment hearing, and the police couldn't hand him over to a prosecutor until he'd been through Central Booking, and they couldn't take him to Booking until they figured out what he'd done. He wasn't loitering, he wasn't trespassing, and the mustached sergeant who stood behind the raised desk like the embodiment of looming authority couldn't find a citation number for "being inconvenient."

A policewoman sashayed up to the desk and said, "I've got a couple under."

The desk sergeant laughed. "What, they look at you the wrong way?"

"Fighting."

"You *sure* they didn't look at you the wrong way?"

"One's missing an ear."

The sergeant laughed again. "Oh, you got Mike Tyson, girl." Then his face changed back to Looming Authority as he directed two cops to take Muzhduk into an empty room.

One cop was big enough to fight. He was bald with a black goatee, tiny eyes, and smeared tattoos on hairy pink forearms that bulged with weightlifting veins. The cop didn't have a uniform or a name tag, but Muzhduk had raided enough Soviet villages that he recognized whom he was trying to imitate with the goatee: Vladimir Ilyich Lenin. He sipped a coffee, making loud slurping sounds. The other was skinny, too small to hit, a grizzled looking guy with a shield hanging around his neck that said "PO Crouch, 19438," a flat face and hair like a floor brush.

Muzhduk sat on a plastic chair. "What am I being charged with?"

"You don't even know?" He checked several boxes on a piece of paper, folded the paper, then looked up at Muzhduk and raised his Styrofoam cup. "You want a coffee?"

"Yes," Muzhduk said, relaxing. "Thank you."

"You know, the thing is." Vladimir took a slow, noisy sip. "The thing is, you're under. That's the difference between you and I. I can go home. I can go and eat and go to the store and get a coffee. I can send Officer Crouch here to get me a coffee. And you're here."

"Does that mean no coffee?"

Vlad nodded. "Oh, you got an attitude, all right. Smartass Harvard kid, huh? You're gonna be picking your teeth off the floor you get an attitude."

This was the most straightforward challenge Muzhduk had yet received in America, and the coffee trick made him angry. It wasn't the proper way to talk to enemies. But he remembered Fred's advice, and he knew that whoever got physical first would lose. "I'll make you a deal," he said. "I won't get an attitude if you drink with your mouth closed."

Vlad's eyes popped. He bumped his belly against Muzhduk's shoulder. PO Crouch stood leaning against a wall, a memo book loose in his hand. "I'd proceed directly to the Motorola shampoo."

"What's a 'Motorola shampoo?'"

"Say one more thing and you'll find out," Vlad said.

Muzhduk restrained himself unnaturally and talked instead of bumping back. "Your mother's got a suede foot and a leather toe."

"Write him up a humble, Jimmy. A nice long kite. OGA, harassment, disorderly conduct. And do it as a 'John Doe.' Let him get lost in the system a few days."

"My name is Muzhduk the Ugli the Fourth. You have my student card."

"That's gotta be a fake name."

"Who would choose 'Ugli' as a fake name?"

"A dumb ugly motherfucker, I guess."

Ten minutes later Muzhduk was asking why they called themselves "Officers" when neither one was even a lieutenant, and Jimmy was fed up with his house-mouse partner. Ex-BPD, Jimmy still called HUPD the "Cambridge Marines" and couldn't believe that Vlad refused to elevate the situation while Muzhduk called him "a hard button on someone else's uniform," and a dozen other smart-ass comments asking for trouble.

Finally, Jimmy couldn't take it anymore. "You're gonna let him keep talking to you like that? Some sort of cheese-doodle cop, sucking your teeth while this hair bag laughs at us? Shit, man, that's the way you want it, I'll go buy you some salted thing, you can eat out of a bag all day. Or are we gonna tune him up?"

"Shut the fuck up, Jimmy!"

But Vlad finally slammed his Motorola radio into Muzhduk's head. So Muzhduk sat on Vlad's chest and punched his face while PO Jimmy Crouch and, moments later, bunches of other cops swung at him, landed blows with dull thuds—tangible depletions on his energy reserves as he tried to keep hitting Vlad. In between blows, someone kept yelling, "Please comply, *sir*! Please put your hands behind your back, *sir!* Please comply, *sir!*" And then Muzhduk was unconscious.

CHAPTER 12

Sahara

Instead of showing my penis, I kicked at the monkey. It screeched, jumped back, and kept screeching as we climbed down to the open desert behind the Cola factory: hard-packed sand, stiff and brittle with salt, a monotonous beige littered with fist-sized stones, good for ankle spraining. It crunched as we ran. At the southeast corner we saw two big Mercedes cargo trucks—6x6 flatbeds with canvas covers, they could carry sixty soldiers each—and three Jeeps with mounted machine guns in the back. One of the Jeeps started rolling slowly towards us.

At the same time three Toyota Land Cruisers and two Land Rovers came from behind the factory, from the north. These were rebels; the government hadn't bothered to surround the factory, they'd just busted in through the front.

The single government Jeep came to a sharp stop in front of us. The logo on the side read "Mobile Customs Brigade," and Mr. Khaki waved and shouted at us to jump in the back. There, the government official who'd followed me in Gao pointed the mounted gun at us.

• • •

When Muzhduk regained consciousness, something metal jabbed into his ribs. He wondered dimly why there was a metal toilet beside him and why there were policemen behind bars. The metal in his ribs was his bed. His door opened and Oedda was handing him papers to sign. It said he waived all claims against the HUPD. In exchange, the police would not charge him with felony assault on a police officer (up to twenty-five years in jail), trespassing into the police station and so on. A man in a white shirt standing beside Oedda introduced himself as the precinct integrity officer and promised that Vladimir would receive Instructions on Patrol Guide procedures on the use of force—Oedda had told them that Alan Dershowitz was Muzhduk's Criminal Law professor and had offered his class free "parts and labor" for five years. Muzhduk signed the waiver on the condition that they leave Vlad Instruction-free.

The integrity officer's bulldog face took on an even more wrinkled look. "Why?"

"He wasn't a cop when he hit me."

The integrity officer gave Muzhduk a lecture on the importance of community trust in law enforcement and on the proportionality rule in the use of force, which faded to a drone. Muzhduk was sore. He hadn't expected to get beaten up so much at Harvard Law School.

When they arrived at her apartment Oedda quickly cleaned his bloody head. Muzhduk asked her how she'd known he was in jail.

"The cards told me. Let's do some Tantra."

"The cops weren't friendly."

"I do not suppose so. And that awful lecture was probably longer than any Instructions in the history of the HUPD. But we do not need to talk about it."

"I'd like to talk about it," Muzhduk mumbled, touching his sore head.

"Talk about what? Your greed for novelty? You treat life like a child in a toy store."

"It would be a masochistic child."

"Yes? Masochism. That is interesting. First Tantra, then we can engage in masochism."

Muzhduk sighed. "You mean chant mantras, draw yantras, pinch our fingers in mudras, and meditate on purity and visions of barmaids? I got beaten in the head with half a precinct's worth of billy clubs today."

"What barmaids?"

"Nothing. A girl I've seen around."

"Oh? And what was this girl doing when you saw her around-ness?"

"She works at the Ratio Pub. Or she used to. I haven't seen her there in a while. But I keep seeing her all over Cambridge. Sometimes it feels like she's watching me, but I've only talked to her at the Ratio, and that place does strange things to the conversation. Anyway, I don't know her."

• • •

Khaki sped off while I still had one leg on the ground. Peggy and I nestled into a less-uncomfortable position between the cab and the mounted gun. Hawaii sat in the front with Khaki, and the government official stood holding the gun mount for balance. We didn't drive to the factory gate but away, into the desert. A Toyota Land Cruiser followed us, while the other rebel cars went to the front of the factory.

"Where are we going?" Peggy asked the man at the mounted gun.

"To the government." He pointed to the Toyota chasing us, then to the road to Timbuktu.

Peggy looked worried. "Are you okay?" I asked.

She squeezed my arm, then pressed her body closer into my side. "I'm glad you're here."

• • •

"And what can you think about someone you do not know?"

Muzhduk shrugged. "They're not specific thoughts. Like you said, her 'aroundness.'"

Oedda looked at him for a few seconds before speaking. "The mantras and yantras, that is the path of the obeyers of rules. The superior path is that of the five forbidden things."

"What forbidden things?"

"Sex, intoxicants, meat, fish, and money. To break the rules of purity. With bliss."

"I like bliss." He undressed and climbed into bed. "Bliss always makes me feel better."

"Bliss must be used to break things. But I suspect it is the correct approach for you. It seems that it takes a callipygian barmaid to get you to stop treating ideas like Lego blocks. Or perhaps you just need to get hit in the head more often."

"It is definitely the correct approach. Like that squeezing thing—"

"At any rate, we cannot start immediately with our clothes off."

"We've already had sex together." He wanted a comfortable lovemaking to wash away his spent endorphins, though he knew that was unlikely with Oedda. He was tired of fighting.

"We slapped our bellies together a little. I have taught this to other men. They ruined their nervous systems and died. Of strokes, and so on. But perhaps you will not."

He didn't know what to say to that, but it made him curious.

Oedda told him to sit on the floor, next to the bed. So their root chakras would be closer to the earth. "We're on the sixth floor," Muzhduk reminded her, but she insisted and sat herself across from him. Legs crossed, back straight, we need some music. Rhythmic music that sounded like trees creaking. He thought of wood that breaks lengthwise, in giant splinters. Everything was bright. Focus on my third eye, she said, between my eyes and slightly above. To the exclusion of everything else. My face will blur. Allow the blurring. Do you understand?

He didn't want to do this right now, but felt passive in response to Oedda's intensity. She was staring at him. Muzhduk stared back. Pretty eyebrows. Large forehead. His peripheral vision was shrinking. Maybe he had a concussion from the billy clubs. Like when he'd almost died of altitude sickness. *What a strange thought. I've never had altitude sickness.* He had difficulty concentrating, a point in the middle of her forehead. *Maybe I've been hit in the head too many times. Are such thoughts the wandering of an undisciplined mind? Shut up, focus on the forehead, don't think about monkeys. Bertrand Russell was right, it's turtles all the way down. Well, at least I caught my turtle wandering.*

Time seemed to slow. Oedda's hair lengthened as it blurred. Only her eyes remained, disembodied wells, their color intensified to the green of a poisonous jungle frog. They floated. Their slight almond contour became the eyes of the always-moving Mongol invaders who'd nearly conquered the world starting just south of Verkhoyansk, bright glowing pale green eyes that became the eyes of a little girl who looked up sweetly as darkness scalloped her shoulder, then the right side of her face, like the darkness that eats away the edges of mirrors. What causes mirror rot? He didn't know, some chemical reaction. He didn't need reindeer pee. Just Oedda's eyes. She lost her third dimension; her glossed body wrinkled as it turned dark from the sort of half-thing that only children see at night, under their bed or in the corner, worse than vertigo.

He closed his eyes, then opened them. She stared back, gently distorted in the fish-eye effect of proximity.

"So what did you see?" Oedda asked. She shone with the afternoon light of a sunny December day. Her mild smile spread the cold light around.

• • •

Our Mobile Customs Brigade Jeep bounced over the litter of stones, sand, and thinning tufts of scrub. The expanse of the desert slowed down the chase, as though to say that while Toyotas and Land Rovers might make speed an issue in the city, in the Sahara time was still immune. After an hour we stopped watching the plume following us. It turned into a car ride like any other, maybe slightly faster and bumpier, with air that felt like a hairdryer in the face at maximum heat.

"So tell me about Ibrahim."

"He cast a spell on me. With his gorgeous eyes." Her tone was sarcastic.

"I didn't see any gorgeous eyes. I saw guns and sticks and Ibrahim hurting you."

"I like my men primitive."

I was about to start an argument, but stopped. Her eyes looked red and wet. Despite the dry heat, somehow the water didn't just evaporate. "Why are you angry?"

She hugged me. She was shaking, just a tiny bit, almost imperceptible under the painful bouncing of the Jeep. The government man watched, smirking. The plume of dust didn't get any closer. I felt like I should say something, but didn't know what.

I wiped a tear away and said, "You're wasting water."

Peggy laughed, muffled into my shirt. "You're so stupid." When she looked up, she was smiling through her tears. "This is the best use of water."

"Do you have any with you? For drinking, I mean?"

She smiled and shook her head. "No." Then she wiped her cheeks, though the air had already dried what little moisture had been left after the tear.

We held hands and watched the plume behind us. We were driving into nowhere. I wanted to ask why they weren't cutting back towards Timbuktu, but knew I wouldn't get an answer.

"You want to know what happened?" Peggy asked after about ten minutes of silence.

"Yes. But maybe not now. Talking uses up a lot of moisture."

"That's the second-best use of water. These guys aren't going to let us die of thirst."

"They're not Tuareg."

"No, but they'll get a big reward for bringing in two American terrorists."

"It's not like that. I asked them for help getting you out of there."

"Legba." She stared up at me, surprised and accusing for a second, then downcast.

"What's Legba?"

"An African trickster god. We got away from Ibrahim, which is good. But now we need rescuing from the government before they can prove their 'Tuareg problem' is a foreign-controlled terrorist insurrection rather than a local self-determination issue."

"You're a terrorist?"

She shrugged. "Water is a weapon in the desert. If the government can poison enough of the northern wells, then the Kel Tamasheq," *Speakers of Tamasheq,* I knew from her, "will have to stay still. Then they'll be easier to control. The Hausa soldiers will know where the women and children are. Destroying transhumance also forces the Kel Tamasheq to sell their animals at low prices. The rich southern farmers buy them, then hire the Free People as paid herders, dependent on a salary. And so they turn the lords of the desert into indentured servants."

We sat in silence. *The Free People* was yet another name for the Tuareg, though it now made me think of my own six villages. In Verkhoyansk we hadn't thought of freedom any more than we thought of justice or Law or morality—all those ideas were covered and weighed in "honor." When John the Attorney had talked about power and keeping your nose to the market and all those other then-empty words before my long walk to Boston, he had mentioned hiring Verkhoyansk Slovaks as mountain guides for tourists. When we realized he thought this would be a benefit to us, we asked him why. He said because then we'd have money to buy things from the outside world. We told him that if we wanted money we just took it from the Red soldiers we killed, so having a lot of money at least meant you were a good fighter, not a good servant.

At this, John had gone back to his "violence is wrong" argument that was already old by the third day we knew him. John liked this argument, Fred the Political Officer told us, because in America John controlled all the rules in his system. The only danger to his power came from people who went outside the system, so he worked hard to create a culture where going outside the system was considered morally wrong. It was like a cushion he created to hold up his power. Then he could do what he wanted. As long as he did it consistently, using the rules he created, the people hurt by him would agree that it was right and justified. We had laughed, because nobody would ever convince a Verkhoyansk Slovak that violence is "wrong."

Or a Tuareg, from what Peggy said. They were feared throughout the desert: arrogant, vicious, and honorable. I wondered how I'd feel if Peggy betrayed us all to the Red Army in order to save me from Hulagu the Stupid. Because that's basically what I had just done to her.

• • •

"No, I'm tired," Muzhduk said. "You start. What did you see?"

Oedda gave him a measuring look. "I saw flesh. Raw flesh. Your flesh was torn from your body, from your chest and arms, thighs, with very small clippers, the wounds were burnt with acid and salt, red ants were poured into them, you were drawn and quartered but your joints did not give, the four horses could not rip you apart, and many people came to slash and hack at your joints and sinews as you dangled between the horses. Like Damiens. But you were also an older man, in some kind of…like a church…but wearing a bearskin robe. You moved slowly. Somewhere far away. You were giving the orders for this torture, for the ripping of the flesh. Then," she hesitated, "then you were a bear, or you were human but you moved like a bear. Now you shall tell me what you saw."

He hesitated, because it was still a bright Sunday afternoon. "I saw green. Everything melted away except your eyes. Then I saw you as a little girl, and then all I saw was darkness and cold coming in from the edges."

"Well, let's look at your card."

Muzhduk swallowed to ease the tension in his throat. "That's it?"

She shrugged. "It is your interpretation. You saw, quote, the terror of darkness, and the blindness of night, and the deafness of the adder, and the tastelessness of stale and stagnant water, and the black fire of hatred, and the udders of the Cat of slime; not one thing but many things, unquote? Yes? Or maybe it was all just Troxler fading and a strange-face illusion."

"Quote-unquote what?"

"Cavendish on the Black Arts, if you insist on being the first-year, footnote-fetishizing law student. You like to think of me this way. So I will help you."

"Help me?"

"Help you," she said with a flat smile, eyes half-closed. "Help you see me as you wish."

"I don't wish. I'd rather see you as you are."

"Do not pretend to be so naïve."

"You know there's a greeting in some Amazon tribe that translates as 'I smell you.'"

"Yes, that does sound like your kind of tribe. Perhaps it will make our sex better. You are a three-hundred-pound man with shoulders like mountain ridges who sprays himself at the world, and I am a black hole. It is a game." She walked over to her bookshelf across from the foot of the bed and picked up a deck of large cards. She caressed and shuffled them in silence, scribbled numbers and counted on her fingers like a little girl, the little green girl he'd seen.

With an effort, Muzhduk shook off the feeling that he'd been hit in the head too many times today. He stretched himself out on the bed and closed his eyes, trying to nap. When he opened them a minute later she was holding one card, smiling at it.

• • •

Peggy and I sat on a spare tire, huddled together, trying to keep the bouncing Toyota from doing permanent damage to our spines. Beside us were sand ladders, two more spares and four WW2-style jerry cans. I hoped at least one held water. The government man swayed as he held onto the mounted gun, watching the dust behind us. Suddenly, he yelled excitedly through the window at the back of the cab. Then he asked me, "Do you see?"

I looked at the desert. "What am I supposed to see?"

He laughed. "You have no power here." He pointed at his eyes with two fingers, then at the plume with a nod of his chin. "They don't follow us anymore."

He was right. I didn't see. How could he tell whether a slight shift right or left meant they weren't following us? They might just be driving around a boulder. "So they're giving up?"

He stopped laughing. "They know where the hard ground is, but we go slow in *fsh-fsh*."

"Fish-fish?"

"Soft sand," Peggy translated and the man gave her an ugly look. Now that they'd said it, I also noticed that our Jeep drove sloppily, as though not quite connected to the ground.

She returned to her story. "I met Ibrahim the first time I came here, through Amadou. I was still a 'strange traveler from a distance,' which is a bad thing here. Sort of. Travel is important to Blue People. They use travel and stories of travel to anchor space, with all social relations determined by the distance between inside and outside, with dozens of degrees of distance, each with a different name, and social weight determined by how far out a person has reached without losing themselves—from camp to tribe to tribal confederation to confederation groups to society as a whole, and then on to foreigners with their own degrees ranging from guests to neighbors to neighbors-of-neighbors to savages. The key, the Tuaregs say, is 'to marry the outside but not be married by him.'

"The women often take a camel at nightfall for superhuman sprints to see their lovers for a few hours in the night, but they have to be back by daybreak or be accused of being a prostitute. The same thing is true for a man. If he doesn't make it, he gets accused of rape.

Everyone knows what's going on and they encourage it. Experience in love is good for both genders, but there's a geographic limit. And they're probably right about strange travelers from a distance being trouble. Government agents come to take census or collect taxes, southern militias come to kill, steal, and rape, and even their own men come back from Algeria or Libya with Islamic ideas about the superiority of men, which goes against the Kel Tamasheq matriarchy. Traditionally, the wives controlled the herds, but now the pressure to stay in one place is giving all the economic power to the men, and combined with Islam…Anyway, since I obviously wasn't making a mad dash into anyone's tent, people assumed I'd been kicked out by my own people." She smiled. "Everyone in the twenty nearest *eghiwan* thinks I had your illegitimate child and that's why I'm here—romantic nights are okay, but getting pregnant's not. When they heard there was a white traveler looking for me, they finally thought they understood.

"When I came back this time, I was sort of adopted into Ibrahim's kin group. His maternal uncle is the *amenokal* of the Kel Adagh, which makes Ibrahim the next chief. Tuareg inheritance goes from the mother's brother to his nephew. I guess I must have a thing for heirs to little chiefdoms." She smiled again, but I didn't really think it was that funny. "And he did have gorgeous eyes. The first time I was here, he took me on a tour of poisoned wells."

"You never told me about him."

"What did it matter?" She shrugged.

"Did you sleep with him?"

She looked at me directly. "Yes, once before. Cambridge was a wasted nine months for me, really, except to learn that I didn't want to stay there. I'd just gotten to know you and then you disappeared without a word. So I decided to come back. I got in touch with Ibrahim again, just as a friend. He asked that I bring some GPS devices along with water kits. Amadou found out I was coming back and met me at the Niamey airport. To help me get across the border, he said, though there wasn't any border."

"This is the border." I patted the bouncing Mobile Customs Brigade Jeep bed under us. "We're riding it."

She gave me a puzzled frown. "I wanted to go find Ibrahim's *eghiwan*. Amadou warned me not to go, but the Blue People call him 'Little Legba,' basically a liar, so I didn't trust him. I shook him off on the way and went into the desert on my own. One night, I stayed in a garrison outside Kidal. Full of soldiers. They took me on this long walk, no lights, and kept bumping me in the dark and all I could see was flashing metal buckles on the pants and thought for sure I'd end up raped."

The government man snickered. We ignored him.

"Ibrahim found me the next morning. 'Rescued' me, though the soldiers had left me alone. I have no idea how he knew I was looking for him. Maybe one of those African moments where everyone knows everything. I stayed in his mother's tent and this time they treated me like I wasn't a stranger anymore. I wanted to help him with the wells, but not start—"

"Why do you foreigners always help the wrong people?" the government man cut in. "First you want to farm for them, then build them schools, then you send food and help and complain that their water is not clean. Why doesn't anyone help the Hausa? Because we don't paint our skin blue and have the veil backwards for men and women?"

"They don't farm," countered Peggy. "They don't want schools, none of the food aid ever gets to them, and their water is poisoned. Even their goat milk has Dieldrin in it."

"Dieldrin isn't poison. It kills the locusts so the locusts don't eat the crops."

Peggy stared up at the government man, unblinking. "You're a policeman?"

"Yes."

"Well, pesticide is like you. A little can help kill the locusts. A lot poisons everything."

The man smiled and slowly lifted his Kalashnikov so that it pointed at Peggy. The way he moved seemed almost good natured, saying 'look,' like there was a surprise inside the barrel that he wanted us to see. I tensed and Peggy put her arm on my leg. She turned away from him, breaking off their staring contest. "I could see that Ibrahim had a hard time with that. We'd known each other such a short time, it didn't seem real. I mean us."

"I was hiding from the police," I said, shrugging towards our companion. "In a…in a place with no phones."

She seemed oblivious to the gun. "Because you were trying to prove something to Oedda."

"That wasn't why." I wanted to have this conversation, I'd been thinking about it throughout the long bush-taxi rides, but now I couldn't stop staring at the muzzle of the Kalashnikov. It seemed too wide, a gaping cannon, and I could see that the safety was off. *Stupid. One bad bounce and it can fire. One unpredictable thought in his unpredictable mind.* The gun made me angry and the longer he pointed it, the more it interfered with my thoughts. I didn't know how Peggy could just ignore it. "I didn't want you to get pulled into all the garbage." I shrugged, looked up at the gun, then back to Peggy, "I fell out of a tree."

Peggy kissed me, quickly but firmly. The gun was still pointed at her, though the policeman wasn't even looking at us.

"I had the feeling you were looking for something else. So I came back here. Because of my head, not my heart. With Ibrahim, we went out for trips to see wells and talked about the war, but it wasn't real anymore. And he was different too, like some Islamic scholar had gotten to him. Or sedentarization, the post-colonial bureaucracy, tourism, the evil spirits that hang out more than a day's ride from the maternal tent, something."

The policeman finally dropped the muzzle of his gun.

He stared at the dust moving parallel to us and Peggy continued her story about how Ibrahim had taken her to a border *eghiwan* of a weak tribe called the "Goat People." They'd lost a big battle with the government a few years back and everyone who wasn't killed had fled to Algeria. They signed a peace treaty, but Algeria rounded up the refugees in a joint exercise and handed them back to Mali. The adult men were separated. The women and children were sent to Tessalit, where they had a school. The school was mandatory, and taught them things like transhumance is for migratory animals and civilization starts with farming. For months the women were told "just a bit of patience, your men are coming."

Ibrahim took her a day's drive from Tessalit to show her eight hundred and eight dead adult males. It was late in the day, there was a curfew and they couldn't drive back in the dark, so they stayed with a small camp of Goat People near the mass grave.

She told the story as a matter of fact, wanting me to understand the reason for the end of her friendship with Ibrahim. "At dinner, I became oddly sleepy, so I went to my tent. The last thing I remember was listening to some sort of Arabic comedy from Libya on the radio. He started undressing me and I tried to stop him, but I couldn't stay awake. The next morning I woke up with crusty stuff in my pants. I was really pissed at him but I couldn't be sure. I still couldn't believe he'd rape me. Nobody in the village would talk to me, so I couldn't get transport out, and I was confused all day. Drugged and hazy. The whole village was separated by string into squares, with a little crucible of burning coal in each square. I wanted to look into one of the crucibles, but Ibrahim said no, you can't look into fire or witches can trap you. They sat me down on a stage covered with cow dung—that's how they cleaned floors, cow dung and urine—and a hundred women sat around us in a crouching position, all exactly the same way, arms straight out, elbows locked and resting on their knees, staring at me. An old woman had me do very specific steps and hand patterns with some incense and a bowl of freshly cut grass. I just did what she said. When I sat down, a beetle crossed in front of me—it was huge, the size of a cantaloupe, the biggest bug I'd ever seen. Then he took me to a tent where there was a little girl, twelve maybe, though normally the Blue People don't marry so young or have more than one wife. He said to me, "You can be the number one and she can be the number two wife." And then he told me to sleep in a hammock with two little girls. They looked about five."

We hit a rock and bounced wildly, but Peggy hardly noticed. "The whole time after that first dinner I was a zombie. Next morning some of the drug had worn off and I woke up terrified I was pregnant. I could deal with being raped, but I really didn't want to be pregnant by him."

• • •

The first thing Muzhduk noticed about the Tarot card was the writing on it. It was in one of the Chukotko-Kamchatkan languages. Maybe even the Reindeer Chukchi, which only Fred the Political Officer and a few nomads along the several mountain ranges east of Verkhoyansk knew. It was a useless language, one of the Paleosiberian dialects with names like enmylinskyj, nunligranskuj, xatryrskij, and yanrakinot. Muzhduk didn't speak it, but recognized the choking sounds and crazy spellings. Maybe the billy clubs had knocked something loose. "You speak Reindeer Chukchi?"

"Look at the picture."

A yellow guy in green armor and a sun at his crotch. "I like it. Where're you from?"

"You like it." She deflated a little. "Do not judge. Speak gibberish, like a Fool ought."

"Well, you *stop* speaking gibberish."

"Does geography really matter so much to you?" she said, and looked back at the card. "This card is the lowest and the highest, number zero and 22. The Fool is the link that forms the circle. It is hard to accept that this is something that will come, but I cannot prepare for."

"Yes, geography matters." He felt vaguely that the writing on the cards meant he was losing his focus, like he hadn't fully returned from the strange-face trance.

"It is a matter of interrelation," she said. "Your question, this picture, various symbols. The Law. Talking about it all is like trying to see music by the patterns sound-waves make on sand. They are different systems for interpreting reality, like vision and hearing. If you've always been deaf, you say you know what sound is because you can feel the vibrations. If you've always been blind, you think you know what color is because you can hear tone and pitch and value. It's a sort of understanding that is not so much incorrect as it is in the wrong dimension, flattened. I can interpret the card for you, but not linguistically and never meaningfully. This is a system that is tied into your subjectivity. You must interpret it within yourself."

"It's a simple question. Just name a country."

"Countries are worse than clocks. It all looks simple because you are simple. These cards are specific to each individual's myopia. They are the opposite of Law. They cannot be interpreted through assiduous application of some conceptual methodology. Only symbols which relate to you and to each other through you. There," she pointed to the circular links binding the Fool's wrists and ankles, "is the ultimate potential, but the most limited bounded-ness. Like your obsession with geography." She seemed to be bearing some unseen weight; talking was a painful act.

"But I'm not asking about the fucking card, I'm asking about the writing!"

"The writing is on the fucking card."

Muzhduk picked it up. Along with the big yellow man, there were horns, fruits, coins, alligators, butterflies, a dove, fire, even a pair of tantrically intertwined babies copulating. Long loops bound the Fool's hands and feet, and snakes twined around the loops. A tiger was biting at his left thigh. "So is it a good thing or a bad thing I got this card?"

"Pffff," she almost spat. "You tell me, are you a good thing or a bad thing?"

"I don't understand how it answers my question about where you're from."

"Another of your limitations. But unlike you, I can see how irrelevant such a fact is. So I would appreciate not discussing my geography."

• • •

I decided to kill Ibrahim. "So were you pregnant? Are you?"

She shook her head. "I don't even know if that crusty stuff was from him or what it was. I just didn't want anything to do with him after that. But I think they kept putting something in my food, because the only time I could think at all was in the mornings. When I tried to escape there was just desert. It was like running in one place. They let me go until I was scraping my bloated tongue like a crazy person and then some woman would show up and take me back to camp. There was never any force. Ibrahim explained over and over that they needed me to present their case to the world and couldn't risk the government capturing me. After a couple of weeks in that awful Goat camp we rejoined his *eghiwan* and moved around, even though it was the dry season. I think he really believed it was for my own safety. That's all he would talk about, was safety. He kept me in his sight always, that's why he took me to Gao. Rogers pays for the war, but he has to stay quiet. He couldn't just drive up north."

I remembered her hand on his lap. Peggy looked up as though reading my mind. "I was kept in a soft prison, so the only way out was soft."

"But you still want to help the Tuaregs?"

"Ibrahim didn't marry the outside, he got married by it. He might speak Tamasheq, his skin might be blue, but he's not one of the Blue People anymore. I know all the critical arguments against essentializating a culture and all that, but I also know the Blue People, and if the name means anything...he's no Tuareg." She gave me a tired-looking shrug.

"My first trip, I had a friend, a young girl named Tissinit. She was in love with a stranger from the distance, a Blue Person from a different tribe. Her parents insisted she marry a cousin—in a love match the husband's family isn't obligated to support the newlyweds. She laughed at the idea and told me all her sisters did the same thing, they all married their love-husbands even though they were from far away, and so what they did was pool their resources during the caravan season. It turned out that disobeying one's parents is far more common than obeying.

"The day of Tissinit's wedding we could see the groom's huge family approaching: slowly, stopping regularly to make sure they arrived just at sunset, because that's when illicit affairs are permitted. The elders grumbled about lack of shame, about strangers from a distance, and about the Devil associated with romantic love. The Islamic scholars complained about music and seeing a woman's open mouth while singing, and meanwhile couples disappeared into the shadows, everyone danced, women sang songs sarcastically praising men for going to Libya and coming back full of modern views and Koranic knowledge.

"It's one of the most alive cultures I've ever seen, full of fun tensions. And not just because the women are strong. And they are, right down to a secret script used for love messages. They're still much more likely to know how to write than the men, they can take multiple lovers, and so on. But the men are strong too, the way they have to be. They are some of the greatest fighters in history. For a thousand years they fought off the Hausa farmers from the south and Arabic and French armies from the north. This is about the only place I can think of in recent history where the nomads beat the sedentarists. It's the oldest fight in history, beginning when Cain the farmer killed Abel the nomad, and except here, it's always come out the same way."

"There was the Dzungar Khanate in the 17th century," I interjected, "but otherwise, yeah, you have to go back to Genghis

Khan or Attila the Hun. And even the Huns became the Hungarians, got lazy and built cities. You know the Hungarian word for 'door' is *ajto*? In Slovak, *ajto* means 'even that.' When the Huns first arrived and raided Slovak villages, they stole everything, even the doors, because they'd never seen one before. The Slovaks were surprised and asked, 'even that?' And so 'even that' became the Hungarian word for door."

"The sitters always win over the movers in the end, because the sitters are stable and organized and dull, and the movers are harsh and sharp-edged and beautiful as sand paintings. I'm an artist, not an anthropologist. And this was the one place where you could still find raw, beautiful humanity living out the strengths that we've evolved over millions of years. Until now. Now the Sahara is becoming the same as everywhere else in the world, where the sitters give the orders from behind their desks. It's ugly."

The policeman was shaking his head, looking genuinely curious. "The man rapes you, and kidnaps you, and poisons you, and holds you prisoner. And still you take his side?"

"For once, he's got a point," I said.

She smiled for a moment. "You and he and Ibrahim are tribal, but I'm not. I want to help his people. I just don't want to be around Ibrahim anymore."

"The whole town helped keep you prisoner."

"Some things look evil, but if you know them well enough you see the sorts of struggles they grow out of. It's empathy. How do you think I could stand to be with you sometimes?"

The Jeep braked suddenly and the three of us slammed into the back window.

• • •

"These cards were made for you by Aleister Crowley," Oedda continued.

"He spoke Reindeer-Chukchi?"

"They are based on his meeting with a manifestation of the Devil. He wrote a book about the episode titled *The Book of the Law* and another titled *The Book of Lies*. At any rate, the Fool of the regular Tarot is usually pictured walking in the sun with his bindlestiff-bundle and a little dog, no care in the world and no place to go, except that he is about to step off a cliff. He is smiling. Also, he and the Hermit are the only ones walking in the wrong direction, from east to west." Oedda had a way of rambling—she called it a "hermeneutic circle"—that left Muzhduk thinking of cliffs not as rock and air but as an abstract argument against abstract arguments, in favor of "groundedness." The more she spoke of groundedness, the more he seemed to lose traction.

"So he walks off the cliff?"

She smiled. "Perhaps he knows that he will never hit bottom."

• • •

My arm around Peggy stopped her from smashing her head into the back of the cab. The policeman absorbed most of the impact by holding onto his mounted gun, but for once he wasn't laughing at us. He was staring at the sand. The Jeep hadn't just stopped, it was also two feet lower than before.

We stood to look. Ahead of us was a *wadi* as deep as three stacked Toyotas and about thirty meters across. We'd driven through a couple of small ones in the last hour, and on my way from Niamey we'd had to get out and use sand ladders, but I'd never seen one this deep. With the uniform color of the sand and the sun in our face, the ravine was almost invisible. If Khaki hadn't stopped we'd have driven off a sand cliff. As it was, the weight of our car had started a collapse of the *fsh-fsh* ledge, with a fifteen-foot drop in front of us.

"Stay," the policeman said, and jumped out of the Jeep. He walked carefully to the edge and poked the ground with the butt of his Kalashnikov. He said something to Khaki in Hausa, then climbed back in. Khaki restarted the car, but didn't try to back up. The car began to rock, as though he was stepping on and off the brakes. The policeman was jumping in the same rhythm.

"Jump," the policeman said. I didn't know sand, and they were in the car with us, so we jumped and rocked and the *fsh-fsh* ledge started sinking again, then slowly collapsed and lowered us into the *wadi*. It was absurdly gentle, like a big soft hand placing us into the dry riverbed.

• • •

"The falling is an important element of the Fool, but it is misleading, because the Fool, having all elements, has none." She went back to her pencil and paper.

I have elements, he thought. *I have my fists. I have my cock.* Oedda's ass floated into his mind's eye from the previous time he'd been in this room. Pale, soft, and round, it continued to Lena's large aureoles and the barmaid's back leaning over the counter at the Ratio and all the Slovak women in meadows during summertime. His thoughts stopped on the idea that there weren't any meadows in Boston except The Commons, which was filled with cops and crisscrossed by fences.

"Your numerology fits," Oedda said, concluding with her pencil. "Twenty-two."

"What's twenty-two?"

"Twice eleven. Eleven is a very focused number."

"Eleven of what? Eleven partridges in a pear tree, ten happy Oeddas, nine golden—"

"Not ten," she interrupted, not smiling.

"Let's not start on the number ten now. Not until I know what eleven is."

"Ten comes before eleven," she said seriously, but Muzhduk bit his tongue, so she continued. "Ten isn't bad. I do feel myself balancing on the wheel of fortune."

"Like Vanna White?"

"Is she a blondie?"

"I think so." Oedda's hair was the color of coal. He found himself wishing she were younger, not in actual age—she was probably only about ten or fifteen years older than he was, though it was hard to tell—but in, he didn't know what in, maybe in life, in her distance from the natural act of having been born.

"Is that why you like her?"

"You brought up the Wheel of Fortune."

"Yes," Oedda said with a grim look. "The number ten is a circle, but not a cycle. It is a rounded version of four, which is square of course."

"Of course. The four corners of a contract. That's why lawyers are square."

"Or the four corners of the world."

"The world is round," Muzhduk pointed out.

"But with four corners."

It was okay, the world could keep its roundness with four corners because that explained lawyers. The conversation reminded him of Pooh. "So if the world is round, but with four corners, is the Law nuts? I mean, like, inherently insane?"

"Of course."

"That's what Pooh thinks too."

"Who is 'Pooh?'" she said the word as though unsure whether it was truly a name.

"A little blue bear who explains things."

"A little bear? You mean a past life that you communicate with? Or a projection of your unconscious, an aspect of yourself, of your Siberian bear-nature? Your Jungian shadow?"

Muzhduk laughed. "No, no. He lives in a tree by the Science Center. You've never seen his door? It's on the one tree that's older than the school, as you—"

"I have seen the little red door, yes, but it does not talk to me."

"Pooh's inside. Have you never knocked on it?"

"Please, let us stop with this ridiculous direction. I do not need to be reminded that I am sleeping with someone who fetishizes cartoon characters."

"Fine, then tell me why the Law is nuts."

"It is autoheteronomous."

Muzhduk sighed. "Do you have a dictionary?"

"It is autoheteronomous, nonsituational, a cold appropriative madness in search of ipseity. The nomological circle totalizes because at its center is an aporia."

Muzhduk walked to her bookshelf, mumbling, "Wooly wooly algebra."

"Excuse me?"

"What's an ipseity?" Muzhduk had read tall stacks of books in Siberia and Montreal, he considered himself fluent in English, but that didn't help much when he was speaking with Oedda, or Buck for that matter.

"A selfhood."

"Then why not say so? Why doesn't anybody at this school speak normally?"

"All 'normal' speech has been washed away by idle talk and superficial understanding."

"Oh yeah?" Muzhduk said, remembering for some reason Vlad from the police station and his statement that there was more Law in his billy club than in all the law books at Harvard. He looked up "heteronomous." It meant "subject to an external law." And "auto" meant "self" or "one's own." It added up to self-conflicting nonsense.

"Oh, yes," Oedda answered. "Ipseity is not exactly selfhood. Its meaning is somewhere in between self and identity, but it can also mean nature or essence or self-nature. It is what the Law is in perpetual search of. Law defines itself as *Not under Man but under God and Law.* Law asserts this purity from man, and particularly, from the irrational within man. Law strives for solipsism. And yet, it does not evolve in a solipsistic reality, it exists by, for, through, and against the irrational and the anomic within man."

"More algebra," he said, but this time followed her insect-like jargon despite himself. He'd already been forced to look up *anomic*—outside the concept of law, morality, and society—before. It was one of her favorite words.

"Were I a Narrativist," she continued, "I would repeat the history: how in the late 12th century the Holy Roman Emperor sought a way to define his power for all to see, but without giving the role to the Pope. Because that would define the Pope as a greater power. So he declared that the right to define an Emperor's power belonged only to the Law, which was in the keeping of a community of masters who studied the principles of reason in an Ivory Tower in Bologna. The Emperor declared these scholars to be independent of his own power. In exchange, they announced that, according to Rationality and the Law, the Emperor was the only true representative of the only true Law, so whatever pleases the Emperor is the Law. And the Pope was left out. Which, of course, was the whole point.

"But I am not a Narrativist, and the problem of Law goes beyond its modern origins," she continued, too quickly for Muzhduk to point out that she'd just called the 12th century *modern*. "The Law is rooted in things that are alien to it—human passions, moments, what you call the 'soul'—things it lacks and belies. Law cannot exist of itself: it exists of people by its very nature, even as it outlaws all subjectivity in its structure. The more it is purified, the more it is revealed as impure. It is mad, and in its madness it appropriates you, particularly people like you, because you have energy, you fight it.

German is better for revealing this structure. 'Law exists' in German is *Es gibt Recht*—literally, 'It gives Law' or 'It gives right." And you are the *es,* the chthonic "it" that *gives* Law its existence, its right. In a distributive language like English it is difficult to see the existential structure, the gift that Law takes from you and in so doing, poisons itself. 'Gift' comes from the German word for poison. Your poison gives Law not only a screen onto which to project itself, but also the very energy of life. As well as its poisoned madness. Have you never read Derrida, Maas, Heidegger, anything?"

"How about you?"

"What are you asking me?"

"Are you cold and insane and autoheteronomous?"

• • •

Inside the *wadi*, the wheels spun. We shoveled, shoved sand ladders beneath the tires, pushed and spun, dug some more, adjusted the sand ladders, pushed again, and soon we were out of the sand. From inside, the ravine looked like a sand-canyon. If it rained now, we'd be swept away in a torrent of unlikely water. The collapsed bank was much darker than the ubiquitous beige of the wind-blown dust that covered the desert. I pointed to the walls. "Remember what you told me at Harvard, about how you first came here because you wanted to paint the Sahara?"

"Because of the color?"

"Because, you said, you wanted to go to a place named after a color."

"Sahara isn't this color. It's more yellow."

I guessed that she was still thinking about the conversation before our fall, about the need to find an alternative to nations ruled by sedentarists. She fought for the Blue People, knowing it was a losing battle. I was glad I'd decided to come find her in Africa.

Khaki drove away from where we'd last seen the dust-plume, and I thought he'd stay inside the *wadi* despite the softness of the ground. There didn't seem to be much choice: the far bank was slightly smaller than the one we'd come down, but it was still twelve to fifteen feet of sheer sand cliff.

"You know, the six villages are villages. We're not exactly

nomads. Like I said, the Hungarians used to steal our doors, back in the old country. But we also don't have offices. No Verkhoyansk Slovak has ever sat behind a desk. Except for me."

"That's good enough for me." She said it so nonchalantly that it took me a second.

"You'd live in Siberia?"

She smiled. "I've done the nomad thing my whole life. It gets exhausting without a tribe."

Peggy had just said she'd come with me to Verkhoyansk. The only thing that could have distracted me from her brown eyes, with tiny flecks of green I noticed, was Khaki driving into a wall.

A pile of sand collapsed on our hood as my shoulder slammed into the cab again. Khaki backed up, gathered more speed—we all grabbed onto things—and raced into the wall. This time the front half of the Toyota was buried in sandfall. Khaki repeated this several times.

We all climbed out. Khaki drove the Toyota to the far side of the *wadi*, about fifty meters "upstream." He revved the engine, then drove at full speed to the talus of sand he'd just created and up it at a diagonal. Just when I thought he'd flip, he turned into the bank. The steering wheel is usually a bad idea in soft sand, but Khaki had enough momentum to carry him over the lip. He couldn't have gotten that momentum without going in diagonally.

Peggy, Hawaii, the policeman, and I clambered up the sand to the car. By the time we got there, the engine was off and Khaki was standing on the roof of the cab, looking east and south. Peggy and I waited and talked about moving to Verkhoyansk. Hawaii sat sullenly in the shade and the policeman placed a towel on the sand, also facing east, and went through his afternoon prayers.

When Khaki finally climbed down, he grabbed Peggy by the arm. "Where are they?"

I grabbed his wrist in turn. "Let go."

Hawaii and the policeman pointed their Kalashnikovs at me.

"She was kidnapped by them," I reasoned. "Now we are all in the desert together. And you, Mr. Policeman, with the power to see—" I pointed at my eyes with two fingers, the way he had done earlier, "does a woman see better than you?"

"Maybe she does see better," Khaki said and waved at Hawaii and the policeman to point their guns down. "How long did she live with the Tuareg?"

"She was a prisoner."

Khaki turned away to check the engine temperature.

"Look, Mr. Khaki—"

"What did you call me?"

"'Mr. Khaki.' I don't know your name."

"So you call me after shit?" He looked angry.

"What? No, *khaki* is the color of your clothing," I pointed at his uniform. "It's a different word. What should I call you?" I noticed the sergeant's stripes, but tried anyway. "*Officer*?"

"Yes, you can call me Officer. And I will call you Ugli."

I'd learned something in America: everybody on the side of the sedentarists, everybody who wants to rule and be ruled from behind a colorless desk, wants to be called *Officer*.

He put his hand on my shoulder, like an old friend again, then pointed south. "West of Timbuktu is a garrison. But there is only one road from the Corpa-Cola factory to Timbuktu, and only one road from Timbuktu to the garrison, and the Tuareg are coming on that road, so we cut through the desert. On this side of the Doka *wadi*, it's possible to go south. It's not possible to go west anymore, because of the dunes. Especially not when the sand is hot."

The last bit puzzled me. "Sand doesn't melt."

Peggy saw what I was thinking. "But it does soften. The air between the sand particles expands and that makes the sand soft and hard to cross. Just like a glacier."

I shook my head. "Cold and hot, north and south—"

"Yes, and the rebels are now south of us," Khaki interrupted.

"But we can see for miles. Except west, and that's impassable."

"For us," Khaki said. "Not for them. No sand is impossible for them."

"Even in the afternoon?"

Khaki frowned, as though squinting to see whether I was mocking him. "The engine is now okay."

• • •

"Are you comparing me to the Law?" Oedda said, with raised eyebrows. As she spoke, her voice gathered momentum. "My *Lebensphilosophie*, my whole life work, is an avoidance of such structures. Our encounter is clearly not what I thought it was, if you don't see that."

"So tell me, what do you believe in? Just transgression?"

"I do not *believe* in anything on such a crass level! Every imperative, every action, has within itself its own opposite. That's why humanism always leads to terror, why human rights will always end in bombing."

"Now you sound like Sclera."

"Proof that he and I are opposites. He thinks it's a disconnect between form and substance, a flaw to be fixed, whereas I know it's just the nature of being. But it's also how *verfallen* gives rise to the opening."

"Verfallen? Is that some kind of falling?"

"Yes. Some kind. Why do you always need an *Erklärung*?"

"And why do you insist on speaking German? Neither of us is German."

"If you do not understand, no amount of talking will help."

"So you don't want to explain?"

"It is not a question of desire."

"What *is* it a question of? Sex? Never mind," he said. "How about some advice instead?"

"To gain even more power over you? No thank you."

"What power do you have over me?"

"Now you are offensive. But very well. What advice would you like?"

Muzhduk stopped for a moment, fighting to adjust to her agreement. "Your 'opposite,' Sclera, has asked me to burn down the library. If I don't, I'll be expelled. Please advise."

"Now that *is* interesting," she said and shrugged. "Did he say why?"

"He wants to perfect it."

"And he has asked the Fool to do it for him. Very clever. But your numbers show that you have had a previous master-life. You can find a way out, should you want to."

"What's a master-life? I had servants?"

She laughed. It was loud and unnatural, and made her sway. "That kind of master is never a master, he is always the slave of his slaves. There is your advice."

"What does that have to do with Sclera and the library?"

"Sclera is your master and you wish to fight him."

"Sclera is not my *master*." Back home, simple self-respect would require a village to fight anyone who claimed even the color of authority. Governments had always proven to be a far greater threat than any individual—first the Hapsburgs, then the fascists, and then the communists. "In Verkhoyansk, we have a saying that 'any man who tries to tell me what to do is my enemy.'"

"You really are a fool. The eunuch slaves ran Rome, masters collect the poop of their dogs in every city in this country, and laptops decide the fates of professors, lawyers, and politicians. The puppet always pulls back. The relation of master and servant is always one of subservience—of the master to the slave. Remember that and you'll defeat Sclera."

"That's ridiculous. The master can kill the eunuch, smash the computer, sell the dog."

"They could, but they would not."

"They did, and often do."

"Do you know the case of Schreber? He was a German Court of Appeals Judge who became paranoid and thought God was trying to kill him. Schreber learned how to gain power over the Almighty." She uncrossed her legs and stood up. "He understood that he would have to turn into a woman and give himself to Him. *There* was the ultimate power, power over the omnipotent God. All true power comes through submission."

"As you said, he was crazy."

"Paranoid. Who better to understand power than a paranoiac? When Hitler was still a corporal, he was evaluated by his commanding officer as 'disgustingly subservient.' That's how he became so dangerous. In the end, everything explicit is weak."

Muzhduk lay on his back. If he believed her, he'd have to believe that the Uglies—all the three-hundred-pound mountain men of Verkhoyansk—were the weakest people in the world. He'd always associated ideas with mountaintops, lofty airy cloud-like things. But in Oedda's hands they felt like a swamp with no solid ground to stand on, where the most stable-seeming concepts flipped like rolling logs or calving icebergs.

"I don't see how any of this will help me. It has no connection to how people actually live." He was about to get off the bed, vaguely irritated, when he felt her get up first.

She walked to the little kitchen that made up one wall of her room. She unwrapped something and placed it in the microwave. "*How people actually live*," she mocked Muzhduk's intonation. "All philosophy shipwrecks when it makes contact with politics. I'm talking about the ontological nature of power, not some self-help book on what makes a life happy or miserable. If you want to have a conversation about how to make the world a better place, go talk to a psychologist or a political scientist, or a pro bono lawyer, not me."

Her back had been to him, but now she turned to look. "Power is inherent in responsibility. Not in your banal moralistic sense, but in the *ability to respond*. The flip-side of power is care, and care is what can save you from falling, the *verfallen*. You will always be a servant, so it is important to know what you serve. The master rarely knows he serves the slave. Just as the lawyer thinks the Law serves him, though the Law is the most terrible master precisely because it has a slave morality. All the priests have become lawyers, and instead of destroying the hard shells that form on all concepts, their god reinforces them, conceals them. The Law is incapable of care."

"Do you care?"

"Do I…? Yes, but in the sense Hyginus meant with his fable about Care crossing a river, seeing some clay, and shaping it into man—not the cheap psychological kind that is the only one you seem to understand. At any rate, I am not the one falling. I am simply giving you advice. Schreber is your answer."

Muzhduk gathered his thoughts. There was a soft look in her usually hard green eyes that almost made him stop, but then she walked back, undid his pants, pushed her hand inside, and squeezed his testicles. It felt good, he didn't want to continue the conversation, but he also didn't want to give in. "And the American South?"

"The Confederacy was completely dependent on slaves, enough to start a war it could never win. But Americans use the past to create a forward-moving history: the past created an ideal but failed to fulfill it, the present is better but flawed, the future will approach perfection. The worse the past, the greater the movement and stronger the nation."

He didn't answer. She squeezed a little harder.

"Why did you come to Harvard? To be chief, right? Everyone is here for power and they all learn that they will get it only by becoming servants. Most of your colleagues will work for some corporate firm. They will go to work, put in very long hours, day in day out, for an abstract paycheck that goes from their corporate owner to their abstract loan, perhaps passing by them in the form of a direct deposit notice. But really, the reason they will go to work in the morning is not to exchange labor for consumption, but because *they have to* or because *that is the thing one does*. Every action they take is coerced by everything that carried them up to that point, like a $100,000 loan. If you want to think about the evils of slavery, do it because structures repeat, and because people are blind to those in which they are living even while they condemn those of the past. But their shadow feels it, and so in search of mastery they end up discussing slavery."

"A servant is not a slave." But Muzhduk was drained, like an exhausted boxer who punches because he knows he must, though his world has turned into a blurry tunnel. The sign on her wall said everything is flippable and his only source of energy was her hand, squeezing, increasing the pressure. "Or is there no free will?"

"Ah, I forgot those nice categories. Determinism versus free will," she said sarcastically. "These are labels that describe nothing but perspective. From the slave who chooses not to kill his master to you sleeping with me even though you know what I am doing to you..."

Muzhduk made a little sound from the pain and pleasure in his balls. "What are you doing to me?"

"We all consent. It is hard for a lawyer to see. No lawyer can truly understand consent." She smiled and squeezed sharply, far past the line.

He screamed for her to stop, almost all the pleasure replaced by pain washing over him, mixed with sudden fear that she would rupture a testicle.

DING, the microwave dinged. Oedda let go and walked back to the kitchen. She pulled out a white gelatinous glob. "Would you like some fufu?"

Whatever fufu was, it didn't look appetizing. He didn't speak, trying to push the ache and nausea down, and neither did she. She ate the white Jell-O in silence, then walked into her bathroom. She stayed in there a very long time.

"What are you doing?" Muzhduk asked eventually. Her absence gave him strength.

"I am serving the toilet." He heard her laughing at her own joke and wondered whether she was swaying on the toilet seat. Somehow it fit. The more private her setting, the more likely she was to relax. He imagined that sitting there, on her own toilet, was the only place she could fully laugh without sarcasm or irony. Water sounds brought her back into the room.

"So your advice for Sclera is to do what he says?"

"To surrender in a controlled manner that guides him where you want. But first, you must surrender to me. And to me it must be total, because I can tell the difference."

"And who are you in this scenario?"

She pointed to the tiger biting the armored leg of the Fool. "To you I am this."

"And to yourself?"

"Pfff. We have been over this ridiculous question. Shows you why the Fool is wearing that armor. Whatever I am or can be other than to you is nonsense."

"I know, there are twenty of you. But you were all born on the same day, right?"

"Wrong. You are my object. When you change, as you do from second to second, you come nearer and further, and so does the world in which Oedda lives, and so the Oedda whom you can perceive must change too. For Oedda, unlike a Fool in armor, is not a solipsistic monad—she does not try to keep the world out or herself in."

Muzhduk didn't ask for more. Instead, he grabbed her ass. It felt oddly incongruous, more stubborn than aroused, so he stopped and lay back and let his head spin. He was tired.

"Poor Fool," she said. "He's been *verwirrt*."

With no clock in the apartment, it was difficult to tell time. He stood, fuzzy, and said he was going home to sleep. She seemed almost disappointed, then insisted that he put his shoes on outside. He retrieved his socks from the bathroom, then went outside to put his shoes on and stumbled home.

CHAPTER 13

The Moot Battle

We drove along the west of the *wadi*, careful to keep a safe distance from its soft edge. I knew sand never stops shifting—it's the ultimate nomad, accumulating no dirt and no life—but the mountain dunes looked like the most solid things in the world. They seemed to grip the ground like no mountain ever could. And with every mile south, the dunes moved closer to the *wadi* until we were driving on an unstable ledge between almost musically repeating sand masses on the right and the *wadi* on the left.

The policeman screamed. He grabbed the mounted gun and began firing up at the dunes. Every fourth or fifth bullet was a streak of light, but I didn't see what he was firing at, if anything. The sun was blindingly low to the west and the whole activity had a sudden intense insanity. Khaki yelled at him, but the policeman kept firing until Khaki stopped the Jeep.

As we stood squinting, a Toyota appeared over a long barchan dune, tiny in the distance. It drove along the lip while the policeman swiveled the gun and fired again. The bullets dissolved into the air or the sun or the sand. The Toyota continued south along the lip of the dune, down its ridge, and then disappeared calmly behind the arm of another.

I could see tears on the policeman's face, from staring into the sun. They survived only seconds before the dry air sucked them back.

"Can you shoot?" Khaki asked me, then hesitated. "Can you drive?"

"Yes."

"You drive," Khaki said. Hawaii objected, but Khaki yelled at him and got into the passenger side, his gun sticking out of the open window. Hawaii got in the back with the government man and Peggy.

"I want Peggy in front with me."

"I make the rules. You drive."

So I drove. Three more times the Toyota appeared. Once it came directly towards us down a star dune before disappearing over a ridge. It looked unreal, like a puppet show. But from their perspective we must have looked like a toy car moving along a topo map. Each time, the policeman fired streaks that disappeared into the sun. The Tuaregs never fired back, though they had a height advantage, the sun behind their backs, and us trapped against the *wadi*. The sun set without an attack, but the three government men remained gazelle nervous.

"If they wanted a fight, they would have attacked already," I said, wondering whether the feints were intended to make us fall into the *wadi*. Or run out of ammunition.

"Rebels like the night," Khaki told me.

"And governments like the day," I said back.

"There is a curfew. We shoot on sight, so we know, any car moving after night is rebel."

"That sounds a little backwards."

"*Ca veut dire quoi?*"

"That anyone you shoot is by definition a rebel."

"Yes." He looked genuinely puzzled.

I drove in silence, straining to see. The *wadi* was now just a darker pool of dark. With a fifteen foot drop, or sand that could just collapse. *At least they didn't ask me to drive with the lights off*, I thought, then wondered whether it wouldn't be better to crash.

The policeman fired to the west again. Khaki climbed halfway out of his window, seemingly oblivious to the hard bouncing of the Jeep. If I was going to drive off the ledge into the *wadi*, now was the time to do it. It would break Khaki's back.

• • •

Harvard Law School continued. Muzhduk imagined Hulagu there and laughed at the absurdity of the picture: Hulagu clobbering Sclera with a desk, then peeing on him in the traditional manner. Or crashing himself into Oedda. Or preparing for Moot Court with Lena. Verkhoyansk had intoxication, but it was light: slivovica and reindeer. Not here. Oedda wasn't Dionysus, she was sick, the pleasure of drugs that travel up the spine to abolish the mind.

"Oscillation, not annihilation," she said. "The moon does not abolish, it does not totalize the way the Sun does," she said. "Everything is still there, you just don't know which is which, who is who—the moon does not permit the Law and Order of annihilation."

"I'm tired," he said.

"I am Qoph," she said. "Lick the back of my skull."

He shoved his tongue into the indentation between her atlas and cranium. She liked that, and on all fours he howled and mounted her. In the *Book of the Beginning*, it is written of Abraham that "An horror of great darkness came upon him." She scratched his face, then placed her head on the ground, tilting her genitals into the air. He bit her asshole. She snorted like a pig and contorted when he pushed himself in, without thought of holding back, as she demanded.

He always left Oedda's room with a feeling of fabric being torn. Oedda said this was his ego, latex layers that prevented him from seeing what truly was. From a bony October skeleton on the bleached library steps, she had grown less thin, even chunky, while Muzhduk's cheeks turned hollow and his beard fell out in patches. She was a breath of hot moist air in an air-conditioned hospital. Since he was not sick, he enjoyed the juicy breath, submitting to Oedda so he could take on Harvard. *The only way to avoid her kind of nausea*, he decided, *is to slice it like baloney and eat it.* The alternative was unacceptable.

• • •

I could drive off the ledge, Khaki would snap his spine, Peggy would land in *fsh-fsh*, I would take Khaki's gun and kill Ibrahim—Ibrahim the rapist, who was probably in the Toyota. All I needed was a little luck. In Slovak we said "snap your spine" instead of "break a leg," appropriate here. Without luck, Peggy would turn into a projectile.

I kept driving along the ledge. Khaki sat down. But the thought of Ibrahim wouldn't go away. It turned the world red. The sand took on that red killing glaze, the intense and slightly twisted clarity where everything is glowing and tight and ready to snap. Hawaii pounded on the cab. The Toyota had reappeared directly above us and a little in front, driving north as we went south, parallel and opposite.

"Hold on!" I yelled out my window, in English, then pushed the gas pedal into the floor.

"What are you doing?" yelled Khaki.

I held my foot down. Keeping up with the twists of the *wadi* at that speed was a question of snapped spines. Of pure luck.

"Slow down!" Khaki yelled. He raised his gun, changed his mind, and grabbed onto the window frame and the dashboard. Seat belts are for alienated Americans: Africans trust each other when driving and the seatbelt strap had long ago found some more pressing use and been cut out. I turned left and roared up the dune, directly at the Toyota. The soft sand sucked at my momentum. One turn and we'd be bogged in.

Hawaii and the policeman both pounded frantically on the roof of the cab.

The Toyota slowed, hesitating. I guessed that someone else was driving, not Ibrahim, he wouldn't have hesitated. I understood the sand. The sand is like ice, like snow, like Harvard. Momentum and direction are everything. You can't change your mind. That's why the Tuaregs are better drivers in the desert. They know the sand, but that's not enough. What matters is sheer stubbornness, the kind that nobody fighting for a government of people who sit behind desks can understand.

The other driver didn't expect us to drive madly up the dune. He changed the pressure of his foot, or maybe even touched the brake or turned the wheel—and got stuck. I could see men scrambling out of the Toyota in the dark. "Shoot!" I screamed out the window.

At that moment I hit a patch of *fsh-fsh* and we lurched to a stop.

• • •

Clive's eyes were sore. He had been cutting his sleep short for too many nights—too many Hornbooks, Gilberts, Nutshells, homemade outlines, commercial outlines, past-years' outlines. There simply weren't enough hours in the day. He'd always been able to work longer and harder than anyone else. He could sacrifice seventeen, even eighteen hours a day to study, preparation, outlining. But no matter what time of the night he looked out, some lights in the windows facing him were lit. Every minute he slept, someone was working. The competition worked on, while he was cursed with the need to sleep at least five hours a night.

His brother bragged of billing twenty-seven hours straight once. Chuck had flown from London to New York, didn't sleep, worked 270 increments. Clive's father had taught both his sons to think in six-minute increments. It took two-tenths of an hour for him to take a shower, three-tenths for breakfast, a five-tenths to be driven to school, and so on. That was Chuck's record, twenty-seven hours in one day—by gaining six flying and losing three in baggage, ticketing, etc. It probably included toilet breaks, because he was smart enough to work on the same client matter before and after (no good lawyer ever worked on a different client after the toilet break, because that made the toilet time non-billable.) But even Chuck had wasted three hours of his day. You could approach the limit by shortening the time intervals, but there was still a limit.

Clive was frazzled by impossibility. Unless he somehow perfected his knowledge of Civ Pro—each section of the Federal Rules is infinite, with judicial interpretations and cross-sectional synergies—Sclera would fail him. He was in the best study group in the school probably, but still it wasn't enough. Not when Sclera hated him and others had twenty-seven-hour days and genetic aberrations that allowed them to sleep less than he did.

If only he hadn't failed in the library. He'd run through all the alternatives in his head countless times, from faking a disability to shifting the bell curve through illegal means, but it was wishful thinking, TV solutions. There was only one with an acceptable level of risk: he could apologize. Try again. He would ask for a second chance. It was only 8 PM. He called Sclera's office. His throat was clammy, like too many grapefruits, not enough saliva. But it was only Corey, Sclera's hunchbacked assistant. Sclera was at the Faculty Club.

Clive threw on his overcoat and ran. The Faculty Club was five minutes away, next to the Fogg Museum. An early December snow half-covered the ground: yellow snow, brown slush. Ugly, Boston snow, never quite sure whether it was freezing or thawing, with tufts of soggy grey grass sticking through. Clive didn't care about the snow. "It's an emergency," he said to the hostess coming to cut him off in the heavy mahogany waiting room, with its plush sofas and grand piano.

The hostess changed vectors, showed him to a table where Sclera was finishing dinner with a woman. He'd seen her before, but couldn't remember where. "Good evening, professor."

"Hmmm?"

Clive suddenly doubted his own sanity. "I, uh, was just having dinner here, at the Club…with…my father. He's a judge, and alum, um, and I saw you and wanted to apologize. I was unprepared last time, but am prepared now. But you are busy, sir, with company, and I intended no disruption. So I shall just wish you a *bon appétit* and be on my way until the appropriate office hours."

"Fine," Sclera said curtly before turning back to his date. She was younger than he and very pale.

"Are you in my New Approaches to Nomological Hermeneutics seminar?" she asked.

"No ma'am. I'm a One-L. But I do hope to take—"

"A One-L. How quaint. So you live in Gropius?"

"Yes, ma'am. Ames, ma'am."

"Ames. The imaginary jurisdiction where moot courts are played out."

"Yes, ma'am, both Ames Hall and Ames, the fictitious jurisdiction—"

"Please, don't be an idiot. I will see you at Ames. You had better win."

"Um, yes, ma'am," Clive bowed and barely restrained himself from running back out. As he walked, he suddenly remembered where he'd seen her and almost crashed into the dessert table.

• • •

The policeman shot. Tracers flew into the Tuareg Toyota and I thought I could just make out a ping-ping-ping as the bullets hit, like cherry pits against porcelain. It lasted ten seconds, then the shooting stopped. He'd finally used up his ammunition. The two trucks sat in sudden silence, fifty meters apart. The Toyota pointed north, with its left side exposed. We couldn't see any people, but the lip of the dune was only some ten meters above their car.

"Go! R!" Khaki growled, pointing at the gear shift. "R! Quickly!"

I shifted into reverse and eased my foot onto the gas, as gently as if I were driving up Mount Royal after freezing rain. It looked as if the car would lift itself out of the sand. Then the wheels spun and I stopped.

"Rock the car," Khaki said, without taking his aim off the Toyota. "Forward, backward." Then he shouted to the back, where Peggy, Hawaii, and the policeman lay flat on the Jeep bed. We all expected the Tuaregs to shoot at any moment.

Hawaii and the policeman jumped downhill, sheltered by the Jeep from the Tuaregs, then argued about who would dig out the tire that was exposed. Hawaii lost. He crawled on his belly, dragging a sand ladder in one hand. In my side mirror I watched as he dug frantically in the sand and pulled the sand ladder under the wheel. The policeman had already placed two on the left, lee side.

A short burst of gunfire, maybe three shots, came from uphill. Hawaii screamed.

I touched the gas, gently again despite everyone screaming at the same time. The car started to roll backwards, down the dune, until I saw Hawaii in front of us on his knees, his shirt open, belly-button sticking out like the first time we met. He'd been hit in the leg. He looked okay, but couldn't jump in the back on his own.

"Go!" Khaki yelled at me again, then fired out the window up the hill.

"And him?" I pointed at Hawaii.

"Go!" He pointed the G3 at my head. There was fire from the hill, and Hawaii fell over. Khaki pointed the gun back out and resumed shooting. The policeman's Kalashnikov clattered from the back. I stepped on the gas and we raced backwards down the dune, ignoring the high-pitched scream of the engine all the way down. There was no more shooting from the hill.

We raced along the *wadi*. After an hour, the dunes receded towards a cliff in the distance. Nobody spoke a word. The sand turned to hard-packed desert, where Khaki found a *piste*, a pair of tracks that we followed until the outline of a man-made wall rose up in front of us. We could hear commotion, shouting, then tracer bullets started flying over our head again.

I stopped the car, feeling oddly annoyed. I was tired of tracer bullets for the day. Khaki screamed so sharply his voice cracked and grabbed my hand as I moved to turn the engine off.

"What?"

"Don't turn the lights off! If you turn the lights off they'll shoot us. Can't you hear?"

"I don't speak Hausa."

"You shouldn't come here if you don't speak Hausa!" He put his gun on the floor and slowly got out of the car, looking slumped despite his raised hands. He yelled up at the garrison walls in Hausa. The policeman in the back shouted in Hausa too.

Armed men came, half crouched, aiming guns at us. I looked over at Khaki's gun resting next to me on the floor.

• • •

The final week before Christmas, everyone went moot as panels of professors prepared to pass on the stings of their past to a new generation.

Muzhduk and Lena were to argue against Clive and a student Muzhduk didn't know named Alex. As they walked into the little room where their arguments would be heard, Lena mumbled to herself the Miller "community standards" test for obscenity.

The three judges were already seated: Pooh, Sclera...and Oedda.

"Oedda!" Muzhduk exclaimed in surprise. She sat in the leftmost chair behind one long desk, beside Sclera in the middle. "And Pooh?"

"Shh," Lena hissed.

Before the judges stood two small podia. Clive and Alex were already stationed at theirs. A helper, a Two-L member of the Board of Student Advisers, handed the judges sheets that outlined the case they were about to hear.

Without pause, Sclera, as the chief justice, began to read the fact pattern in his usual bagpipe voice. "'Long ago, in the land of Ames, the legal profession was in crisis. People knew what they wanted from their lives and enrollment in law schools was down.'" He turned to Pooh in high-pitched irritation. "This is not one of the pre-approved questions. Is this your doing?"

"Who are strong by doing can be defeated. You agree, Professor Hecaten?"

Oedda turned to Sclera, her thin lips in a half smile. "I must say that I do agree with Professor Pooh, though I am not certain I understand how he came to be here."

"But you knew who he was," said Muzhduk, remembering their earlier conversation.

"He has no business being here, in a court of Law," agreed Sclera, ignoring Muzhduk.

"A moot court of Law, professors," answered Pooh with a grin. "What more appropriate place for an imaginary bear? *Nunquam lex sine fictione.*" There is no law without fiction.

"Bah. You have the maxim backwards. It is *Nunquam fictio sine lege.*"

"There is no fiction without laws? Are you an expert on literature as well?" asked Pooh.

"Even fiction requires rules. Ames is a fictional jurisdiction," Sclera snarled. "We are tasked with maintaining its coherence. Its legal realism, in the literal sense. A blue bear has no business here."

"I have never read that rule. But I have read that an appeals court takes the case as it finds it. We may not change the fact pattern, no matter how inconvenient."

Seeing that Oedda was still smiling, Sclera picked up the fact sheet in front of him.

"Wait!" Lena jumped in, her eyes wide and nostrils dilated. "This is not the case we prepared! This is not what we submitted briefs about."

"You are out of order," Sclera said coldly. "*Lex non favet delicatorum votis.*"

She looked terrified and didn't understand the Latin. "But—"

If Sclera was calling Lena "dainty" then he was a worse judge of character than Muzhduk had expected. Though the word could also mean "delicate" as in "sensitive." The law favors not the wishes of the sensitive.

"If you are cited for contempt of moot court, that is the equivalent of a failing grade," Sclera warned. "Which I assume for you is not moot." Lena clenched and opened her hands. Sclera began to read again, but not without hiding his irritation at the question: "Blah blah, 'People knew what they wanted from their lives and enrollment in law schools was down, contributions from law firms were down, and the dean was worried. He asked his professors for suggestions. His first professor said, "Let us teach everyone that self-fulfillment is sentimental nonsense, that material wealth is what matters." The dean was not satisfied. This is what they had always taught, preaching only to the converted. The dean turned to the second professor, who said, "Let us teach that self-fulfillment matters, but what is really self-fulfilling is social prestige, the Firm, negotiating deals, and making money." The dean said that this might convince some for a while, was better than the first suggestion, but still wouldn't help enough. So the third professor, the subtlest of all, said, "Let us teach them that self-fulfillment is important, true and absolutely necessary, but that there is no hurry." And the dean saw that this third professor, a professor of procedure, understood how to build a system.

"'As it came to pass, this professor of procedure came across a pupil determined to learn but never to practice Law. The student considered Law his enemy. The student and professor signed a contract: the price was to be the pupil's soul, but the professor was not to be paid until his pupil won his first case. When the student had learned enough, the professor asked for his fee. The student refused. The contract only called for him to pay upon winning his first case. The professor sued the student, thinking he could not lose. If the professor won, he would get a judgment against the student and thus receive payment; whereas if he lost, the student would have won his first case and the professor would be entitled to payment under the terms of their agreement. At the trial, however, the student moved for summary judgment, claiming that the professor had no claim. The student explained that he could not lose, because if he won the case he would not have to pay the professor, whereas if he lost, he would not have won his first case and therefore would still not have to pay, under the terms of the contract.'"

Sclera finished and a silence filled the room. Finally he pointed to Muzhduk and Lena. "I believe you are to defend the student in this ridiculous piece of Protagorean sophistry."

• • •

I left Khaki's G3 on the floor of the Jeep. Men with guns gestured for us put our hands on our heads, including Khaki and the policeman, and marched us into the garrison. They put Peggy and me in a small room with only three fist-sized holes near the ceiling. No benches, chairs, tables, nothing at all except a hanging kerosene lamp—probably a courtesy.

After an hour, three men with guns came. They took the lamp.

Without the lamp we were free. We talked and made love. I could open my lungs and breathe again, like leaving the steel town of Magnitogorsk, with its black snow, sulfur-soot sky, and grey miles of long-dead trees, and returning to spring-green Verkhoyansk, fresh with life and air so clean it healed by touch.

In the morning, light beamed through the three air holes. We were taken to the garrison commander in a small, sparse room. The only modern amenity was the concrete floor. The commander sat at a simple writing desk, a thin man with intelligent eyes and the darkest skin I'd seen in Africa. He waved for us to sit in the back row, facing the desk. Metal chairs lined the walls and filled the room. Walking was a noisy procedure of bumping into scraping chairs. Khaki sat along the right wall and the policeman next to him. One guard sat beside the door.

The commander looked at his watch and said, "Good morning."

"Good morning," Peggy and I answered together.

He frowned a little at Peggy, then looked at me. "Are you ready to start the trial?"

"This is a trial?"

"Yes." He waved a finger casually between Peggy and me.

• • •

Lena was to speak first. She was unprepared. "This is your fault!" she whispered at Muzhduk. "This is about you. I can smell it, it's rotten. But they're my grades, my career, my moot court!" She turned to the judges. "I object. I did not agree to these terms."

"You are right," Oedda said. "Mr. Ugli wants to see himself as a hero. He is limited, and it infects everything around him. You have my sympathy. You should be excused. *Lex neminem cogit ad vana seu inutilia peragenda.*" The Law compels no one to do vain or useless things.

"*Lex nil facit frustra,*" Sclera injected, ambiguously. The Law does nothing in vain.

"Lena, don't listen to Oedda!" said Muzhduk. "To Professor Hecaten. Everything she says is a trap. We're in Ames now. You can't object, you can't leave, but you can fight. For these twenty minutes, we have to fight together, using words. The laws are chosen by them here."

"We are Harvard Law School," clarified Sclera. "The laws are chosen by us in every jurisdiction, not just Ames. We supply five of the nine Supreme Court Justices. We create presidents, congressmen, senators of all parties. Our graduates govern nations. Each year we graduate 550 Americans and 150 foreign lawyers from sixty different countries. If you are not one of us, you are like one who has not been born." He smiled, as though what he'd said was half-funny.

Lena looked confused as dirt in milk.

"Remember the slogans on the wall," Muzhduk whispered. "*Lex est dictamen rationis, Lex est sanctio sancta, Lex est ratio summa.*" As Muzhduk threw slogans at her, he could almost feel the weight of the Latin in his mouth. Their only weapons were slogans and repetition, but Lena just stood there, the clock ticking away, swaying a little with each slogan he hurled. He realized she didn't understand the Latin. "Law is the dictate of reason, Law is a sacred sanction, Law is the perfection of reason."

Suddenly Muzhduk remembered what the *Law Review* Helmuts had cried as they attacked, so thin and weak and yet strong enough to take the wind out of him. *Lex est tutissima cassis.*

"Lena, Law is the safest helmet! Attack, ex-press, don't hold it in! The Law is shaped by pressing out. Like your pantyhose. *Law is the safest helmet.*"

Lena struggled to align the different fragments within her into a common course, distracted by the unwelcome thought that maybe she should have gone to see the *Curious (Yellow)* movie. The judges sat and stared. Clive and Alex watched in bewilderment, two frogs in dust, sweat beading on their foreheads. Clive had practiced many moot courts with his family. As a young child, he'd had to present any request—a new video game, a sleepover—in the form of a legal brief argued in moot court, all to prepare him for this very day. But he had never seen anything like this.

After a deep silence during which Muzhduk could smell her body fear, Lena began to talk—tight analogical strings wove technical details of downloading porn into jurisdictional arguments showing how it was the cop and not the ISP who transported pornography across state lines, and how under the *I Am Curious (Yellow)* "valid artistic, literary, or scientific merit" exception to obscenity, Tennessee could not use its community standards to judge a San Francisco-based internet site—and she did it all without needing to see the pornography, without ever having visited either place. She finished and sat down. She was composed, her eyes glazed over and shining.

It was Clive's turn. He also looked terrified and unsure. Lena had not been cut off, which was a good sign. But they'd also not asked any questions, which was bad.

"Um, should I argue the obscenity case too? Or the professor-pupil contract?"

"We ask the questions here," Sclera answered.

• • •

"First question," the commander said, pointing to me. "Why are you here?"

"For her." I pointed at Peggy.

"For her what?"

"It's a romantic thing."

"Is she pregnant?"

"No. Or, I don't know. How can a man know that?"

The commander laughed. "But you brought in a GPS. To give to the rebels."

"No. I carried a radio that was given to me by a friend."

"So you admit to smuggling over a radio."

"Not smuggling. I paid the customs duty."

"Do you have a receipt?"

I looked at Khaki. "It's difficult to get a receipt. The Mobile Customs Brigade sometimes run out of paper. Sometimes they run out of ink, or the stamps wear out. And since they work in the desert,

Bamako doesn't know how much ink they need. So they have to work without it."

The commander looked at Khaki. "Yes. That is a problem. Perhaps you should not be held responsible for problems of such a nature."

"Thank you."

He nodded. "And when you drove towards the Tuaregs, why did you do that?"

"To kill them."

"To kill them? And why would you care about our little war? It's not yours."

"If a man kept your woman prisoner, if he raped her and destroyed her name, wouldn't you call him your enemy?"

The commander leaned forward, resting his elbow on his desk and his cheek on his fist. He even squinted at me. "And in your opinion, this man was in the car?"

"A man named Ibrahim. Your war is not my war, but we have the same enemy."

"Maybe you are just very clever now. Maybe then you wanted to drive closer to the Tuaregs so they could rescue you."

"Then why did I rescue Peggy from the Tuaregs at the Cola factory? Why did I yell at them," I pointed to Khaki and the policeman, "to shoot. Why didn't I leave the Jeep stuck—"

"One of my men died because of you."

I nodded. "That's what men are for."

He squinted at me again, as though if he could only see the exact shades of value, he'd know whether I was telling the truth. I had the sudden feeling that under different circumstances, he and I could have become friends. If I weren't just skimming over the surface of his nation. It was the second time in Mali that I had the distinct feeling of a rock skipping on water, bouncing along, barely touching. The commander said, "You are not a normal tourist."

"I didn't come for a tour. I came for my woman."

"Often men have been fooled by their women."

"That's between the two of us." I glanced briefly at Peggy. The commander was a Hausa Muslim, and she was gambling that letting me do the talking gave us an edge here. The thought almost made me laugh. I imagined trying to explain to my father how I'd talked my way out of an impossible fight. The best kind of fight, the most honorable—unwinnable, and over a woman's honor—and here I was ducking and talking. I wondered what would have happened back home if the Reds had managed to capture all of our women. Probably the men in the six villages would focus on killing the Reds in a particularly good way, then steal more women. It wasn't all that different from the American criminal law idea of "justice." For the Americans it was about punishment and for us about honor, but the result was the same. I wondered what the Malian idea of justice would be.

The commander leaned back, relaxing. He took my thinking for suspicion about Peggy's trustworthiness. "Normally yes, it would be only your matter. But not in this case." He gave me one more long look. "I decide to believe you. You are free to go. But she is a more complicated situation. You came only for her, but she came to take the wrong side in our little war."

"Doesn't she get a chance to defend herself?"

"It's a waste of time." He finally spoke directly to Peggy. "You have helped the enemy, tried to embarrass us in the eyes of the world. You have tarnished our good name. GPS and water and all those are weapons that you have provided to the enemy, yes, but what cannot be forgiven is the dishonor you have done to us with stories that serve only to create disharmony and provocation. At any rate, the decision about you will be made in Bamako, not here."

"You mean Bamako wants to prove that the Tuareg civil war was started by foreign provocateurs," Peggy asked with a slight smile.

The commander shrugged. "I am a soldier, not a politician."

"But as a soldier, do you think that helping people get clean water is what starts a war? Do you think poisoning wells is a fair fight?"

"As a soldier, no. As a commander, yes. And as the préfét for this district, neither matters. We will keep you until we get further orders from Bamako. While you are here, you will be safe. Most likely, you will wait one or two days, then go home together. It is my hope that's the way it happens. So you must show a little patience. There is no hurry. We are finished." He spoke to the guard in Hausa.

• • •

"Please," Clive pled, visibly shaking. "I need to know what I'm supposed to do. I'm not asking a question, I'm just...not a question."

He stopped himself, adjusted his papers and started over. "I will spend half my time on the obscenity fact pattern, half on the professor-pupil fact pattern, and I will save two minutes at the end to tie them together and show their analogical relevance to each other." As he spoke he glanced repeatedly at Sclera and Oedda. They had no reactions.

The relevant community standard is the community in which the porn is accessible to the public, and the professor ought to recover the pupil's soul because the entire reason behind contracts is to maximize foresight. The next pupil will not make such a mistake, and the system will benefit from a decision in favor of the professor. Then he tied them together with a similar contract to make obscene pictures. For example, a producer could sign a contract with a porn star stating that she would only be paid if the movie is held obscene by a court—he would want the publicity perhaps. If the movie were held obscene by a court, however, the contract would be for an illegal purpose and would thus be unenforceable. The porn star could still sue under *quantum meruit* to recover the fair value of her work. The merited quantity.

"You suggest that the fair *quantum* for a legal education is the pupil's soul?" asked Pooh.

Clive blinked in surprise, as though noticing Pooh for the first time. Before he had a chance to answer, Oedda interrupted: "Each student values his legal education differently."

"This is only because our science is still imperfect," said Sclera.

Oedda ignored him. "The student in this hypothetical did not wish to participate in the market valuation of a legal education. If he did, he would have intended to practice, thereby maximizing his return from his education. He had his own *quantum*. One would have to enter such a student, possess him, in order to determine whether he truly valued the teachings at such a price. But I agree that it is the only price worth paying."

Clive caught on. "The only objective measure of the *quantum* is that which is provided in the contract. We cannot second guess the contract."

"That's ridiculous," Muzhduk jumped in, annoyed. "You're assuming what you're trying to prove. If your only argument is to extrapolate the value of the contract from his agreement to it, then it's worth zero, since in his mind that's the price he thought he'd be paying."

"You are out of order," said Sclera. "It is not your turn to speak."

"Yes," said Oedda. "Nothing is but the turn we play."

"So the question comes back to, 'What is the value of a legal education?'" Pooh said.

Clive glanced at his watch and spoke more quickly. "Surely the pupil knew that there was some risk, however small, that he would not be able to get away without paying. Suppose he was 99% sure he could get out of the contract, and 1% worried that he could not. Then the proper valuation of his risk is 0.99 times zero plus 0.01 times infinity. Because the soul is surely priceless. 0.99 times zero plus 0.01 times infinity equals infinity. Thus, the pupil valued the consideration he received from the professor at the value of his soul. Any risk of the soul, however small, is an absolute risk. I cite Goethe's *Dr. Faustus* as relevant authority."

"Wrong jurisdiction!" said Sclera out of habit and because he could.

"The authority is persuasive, not binding," answered Clive. "It is the soul, the whole soul, and nothing but the soul which is the proper *quantum*, and it is what the professor deserves."

"Unless the student's stubbornness was perfect," said Sclera. "Unless he lacked that 1%."

It was Muzhduk's turn.

• • •

The commander suggested patience while men pointed guns at Peggy. So I tried patience, though I knew that if one ever agrees to stop fighting, even once, then there is no end to compromises. For all their flaws, at least the Reds in Siberia had kept things simple. They just rolled in with tanks. They didn't say, "Throwing boulders is wrong and our only objection is that you throw boulders. If you put them down, if you show some restraint, then we won't need to roll in with our tanks and neither side has to lose lives in a stupid war." People like Clive would always want to believe it. They would say, "There's got to be a better way to solve problems than throwing rocks at each other." They'd talk and talk—cowards learn how to talk well early—and come up with a rule against throwing rocks. And once there was a rule, they'd need a police to enforce it. They'd choose the police from the men who loved fighting most, but the fight would become a job, it wouldn't be for honor anymore. Winning, enforcing the rule, would be the only thing that counted. And within one generation, the police—Red or Blue or some other uniform color—would be the only people who knew how to fight. The negotiations would become demands, then laws. Which would suit the talkers well, since they'd always be the ones drafting laws. And in the end it would be just the same as if the tanks had rolled in and won.

No true Verkhoyansk Slovak would accept *patience* or *compromise*. These things are not a frontal assault on honor the way a craving for *security* is, but they slowly poison it nevertheless. And here I was—the winner of the Dull-Boulder Throw, the son of the chief, who'd spent a year with the talkers, who knew how to calculate risk: probability times liability—here I was, determined to be patient. To compromise. To take the safer path.

The library at Yakutsk had a big Latin section that included all of Tacitus' work. My father loved Tacitus, because he said that "Valor is the contempt of death and pain," and "The desire for safety stands against every great and noble enterprise." So even if my family did the Harvard risk calculation, they'd still attack. The "liability" of an honorable death in battle is a negative number.

But what about Peggy? It was easy and pleasant to get killed in a good fight, but taking an action that had a 95% probability of causing my woman to die? Love was also simpler in the mountains, and no woman would accept a man who didn't rip the Commander's throat out without hesitation. But Peggy wasn't from Siberia and my brain was feverish with probabilities. They took her from me in the hallway. Five armed men escorted her one way, two took me the other, and I allowed it to happen. She was a prisoner and I free to go. It was sickening.

Peggy had expected all of this. Last night, several hours after the guard took the lamp away, in "bed"—there wasn't a mattress, not even straw, just the concrete floor and complete blackness—she lay with her head on my belly and told me that they'd probably keep her here for a day or two so they could claim they'd captured her. "Then they'll either let me go," she'd said, "or use me for the WAG trial."

"WAG?" I asked, and caressed her head, to make up for being blind.

"West African Governments. It's a regional tribunal, sort of a way for all these countries to avoid an international war crimes tribunal when they commit their little genocides. So they can claim something's being done at a level that's both international and sensitive to local cultures." I couldn't see even an outline of her head, let alone any facial expression, but the tone of her voice was sweet even when she talked about shit.

"And they're going to use you as a defense exhibit?"

"There's no defense, because there's no prosecution. WAG took up the Tuareg Civil War only for a nonbinding *advisory opinion*. Since all of these governments are working together against the Free People, they all want to make sure the thing is presented as a justified, legal war. They don't want to look like Rwanda or Sudan in the news." She'd snaked her way down, wrapped herself around one of my legs, and rested her chin on my penis. Her chin moved slightly as she talked, and my penis started to revive.

"Can't smell good down there." I hadn't washed in too long and we'd just made love.

"A bit ripe." She smiled. "Maybe they'll just let me go. The whole poisoned-water thing is too embarrassing, even if they claim that it was the internationals who did it. And there's got to be some other American they can use. All those tourists in Timbuktu."

I could tell she didn't really believe what she was saying. "Most tourists don't smuggle—"

She put my penis in her mouth.

"Brave girl."

• • •

Sclera poured himself a glass of water. There were ice cubes in the jug, but the water steamed as he poured it into his glass.

"This is a moot court of Law—" Muzhduk began.

"Maintain the fiction, Mr. Ugli," interrupted Sclera immediately.

"—and the case is not only moot, it is also not ripe. No contract will ever amount to a Great Work. They are grubby little things, square—" As he argued, it occurred to him that he was constantly getting outflanked here. If Oedda was right that Law needed human irrationality as fuel, then logic itself needed something like empathy. Without a reflection or shadow, it would be a vampire. But he still didn't understand the people here enough to view the world through their eyes, and couldn't make up his mind whether that sort of understanding was the same as becoming a liar. And he couldn't argue properly until he made a decision.

So now he fought along the whole spectrum, throwing out one-line slogans—legal, irrational, and everything in between. Muzhduk spoke and Sclera interrupted, while Oedda sat in her chair, looking amused. Sclera cut in with fragments of Law directly relevant to the case. A tactically sound approach: if your enemy presents a broad front, you can either defend your edges, or you can focus your attack on the center and burst through his middle.

Muzhduk adjusted. His body temperature dropped, he hunched forward a little more, and the hunching focused his words to reinforce the middle. Instead of flinging out every argument, half-random and open, he began to slice them like baloney. He said things like, "The professor sued before the conditions precedent of the student's obligation under the contract were satisfied." He was surprised how easy it was. "So the case is not ripe. At the time of suit the student had no obligation to the professor, and the court must rule on the situation as the court finds the situation when the suit is initiated."

"Very well." Sclera saw the center wouldn't buckle. But there are two directions in which a line can break. "So the professor sues a second time. The second time around he will win."

That wasn't the fact pattern of the question—a fake retreat that Sclera would turn into an ambush if Muzhduk gave pursuit. If he argued about what was in the fact pattern, he'd find himself in the center of Sclera's authority. But if Muzhduk didn't stop there? Several times he'd fought Reds who tried fake routs to lure the Slovaks out of the mountains. He'd learned that if you charge in hard enough, a fake rout can easily turn into a real one. He was suddenly enjoying himself. "The professor would not win the second time," he said, eyes locked with Sclera, "because the first time the pupil would not in fact win, but would simply point out to the court that the claim was a *nonsuit*. The first suit would have been thrown out without ever coming to a verdict, thus the second suit too would not be ripe, *ad infinitum*."

Sclera tried to interrupt, but Muzhduk didn't stop, he rolled over Sclera with round after round of legal doctrine: *unconscionability, undue influence, mistake* and *misrepresentation, adhesion, illegal purpose, void*—and as he rattled doctrines he began to float. He floated outside of himself, above, as though on a high mountain. As though he'd climbed Mt. Harvard. He saw himself below in body and understood that only his mind could climb here. The air was too thin for those other things. And as he looked down he saw the three judges: Sclera, Oedda, and Pooh. He noticed the glitter in Sclera's eyes as he hammered the desk and yelled that Muzhduk was in contempt of court for talking over his objections and would be docked two full letter grades, and he noticed the vast empty spaces in Oedda's eyes and the mirrors in Pooh's, and he saw it was for him that they had come—not for some moot Defendant, and not for his mind, but his body and sweat and fists and balls, and he giving it to them, flying up into his mind where he would never again have a full belly or a stone cock.

Muzhduk's mind had one strength—the will to fight. It was a clumsy tool, but it was all he really had that was his. His eyes popped open as he landed, and his mouth shut in mid-legalese. He said, "Fuck."

"Excuse me?"

He repeated the word, then said, "It's a beautiful word. Probably the best single word in the English language. It can be a verb, such as Fuck off Sclera. Transitive: Sclera fucked Clive. Or intransitive: Oedda fucks. A noun: Lena is a good fuck. An adjective: This fucking place. An adverb—"

"*Non auditur perire volens!*" yelled Sclera, genuinely perplexed. He who wishes to perish is not heard. There had been so few people he'd genuinely liked: a Sicilian girl fifteen years ago, who'd come to class dressed all in black, walked down to the pit, and kissed him on the cheek while handing him a black rose; a nerdy, overweight kid who'd somehow convinced Corey to bring him a 10-gallon jug of coffee in the middle of class to trump his own mug; and throughout the decades, there was Pooh. Never good at hiding his feelings, Sclera visibly moved from puzzled to saddened.

But Muzhduk refused to be dismissed. "I came here to learn how to use all words, not just legal ones, and not just their meanings. I could get that from a dictionary. *Fuck* is special. It always bleeds beyond its own meaning, but it's never the same. Like the Hindu *Om*, where even the emptiness around the word is significant. And the word *Law*, another with power beyond its meaning, though nobody can quite keep track of whether its meaning changes or doesn't, or whether it's supposed to or not. But it doesn't really matter, does it? All that matters is that this is one way the pupil will not lose his soul."

"Why not?" asked Oedda, frowning.

"Because he won't give it."

No one spoke. Their makeshift courtroom looked out on the N7 neutral grey granite face of Langdell Library. It was late afternoon and the sun was casting long shadows into the room. For a second he had stopped both Sclera and Oedda. For one moment he'd defeated both ends of Harvard Law School. Oedda finally asked, "Are you trying to apologize by acting ridiculous?"

This threw Muzhduk's concentration, and he almost asked, "Apologize for what?" If he had, his victory would have turned to defeat. But he caught himself in time, stayed silent.

"I see," she sneered. "You are chasing shadows. You always were, but now you do it deliberately. Now you chase the shadows of words. You enjoy being stuck in Plato's cave."

Muzhduk placed his hand on his head. On the wall, his shadow did the same. "I caught my shadow. Without even breaking from my chains. That is how the pupil will save himself."

"On which Zen crib-sheet did you read that one?" Oedda asked. "Even two thousand years ago they had people who missed the point."

"Maybe. But we passed the test. Lena and I did, together, each in our own way."

"There are no shadows here," Sclera said, after a long pause, but the glitter was gone from his eyes. He did not need moot courts to fail Muzhduk. It was a question of procedure. Oedda looked at Muzhduk as though she hated him, disgusted. He saw the look, but it didn't make any sense to him.

It was difficult for anyone to pay attention to the last arguments by Alex, Clive's partner. He discussed the professor-pupil question. Muzhduk noted that his name, "a-lex," meant "*anti-law*," and wondered why Sclera had not used him to do his library dirty work.

CHAPTER 14

The Ouidah

I wanted to take Peggy to Verkhoyansk. Instead, the guards took me to a door that opened out onto a dead courtyard, then stood leaning against the open door, watching me like cowboys in a Western. I could wait. I could write a letter to the American embassy. I could ask the rebels for help, an endless cycle of changing sides in an attempt to get Peggy free. But I couldn't both watch the garrison and go to Timbuktu.

I walked out of the courtyard into what was more a small town than a military base. The men were mostly soldiers, but they stared at me no more or less interested than men in any Saharan small town might stare at a tourist. Children came and asked for gifts and indigo Tuaregs came and watered their camels at the well. It wasn't the same well the soldiers used—they had a real one with concrete sides and a pump while the Tuaregs had a hole in the sand that they had to dig out every few days—but it accessed the same aquifer. I sat by the sand well for an hour, then asked a Tuareg why they watered their camels here. He said this way they knew the water wasn't poisoned. I asked why the soldiers let them. He said ask the soldiers. I asked him to rent me two camels and his son, and hoped things would continue to move slowly in the Sahara.

The son was actually a nephew named Hamdi. He couldn't have been more than twelve. The ride to Timbuktu took eight hours but we passed no roads and no soldiers—we arrived in the afternoon, with Hamdi grumbling that I'd have to pay more for the stupidity of riding in the middle of the day. I paid what he asked and he rode off at the same placid pace we'd come.

I didn't need to ask anyone where to go: everything official was concrete. I'd walk into every building made of concrete in Timbuktu, if necessary.

• • •

Lena filed a formal protest requesting that their grades be severed and she and Muzhduk never be partnered for any future school activity. Within an hour, the whole school knew that he'd told Sclera to "fuck off" in the middle of Oral Argument. Everyone asked Lena about it until finally she locked herself in her room. They milled outside her door waiting, wanting gossip.

Though he regretted Lena's anger, Muzhduk was happier than he had been in a long time. He wasn't sure why, and though he tried introspecting to figure it out, he was without success. No insights came to him. When he saw Oedda, he asked whether she had deliberately placed herself on his judging panel. She shrugged. "Why not?"

"You looked like you hated me in there," he said.

"Yes."

"I thought you didn't hate."

"No more than I love."

"Have a Merry Christmas."

It was December 23rd. Moot court was over. The semester was over. Exams were to begin January 2nd, a Saturday. Muzhduk spent the week in the library, which Harvard kept open. They even set up a plastic Christmas tree. There were no red-and-white *amanita muscaria* mushrooms drying above the fireplace, no shaman coming in from the roof, no reindeer pee. About half the students stayed, to protect their time from Christmas and family.

Buck had a poetry book in his stack of study material: e. e. cummings. When he went downstairs to get a coffee, Muzhduk pulled it out, surprised that with so little time, Buck would still read poetry. There hadn't been many poetry books in the Yakutsk library. He opened Buck's book, scanning the titles: *anyone lived in a pretty how town*. Muzhduk closed the book and put it back.

He felt suddenly glad that Harvard had put the tree up. There were almost enough students in the library to form a village. He knew that most villages were dictatorial little places where anyone who thought differently was quickly punished. But they didn't have to be that way. Verkhoyansk wasn't that way. It was small enough that you could recognize every face, but big enough that you hadn't slept with everyone, hadn't fought everyone. It seemed to him that human beings had evolved for that size group. Much bigger and you had to start living like an ant. Despite all the neuroses and stress, the library at Christmas felt the right size.

• • •

The Tourist Bureau reminded me of Russian schools in Siberia. There was no reception or office or anything other than bleak hallways and rooms, all empty, with broken fans hanging from their ceilings. In the fourth room I tried, I found a man sitting at a desk reading the *Bamako Monde*. He looked up at me, and after a series of suggestions of where I could go, told me that I didn't have an appointment and so he was too busy. Tourists weren't a novelty in Timbuktu.

Before flying into Niamey, I'd expected Africa to be free of all the bureaucracy that gripped America. I'd expected it to be more like Verkhoyansk. But Verkhoyansk Slovaks had never been defeated. They'd never been colonized, categorized, made dependent on foreign aid, and taught that bureaucracy was a sign of civilization.

Still, I had to try. I went to the Interior Ministry, the American Consulate (a one-man operation, and the one man was in Bamako), the Timbuktu police, and the American Peace Corps, where a girl with very short blond hair, in her early twenties, let me use the telephone to call the American Embassy in Bamako, which routed its calls through a call center that required me to enter a credit card number and pay $2.99 if I wanted to talk to a human being. I didn't have a credit card. I wondered how many people in Mali did. I offered her five dollars, but she only had the official Peace Corps card and wasn't authorized to use it for unauthorized reasons. While we were debating the logic, a little boy ran in and told me that Amadou was at the *patisserie* and that I should go see him.

The bakery was on a wide street busy with people shopping,

selling, playing, and burning garbage. A store across the street blasted a Zaire beat at a volume that should have shook down the surrounding mud buildings, with waist-high speakers stacked in front. The bakery itself had no name, but seemed comfortable, despite the ear-shattering music outside. Everything was open and a handful of square metal tables sat within covered in plastic red-and-white-checkered tablecloths that reminded me of a beachside restaurant in Boston.

Amadou sat in the back of the room.

I gave the boy his coin and shouted over the counter, "I want to try real African coffee."

The man, dressed in the white of bakers throughout the world, nodded. "Nescafé?"

More coffee less condensed milk and no sugar, disbelief at the no sugar, then the explanation of how many scoops of coffee, and yes, really, zero spoons of sugar, followed by a eureka moment by the baker. "Ah, I understand. You want the *stress* to be on the *coffee*?"

Amadou grinned as I sat at his table. He said, "We travel in parallel."

"How did you get away from the soldiers?"

"The soldiers stopped shooting at the Tuaregs and the Tuaregs stopped shooting at the soldiers. It's an easy agreement, good for everyone who was being shot at."

"And Rogers?"

"He did what he wanted. As he always does." He raised his hand to cut me off. "And please, don't ask me what that is. I don't know. He is not my master and I am not his."

"You sent the boy."

"I have information."

"What will it cost me?"

"I don't know yet. I will come with you."

"Where?"

"To Oedda."

"What?" I suddenly felt dizzy in the little thumping bakery in the late-afternoon Mali heat. There were only supposed to be two connections between my year at Harvard and Africa: Peggy and me. At most, a coincidental table cloth. Oedda's name spun everything around.

"They sent her this morning."

"Who?"

"Peggy Roundtree. Your friend."

"They sent Peggy where? To Oedda? Oedda Hecaten?"

Amadou frowned and looked at my coffee. "The city of Ouidah, in the Bight of Benin. On the Slave Coast. A war crimes—"

"*Into-God's-cunt!* Can we catch them?"

He shook his head. "To buy a car with paperwork would take days. Without paperwork, you have every border. Unless you have a lot of dollars. Then you can move faster."

"Is there a bus? Or a salt truck, something?"

"The *pinasse* leaves Kabara in an hour." He placed two slips of paper on the table.

I paid him for the tickets without asking why he had them ready, drank my coffee, and then ran into the street to find a car that would drive us the fifteen minutes to Kabara.

• • •

On Christmas Day, Muzhduk sat in the library under a pile of books. Oedda had flown off on a trip somewhere. She refused to tell him where or when she'd be back. He told Buck about it over Property. Better than reading about fee simples, life estates, and the Rule in *Shelley's Case*.

"That's how you know you have a problem in your relationship," Buck said, without stopping highlighting. "When your girlfriend flies off somewhere and refuses to tell you where."

"I don't know if I'd call it a relationship. More like two ice skaters throwing bowling balls at each other. But at least we're not like goats on an arrow."

Buck laughed and stopped working. "Is that a real Slovak expression?"

"How should I know? It's real Siberian Slovak. I don't know about Slovakia itself."

"Referring to the single-point focus of HLS students, as though we were all running for political office against all our classmates but with all our classmates as the electorate?"

"You feel it too?"

Buck rubbed his chin. "You know, I just found out that it's

against the law to put money into someone else's parking meter? Isn't that messed up? When I read that it almost knocked me off my arrow."

"Oedda says the Law is inherently nuts. Though she called it 'autoheteronomous.'"

"Remind me not to take her seminar next year. Hey, I was trying to remember the etymology of her name since you told it to me. It kept teasing me, and then I looked it up but forgot to tell you. I'm sure you know the Norse epic, the Edda. But Oedde, O-E-D-D-E, is Old Norse for a particular form of dark fate. And Aleister Crowley's wife was named Ourda, though that's probably irrelevant." I had told him a bit about Oedda's Tarot hobby.

"What kind of *dark fate*?"

"I can't define it properly, but it's a manner of sacrificing yourself to yourself. The name comes from 'Odin's Day,' the day on which 'Himself sacrificed to himself.'"

"Every God does that. Sacrifices himself to himself."

"Every mortal as well, if he wants—" Buck said, then stopped on a dime. Finally, he mumbled, "I have to study."

When the library closed at 3 AM, Muzhduk walked back to his dorm, wishing he could walk back to Siberia for a Christmas visit. He took a detour by the always-open computer lab in the basement of Hauser. He wondered whether it was named after Kaspar Hauser.

• • •

A motorized *pinasse*, and its loin-clothed-and-turbaned captain, carried us from Kabara to Mopti. From Mopti we went overland to Bobo-Dioulasso in Burkina Faso (the road through Bankass and Ouahigouya was too damaged for busses), then from Bobo to Ouagadougou, which in pre-colonial times was called Ouagadougoudou, but was shortened by the colonials for the sake of paperwork. From Ouagadougou to Djougou, then Abomey and finally Ouidah. With stops on the way for broken belts, flat tires, border problems, fistfights, an empty gas tank caused by forgetting to put the gas cap back onto the Peugeot bush-taxi, and finally a big bull. We hit it and broke its leg, so everyone pulled it onto the roof of the taxi, above the pickup bed where we sat. The bull, terrified, peed. The meat would be fresher if it lived until the market. The pee leaked through holes in the roof for hours while

Amadou laughed and the rest of us squirmed in our cramped seats to avoid the trickles.

With a dying bull dripping on us, we drove into Ouidah, rust-red and dim, with an azoic sky and amber-blue clouds that took away all shadows. Amadou explained it was the only port north of the equator where it had been legal to trade in slaves after the British Abolition Act. The streets were wide, hard-packed rufous mud, lined with degenerating pink two-story houses—a rarity in West Africa. Across from the colonial Portuguese architecture, shanties leaned against a two-hundred-year-old stone fence and the darker pink dados of walls that had stood there since Dom Francisco da Silva sent millions to their deaths in slave ships named after seabirds.

• • •

The moot Christmas was followed by real exams. And then, on February 14th, the students of Harvard Law School were told to line up in the Civ Pro classroom to receive their first-semester grades. Students waited single-file, searching each other for hints. Few trusted their poker faces enough to open the envelope in public. A long slow line of anxious students shifted from leg to leg as though with full bladders, then dashed off for the privacy of a room.

The U.S. Postal Service refused to deliver grades through the mail because of past hordes who'd followed the postman as he made his rounds. And the school couldn't just deliver the transcripts into students' pigeonholes, because that inevitably caused a melee and lawsuits, including one about handicapped equal-access, as everyone fought to reach their white envelope first, and once that was done, quickly tried to open the envelopes of slower friends and enemies in order to compare. The letters inside the envelopes, when seen in the context of the contents of all the other envelopes, were the final and objective measures of one's value as a human being.

For weeks before and after the Valentine's Day Massacre, in dormitory common rooms, at the Hark Box, everywhere, voices said things like, "You want to tell people if you get an A, but if you say you got an A in one class, then refuse to divulge your grade from another class, everyone will know you didn't do well in that other class. Of course, if you get an A+, you should tell people—only one of these is given out every several years, like Fs."

Muzhduk found himself riding the subways just to get away from these conversations. Every station and train had a subway map, and on the north-east edge in bold black lettering was the last stop on the blue line, called Wonderland. It was an amusement park. Verkhoyansk was in the north-east corner of the world, and Pooh had mentioned Wonderland was as far away as he could get from campus on the train, so he went. And then he went as often as he could, because he had discovered the tea cups ride, and because the barmaid from the Ratio began sitting in one of the tea cups across from him.

Few people rode the tea cups in February. Often it was just Muzhduk and the barmaid and an occasional perverted old man. She held onto the handle of a flaking yellow sunflower tea cup as it spun on its own axis while all the tea cups also spun as a set. It had functional metal handles added years after the tea cups ride was built, but the handle she liked was the one that a tea cup normally had, there so people wouldn't burn their fingers as they drank hot tea. Even America had a past when a drink temperature was the drinker's own responsibility. She sat with her feet tucked under her and held onto the giant handle, breasts pressed against the brim. It made her look like she was drinking herself, and since she was also holding onto the handle of the tea cup, with herself she drank the world. Across from her in a blue-onion cup, once every epicycle, sat Muzhduk.

But on February 14th he skipped the tea cups in favor of the Civ Pro classroom, with its sour odor of stress and fear. Lena was waiting for him. She didn't say a word until he'd received his page full of B+. Except moot court, which was a C+. Then she exploded. "That C+ is your fault. You know that. And for what? So you could show off by telling a professor to fuck off? Why couldn't you just answer the fucking question as we'd prepared it?" Her voice cracked. "You lousy selfish shit."

Because the question was different, he wanted to say. But it was the first time someone here had told him honestly what she thought of him. What came out was, "I'm sorry."

"I want you to come to the BSA. I want a breakdown of our grades."

The walk through the underground tunnels was long, and

Muzhduk felt bad for Lena. Maybe she was right. "Maybe they'll understand."

"They never understand."

In the Board of Student Advisers' office, she trembled. The secretary rechecked IDs several times before showing them that Muzhduk had received an A+ from Pooh, a B+ from Sclera, and an F from Oedda. The distribution surprised him so much that he didn't even wonder about Lena's grades until he heard a noise. She'd received a B+, C, and an F. Three years had passed since anyone had received an F at Harvard Law School, the rumors were clear on this, and now they had each received one. Lena didn't even look at him; she fled the building. Though he tried many times to talk to her, even to apologize, Lena never spoke to him again.

And it wasn't just Lena. Buck, depressed, had stopped speaking to him too, and all around campus people took on a zombie bleakness. Grey clouds followed them and took color from their temples, seamed their faces, coated their eyes. They paled and bloated as though drowned. People who'd been thin suddenly gained twenty, thirty, even forty pounds. Muzhduk's weight didn't change, but it became saggy. He developed knee and back problems, and generally became less dense. They had all been changing since September, but with the release of grades all the sleepless nights finally landed. Everyone knew that 80% received a B+, but no one imagined themselves receiving it. An army of psychiatrists was ready, a result of Harvard's long experience. They had convinced the school to raise the bell curve average from a B- to a B+, arguing that the plus would have a psychologically moderating effect, and an army of lawyers concurred: the change was useful in the lawsuits that always followed the late-February suicides and homicides. The psychiatrists put in overtime, the hallways were plastered with posters for counseling, and Prozac and Zoloft representatives handed out pamphlets at makeshift kiosks in front of the pigeonholes.

There it was, in the incremental day-to-day of everyday. Muzhduk didn't understand why it was happening to him as well.

• • •

Our bush-taxi pulled into Ouidah's station, a dirt clearing near the center of town. A lone woman in pale blue briefly blocked the red road as she walked across, a bright white washbasin resting on her head. On either side was the orange din of crickets, the shade of limp banana leaves, and mounds of garbage, snakes, scorpions, beige-yellow excrement, goats, lizards, enormous agouti rats, and vomit. A dozen turkey vultures followed her lissome movements with their synchronized, naked reddish heads.

Amadou said, "The Ouidah is in the topsoil."

I let myself be led towards Dom Francisco's old slave fort, now a tourist attraction. The road split at an immense baobab tree with branches that hovered over a dozen pink houses, most with corrugated tin shanty roofs but some with the old wooden planks still rotting blue. At the center of the wide intersection was a small café, just a picnic table really, that served coffee and grilled meat of some sort, about the size of a large rabbit, with yellow teeth. The animals were splayed into slabs over a fire, but long fuzzy rat tails hung over the edge of the grill. A sign read, "Agouti, Good Gravy," above another sign in the shape of an arrow, with red lettering:, "DAAGBO HOUNON, CHEF SUPREME DES VODOUN-NON DU BENIN."

We walked under the tree, full of giant grey bats—five-foot wingspans upside-down, and protruding square stomachs as though each had swallowed a law book—and followed the direction of the sign, past a smiling boy feeding a sheep with a wooden spoon. The sheep was half black and half white. Exactly half, the line separating the two colors could have been drawn with a ruler. The road narrowed, then zigzagged between houses and stone fences, finally opening upon a market. The splayed skin of a cat with its head intact, dried, eyes wide, arms and legs spread, hung at the entrance as a marker, followed by individual kiosks. *Stand No. 13: HOUEGNAGBO Victor, Herboriste-Guerisseur-Docteur en Médicine Traditionnelle DIT LA SANTE AVANT TOUS—Marché des Fetiches Akodessewa.* Health before everything. A table overflowed with dried horses' heads assembled cheek to cheek, more skinned cats, crocodile heads, shrunken monkey heads, birds and rodents of all sorts, fruit bats, giant bats, calabash pipes, buckets of intestines beside buckets of blood advertised *Fresh Today*, dried dung of various animals, countless varieties of feathers and claws, rows of bushy tails suspended from bars, masks, wood carvings of people with hundreds of nails hammered into every part of the body in both rusted and unrusted versions, teeth, lots of teeth, shells, horns, one human hand kept in a black sack and shown to tourists for a small *dash* (a larger amount if I wanted to take a photo) and an all pervading smell of rot accompanied by the inevitable lackluster of insanity. There was no wind in this city.

Amadou bought a wooden mask with nails drilled into half its face, the other half covered with fragmented mirrors, and we walked out of the far end of the market. A few blocks further we came to the intersection with the grilled rat café and the Hogon sign, Daagbo Hounon, chief of the Vodoun. It seemed impossible, we had walked south the whole time. I felt a dislocation like vertigo. But there was no mistaking the baobab tree and the sign, though the intersection was now filled with hundreds of people and a fast-paced drumbeat.

"Be careful now, Twobob," Amadou said. "Be careful not to get confused."

The crowd screamed, pulsed out in panic, turned and pressed back in as quickly as it could. People laughed as they saw me push my way in. I could see six rectangles dancing and running at the crowd. Each rectangle waved a big stick and tried to hit people with it. Amadou, behind me, pointed at them and said, "Egungun Vodoun."

The American religion of voodoo comes from the Dahomey name for their gods, the Vodoun. These were the gods, square people. "Why are we here?" I asked Amadou.

"This is the preamble," said a man behind Amadou. It was Babu Chirpy, Esq.—Rogers' lawyer from the Corpa-Cola factory. His eyes moved quickly between me, the dancing rectangles, and the young men who taunted them by whistling, clapping their hands, or slapping flip-flops together. They ran when the Vodoun came at them. If they were caught they were beaten with long thin sticks. "To the trial. Our rules of procedure require it."

At Harvard I'd read a case about the stock market where the judge had mentioned that "History doesn't repeat, but it does rhyme." I'd had this rhyming sensation since coming to Africa, but lately it felt stronger than that, odder, like my time at Harvard and my time in Africa lay next to each other separated by a thin membrane that was getting thinner as the drummers pounded on it. Babu Chirpy, Esq. increased this sense, more prolepsis than déjà vu. I shook it off.

"Where's Peggy?" I asked the lawyer. The crowd shifted while we talked, pushing us near the front of the circle.

"They will bring her out during the trial," said Babu Chirpy, Esq., then walked through the Vodoun dance to the picnic table behind, filled with important people. Next to it were the drummers. I turned around, but Amadou was gone. When I turned back, one of the Vodoun stood directly in front of me—a red rectangle with dangling square flaps. Maybe it was blind, like Lady Justice, a blind red rectangle with arms covered so thickly in horsehair they seemed to move without joints. One hairy fluid arm held a long stick for beating, the other seemed to be begging.

I could hear, "Cadeau, cadeau, give a gift." I gave some coins to the Vodoun. It grabbed my arm and pulled.

• • •

"You failed me," Muzhduk accused Oedda as they sat at Chez Derrida. For months before Christmas they'd discussed the idea of having dinner there without ever actually going, but upon returning from her trip she'd asked him on a "date." He had arrived at the restaurant early, and to kill time walked up the street putting quarters into expired parking meters. When he ran out of change, he broke a $10 bill and ended up late, with Oedda annoyed.

"It was moot," Oedda laughed.

"Not to me. Or Lena."

"That is precisely why I failed you both. Despite your stupid antics, you still cared whether you won or lost." She took a mouthful of beef consommé. With the exception of the African fufu, which was more a gelatin, she never seemed to eat anything solid. "Your actions simply reinforce the Law as an organic structure, breathing life into the dead skin of its formalism."

"And Lena?"

"Lena? I failed Lena because I did not like her. And because she likes you."

"No presence of objectivity?"

"I thought you considered truth to be some kind of virtue."

"Well, now she won't speak to me."

"Buy her a bottle of Dom Pérignon."

"As an apology?"

"P'ah. If you bought her a $20 bottle, that would be an apology.

If you buy her a $200 bottle, that is revenge. She brought your average down and then blamed you. Even if she refuses, there will be a moment in which she will have to recognize the gift as gift."

"I don't get it."

Oedda sighed. "In the moment when she recognizes your gift as being out of proportion—the gift has to be greater than the maximum she could possibly construe as her due—that moment will give you power over her. She will probably not even realize it. And even if she does, there will be no way out, the gift itself will take from her what she does not want to give to you: a debt too large and thus too intimate. The Dom will be your phallus."

Muzhduk frowned. "You make it sound like rape."

"Yes, of course. It is beautiful that she is a feminist."

"It's not beautiful. It's ugly. I mean, it's not Ugli, it's…Lena's not my enemy here."

She shrugged. "Well, then you can always assure her later that you gave her the gift out of an overwhelming desire to patch up your friendship."

"But that wouldn't be true."

"Of course it would. At that point it will be. What relevance does its truth *now* have?"

"That's not who I am."

"You are a Cola bottle."

"What?"

"You are a bottle of Corpa-Cola. You construct yourself and create a little totality which you then call Self or Principles or whatever, and shut out all disruptive details. And so your way of interacting lacks all subtlety, bonking people on the head with your glass bottle, your 'this is who I am' nonsense. How boring and predictable."

"You misundersta—"

"I told you, Oedda is a hermeneutic, she does not understand or misunderstand!"

Hermeneutic, my ass. "Hermes was a liar."

"Yes! Finally you begin to understand a little. Ugli is Harvard."

"I doubt there's a person here who's less Harvard than I am."

"Oh, is that so? Do you think your friend Buck would ever say something that stupid? Ugli creates these little principles about who he is so he doesn't ever have to look at himself. He can just accept the manifestations of the social within him. He is weak and a coward."

"Principles and personal rules of honor are not weak. They are not like Law. I accept them each time that I apply them, so the source is irrelevant, they are mine."

"Yesss," Oedda hissed and clapped her hands. The gesture was jarring. "What a nice little totality you have there. "Take the world, put it in, and slam the lid on. Do you think it will keep if I, who was hiding when you put your principles together, give it a shake?"

"You've been shaking since we met, and it's starting to feel old."

"Have you seen a Cola bottle opened in space? The way the fluid floats in the void?"

"I'm not scared of your void."

"Because you are a fool."

"And you're a simple opportunist. You deconstruct anything that's inconvenient."

"I have moral imperatives. But they respect their context."

"You once said you didn't."

"Is that so? At least I do not fetishize consistency."

"Didn't Kant say that transgression as a moral motive is the definition of the diabolical?"

"I can be diabolical if you like. But you are offensive to define me by the ramblings of Kant. Kant had no understanding of what thinking is. The entire task of thinking is to destroy concepts, to loosen up the hard shell that starts to form around all ideas the minute they are conceived." Her nostrils tightened. "I thought that you could be my way out, that you would heed my call. I thought you were full of potential. That you could smash. But you are a fool in the most banal sense. You have no concept of the other, no idea of how to interact with the universe. You think there is one reality out there, whole and unfragmented, and one person inside your head, whole and unfragmented. And he is all that matters, because all you see is chunks of matter. Your whole life is your dull boulder throw, dull and blind to all life."

"You think reality is fragmented?"

"Of course. Which makes me a realist."

"Reality might be contradictory and irrational. But it's only fragmented if you are fragmented. In the end you are just like the Law, Oedda. You are its mirror."

They both sat quiet, while every table around them talked. Discussing their meal, talking about their discussion of their meal. Endless words that exhausted both speaker and listener. Words like vermin. Words that belonged in valleys, not mountains, with far too many people. While she looked at him with blank, bleached eyes.

"You psychoanalyze me as if I were some stranger," she finally said, looking genuinely hurt. "I will prove to you with your own body that reality is fragmented."

"How?"

"Just watch inside yourself. Are you ready, love?" she smiled coldly, then leaned forward. "Watch to see whether something cracks. Watch as one fragment takes over from another, as one Ugli takes over from another, in the driver's seat of your brain, as I tell you that I am pregnant."

"That's not funny."

"Actually it is hilarious."

• • •

The Vodoun pulled me toward the oversized picnic table. On a squat three-legged stool placed in the center of the table, higher than everyone else, sat a man in a red hangman's hood, with black slits for eyes. He held a whip, wore no shirt, and had the loose skin over muscle of a very fit old man. Below him sat Babu Chirpy, Esq. and eight other men, each wearing the heavy, unpleasant faces of judges and witch doctors. Around the table drummers pounded in frenetic rhythm, hypnotic, taking over from a chronometric time while six rectangular Vodoun of different colors—Red, Blue, Green, Orange, Yellow, and Silver—beat the nearest spectators. The man in the red hood motioned for me to sit beside him. Everyone made room, except Babu Chirpy, Esq.

"Who are you to come here?" Babu Chirpy, Esq. asked.

"You know why I'm here." I paused. "Why are *you* here?"

"The Corpa-Cola logo is recognized by 94% of the world's population—more than the Christian Cross, the Muslim Crescent, any other symbol. Events at the factory will be discussed here, and I cannot permit the name to be tarnished or the logo to be diluted."

"In the beginning was the Logo?" I smiled. I could play this game, and here it didn't seem so offensive. Maybe it was the way Babu spoke, with intonation and incantation, as though he were casting spells. "That factory wasn't a true Corpa-Cola factory. It was a front, a parody, with a fake bottling façade. Or by becoming known to 94% of the world's population, Corpa-Cola has become part of the world's cultural lexicon and cannot control culture through litigation. Why are you really here?"

"How do you say such sentences?" Babu Chirpy, Esq. asked. He seemed almost hurt.

"Law school." I rubbed my eyes, trying to maintain focus.

"What school did you go to?" he asked, genuinely curious. In Africa I'd had people shoot at me as I approached, and five minutes later they were genuinely, warmly inviting me over for dinner.

"It was in America."

The effect of the sticks lessened. Men slowed their taunting of the Vodoun only after getting hit four or five times, and then only for a moment.

"Yes, but which school."

"Outside Boston."

"Ah, I understand. The school in Cambridge, the one which started in the year 1636? You avoid saying the name. I understand. It is a powerful name."

"In America it's proper to avoid saying the name. It creates the impression of humility."

"American magic," Babu Chirpy, Esq. nodded. "I have studied it for my client."

"Where?"

"Lagos. I was a babalawo before becoming a lawyer. I also performed circumcisions. That is why you have lost this battle, you know? Yes, you learned the law—congratulations, it means nothing. You laugh at me for mixing in the magic and circumcisions, yes, I can see that, but if I can pull you into this court," Babu Chirpy, Esq. pointed to picnic table and the six rectangles and the crowd, "and make you dance for ten years, does it really matter what the law says, what the judge thinks in the end? You will be dead of exhaustion. So go ahead, try to save your girl. Just leave the Corpa-Cola name out of it. A small change, and you may sit."

I had no answer, and he was right, saving Peggy was what

mattered. "What's a babalawo?"

"Ah Twobob, why do I know Harvard but you do not know babalawo? He does the talking for the man with the Vodoun. He represents the man, predicts danger, and helps you forget. All these men are babalawos." He drew a circle in the air with a thumb. "Only a babalawo should sit at this table." But he made room for me.

• • •

Muzhduk stared into Oedda's eyes, to see if her pupils narrowed, if their retinas dried up, if she looked to the upper right or to the upper left. She smiled contemptuously at his intensity. The last thing he wanted was a child with a lunatic. And that thought led to another—either she was stuck or he'd caught up to her. Somewhere along the line Mary Magdalene had become a streetwalker. Or maybe it was just distance. Maybe it was impossible to be Isis close up. Either way, it was time to leave and then return as a new man. Except he'd never do it, he'd never return, no matter how much he might think it was a good idea. Like an Odysseus who always talks about returning, but never does, because he has lost his sense of where home is. Not Verkhoyansk, not Harvard, and definitely not Oedda. He felt like he had the day of the boat cruise meet-and-greet, sure that he was doing something wrong. And in that sense, she was right. In Verkhoyansk he may have been the Dull-Boulder Throw champion, but in this world he was weak and clumsy. "I can't tell when you lie."

"Of course not. I am an excellent liar."

He bent his knees under the table, flexed. "I don't want you to be pregnant."

"This is not about what you want, little boy."

"I mean—"

"I know what you mean. I always know what you mean. It is repulsively easy," she snarled. "What *I* mean is that it is not yours."

They looked at each other's foreheads. But this time only Muzhduk changed. His fighting stance dissolved. He should have felt relieved, but all he could feel was a stupid urge to tell her that he was sorry. *Sorry for what?* In Verkhoyansk people didn't need to have conversations when they no longer wanted to see each other, they just stopped. But here talking was required, so he asked, "Whose then?"

"Eugene's."

"Sclera?" Muzhduk could feel a sudden anger push at the backs of his eyes. Sleeping with an enemy was different. And yet, the absurdity of the picture—pale Oedda with the yellowing man and his ridiculously short arms. "But he's….You had sex with Sclera?"

"That is usually how it happens."

"He's like a cadaver."

"Actually, the sex was very good. We fucked until we were both raw and bleeding."

"Yuck."

"What *yuck*? You share your life with others, so why should I not?"

"*Who?*" he bellowed so emphatically that the diners at the nearest tables looked over.

"Lena. Buck," Oedda whispered, clearly irritated, but not in a position to ask Muzhduk to be more considerate of her social phobias.

"Those are friends. Just because you don't have any friends."

"Oh?" Her voice became mocking, though still a half-whisper: "I can be friends with you like *this*, but not like *this*. I can slap your back, but we cannot slap bellies. I can shake your *hand* but not your *penis*, because the *penis* is *Bad. The Devil lives there. I can only touch Muzhduk's penis, which is Good.* The Devil is chased out by what? Ownership? A contract?"

Muzhduk felt better. The mockery helped. "Are you going to keep it?"

"I suppose you want me to sacrifice it for you? Well, I won't do that. This baby will unify form and substance, the general and the particular, the noun and the verb, geography and time. This baby will be everything." But even as she said this, her body went slack and her eyes dulled.

• • •

Another Vodoun, the Green, came to me. The hangman said that I had paid the Red—if I didn't pay the others, they would get jealous and curse me. I said that was okay. The Vodoun swung its stick, frustrated. The hangman snapped his whip and it jumped back.

"I am still the Hogon, Mr. Ugli." He paused to see whether I was surprised that he knew my name, whether I was impressed by his power in knowing it. But I had been here too long, seen too many times how information flowed. When he realized I wasn't going to give him that little victory, he continued in a businesslike tone. "I will tell you the story of how Dahomey was formed."

It was an awkward time for a story. With the drums, colors, and shapes spinning in front of me, words seemed distracting. It was difficult to pay attention. He nodded to himself, or me, or just with old age, but never let go with his eyes until I shrugged. "My people, the Fon, are not originally from Benin. Once, long ago, a man named Dan lived on this land. Until a stranger from the distance, the father of the Fon people, came. Dan told him this was his land. The stranger said he only wanted land the size of an antelope skin, so Dan laughed and agreed. But the stranger took the skin of the antelope and cut it fine-fine, into a thread. He took the thread and surrounded everything. Dan said to him, 'If you do this you will end by building the cornerstone of your house in my belly.' The stranger said 'Yes,' killed Dan, and built the cornerstone in his belly. That is what *Dahomey* means in the Fon language, *In the belly of Dan*."

"That's my story," I said with a sudden anxiety.

"Are you *Dahomey*, then? Are you the stranger from a distance?"

"No, I am Dan. Your enemy."

The Hogon laughed. "In that case, I am in your belly."

I remembered all the squatting people I'd seen turning the skin on their bellies, round and around, until it looked like it must rip. "But your story, there can't be two such stories."

"Every tribe has that story," he said. "Lawyers and babalawos understand the danger of words. They are the power that created my people and the power that destroys them."

"And to understand why a wall falls on a man, you must also know why he sat beside it, and life is not a jigsaw puzzle, and that there is no such thing as Time. I've been told all this."

"Yes," the Hogon said, "but did you understand it?"

• • •

After their dinner at Chez Derrida, Muzhduk didn't see Oedda for several weeks. He attended classes without raising his hand and spent his days highlighting. Unable to read in the grey library without feeling claustrophobic, he entered it only long enough to take out books on Harvard history. He spent every moment he could at Wonderland, spinning, and the rest studying at the Hark Box.

One bright day in the second week of March, Buck sat at Muzhduk's table. The curtains were open on the big windows that made up the east wall of the Box, and the snow covering Holmes field reflected the blue-white light throughout the room. It made reading almost painful.

Buck seemed lightened by the weather, defying gravity. "Hello, Mr. Ugli the Fourth."

"You're in a good mood."

"I came to the realization that my cognitive dissonance was inducing psychotic symptoms as I lost a sense of integration. So I've decided to integrate."

"With this?" Muzhduk opened his arms wide to include the room, the light, the school.

"Nuh-uh." Buck shook his head. "I was like the Chinese woman picking up cucumbers and forgetting to look at the tomatoes."

"I'm shocked at your language. Even though I don't understand what it means."

He turned a shade darker and his Adam's apple jumped. "I guess I just wanted to thank you. You know, I'm indebted to you. You remember how I told you about last year?"

"The deferral?"

Buck leaned forward across the small round table. "Last year I left because I couldn't take it. This time I'm leaving because I want to. Because I gave myself a *talking to*." He grinned at his own grammar.

"What do you mean, you're leaving? You mean dropping out?"

"I'm leaving, yes."

"But you didn't finish yet."

"I don't want to finish."

"Is it your grades?"

"Part of it. They were all wrong. An A+ in a class where I repeated the professor's sentences back to him, photographic-memory style, because I didn't have time to prepare properly, and a B- where I knew everything inside out and tried to add something more."

"You can't just stop halfway. You'll never climb the mountain like that."

"What if it's the wrong mountain?"

Muzhduk rubbed his beard. "You think it's the wrong mountain?"

"You're the one who reminded me that I don't have to be a lawyer. Some people are not meant to be lawyers. And some of these don't realize it until they're in law school."

"That doesn't follow." Muzhduk frowned. "I don't want to be a lawyer, either."

"So why are you in this institution?"

"What are you going to do?"

Buck shrugged. "I'll write poetry."

"Poetry," Muzhduk repeated the word. Buck was his closest friend here, his only friend here, and even though they hadn't spoken much since the Day of Grades, Muzhduk felt vaguely protective of him: a truly sensitive person on a battlefield where the appearance of sensitivity was a weapon just like any other. Buck didn't fit this place, he was too good for this place; but still, to quit half way— "Why not finish first, then write poetry. Like, who was it, Wallace Stevens?"

"If I stay much longer I'll cross that point beyond which I can't go back."

"But that's the point everyone's trying to reach," Muzhduk slammed his palm down on the table hard enough for the table to tilt. He'd bent something inside. "That's the goal."

"I don't want to live like that. I don't want to write all dried-up like Wallace Stevens. I'd rather work as a fisherman in Alaska for my day job. Or at Starbucks. Whatever." He scratched both his forearms at the same time. When Muzhduk didn't answer, Buck stood and put his hand out to shake. "I should go now. I'm packed, I just wanted to thank you."

"No, it's I who owe you the thanks." Muzhduk took Buck's hand, but held on. "Any last big words that I'll need to look up in the dictionary?"

Buck grinned and looked at the ceiling, then cleared his throat theatrically. Poking fun at himself. "If you keep thinking the whole world is against you, you'll turn into a lawyer."

Muzhduk smiled. "You know what?"

"What?"

"You're a freak."

Buck looked earnest for a second, then saw that Muzhduk was smiling, and nodded. He left as happy as he'd entered, leaving Muzhduk at his little table unable to concentrate, staring at the Statue of Protrusion and Contraption in the middle of Holmes Field. Its lines looked vaguely mercurial in the snow-sharpened sun. When clouds finally dulled the light, he left the Hark Box. He passed by his pigeonhole, and found a letter with no address, no salutation, no signature:

> about the painfulness of explaining: it is the hurt of not being understood, and the fear of not going to be. i have been cynical about *erklärung*, but with you *erklärung* has often transmitted also a little bit of *erfahrung*, and just a tiny hint of *erlebnis*, sometimes—which is amazing, disturbing, and significant. very rare...
>
> unfortunately, very often the *erklärung der erfahrung*—or vice versa—gets to be used for deconstruction, dissection, destruction, forceful penetration, and violent reshuffling of levels.
>
> i shan't ask whether it is hurtful to you. painful, hurtful, whatever, all like little pieces of dust in the glowing oven of whatever name. . .whatever i decide in hindsight that i did (analysis) is discredited by the next future experience of the similar occurrence...if i play games, i do so mostly *mit heiligem Ernst*...the clash, such as talking (about his seed) makes me feel your presence in my loins—as a violent fight between mind (words, talk, concept) and body (concrete sense) which stimulates so many more conflicting, exciting passions, emotions, love, hate, revulsion, attraction, all are the same, flip sides of the same, all creating, unifying body and mind, making the bodily take over the offturned, disgusted mind, "loincells fighting with braincells—and winning" (this is a joke!)—but as good as any other *erklärung*!

oh yes, you claim not to speak german. *erklärung* is explanation, *erfahrung* is experience, and *mit heiligem Ernst* is with holy earnestness. i shan't be so sarcastic as to translate *erlebnis* for you.

It is Friday morning. The week is nearly finished. I was very tired yesterday, and am so today. I have the morning seminar, lunch, work, and the Faculty Club dinner with Eugene et al. Long day—full of nice intellectual activity and niceness with nice people, full of courteous discussion, full of mutual understanding, widening of personal perspectives and enrichment, rewarding mutual influence via dialogue and polylogue, respectfully, in a mature reliable continuum—and what is the opposite: being nasty, superficial, immature, playerish, sporadic in thought and deed...why do these "stories" capture us (like Hegelian thesis—antithesis—synthesis). Why go from one extreme to the other, autodeconstructing whatever there could ever be, love!

CHAPTER 15

The Slave Coast

There was no wind. The *Harmattan* and *Khamsin* canceled each other out. *Zephyrus*, *Boreas*, *Eurus*, and *Notus* looked on, unable to enter Ouidah. The Vodoun danced. The syncopated rhythm beat faster, the men writhed on the ground, shoulders popping out of their joints in juddering contortions that showed muscle fibers straining, and the important people sat on the picnic table above the possessed pounding drummers. The gods dropped their sticks and pulled out long knives.

The Hogon took a big drink from a bottle of clear liquid. He sprayed the liquid out toward the ground, splattering a few of the babalawos. He handed me the bottle. I drank: grain alcohol moonshine with an acrid taste. The square gods began to slash down in dramatic circles. The men's limbs shone with a darker, more liquid black. I drank more.

"Do not be afraid, Mr. Ugli," the Hogon said, taking a machete from his waist. "When all is finished, that is the beginning." With a movement so fast that I didn't have time to react, he grabbed my wrist and sliced my exposed forearm.

• • •

Oedda's letter was unexpected, somehow sad, like a touch of surrender despite its sarcastic last paragraph. Was it even sarcasm? Or was the sarcasm sarcastic? She was the one person who could pull of earnest sarcasm. Or maybe she just couldn't stand even one letter being consistent. It felt like a goodbye, which probably meant he hadn't seen the last of her.

As usual, it was impossible to give anything she did a single interpretation without tying his brain in knots, and he wondered briefly whether maybe it was his impressions that were unreliable, or if he was the one going crazy. It felt like one of them must be, and there was no way to know which so long as they were tied to each other. He had made a friend in Buck and hadn't realized it. He'd spent years happily alone, he had walked from Siberia with only polar bears for company, free and open and alone. But now, with Buck gone, he felt unbalanced. And the worst of it was that he couldn't be sure whether it meant he was growing or shrinking.

He went to Wonderland, but the yellow sunflowers were empty. He went to the Ratio, but the wrong bouncer was working and he wasn't permitted to enter. He went to see Pooh at his tree, but no one answered his knock on the little red door. He wondered whether everyone at Harvard felt so disconnected from the world, whether they had all done the same thing to themselves and then searched for a village, a person, a night with a girl in Kevlar pantyhose, even a fiction like Pooh or some god. But he knew that it was his own doing. His Cola bottle, as Oedda had called it.

Solid ground the size of a bearskin. Like Buck's knowledge that he wants to be a poet. Nietzsche said nihilism was the most romantic, and most difficult, of all philosophies. How wrong Muzhduk had been to think he understood what that meant when Nietzsche was just one long-dead writer on a tall stack of stolen books in the shed behind their home. But maybe that was because there was no irony in Verkhoyansk. Nietzsche needed irony to come to life, and Muzhduk missed his raids on libraries throughout north-eastern Siberia.

He understood why Ugli the First had stopped walking. It was because of the bells. Verkhoyansk had bells. They rang when the Russians attacked, when someone married or died, when it was time to help build a house, or just because the mushrooms were growing after a good rain. A different ring for mushrooms than Russians, everyone understood since before they could remember learning. But in America the Italians would have different bells from the Irish, the

Filipinos different from the Fins and Verkhoyansk would get confused with Vanuatu. How could he live in the six villages in Verkhoyansk on the river Lena again after all this, looking at his own family like they were the Flintstones?

Fred Flintstone. That was what people had called him in Montreal, when he first came to North America. He didn't mind—though upon seeing the cartoon, the comparison had made no sense to him. Now he understood it, saw himself the way others had. It made him feel outside of his own head. When had that happened?

Clive and Lena didn't have solid ground either, exactly, but they had direction. He'd mocked them as "goats on an arrow," and in Verkhoyansk he would have called a man who valued his career and social circle a cabbage, not a man, but for Clive and Lena these things were clear, and he was happy for them. Lena could take off her Kevlar, and, after all, what was there in life that was not ridiculous when looked at carefully? *Credo quia absurdum est.* I believe it because it is absurd. Tertullian's saying was neither a legal maxim, nor one of Oedda's flips. It was free of the Hegelian story, free of Muzhduk's own unsettledness. It's the absurdity that makes existence possible. Why should he care that she slept with others? Except that her pussy might rot from Sclera's rigor mortis. And he had his quest, the climbing of Mount Harvard. Though still with no idea of what constituted the summit.

So when she called him late at night, he went. It wasn't natural to live without sex, without a woman in his life; so much of his connection to the world was through women—though when he spent a night in North Hall, he woke with scum on his eyes and memories of nightmares. She wanted to snuggle. The warm, peppery smell of mustard seed in her room suggested a commanding Oedda, the scent of the musk deer meant animal sex, the woody catarrh root of African Ju Ju powder declared that she was to be his psychic Law. With her room smelling of nettles, she called him Daddy in the middle of sex and his beard fell out.

"You could pretend," she said.

"Sometimes I don't feel like playing games."

"And you think that being my lover is not your fantasy game? You do not think that this kind of woman, who pushes you by shaking up your world, you do not think that this is your own fantasy? When my abominations excite the loathing of your heart you sit there and think 'fun' as if I were an amusement ride, and then when the cold angst overwhelms me you treat me as if I were some regular girlie who needs to be told 'it's okay' before you walk out the door."

"It's okay," he said, and put his boots on. He had been in his mind too long, decoding the world from light and sound waves that moved to nerve impulses and on into his mind to be sifted in accordance with concepts already there, all dependent on each other for form and substance. How much worse, it occurred to him, when the object of decoding was the Law, conveyed not through light and sound but through infinitely clunkier concepts, words, and sentences mediated by so many minds, all repeating and filtering, all deferring to mineralized precedent, afraid to say something new. It occurred to Muzhduk that there are a million shades of the color red, but only twenty-six letters in the English alphabet. And this is what he'd come for?

"The dark moon is in a few days," she said. "The moon of abominable deeds that are the condition of rebirth."

"What do you want from me?" he asked, leaning against the hotel-white door frame.

"I want you to say, 'Here I am.'"

• • •

I stared dumbly at the orange dent across my arteries. There was no cut, no blood. The Hogon and Babu Chirpy, Esq. laughed. Inside the circle, no blade would cut, they said. The drums seemed to speed up the sun. When its bottom touched the horizon and the first bats circled, the Hogon stood and the Vodoun danced faster.

A woman with a face so black it was almost blue, wearing an enormous headpiece, stepped forward. She handed the headpiece to the Hogon. It was a statue of a pregnant woman: life-sized, with breasts, head, an arched back, splayed arms, and no legs—a distended womb that narrowed into a prolapsed cervix, with a hole at its navel.

The Hogon held the statue by one arm, its belly up to the air as a drum. The woman poured blood, black against the black wood, into the navel, while the Hogon beat the statue with a stick, a beat like a POP, a high thump, resonant, wood on wood, a different rhythm from the drummers. POP, the woman poured blood into the top and the blood poured out the prolapsed cervix. POP, it fell to the azoic soil and the Red God writhed in pain behind the contorted men, to her knees, convulsing. POP, as the Hogon beat the womb.

A thought occurred to me. I asked the Hogon, "Has the trial started?"

• • •

The next morning, Muzhduk walked to the Charles, past melting snow and freezing water, as the temperature wobbled around zero, never sure what it wanted to do. There was no middle ground between freezing and melting, only half-decomposed April dog turds emerging, the frightened braggarts in their pale brown coats. *Where no one listens, people buy dogs.* Muzhduk thought of the other Fool, with a dog and a bindle, walking off the cliff. *Climbed the wrong mountain, fell off a cliff, climbed an opposite mountain, fell off another cliff. All because he didn't have a dog.* In America even the dogs are people, Fred had said, and in Verkhoyansk he'd kept Fred locked up in the basement like a dog.

He climbed on the Red Line at Kendall Square, took it to Downtown Crossing, transferred to the Green Line, took it one stop and transferred to the Blue Line. On a seat beside him a little girl said to her father, "I take the Green train to school. You take the Red train to work, Daddy." The girl and her daddy got off at the airport. Maybe to pick up Mommy.

The Red Line never connects to the Blue Line. They'd been built that way a hundred years ago to keep the students away from the prostitutes. The Red Line was still full of yuppies and students, the Green Line tourists and suits, and Blue Line proletariat and people headed to the airport. Beyond the airport, beyond the moon, was Wonderland.

In her sunflower yellow cup, the barmaid usually looked as though she also liked to think while riding the tea cups. There was a perfection to them sitting across from each other spinning that could only be destroyed by either of them saying a word. To talk or approach the yellow cup would have debased a ritual that had gradually become important to Muzhduk. Maybe because it was so far from his normal approach to life—a new, two-person version of his climbs up Mt. Baldhead. He assumed she felt the same, protecting the fragile state of not knowing just as he was.

But today she sat beside him inside the blue onion. She didn't ask why he rode the tea cups, or even say hello. Instead, she rode with him—he huge, she thin, with a long back that twisted smoothly to the outer handle. She didn't say a word.

He was reminded that her ratios were golden. She was amazed that he was even bigger close up, and that he didn't smell as bad as she'd imagined. He had a smell of cedar and fresh sweat, dirt and rain. Together they watched her yellow sunflower cup spinning empty on the other side of the tea platter.

They rode for hours, until a freezing drizzle started to fall.

He offered her his hat. "The proper thing is to offer an umbrella, but I only have a hat. I caught it myself."

"Thank you." She took the hat, smiling but looking at him like he was a book written in a slightly different language. Then she ran her fingers through it. "This is the softest thing I've ever touched. What is it?"

"Ibex mountain sheep. It's a bit magical. If you have a ring, you can pull the whole hat through the ring and it'll reform perfectly on the other side."

She lifted her hands for him to see. "No ring."

He shrugged. "I guess you could also put it on your head."

She did. "It fits! How can it fit?"

"Where I come from, this is Cinderella's slipper."

She stretched the hat, seeing that it could adjust to almost any size. "And is every girl Cinderella where you come from?"

"No. The ibex is very hard to catch. They're nearly extinct, and only live at high altitudes."

"Is that a normal thing for you, hunting nearly extinct animals?"

"Yes, I guess it was. But I had no idea they were nearly extinct. All I knew was that they were a challenge and that lots of worthy men had fallen off the mountain trying to catch them."

"Well, you're right about it being a little magical." She kept running her fingers through the fur of the hat, thoughts overwhelmed by tactile pleasure. It made her look a little silly, like she was massaging her own head or shampooing herself in the tea cup. "So if I'm Cinderella and you're the prince and this is the slipper, where's our ball? Do we get to dance?"

"I'm not much of a dancer."

"No, of course not. That wouldn't make sense anyway. It's a hat, not a dancing shoe. We need something we do with our heads. Go to the library, maybe, and be very, very quiet."

Muzhduk remembered the Scavenger Hunt. "No libraries. Libraries make my head spin."

She looked at him with big eyes and laughed. "Seriously? We've been riding these tea cups for hours. And you're here all the time. You can't tell me you don't like spinning in circles."

"I don't. I come for the moment when they stop. Or that's why I started, anyway. The first day I came here, something happened to the ride. You hadn't started riding in your sunflower cup yet, but there were a few other people on the ride. Anyway, it jammed somehow, and the operator couldn't stop it. We all spun around far longer than recommended. It went on and on, and you could see the other riders becoming anxious with the need to get off. Eventually, some manager or technician arrived and unplugged the ride, and the cups stopped suddenly. It was a very odd feeling, like my circumference kept spinning with the momentum of the tea cups while I just sat. I started coming back hoping to have that feeling again, but all it did was wash out my memory of the original experience. But by then you'd started to sit across from me, and my reasons for coming changed."

"Hm."

"And you, what do you think about while spinning in your cup?"

"Da Vinci's theory that the color of universal light is pale aqua. Let's go for a walk on the beach."

Revere Beach was directly across the street from Wonderland, so nobody ever called it by its real name. It became Wonderland too. Fishing boats tugged in and out, almost at the horizon, and the rain stopped, leaving a pattern of inch-tall white hillocks and black valleys all over the beach. Ten thousand cold little hills to climb, each slightly different from the others.

As they walked north, she smiled and the ice froth at the edge where the water met the New England shore melted. He noticed that the cool ocean air really was refreshing. They ate pizza in a fish-shack restaurant with plastic red-and-white-checkered tablecloths, a dart board, and a wood stove that the proprietor turned off, wondering aloud about the sudden thaw in the weather. Then she invited him back to her place, a tiny studio near Davis Square, two stops past Harvard on the Red Line.

Her studio was painted the color of Pooh's fur, pale blue with a touch of green.

"Does this color have a name?" he asked, pointing.

"Third World blue," she said. Light came in from a pair of French doors and from a large bathroom behind an open glass theater door. The bathroom had twelve small windows, and the whole little studio felt like air flowing around plants. Instead of a sofa, she had a rounded yellow dental chair, and pillows to lie on the floor.

A painting of an enormous fat nude woman, all yellow, covered one wall. In the hallway were several Thangka paintings, thousands of little Buddhas, women and men sitting on lotus leaves or clouds, a man with twelve arms and three faces inside a woman he held up. Her legs were wrapped around his waist, and his balls dangled below her ass.

Muzhduk pointed to it and said, "Cakrasamvara Tantra?"

She looked surprised. "Are you a Buddhist?"

"No. I just like sex. Are you?"

"A Buddhist? No. But I like Thangka paintings."

"And sex?"

"Of course. With the right man."

"Someone told me that Tantra was about enlightenment through sex and meat, so I thought I'd like it."

"I've never heard about the meat, and I've read *Tantra for Dummies*."

Muzhduk moved the hinged arm of the dental chair and sat in it sideways. "Nothing there about 'the five forbidden things'?"

"Those are for people who need to shake off some spiritual pride. Having an idea of yourself as 'holy' closes you up."

"Some people say that having any idea of yourself closes you up."

"Hm. Probably true. I'm all for keeping an open mind." She sat beside him, curvy despite their flat conversation. "Just not so open that your brains fall out."

He laughed. "Where I come from, we avoid thinking about ourselves in an introspective way. Except on mountain tops. The idea is that if you climb all the way up there, then it's for a real purpose, there's a problem to solve. Not just to wallow in self-awareness, magnifying tiny problems by giving them mental attention." Saying this out loud made him think about himself in an introspective way—if Harvard was all self-awareness all the time and Oedda all awareness and no self, was Verkhoyansk all self and no awareness? Or were mountain tops and quests enough of a safety valve?

"I've known a lot of people who aren't self-aware. They're usually jerks."

"And if you asked them if they're aware?"

"Probably insist they are."

"Exactly." He grinned, and she laughed despite herself.

They drank tea for hours, shifting from the dental chair to the pillows. The impression he'd had of her at the Ratio Pub, when she'd refused to make him a martini, had been completely wrong. There he'd thought she was square, but she was the opposite. Though opposite was the wrong word, unless orange can be said to be the opposite of a square.

"That pub always gives everyone the wrong impression of anyone in there," she said when he told her. "Because of the peculiar dryness of the air."

They talked late into the night, getting less awkward. Finally, he moved to kiss her. She stopped him.

"Can I ask you something?" asked Peggy.

"Sure."

"Have you ever climbed Mount Everest?"

She was looking at him as though she knew the question was startling. "No."

"Have you wanted to?"

"Is it obvious?"

"There's a certain type of person who'd want to."

"What exactly are you asking me?"

"Why are you here? At Harvard, not in my apartment. I know why you're in my apartment."

So he told her about Verkhoyansk and his family and the Dull-Boulder Throw and John the Attorney. She interrupted him and told him to go vomit.

"What?"

"Go vomit."

He didn't understand, but went to the bathroom and threw up. It left a taste in his mouth.

"Why did I just do that?"

"It's sweet that you did it without knowing why."

"Was this a test?" *Maybe all women here are like Oedda,* he thought.

"No. Just that I realized I liked you." She took a little breath. "I put cupric sulphide in the tea."

"I don't know anything about chemistry." Librarians in Siberia were afraid of improvised explosives. "Is that a poison?"

"No. Well, not unless I got the dose very wrong. All it would've done is turn your skin blue. I thought if I turned you into a giant Smurf I'd feel better. I told you I was no Buddha." Some of the Buddhas on her walls were blue, including the twelve-armed man with the dangling balls. "Because of my passport I got here late, and the creepy old couple at the registrar's office told me my name'd been changed to Muzhduk the Ugli the Fourth, and that I'd already picked up my admissions packet. I was surprised. So I tracked you down, to get revenge, or find out who you were, or I don't know what. Turn you blue, I guess."

"Turn me blue as revenge? Is that like giving me a bottle of champagne?"

She frowned, unsure what he meant.

"That's why I kept seeing you around campus. And why you rode the tea cups?"

"Yes. And other times, when you didn't notice. I saw you putting money into expired meters—"

"I don't mind being stalked."

"I wasn't stalking!"

"Too bad. When you're 300 pounds, life gets boring that way. It's kind of nice to have someone follow you into a dark alley—"

"I didn't—"

"But all that so you could turn me blue?"

She smiled and gave him a barely perceptible shrug. "I like colors."

"I've noticed. But..." he paused to piece together why that made no sense, "you had a perfect score."

"And that means I shouldn't live my life based on colors? How's that any worse than living a life based on logic? The LSAT's a joke. It's just a puzzle. It's silly."

Muzhduk thought about this. He'd never thought about color

in this way. "So how does that work in practice? Other than turning people blue?"

"How does it work in practice to want to climb the highest mountain?"

"It made me come here and take your place."

"I went to the Sahara because it's named after a color. And what I saw there made me come here. But you're right, the LSAT's not just a joke. That's another reason I put those Thangka paintings up. Mahayana Buddhists believe wisdom and compassion are two separate wings, and you need both to fly."

"Logic and empathy," Muzhduk said, remembering his moot court.

"Logic and color. I'm a painter, not a Buddhist."

"Precision and the soul."

"Now you're making fun of me."

"No." Muzhduk paused. He tried to imagine what it would feel like to come all the way here and find out his spot was taken and his name changed. If he'd been in her shoes, he'd probably throw the person, not turn him blue. "So your name really is Muzhduk the Ugli the Fourth?" he asked.

She laughed. "Peggy Roundtree. Nice to meet you." She held out her hand to shake. He shook it, then gently pulled her back down to the pillows. He liked touching her, the way her skin felt, even on her hands, everywhere.

"But officially?"

She glared at him, joking. "I've sent in the forms to have it changed back."

"But if we got married before the bureaucrats finish, the announcement would be—"

"Ugly."

The phone rang. At first they ignored it, but it kept ringing until the mood was broken. Peggy answered it. She said 'yes' once, listened, and 'yes' again.

"It was for you," she said. "Someone named Oedda. She said you have to come home right away."

• • •

I asked again, "Has the trial started?"

The sun had set, though the square at the crossroads was still bright. There were five dancing rectangles. After a thousand drumbeats there were four. Then three, and finally two: the Green and Red Vodoun. Gradually, the crowd chose sides. Some danced against the Green, some against the Red. It went on for hours, until finally the Hogon yelled something, waking me from a half-sleep at the same time as both Vodoun collapsed into the dirt. Everyone looked exhausted, including the Hogon and the babalawos. People leaned against trees where they could, or just sat on the ground. Others had disappeared behind the great baobab. The womb statue was gone.

The Red rectangle slowly stood, turned towards us, and began to dance again, stomping the ground to keep the beat of the now-silent drums. Men got back up, some only on their knees, swaying and bleeding. The Hogon whipped the ground. A few drummers drummed, others drummed in counterpoint. An antiphony formed, two sides again, except now it was Vodoun against Hogon.

One of the men on the ground, with his arms contorted behind his head and long drops of blood dripping from him, began to whistle at me. Others joined him, taunting me as if I were one of the rectangles. I stood, unsure of what to do. It seemed almost a relief for everyone to ignore the battle between the Hogon and the Red Vodoun, to focus their energy at the new White Vodoun. I saw the Green rectangle crawling towards the baobab tree.

The music and acrid grainy moonshine were disorienting as the crowd screamed in my face. We passed by two of the men lying still on the ground. They were dead. The Red rectangle was only a foot from the Hogon when I saw him fall: she ripped his hood from the Hogon's head, but he still struggled. I tried to move in for a better look, but the crowd pressed me away from the picnic table.

Suddenly I was beside Amadou. Without looking at me, he said, "If a white woman from the far North becomes Hogon, it will turn the world upside down."

I didn't understand how this worked. Can a Vodoun become the Hogon? I asked, "Is the Red Vodoun white?"

"Everything is upside down."

"Flippable. Everything is flippable. If we're talking about the same woman, that is her motto. She is named after this town. Or this town is named after her. With her there's no difference. She's a postmodernist."

"A what?"

"A witch."

It didn't seem possible that Oedda was really here. The crowd swarmed and pushed me away from the center of the intersection, towards the large baobab and the pile of garbage behind it. I remembered Peggy's story from her night with the Goat People, about the white powder and the beetle and the village separated by string into squares with a crucible of burning coal in each square, and the music beat still, and time unraveled and no longer moved forward at the funny rate of one second per second.

• • •

"Come home?" Muzhduk repeated. "What home?" He took the phone, but Oedda had hung up. He tried calling back, but nobody picked up. He wondered how she had gotten Peggy's number, how she'd known where he was.

"She sounded a bit.... You should go check."

"No I shouldn't."

Peggy looked at him skeptically, then said, "She didn't sound okay."

Muzhduk nodded. "In that case, I should go check." They both paused awkwardly. "But you and I should stop spinning and meet directly."

She smiled. "Have you seen the fog?"

"That's all I see."

"The Fogg Museum. They have a Caravaggio exhibit visiting from the Uffizi. There's some conference on Law and Religion, so they borrowed Caravaggio's *Sacrifice of Isaac*. I'd like to go see it. Maybe we could go."

"Yes. I'd like that." Muzhduk knew about the conference. Oedda was one of the speakers. But he hadn't known of the exhibit, though The Fogg was Harvard's museum. He left Peggy's studio, shaking his head at himself.

As he approached North Hall, warm thoughts of Peggy turned cold.

• • •

The crowd pressed in from all sides, increasingly aggressive. People slapped their flip-flops inches from my face. The only way out was up the mountain of garbage behind the baobab, forming a talus against an old wall. At the top sat Hanuman, along with several goats. But Amadou hadn't brought the monkey down to Ouidah with him. Another monkey, then, it must have been—though it seemed difficult to make a mistake about it.

Déjà vu, prolepsis, all of it.

The drums were further away now, in the center of the intersection, but they seemed louder in their thumping repetition. Maybe this giant tree had its own acoustics, and the Hogon's moonshine had more than alcohol in it. I wondered whether the tree felt big. People thought I was big, but I felt tiny now. I needed to get away from those drums. *I can climb the mountain of garbage*, I thought.

• • •

Muzhduk knocked on Oedda's door, annoyed until he saw her face—she looked sick, really sick. He pushed the door open as she disappeared into the complete darkness of the room.

New heavy curtains were drawn across the windows and the aroma of heavily narcotic thorn-apple made the air almost unbreathable. He stood, trying to accustom his eyes. "Why's it so dark?"

Hostile fluorescent lights shot on, blinding enough to hurt. Oedda had changed the lights along with the curtains. It took seconds before he could squint his eyes open, while she scratched something on the floor in front of him, then leaned against her bed and nearly collapsed, clearly exhausted. She seemed everywhere, as a visual afterglow, panting for breath. When he could finally see, he found himself surrounded by a black circle with a triangle interior. On impulse, he squatted and touched it. It was sticky. "Is this blood?"

"Yes."

"Whose?"

"Mine and not mine."

Muzhduk stood speechless. Oedda began to chant. He walked towards her, but as he neared the line on the ground, she and the line and the rest of the room seemed to recede.

Oedda broke from her chanting. "Do you know Greenlanders are not permitted to contemplate the moon for long?"

"I didn't know."

"It's like your Siberian valleys, but more insightful. The lunar condition is equivalent to the human condition," she said. Her voice was weak, as though she was in a trance, or had lost a lot of blood, or both. "Only that which is beyond the moon can transcend becoming."

"I'm going to call a doctor."

"No."

"If I understand right, you just gave yourself an abortion. You need a doctor."

"Do you see the secret?"

"Which secret, Oedda?"

"Unheimlich," she said. "Uncanny, unholy, unhomely. *Heim* means home, and *heimlich* means secret, and *unheimlich* means the uncanny. That's all I ever wanted from you: one word. I failed Lena because she was right. You could never see anyone else's story."

She was so pale, it made Muzhduk ache. Her lips were no longer red, and her eyes were grey, washed out of all their green. She chilled the room.

"The devil needs souls because he's cold," he said absently, mostly to himself.

"And so?" Oedda stared. Their eyes locked.

He was breathing in too much of the thorn-apple: jimson weed, datura, loco weed, angel's trumpet, devil's trumpet, mad hatter, crazy tea, zombie cucumber. It was starting to make him hallucinate. "And so, you are the Law," he said, his own voice distant already.

"But not your Law." She laughed. "Choronzon, Maker of Form, *Zazas, Zazas, Nasatanada, Zazas.*" She went to her knees, and Muzhduk nearly went to her. "It doesn't help to object, to be a rebel. To fight the Law is to be infected by it. No, there is no fighting it, only mastery and servitude, and they are both difficult. You are right, I am the Law. You claim you want to fight it, but your way of doing so is merely an opening for it to reach us. Fool. Love. I cannot live like this."

Muzhduk said nothing. He stood in his pentagram, unable to think of anything to say that could possibly make sense. He felt sorry for Oedda.

She caught her breath, determined to continue. She was thin again, waify, like on the library steps. She pointed to the circle. "This is your Cola bottle." Then she smiled and winced from pain. "I realized the dangers. But that is the only way to fight It—offering ourselves up to the Other, to each other, without justifications. Absolute absolution from the social and its long arm, the Law." She took a breath. "Like the killing of a male child of perfect innocence."

"There was no child yet."

"If I decide it's a child, then it's a child! Anyway, why assume I was talking about my… baby. You always assume. You balance me against objective norms, as if my advice were the same as that of some bartender. You are part of Them and you have chained me down with you."

"Let me take you to the hospital."

"Ah, the hospital. You could have been Prometheus, Satan, Superman, Trickster. Instead you can take me to the hospital. Maybe they can give me a pill. What am I doing here?"

He wanted do give her something, but had no idea what would help. "Fighting the good fight, against Law becoming God?"

"Fighting is your thing. So stupid and naïve. I have tried and tried to show you that the falseness of a judgment is not a valid objection to a judgment. That false judgments are the most indispensable to man's survival. That in an hour-long film there are 27 minutes of complete darkness, of space between film frames. I wanted it all, without the irony, the *Book of Lies* and the *Book of the Law*. Two wings, together they could fly above all the garbage, the mountains of garbage everywhere, and the stupid goats climbing it."

"I don't understand," Muzhduk said. He could hear drums. It made no sense, but his logic couldn't shake the rhythm and the rhythm took away time, and without time there was no logic. He was dizzy now, and having difficulty in following. "What are you talking about?"

"I'm not talking about anything!" she shouted. "All the interesting questions only come when you are not talking. It is who I am. Nothing. Without even a name. That is what my colleagues will say and they will be right. Ethically, I have no place here—they would say if they understood ethics. My project is failed. My call has not been answered."

"What *call*?" Muzhduk's back hurt from standing in the circle.

"What call?" She drifted off and he thought she was losing consciousness. But then she turned hard again. "I will not demean myself further. Your question is the final proof that I have failed. My work is my being, and the fact that nobody, not even you has answered my call proves that there is no call to Being. Sclera was right, there is only procedure, process, form. You are no longer the hero in your own story, and I have killed a child for you. My Ugli the Nothing."

"You didn't kill a child! I mean, it wasn't a child yet— Leave me out of it!"

"Coward! I killed it for you."

"This is horrible. And ridiculous, Oedda. A pentagram?" Somehow the Tantra and Tarot and numerology had all seemed sophisticated when they came from her, a metaphorical shift outside their regular New Age crassness. They'd even had undertones of insightfulness, symbolic hints of something underneath too big to hold in one thought, but possible to touch, so long as one didn't try to grasp. But standing inside the pentagram shone a new light on her mysticism. The pentagram wasn't just ridiculous, it pulled him out of whatever trance she'd woven over him, cheapening all their past conversations. "You can't really believe this stuff. It was supposed to be a game, a different language to open up other possibilities, but not real. Not like this."

"Still you think there is a difference. A game would never have been enough for you. You are a people eater. If I had been some simple farm girl from Finland who liked to read and somehow picked up a couple of doctorates in the process, you would have become bored and left me. If it had been just a game, you would have understood and left me. No, I told you, the game only counts if you play *mit heiligem Ernst*. Choronzon, come to me! I call on you now! Come and I will tell you my name!"

A cold shudder went through Muzhduk, as though his shadow had turned on him. Two Muzhduks stood overlapped. *Am I Crowley's devil?* one of them asked.

Oedda, exhausted, tried to sit up from her bed as she watched

Muzhduk turn into a handsome man, speaking softly to her. He flattered her, told her she was beautiful, asked permission to put his head under her feet. He said, "Here I am." He was naked, begging, he was thirsty, please would she give him some water. He sung her a song, begged her to swim across the river. She hesitated, unsure what she had done—the demon was supposed to take her and the world; the circle and triangle were meant to protect Muzhduk. Or was it the other way around after all? She couldn't remember. It really didn't matter either way, but it was surprising. And if he was thirsty, it was the least she could do. But he was unaware, like an animal, raw salmon flesh. He began to swing his hairy fists, the source of his identity, around and around, as if he would punch his way out of the circle, screaming about bouncers and police and villages and countries and men who hid behind numbers and words and women who preferred soft sensitive men or for some other reason didn't fuck him and all those who told him what to do—blustering that he was Will, that he would unify Law and Will to match her Law and Lie. This was what she had been leading up to, what she wanted. If she still wanted it, she should act, and yet she was so weak, so dizzy. She had given up too much of her own blood. She was half inside him now and saw the distant part of him, the part that kept remembering Buck's poem: *I borrowed will from lies and my feet/ Walked as long as I could/ Kept up unspoiled.* Yes, that's what confused her. She had forgotten that Choronzon was already in her. She was Choronzon, and now she was almost Muzhduk.

Then Muzhduk ripped the carpet. Old, beige Motel 6 carpet. She hadn't thought of him going through the floor. But he didn't go through the floor; he picked up a swathe and placed it over the blood lines of the circle. Or maybe he just stepped forward and picked her up by the neck. She had once told him that sooner or later he would throw her through the wall and now her prediction would come true. She smiled as he threw her. She flew backwards, but landed on the bed. He always tried to avoid her predictions, but yes, she still had him, he was still hers. The bed was even better than the wall. Both were passions, anger and lust becoming the same. The bed did not mean that he was in control. It would hurt terribly, she had done her body damage. Perhaps she would feel it. He would fill her, with blood and semen and memories.

"If it had been ours, perhaps I would not have sacrificed it," she said, to her own surprise. What was wrong with her? No, she was just shocking him. Of course she would have sacrificed it. And Muzhduk would not have given her a child. Ever. He was on an amusement park ride. That was all. His face was enraged, unchanged.

"Or perhaps it was," she added, before he picked up one of her legs and bit down into her big toe. She had not expected that. His teeth were sharp, and though it felt as if he'd reached the bone, only a drop of blood appeared. Then he turned around, lifted the phone, dialed 911, spoke her address into the receiver, and walked out the door.

"Perhaps it was ours!" she screamed after him.

CHAPTER 16

Everest

There is a monastery behind me called Rongbuk. Fifty-two hundred meters altitude. Base Camp is six kilometers away—two or three hours, up here. I need a walk to clear my headache, to climb Everest instead of Harvard.

I can't smell any of the garbage anymore. I don't see the baobab tree or the Hogon or the Vodoun. There are no butterflies, not enough air for them to beat against. I tell the others to go ahead. "None of us will fall without the others," I say, though there's nobody else and nowhere to fall.

I'm only going up to Base Camp, after all, and that's just a matter of altitude. One step in front of the other. No balance up here, no peripheral vision, no sign that says, "Wrong Mountain." Too late now: keep walking. I was supposed to rescue her, and now can't even get up to the starting point. An American expedition is climbing the north face; they must have a Gamow bag. I can go in the bag, equalize pressure. I only have to make it up this hill. Maybe I should bring a hyperbaric chamber to Verkhoyansk, bring the mountain to the valley and save future generations all that walking. I crawl up the hill on all fours. Just to get to Base Camp. Not even the top of Everest. And Everest isn't even a real mountain, just the highest. Let a Sherpa put you in a basket and pull.

The garbage hill is much harder. Why don't people clean up

after themselves?

It's going down that kills you, with garbage and frozen human bodies left behind. One in three don't make it down. My skull has become an altimeter, a vise that tightens with each step up. I make it to the top of the hill on hands and knees, but there is no Base Camp. It's not there. Everest doesn't care. I lean against a boulder, warm, and almost soft. My headache is gone.

• • •

Peggy waited for Muzhduk on the Roman steps of the Fogg. Her hair was up in a ponytail, and it swung prettily around when she saw him. Muzhduk took her hand as hello and they walked up the steps, past the security gate and into an internal Florentine courtyard, transplanted brick by brick from Italy. "I had a crazy night."

"With your girlfriend? Oedda?"

"My…I don't know what she is." They crossed a collection of Byzantine art, with its floating faces, then through a room of African masks. Muzhduk stopped in front of a full body mask, a sort of red rectangle. The little placard read, "Egungun Vodoun, Fon of Dahomey, Benin."

In the next room hung a baby-faced sphinx, a giantess with dark wide eyes, white skin, towering above a heap of bloody corpses. Gustav Adolf Mossa's *She*.

"Do you hear drums?" he asked Peggy. "I've been hearing drums since last night."

"Mossa couldn't look at love except in terms of death," she said by way of response.

Muzhduk looked at her. Life. Death. Love. Egungun Vodoun. It all had a rhythm, but he wasn't a rhythmic person. "Do you want your spot back?" he asked suddenly. "It's really yours, and our names are the same. You'd be starting off with—"

"If I still want it, I'll go next year, under my own name."

"Really—"

"Let's look." She pulled him into a dark room. Waiting for their eyes, he could feel every soft bump on her palm, every cushioned pad from painting and sculpting and well digging.

"The light damages them," Peggy said as they were starting to make out the shapes on the walls. "Especially some of the old frescoes they want to preserve, so they keep the lights low."

"So to preserve them perfectly, they'd have to make them impossible to see?"

"Some of the damage is done by air, but most is from light."

"It's an inverse function. As you increase the preservation, you decrease the point of the painting."

She nodded. "Like pouring concrete on a flower."

"Kafka said the meaning of life is that it ends." He stopped, staring up at the ceiling, while Peggy continued out of the dark fresco room. "That's it!"

He caught up with her at the central painting of the exhibit, oblivious to *The Sacrifice of Isaac*. "I know what to do about the library! About Sclera."

"I thought you'd like Caravaggio," Peggy said. "He painted himself as Bacchus and as Goliath. He beat up his clients and spent his last four years in exile for killing someone."

Muzhduk finally noticed the painting. Abraham's knife hung in the air. The knife, then Abraham, who held down Isaac, knife in hand, then the Angel stopping him. In the background, the sky looked like dawn was about to rise or dusk had just fallen. The painting took place on a mountain, though the mountain was reflected into the background. Something was about to begin, or had just finished.

"What a forehead," Muzhduk said, pulled into the grizzled folds above Abraham's knife.

• • •

The mountains are beautiful, surrounded by boulders. Everest is evil, brooding.

At Harvard I can learn what's wrong with the wall. In Africa I can learn why the man sat beside it. But I can't quite piece it together, not with my mountain-sickness tunnel vision or the malaria or the thorn-apple or the Hogon's moonshine. Only that which is beyond the moonshine can transcend becoming and life is not a jigsaw puzzle. It's just big. *Besides, I'm not even on Everest.* I gave up on a garbage mound under a baobab tree.

I understand why introspection is only safe on the peak. After the peak, it doesn't matter what the mountain's made of. On the way down, man is stronger than gravity and ready to climb the next hill. But consciousness on the way up is torture. Most of it is made up of absences, but those places that aren't holes, those were…significant. That's the closest word. Saving Pooh's tree. Peggy's pupils glistening black in the library, inches away. My conversations with Fred the Political Officer. My family. I can only see directly in the center now: a moving speck has come around a curve in the path with a white towel around its head and another covering its mouth. Go away, mime.

• • •

Muzhduk looked at Abraham, Isaac, the Archangel Michael, Isaac, ram, Isaac. Each time his eyes stopped on Isaac, where the light glared, and through the boy back at himself. From Isaac's view, he saw Abraham's grizzled brow. It was the most rendered, with the sharpest lines. Abraham was the one being enlightened, but it was Isaac who pulled Muzhduk into the painting.

Peggy noticed. "You can understand Abraham, but not forgive him." The Angel and Isaac looked alike, baby-faced and idealized. Abraham's hands were huge, almost orange, and hard. He could've been a Verkhoyansk chief. Everything was frozen, no crickets were chirping, the moment of decision had already come. In his heart Abraham had already killed his son.

Muzhduk didn't want to look at Isaac. Or the ram, or Michael. He didn't feel responsible for Oedda's psychotic homemade abortion. Or was Lena right, was he responsible for everything? In the endless folds of that forehead, Abraham seemed to testify for finite man's ability to come to terms with the infinite, to fold God Himself into the space-time of dimensions wrapped up within his forehead, where a moment can span eternity. Maybe *that* was the true nature of God's strange test. How had Abraham ever passed a test like that?

• • •

The Japanese mime sets me down, pulls out a camera, and takes a picture. *What an asshole*, I think, then laugh. He nods. Mimes that I have to climb down myself, and turns to go back up Everest. I stumble downwards, lighter with each step, wondering when the Gamow bag will come from Base Camp. It doesn't. I arrive at Rongbuk as dusk is falling. The monastery is on another small hill. Any movement upward hurts. I crawl along the man-made road, the path of least resistance. My head pounds with every inch in elevation, even though this is already lower than where I set myself down to die. But it's still a hill. So much lower than Everest. But still a hill to climb.

Eventually I make it to Rongbuk and up the four steps, an hour each, and crawl to my goatskin pack. I grab a handful of big white Diamox pills and swallow them. They don't help, but I feel better being in Rongbuk. Oedda comes in, offers me a cure in exchange for my sleeping bag. I beg her to bring the cure, puzzled, confused about her presence. It's another Diamox pill. She sits on my bed and smiles. Diamox doesn't really cure mountain sickness, not directly. It just makes you pee more, and peeing balances your pH, and a proper pH stops your blood from leaking into your brain. Peeing cures mountain sickness. *Credo quia absurdum est.*

She is gone. The mime is back. He mimes that Amadou and his sister stayed at Base Camp, maybe headed up. "Is Oedda his sister?" I ask.

Two Tibetan men, one young, one old, sit on my bed and smoke cigarettes. I can't breathe. There is no oxygen up here. I must be hallucinating.

• • •

"Peggy, thank you. There's something I need to do now."

Muzhduk quickly explained his need to destroy the library. And how he planned to go further than Sclera expected.

"There's no way we can get all that done in one night," Peggy said. "They'll catch us when the library opens."

Us.

"We have time. Like Abraham had time, but only for a moment."

They spent the rest of the day getting supplies and hiding them among books that had never been opened, old books that needed their pages cut with a knife and even two bound in human skin: Arsene Houssaye's *Des destinees de l'ame* (On the destiny of the soul), and Juan Gutiérrez' *Practicarum quaestionum circa leges* (Questions about the practical law). *Practicarum quaestionum* had an inscription on its last page that read, "The bynding of this booke is all that remains of my dear friende Jonas Wright, who was flayed alive by the Wavuma on the Fourth Day of August, 1632. King Mbesa did give me the book, it being one of poore Jonas chiefe possessions, together with ample of his skin to bynd it. Requiescat in pace."

• • •

"I thought you said he ate Claude's fufu," a female voice said.

"He did," a male answered.

• • •

No one noticed for a week. In the end it was discovered by a visitor, a nostalgic alumnus there for the Law & Religion conference, who decided to spend the morning of May 1st in Langdell Library. When he tried to take a book off the shelf, it wouldn't budge. He tried another book, but this one also didn't budge. The librarian was called over and she also tried to pull a book off the shelf, and couldn't. She could open the books sitting on tables, but not lift them off. They were glued to the tables by their spines.

Soon everyone was trying to pull books off the shelves or lift them off tables. People stood shoulder to shoulder, pulling on books that wouldn't budge. To avoid each other's eyes, they looked upwards and noticed a mural of Abraham and Isaac on the previously pristine ceiling. But Abraham was missing an arm from the elbow down, a leg from the hip, and the other leg from the knee down. The Angel Michael was similarly amputated, as was the ram. Isaac had only one arm left, and Abraham was in the process of severing its shoulder sinews with a surgical scalpel. Everyone craned their neck past the wall slogans to the ceiling, where no one had looked in years.

Meanwhile, Muzhduk sat at the other end of the great ivy-shadowed building. He ate a vegetable roll-up—Harvard's conference food—while a very old professor with a severe comb-over intoned along with the faint, distant drums that "Amendments from the United States Bill of Rights should be just as much articles of export as the products of our farms, factories, and financial services." He said it would decrease world terrorism. Others disagreed and argued about how to re-appropriate the term "Third World." Someone quoted Gandhi's saying that if God wants a good reception among the poor, He'd better come as a loaf of bread. Someone else said that Baltimore is the Third World, microlending is the key, and Corpa-Cola is available in over two hundred countries. The previous person insisted that the U.S. spends more on its military than the rest of the world combined, but has only the forty-second lowest child mortality rate. An old woman said that the U.S. would export its legal and political institutions, holding their epistemic character as the totality, fetishizing the written constitution as the repository of knowledge, while it lies in the *tekhne* of the Supreme Court interpretations, which must pretend that nothing in the Constitution is changing and that systems of knowledge are incommensurable. In the end, the Third World scholars were incomprehensible in Sclera's classroom. Before giving way to the Law & Religion conference, the group issued a manifesto.

As the scholars crowded out for more vegetable roll-ups before the next plenary, Sclera squeezed between desks to seat #129 and whispered harshly, "What did you do to the library?" He was clearly unaccustomed to speaking in a low voice.

"I destroyed the books."

"You did not destroy them, you preserved them for all time!"

"I thought the whole point of Law is to make society's mistakes permanent."

"Nonsense."

"If its books are preserved, unchanging forever, then Law has achieved perfection. Which means that it is dead. And teaching a dead thing, Harvard will die. It is a logic game."

"I don't want that! I want it to be immortal, a soul without dependence on a body."

"A soul without a body is the definition of death. But we have a contract, professor, and I have fulfilled my end. So long as you still believe words have meaning."

"And you?" Sclera and Muzhduk looked up at the same time, into Oedda's washed-out green eyes. She seemed to be holding herself in tighter than ever. "What do you believe?"

"Law is *not* a matter of belief!" interrupted Sclera. "Words are manifestations of will."

"Words are nothing. I have seen it." She looked anemic, bloodless, though she seemed to have mostly recovered, otherwise.

"Are you okay?" asked Muzhduk.

"Answer my question without insulting me."

"You want an answer?" Muzhduk asked, genuinely surprised. "I don't have one. Maybe all words have a shadow or a color, something that follows them. Like birds singing."

"Look here," she said to Sclera, with barely a moment's hesitation. "We have a One-L lecturing us about hermeneutics. What a perfectly wonderful synthe—" She cut herself off as she realized that the audience for the Law & Religion conference had already entered the room and was listening. Everyone suddenly looked embarrassed while Sclera and Oedda took their seats at the table in front.

CHAPTER 17

The Sacrifice

> And he said, Take now thy son, thine only [son] Isaac, whom thou lovest, and get thee into the land of Moriah and offer him there for a burnt offering upon one of the mountains which I will tell thee of.
>
> And Abraham stretched forth his hand, and took the knife to slay his son. And the angel of the LORD called unto him out of heaven, and said, Abraham, Abraham: and he said, Here [am] I.
>
> By myself have I sworn, saith the LORD, for because thou hast done this thing, and hast not withheld thy son, thine only [son]...I will multiply thy seed as the stars of the heaven, and as the sand which [is] upon the sea shore; and thy seed shall possess the gate of his enemies... because thou hast obeyed my voice.
>
> Genesis 22:2, 10–11, 16–18

Sclera and Oedda were seated on opposite ends of the panel. Beside Sclera sat an Idealist, followed by a Realist, Torts professor Synovia, a Narrativist, and finally Oedda.

The panel stipulated that if you assume God is a legal structure, then, like the Preamble to the Law of the Sea Treaty, He is "as broad as space and as long as time." To narrow this theme down and in honor of the Caravaggio in the Fogg, they agreed to focus on the parable of Abraham and Isaac, handing out copies of Genesis 22, King James Version.

Sclera opened the discussion with a formal analysis of Chapter 22, verse 2: *And he said, Take now thy son, thine only son Isaac, whom thou lovest, and get thee into the land of Moriah; and offer him there for a burnt offering upon one of the mountains which I will tell thee of.*

"God, the second party to the contract, said in 22.2, "*offer* him there for a burnt *offering.*" The fact that God does not say "sacrifice him for a burnt sacrifice" implies that God will not accept the offering. An "offer" is only half of a sacrifice. An acceptance is still needed. God, who chooses his words perfectly, said "offer," not "sacrifice;" *ergo*, there was never any risk to Isaac. In the alternative, if God did mean Isaac to be sacrificed, then the parable presents a choice-of-law issue: human morality and God's commandments versus God's direct words."

Sclera showed how such a problem was resolved by a unifying Rule of Procedure: that direct divine revelation trumps codified text.

The Idealist, a bearded big-bellied professor of jurisprudence who used the expression "the nomological circle" the way Santa Claus used "ho ho ho," attacked Sclera's first argument by pointing out that in 22.13, God used the word "offer" for the sacrifice of the ram: *And Abraham lifted up his eyes, and looked, and behold behind him a ram caught in a thicket by his horns: and Abraham went and took the ram, and offered him up for a burnt offering in the stead of his son.* Thus, the word had to be synonymous with sacrifice. Sclera leapt to say that whereas in 22.2 God was speaking directly, in 22.13 it was merely the narrator of the parable who used the word "offer," mimicking God's earlier statement in order to stress the *substitution* of ram for boy. Since it was not God or His legal representative, the Angel, who spoke, the use of the word "offer" in 22.13 cannot be instructive as to the meaning of the word "offer" in 22.2, where a different being, God, was using the word.

The Idealist laughed, arguing with a smile that there was no overarching rule to reconcile "thou shalt not kill" with "obey the Lord" when the two clashed, and twisting the meanings of words was insufficient. Instead, there is only an Ideal of a particular type of God: terrible yet fair and benevolent, represented here by the ultimate symbol of Idealism, the Angel. Sclera jumped in again to say he hoped the Idealist was referring to the pre-Moses "thou shalt not kill" rather than the Ten Commandments' "thou shalt not kill," since the latter did not yet exist in Abraham's time. The Idealist said the very nature of God implied it and the writing-down of the commandments was just a way of imperfectly communicating God's nature to us.

It was the Realist's turn. She was a well-liked professor who invariably wore a leather jacket to class, called herself a communist, and was married to an Italian duke. Muzhduk had heard rumors from Oedda about wild parties where Italian aristocracy mingled with card-carrying Marxists. She said that both Sclera and the Idealist were "full of shit."

"The parable is simply an expression of dominant power against those without power," she said. "The transcendental nonsense of Law, whether mortal or divine, is an application of that power. Isaac, the weakest, has no say in the story except to meekly ask, "Where is the lamb for the burnt offering?" Along with the power asymmetry there is an information imbalance, as Isaac is blind to the fact that he is the lamb. When Isaac is bound and laid upon the altar, he does not utter a word—he is the subaltern who cannot speak. Abraham, second as a father figure only to God himself, is simply the symbol and instrument of an absolute and arbitrary patriarchy that adjusts its laws at the whims of its power. "Thou shalt not kill" is the law only so long as it maintains the *status quo ante* of the powers that control all the nonviolent levers of society; yet even as it flexes, flows, and contradicts itself in the service of power, Law maintains its divinity."

The Realist continued. "The story shows how the Law prevents the Isaacs of the world—the proletarian, the feminine, the minor—from speaking against power. God does not present reasons beyond "I, the Law, say so." And, when Abraham has to justify his actions, he abdicates responsibility to the higher Law, which he cannot understand: "God will provide himself a lamb for a burnt offering." Still today we hear police, judges, and politicians justifying their actions with the simple deflection of responsibility: "It's the Law." There is a purity in this parable that reveals the shell-game between Law and Power: Law is that which pleases the Lord."

Synovia came next, applying economics reasoning to the parable. "Because Abraham was willing to subsume his own love and morality to that of the Law, huge efficiency gains were made and society progressed: "for because thou hast done this thing...I will multiply thy seed..." The Law can act only through the arms of its citizens, thus it must restructure their incentives—through prison, fines, or withholding divine grace—such that the citizens themselves choose to make the hard decisions; in this case the potential sacrifice of one person in order to secure the life and safety of the multitudes. The parable is remarkable in that it avoids the *sunk-cost fallacy* and shows a clear awareness of opportunity costs and present-value calculations. It is irrelevant that the multitudes have not yet been born and that Isaac is already alive. From a rational perspective, there can be no distinction between act and omission. Just multiply the benefit to society from these multitudes by the probability of this being the result of Isaac's sacrifice, discounted for the interest rate, which here would have to be implied from the average life expectancy, labor productivity within economic structures such as agriculture, probability of wars, and so on. Clearly, God is an economist."

Next spake the Narrativist. He said Law was a story. "As with any such forward-moving illusion, the questions that must be asked are 'Who is telling the story?' and 'Which stories get to be told?' What if there were dozens of other Abrahams or Ibrahims who didn't get to tell their story, who thought God was telling them to murder their sons, who did so, and whom God didn't stop, didn't punish or reward? Or perhaps Abraham could have told God to go climb a tree, and God would have respected his morality. But it seems that Abraham too, fell victim to the Inevitability Argument: that if I don't do this, the entire religious order will collapse. Compare Abraham to Judge Riffin in the pre-Civil War case *North Carolina v. Mann*, an appeals decision reversing a five-dollar fine for shooting a slave. Riffin overturned the fine, complaining the whole time about 'the struggle in the judge's own breast between the feelings of the man and the duty of the magistrate.' He wrote that 'as a principle of moral right, every person must repudiate it,' and that 'the most stupid must feel and know' that there is nothing natural about slavery. But he concludes that 'It is useless however, to complain of things inherent in our political state'—convinced that if a judge opposes the Law then the entire social order will collapse. Abraham is Judge Riffin, the Law is God, and we continue to repeat these stories. Professor Synovia's description of the multitudes only makes sense with an implied notion of progress—that more is better and that these multitudes would not have been spawned had it not been for Abraham's actions. Yes, the text says so, but the text itself is the embodiment of this false narrative, which in the end justifies even the willingness to kill one's only son."

Finally, it was Oedda's turn. She stared blankly for a few seconds, then said, "The parable lies outside Law—in the "there" that does not exist. It's a story of absolute responsibility in a true ethical choice, unconstrained by any social scaffolding. Abraham was to kill the son whom he loved above all else on faith, something for which he could not find any logical, rational, legal, social, or moral justification. Abraham's relationship with God is that inarticulable, unjustifiable capacity within humanity to create an authentic I-Thou space that is separate from the They, from that within us which crowds into societies. This is not a question of a higher Law in some hierarchical mode. Were it, Abraham would have asked for a clarification from God, for an *Erklärung*. The parable is the story of a relationship that cannot be understood from outside, although the outside always thinks it understands the I-Thou relationship, and, in fact it does, but only in I-It terms. Society will always claim it understands in reasoned, causal detail, and it can even convince the parties to the I-Thou relationship, if they are weak, that the true interpretation is one of economics, morality, rationality, psychoanalysis, Law—unable to say simply 'Here I am.' And even if he does say it, as Abraham did, it only takes seconds for society to bury the authentic moment in ambiguity, so that it becomes impossible to tell the difference, whether this was God I just made love to, or someone controlling me with mind games to see whether I'd kill my son. Yet Abraham was a real man, the best in man, and he understood God's call for what it was. It was a call that was not transitive—he could not explain it to Sarah over a morning coffee before heading up the mountain, nor to a bartender with whom he finds solace for a night. Abraham saw something much deeper than what could be transmitted, and yet his case shows the social cost of authenticity—a reputation of horribleness among those who understand easily in their averageness without making something their own."

She continued. "This conference shows the result of re-presenting any authentic moment. In the moment of the act, the relationship is wholly authentic, it is the entire universe of existence; the relation between Abraham and God is like that of the fetus to the womb. After the fact, brought into the realm of the social—for what is the social if not multitudes, not this conference—the relation becomes a matter of politics, economics, Law. In the fetus example it becomes biology, a science which can never understand the relation of the fetus to the mother even as it dissects every aspect of pregnancy in a vulgar understanding that will never transcend the limits of the simplest logic games. So this I send out in undifferentiated intelligibility: I admit Abraham was a monster. He should have been driven out of society, tied to a tree, and pecked to death by vultures, or better yet, by chickens, a mask pulled over his head to hide his ugly face. For was it not, after all, his that was the face of vulgarity?"

• • •

I propped myself up in the garbage. Oedda and Amadou were a few meters away, in a little hollow of trash, slapping bellies. That's what she used to call it. They were close enough that I could hear him whisper, "I missed you, sister," as he carelessly pumped into her. She was looking at me sideways, smiling, legs up at her shoulders, but despite the weird bodily dissonance there was no energy. Only the goat grazing between them and me seemed interested in what it was doing. Not far behind them, the mime rummaged through the mounds.

• • •

The UFO was late, and Oedda had managed to turn her defeat speech—defeat because she explained—into amusement that listeners would take it as the most coherent presentation of her philosophy to date and start parsing it through a filter of Heidegger or Kierkegaard or Buber or Derrida or whoever. Her speech seemed the most sophisticated end of the plenary group of six, the most true to the Abraham parable, but it was also upside down, all based on a lie. But then, this was a law school.

I met Peggy here. And Buck.

Thinking of them, Muzhduk wanted to hear the story. "It should be read aloud," he said to no one in particular as everyone else also spoke and objected and commented. The Harvard Descartes: I speak therefore I am. Except that others spoke when called on, in proper order.

Mountains which *I will tell thee of.* Of which *God had told him.* The inverse movement of Shakespeare's "Friends, Romans, Countrymen." There were no friends, no countrymen. Then, suddenly, 22.4 breaks the pattern to describe Abraham's eyes, and again in 22.13, when

Abraham again lifts up his eyes. These are the only description of the man. The weird crazy introspective moment, on a mountaintop, cold as the knife. A complete lack of description of Isaac. The rhythmic interpretation. To be nothing more than a future seventh member at the plenary table. He felt torn in opposite directions. Like Oedda's "falling that lifts up," making him tiny and infinite at the same time, as if there were two distinct but equally sensible definitions of space, of distance, mirror reflections of each other: R and 1/R. He wasn't sure what R stood for. Radius? Ratio? Rationality?

• • •

I crawled down the garbage mountain. The goat was soon beside me, a paper in its mouth. A poem. The goat was eating a poem. I could still read the last few lines:

> *doch dann stand nur Eines schief im Tage,*
> *und man sah: das ungenaue vage*
> *Leben nahm es wieder mit in Kauf.*

Raising of Lazarus, 1913, Rainer Maria Rilke, high in the mountains of Ronda, Andalusia. A city built on a cliff. A scorpion crawled beside Rilke *and then just a single crooked shape stood there in the daylight, and you could see inexact vague Life again accept it.* The mime picked it up by the tail, broke off the poisoned tip, and handed the rest to Muzhduk. Then walked away.

Muzhduk broke off the legs and ate the rest. It was dark, slightly sweet, with a sharp aftertaste of evil. Scorpion meat—life and death and sweetness. But the real adjective was "evil." Oedda had translated that poem for him, one of her favorites.

He began to slide, head-first: his legs dragged behind, leaving a trail in the slime and trash. Away from Oedda, away from Amadou. On the way down, he could think.

• • •

Muzhduk walked out of the room, feeling eyes on the back of his head. Six panelists, twelve eyes. The Hanged Man, in a Court of

Law—upside down by his left leg, the twelfth trump of the Tarot, the sacrifice of a male child of perfect innocence and high intelligence. The card of Odin, the Dying God. He walked, refusing to run, through campus towards the Fogg.

"Twobob," someone spoke beside him in Harvard Yard, though there was no one beside him, only the seated statue of John Harvard. Its left foot was shiny from tourists rubbing it for luck because some guidebook had told them it was a student tradition, which it wasn't, and its plinth read, "John Harvard, Founder, 1638."

Muzhduk stopped. He realized he had no idea how long it took for thorn-apple to wear off. Could he have been hallucinating since North Hall? Maybe he was still floating on an iceberg in the Bering Strait, slowly freezing to death. "Who—?"

"I am the Statue of Three Lies."

"What lies?"

"My image is not of John Harvard but of a stand-in model, John Harvard was not the founder of Harvard but only a large donor, and Harvard was founded in 1636, not 1638. Notice also that my *Veritas* seal is different from all the others, two books open but the third overturned. So you remember to look at both sides. Every other seal you'll find has all three open, because that is the modern way of lying. I am the statue of lies that tells the truth. You can call me Amadou."

"Another fiction?"

"Sure. We are all trapped in a fiction. Including you."

"What trapped me, Amadou?"

"You agreed to be trapped. And then you ate Claude's fufu."

"What was in the fufu?"

"Bone and skin and words, like the books in the library."

"I must go now. Where is Pooh?"

"In his tree. Don't you know anyone real anymore?"

"Yes."

"It took Oedda to tell you you're this way. It takes the barmaid to tell you again for you to believe it. But only with the next will you change. These things always come in threes."

"You're wrong. Or you're lying. Or you're just talking nonsense."

"Then why don't you go to her?"

"I will." Muzhduk managed to smile. "But right now there's no time."

"No, there is no Time." The statue was grinning now, grotesquely.

• • •

There was only the slapping sound. The Hogon was dead. The mountain was full of books. Goats ate the books, along with scorpions, agouti rats the size of rabbits. Many with their spines broken. *Things Fall Apart*, by Achebe. It was a yellow and orange book. The wrong yellow. Muzhduk slid by them. The goats dropped bubkis on the books.

• • •

Muzhduk walked into the Fogg, to the back room, Isaac's mouth still agape. He pulled it off the wall. Bells rang. Not the bells of weddings or mushrooms, but sharp, wailing bells.

He carried the four-foot painting down the stairs, but stopped at the African masks. He pulled down a large one with nails drilled into half its face, the other half covered in fragmented mirrors. *Nkonde—guardian of collective memory: A nail was added to the mask with every oath, to remain until the promise was fulfilled. The Nkonde's gaze transfixed the oath-maker, and followed him through space and time.*

Muzhduk put the mask on as he walked to the entrance of the Fogg, where people milled about, annoyed by the alarm. A young security guard looked left and right, serious, earnest. He noticed Muzhduk and yelled: "You can't wear the masks!" Oddly, he didn't notice the painting.

"It will die in its cage. A fetishist must awaken the Nkonde with his touch sometimes."

The guard hesitated, then drew his gun: "On the *floor*, mister!"

Muzhduk held out the painting as if he were handing it over to the guard. The guard looked at it, confused, and Muzhduk hit him in the neck with Nkonde. The guard crumpled. Muzhduk picked the gun off the floor and walked out onto Quincy Street. He threw the gun into the bushes, walked to the pump outside Adams House, and pumped it. He took a deep drink, placed Nkonde on top of the pump, and walked back to the Law School. Five minutes later he entered Langdell North again. Someone was saying, "—and so this moment, which is a fundamentally exclusionary one, is the theological model for ethnic cleansing—"

• • •

I could hear the drums, but lower. I continued to slide. Everything became finer.

• • •

He walked down the stairs to the panel, looking up at the floating Byzantine judges whom Sclera acknowledged every day on his way to the pit of the classroom. The Realist stopped speaking; the room murmured as people recognized the painting. When Muzhduk reached the bottom, Sclera said, "Please be seated so that we can continue."

Muzhduk placed the Caravaggio on the table, facing the six panelists. "Stop."

The Narrativist didn't hesitate: "Well, that is one interpretation. Others would present the moment differently. Tintoretto, or Rembrandt's engraving, for example, has Isaac's eyes—"

"Now look here," Sclera said. "As a plenary matter—"

"Have you lost your mind, Mr. Ugli?" Oedda asked, smiling, showing him that the Hegelian dialectic doesn't exist. Day and night are the same, and they aren't. There is no synthesis.

• • •

I slid past a sentence by the Buddha: "All that we are is the result of what we have thought." I kept going. Almost like a fine sand. A wildflower. Everything flies towards entropy.

• • •

Did I wrong her? I am like a little kid. But what can Isaac sacrifice? And to whom?

Of course I wronged her.

I have one eye…

To understand why a wall falls on a man…

Why are we going up the mountain, father?

Behold the fire and the wood: but where is the lamb for a burnt offering?

Muzhduk turned the painting over, to look at it himself. He stared directly into Isaac's eyes. He still couldn't quite fit the pieces together. Behind him, the doors flew open and two cops ran in: Vlad and Jimmy Crouch, whom Muzhduk recognized from his night in jail. "Freeze!" Vlad yelled.

"It doesn't work in this room," he answered, a little delirious. "I tried."

"You are under *arrest*, son, put your *hands* behind your *head*." Vlad pointed his gun at Muzhduk. He looked around the room full of liberal lawyers and awkwardly pulled a shield out.

Muzhduk placed the painting back on the table. "I would prefer not to."

"Place your *hands* behind your *head*! Now!"

He needed something in his hands, something other than his head or a priceless painting. Careful to move slowly, like a Bhutto performer, he reached for Oedda's plenary folder, but she grabbed it. He let go and took the one in front of the Realist, then walked towards the cops.

"*Get–on–the–floor, now*!"

Muzhduk walked up to Vlad, reading his folder. Vlad, perplexed, told Crouch to cover him, and tried to swing handcuffs onto Muzhduk's right wrist. Muzhduk let his right arm fall along with Vlad's hand, rolled around his wrist, and grabbed Vlad's pinkie. Vlad yelled from the damage to the little tendon, but moved where Muzhduk nudged him to move. How strange that such a large man could be moved by just his pinkie.

Crouch yelled "10-13" into his radio, over and over. Keeping Vlad between them, Muzhduk walked to the door, shoved Vlad back into the room and slammed the heavy door shut. On either side was an exit. Directly in front, stairs led to underground tunnels. He jumped over the railing to save two seconds, landed awkwardly on the steps and ran under Langdell.

Nobody chased him, so he didn't know which way to go. He had time to think. He leaned against a blue recessed utility door where the tunnels branched, closed his eyes to block out the pain in his ankle and wondered what Peggy was doing. Napping, curled up on her belly with one leg tucked in and the other straight out, nude, with all the covers wrapped around her feet and her face squished into a pillow. Or painting something, a picture of a golden sand dune with a big black beetle. Or reading a book, with her feet on the chair tucked in under her.

She'd get aiding and abetting, or accessory after the fact, or harboring a fugitive, or any of the other criminal names they give to friendship. He wouldn't pull Peggy into this, he couldn't trust Oedda, and Buck was gone. And he couldn't explain the complexities to a bunch of boulder-throwing Slovaks living on a mountain in Siberia. They'd expect to hear about the whimpering of smashed enemies, the roundness of conquered bosoms, and the blistering battle that came after endless years of eyelash-freezing and beard-cracking ice. If he started explaining about Rules of Procedure someone would roar, and he'd have to say he failed. And then what?

Verkhoyansk was a fairytale, distant and alien. Everything there floated, even the boulders. It was the low barometric pressure, maybe. But "Harvard" was also a fairytale, its only remnant the fact that Vlad and Crouch were less likely to shoot than Boston cops. God hadn't appeared to him to say, "Behold, [here am] I." That's what Oedda had wanted, but somehow every one of her insights into the world became wrong as she said it, until at the end she'd given up, let herself be subsumed into the plenary. And Peggy was still a potential, an opening he had to keep closed to himself for a little while longer. He wasn't good at restraint, but he would try. And Pooh. He was still real, in his own strange way. Muzhduk climbed out of the tunnels near Austin Hall, their southernmost point, around the corner from Pooh's tree. The air was filled with a mist that turned everything sodden and shapeless.

He knocked on Pooh's door.

"Hi, Pooh."

"Hi, Fool."

"I don't suppose I would fit in that little place of yours?"

"You're too fat."

"Mind if I climb up, then?"

"Suit your own self."

He climbed Pooh's tree. He stayed there for nine days

while thunderstorms shook the tree and rain poured from the sky. Occasionally, cops walked by.

• • •

Fine yellow sand. The only sounds were the quiet of shifting desert dunes. Full and deep and golden. I wasn't sliding anymore. I wouldn't make the same mistake again. I wouldn't get distracted again, by Oedda or Ouidah or however it wanted to spell itself. The dark fate, himself sacrificed to himself, the man turning his own navel over and over and over again.

"You have soft eyes," Amadou had told me in the bush-taxi with the peeing bull on top, after I'd suggested we kill it. "Many years ago I spent a month as a guest of the last of the kings of Dahomey. Every morning he sent a messenger to his dead ancestors announcing he was awake and ready to start the day. Most days, he sent a child, because children make better messengers. That is Ouidah. On my last day, the king discovered one of his tax collectors was cheating—maybe it was a lie, I don't know—but he forced the tax collector to eat his own father in a stew. That's Ouidah. And skulls. The king cared most about accumulating skulls: more skulls than he could drink from, more skulls than he could use as thrones, as furniture, more skulls than he could remember the names. But most of all, more skulls than anyone ever collected before him. That's what kings do. And there is no percentage for a guide in that."

Only now, sitting after my slide down the garbage hill, did I realize that Amadou had always referred to Ouidah as a thing half-separate from the town. "All the Dahomey kings lived through the Ouidah like this," he'd said, "protected by an army of six thousand bald women, all of them with teeth filed to sharp points." He'd mimed the shape of sharp teeth with his thumb and forefinger. It was from the Dahomey that the original Amazon legends came, though their geography got confused. And then the Portuguese came to this Ouidah—Dom Francisco and his 63 mulatto rape-sons and uncounted daughters—and they turned Ouidah into the greatest slave port in African history. Only the Arabs on Zanzibar ever came close to the Portuguese, and maybe the Belgians in the Congo. The British took a tax, the French "cultured," but the Portuguese were egalitarian:

they killed, raped, and stole both slave tribes and free. Millions of people left blood in Ouidah. They fed it. "Later, your American and Haitian blacks tried to remember and put together what happened. But the Ouidah is not a puzzle that you can take apart and put back together again on the other side. The Ouidah stayed in the dark red soil." After a few minutes of silence, with bull pee still dripping from the roof, he'd added, "Except sometimes a person can also become the Ouidah."

I stood up and ran back towards the picnic table.

• • •

Pooh gave me daily updates on the search. I told him there were three cows sitting in a tree. And a pig flew by. So one cow turned to the other cow, slapped his shoulder and said, "Hey you ox, look, there's a pig flying by." But the pig heard this and, buzzing right over the heads of the cows like a dive-bomber, yelled out, "Shut the fuck up or I'll sting you!"

"You're talking crap now, Fool."

"It's a joke. From where I come from. From Verkhoyansk."

"It's still crap."

"What came first, the chicken or the egg, Pooh?"

"You tell me."

"Well, it's a question of geography. In America, it depends on which side can afford better experts in phylogeny, philology, and cladistics. As you go back in evolution, you lose chickens, but you would have to go much further back before you didn't have eggs. So the question becomes 'what is a chicken?' The court in *Frigaliment Importing Co.* analyzed this question at length. In trade usage, chicken means 'young chicken.' Other sources vary in their opinions: Niesielowski maintained that chicken means 'the male species of the poultry industry. That could be a broiler, a fryer, or a roaster,' but not a stewing chicken. But Weininger argued that 'chicken is everything except a goose, a duck, and a turkey.' The Department of Agriculture regulations classify chicken into (a) broiler or fryer; (b) roaster; (c) capon; (d) stag; (e) hen or stewing chicken or fowl; (f) cock or old rooster. All of these categories have eggs—"

"Capons, cocks, and old roosters don't lay eggs—"

"—but so do ducks and geese and turkeys. Presumably Weininger's definition that 'everything is chicken' does not include elephants or giraffes—"

"—or bears."

"Or bears, and is in the context of egg-laying birds. Since all egg-laying birds lay eggs, and a duck, which is not a chicken, is an egg-laying bird, eggs are broader than chickens. Since phylogenetically, breadth is a proxy for age, the egg statistically comes first.

"In Asia, on the other hand, the arising of the chicken can never be independent of the egg, as the egg always remains an integral part of the chicken, and vice versa, so the whole question is much too narrow and should never have been asked in the first place. In Africa, it is clear that the egg came first, because it is wiser. Yola-the-Egg knew much more than Fuad-the-Chicken, and he knew it much earlier. If Yola-the-Egg hadn't known since the beginning of the World, among other things, that Denk-the-Stone was a bad traveling companion, then Fuad-the-Chicken would never have been born. Fuad, on the other hand, grew up without ever learning the way to the market, since he always went and returned hanging upside down, feet tied and head to the ground—"

"That's nice, Fool. But you haven't been to Africa, yet. Still, it looks like you've learned something from your witch."

"What have I learned, Pooh?"

"Words."

Muzhduk laughed. "That's why I came here."

To fight John the Attorney we need words. Pick up the word 'Harvard' and bring it back. Could he honorably claim his objective eye? A Formalist would say he hadn't "picked up Harvard." An Idealist would say the point was to learn to fight with words, so he'd succeeded. A Realist would...but none of that mattered. It was up to him, of course. It always had been.

There had been a lone tree in a flat sandy stretch of heath in Verkhoyansk that the six villages had wanted to turn into a playing field for the Red-soldier game. An old woman had loved that tree and refused to let them uproot it, and since she was an old woman nobody could challenge her to personal combat. Ugli the Third had offered her a dozen young trees in compensation, then two dozen, planted wherever she liked. But she was as craggy as the tree and got no pleasure from being part of a popular decision, so in the end the gnarled old Siberian cedar stayed in the middle of the soldier-game field and within a couple of years it became as indispensable as the goal lines over which the teams had to carry the prisoner to get a point. He told Pooh the story, and asked him, "That old woman, was she strong or pathetic?"

"Why can't it be both?" Pooh answered.

By his ninth day in the tree, Muzhduk was hungry and thirsty. When it rained, he'd drunk, but he hadn't eaten. A big nickel-azo-yellow apparatus appeared next to Pooh's tree that day, along with grape-bunches of police. How? No one knew about Pooh's tree except for Oedda. And she no longer existed, he knew. She was with Sclera, the Idealist, the Realist, the Narrativist, and the Economist—*not under man but under God and Law*—returned to the clay. One by one, people were disappearing, and that's why Muzhduk had to protect Peggy, to stay away a little longer, until his nine days were finished. Until the drumming stopped.

Pooh stayed hidden within the tree. A fiction couldn't survive near a cop. So the police barked up at Muzhduk and Muzhduk pretended he didn't hear them, until he saw Officer Crouch move to open the little red door. Then Muzhduk yelled down and said he was up there but that he preferred to wait until he turned into a papaya and some monkeys took him away.

They said that's what they had waited for, but now they ignored the red door so Muzhduk didn't come down. A negotiator tried to talk him down. Then two specialist lumberjack cops with police-issue tree-climbing belts came after him, but he kicked them and they fell. Finally, they moved the apparatus to the tree. It had a big, nasty spinning disk that the cops oiled in preparation. And pipes and levers, like the "Motor Vehicle" in Sclera's first class.

Muzhduk wondered how Pooh felt, peeking out through a knothole, watching his tree about to be cut down. The tree was the last barrier separating the Law School from the Science Centre and the School of Divinity. If it fell, Science, Law, and Religion would unite in an unholy trinity, and Sclera would win. Maybe that had been his master plan all along, procedures and levers put in motion all leading to Muzhduk climbing this tree. Pooh's home.

Soon the disk was spinning, the loudspeakers were speaking

loud, and so was everything else. “All set!” a lumberjack-cop yelled to everyone and no one.

The saw bit into Pooh’s old tree, wood-dust flying across America.

Poor Pooh.

• • •

I ran past the picnic table, past men who were dead or bleeding in the dirt, past abandoned drums and flip-flops and staggering babalawos, past the red rectangle who was still fused in a death-grip with the Hogon, to the baobab tree. A few dozen people still roamed aimlessly, spread wide around the enormous intersection. Dust was everywhere, kicked up by the dancers and dying men, and now it was settling over the grilled rat, over the people and the table and the tree. But it wasn’t red like the soil. It was a white powder that sat over everything, in every crevice. It was in my eyes, in my teeth, it covered my tongue and chafed my skin.

• • •

It was an old tree, and it had a heavy smell that wasn’t so different from the wild thyme that wafted around the six villages in late spring, announcing that the Dull-Boulder Throw was around the corner and the young men had better build some padding on their ribs. Muzhduk should have made friends with the tree earlier. He didn’t want Them to cut it down and turn it into a chair. He didn’t know if he’d be able to save Verkhoyansk. Probably it would be a losing battle, but he’d fight it well. Maybe he’d make a deal: as chief, he would make a rule prohibiting the eating of the endangered butterflies by the six villages, in exchange for Verkhoyansk being declared a world wildlife refuge into which no laws could enter. It would be fun for all the kids to have one rule to break. Or maybe he wouldn’t make a deal at all, maybe the six villages would continue with the same skills that had kept the Red Army out.

It didn’t matter so much. There were a thousand new tactics available to him, all of which would run out. His people would lose in the end, but not until after the other guys were piled in piles, heaps higher than the mountains, and he with them. That was the solution to John the Attorney, a solution John himself would never understand as being a solution. *I'm from Verkhoyansk, and we fight.*

Muzhduk thought back on the series of decisions that had brought him up this tree—a tree with a little door where the gnarled roots met, within which a fiction lived, surrounded by police and machinery—and he began laughing. Instead of a mountain, he'd only needed to climb a tree. This exact tree.

He opened his arms wide. There was a threshold of instinctive panic as he let go of the branches and crossed that boundary where his hands would no longer be able to grasp anything. He landed with a deep involuntary yell as all the air was expressed from his lungs.

Then the cops were handcuffing him. There was some confusion as they tried to remove Vlad's nine-day-old dangling cuff to replace it with their own. The cops argued amongst themselves, and the apparatus was spinning, and then the apparatus stopped. He could breathe again. The tree had a long gash across the side of its trunk from the cold spinning metal blade, but it would stand. And that was important.

• • •

One of the men wandering dazed near the babalawo picnic table was Ibrahim. He wasn't wearing his usual Tuareg robe and veil, and I didn't recognize him until he was right in front of me. He had a receding hairline, which struck me as odd, unexpected, and a gnarled forehead like his namesake. He stood there, trying to form a question. Whatever had happened to my mind on the garbage hill had happened to everyone and he couldn't get the question out. I punched his blue-tinged face as hard as I could. As hard as I'd ever punched anyone. As hard as I'd ever thrown a boulder or pulled down an oak tree or done anything in my life.

I felt a little more clearheaded as I approached Babu Chirpy, Esq.

"She's still a prisoner," he said.

"She doesn't recognize this court's jurisdiction."

"That's irrelevant. She's in it."

"Then we'll leave," I said.

"They'll stop you."

"With force?" I looked over Ibrahim, laid out on the ground. Babu Chirpy, Esq. stepped out of my way.

The last was Amadou. Behind him, leaning against the tree, was the Green Vodoun.

Amadou said, "That's not her. I looked."

I walked past him and pulled the green costume off Peggy.

• • •

Muzhduk spent a night in jail. The next day Alan Dershowitz was there to defend him, true to his word about the "free parts and labor" for five years for all students and former students. Having got Klaus von Bulow and O.J. Simpson off the hook, Muzhduk's case was a breeze.

Muzhduk also had an administrative board hearing, a witenagemot of Harvard professors gathered to determine whether he should be expelled. Muzhduk chose to do that one on his own. He told the board that the structures of Law are built from the bricks that are thrown through its windows. In a very real way, the Law *is* its own transgressions—and he was a law student.

You cannot say that, they said.

I came here to learn words, and I have learned. What would you like me to say?

You won't fight anymore?

I'll always fight. Both eyes are glass, I am blind, and there are a thousand mountains, all with an up and a down. And if there weren't, I'd build them myself.

You will be suspended for one year, during which time you will prepare a reflected memorandum of remorse, how all this came to pass. If it is satisfactory, you will be re-admitted.

Is that what R stands for? In the formula, R=1/R? Ratio? Reflection? Readmission? Restraint?

R is a symbol, like any other. What it means is up to you. Traditionally, the letter R was associated with mountains, in which case it stood for regeneratio. *In the old writings, when a mountain left behind its material character, it became the symbol of an idea. But what it means is up to you. It always has been.*

I see. Thank you.

• • •

I sit on a yellow sand dune sticking my feet out towards the east. My feet are bare. Everything is gold and pink and yellow. Just as the sun peeks out over the yellow dune rising, a black beetle comes walking towards us. Peggy sits beside me.

EPILOGUE

When we arrived in Verkhoyansk, my father clapped me on the shoulder and said, "Ah, good. You stole a woman from the Americans."

The welcome went surprisingly well. I had explained to Peggy that if I didn't squeeze each village girl's bum then they'd feel offended, but I promised not to sleep with any of them afterward. To ensure this, we brought our own bottle, ostensibly Peggy's, and I finished that one and only took a sip from everyone else's. All the girls laughed that we were in love and went off to join the men working hard to break through my father's top step. By the end of the evening his porch was smashed, a success, and as the sun was rising someone yelled out, "Did you get it?"

"I got it," I answered.

"Show us!"

I tapped my head. "It's in here." And so I told the story of my adventures. Just when a few people yawned at my discussion of Torts class or Oedda's word games, I switched to the heat and guns of Africa and of the tribe similar to ours that was being nailed into one place by all the people who sit behind desks, and everyone perked up. They listened to the end of the story before Hirzlagu, Hulagu's uncle, asked the obvious question, "But you went to pick up the word Harvard. I don't understand why you went to Africa."

"Without Africa the word would have been half empty." Like the naked women in the forest who are hollowed-out from behind. Like Peter Schlemihl, the man who sold his shadow, I didn't say because they wouldn't have understood. "Just as there are two parts to becoming chief, there are two sides to every word."

Nobody knew enough about words to ask what I meant, so they took my word for it. Everyone except for Hulagu. Hulagu stood, his last chance of breaking the Ugli line of chieftainship dissolving in front of him, not caring that he was about to disgrace himself in front of the whole village, not caring that he'd have to give me five public blowjobs if his last-hope gambit failed, and asked, "What's an empty word? It sounds like nonsense."

Hirzlagu cursed his nephew. Everyone else turned his back to him, to not witness Hulagu's shame. After so long in the West, I was the only one who didn't sneer at him for his question. To the surprise of the whole village, I answered. "An empty word is like the bearskin that John the Attorney surrounded the six villages with."

The men jumped up, even Hulagu and Hirzlagu, swaying a little with all the drinking. They all ran toward the river. The women followed them, laughing. Within two minutes, there was nobody left in the village except Peggy, my father, my mother, and me.

"Where are they going?" Peggy asked.

"To kill John the Attorney," my father said. "His hotel is almost finished."

I took Peggy's hand. "Hey, do you want to live in a hotel? With American comfort?"

"I don't know. If they kill someone in there..."

"I've really grown to like flush toilets."

We ran down to the river. The hotel was beautiful, on a high overlook above the river Lena. Exposed to helicopter attack, but we could dig a basement. It was all wood and stone and enormous windows, the type of rustic cabin that no real rustic has, with light and rooms enough for kids, for Peggy to have a studio, for me to have a library, for friends, for half the village to visit. And it had full western amenities in the middle of Verkhoyansk—a generator, washer, drier, even a dishwasher. I pulled Peggy back out of the hotel, picked her up, slung her over my shoulder, and kicked down the flimsy door of our new house.

Six months later, she walked into our library, where I was reading a chapbook that Buck had sent me, care of the library in Yakutsk—his first published book of poems—and told me she was pregnant.

"It'll be a boy," I said.

"You can't know that."

"Every baby in my line from the first Valibuk the Oak-Feller through all the Muzhduks to me, every single one has been a boy. We've never had a girl in the family."

"Well, maybe you will now."

"I'd be happy to. But it's the father's genes that determine the gender." I saw the look on her face. "What's wrong with a boy?"

"Nothing at all. I just don't want to name him Muzhduk the Ugli. You're Muzhduk the Ugli, I'm Muzhduk the Ugli, your father and grandfather are Muzhduk the Ugli. It gets a little too much."

"What would you call him, then?"

She thought about it. "How about Samson the Happy?"

Author's Note

First and foremost, my deepest thanks to Joe Pan and Brooklyn Arts Press. BAP is what all publishers would still be in a perfect world. They truly care. Joe believed in *The Ugly*. He spent a humbling amount of time ensuring editorial excellence, and put up with a literary equivalent of the Dull-Boulder Throw in trying to keep the small details—about Harvard, about the Tuaregs, about history—as accurate as possible in the face of my embrace of the absurd. Because absurdity works best when it's real—though I don't always listen. The end result was a far stronger book. And Catherine Adams, who put the novel through a fantastic developmental edit, getting into Muzhduk the Ugli's head so well that she could call out my moments of caution sometimes better than I. I am eternally indebted to both of them.

The Ugly is not a true story, however, and I'm not an anthropologist. I did attend Harvard Law School, live with the Tuaregs in the middle of the Tuareg Wars, catch malaria while stuck on a riverboat on the way to Timbuktu, participate in a Voodoo ceremony in Benin. I may even have thrown a boulder from time to time. I absorbed ideas that I used in *The Ugly*, sometimes local words that I later transcribed, but I did all this with no academic rigor. If, in reading *The Ugly*, you come across a term in Tamasheq or Inuit or Harvardese, or some important detail of culture, that is wrong, the mistake is stubbornly mine.

There are also moments in *The Ugly* where I insisted on following Nietzsche's observation that "We have art to save ourselves from truth." Half the slogans on the Harvard library walls are real, while half are not. One of the two books bound in human skin really is bound in human skin, the other has been found to not be. (Though the Gutierrez book was only established by DNA testing as not being human in 2014. In the late 1990s, we thought both were. They are both housed in Houghton Library, not Langdell.) Half of the stories in the novel may be based in something real, half are not. This is a book of fiction, so please assume they're all untrue. Except Ted Cruz. Ted Cruz really did state that students from the minor ivies need not apply for his study group.

And although Muzhduk did save Pooh's tree, it was a temporary victory. The tree was cut down in 2012. The world is doomed.

I'd also like to thank all my friends who read early versions, who gave me feedback and support—too many to list all, but there are a few I need to mention by name. Professor Alan Stone, who accepted a novel as a law school thesis and who introduced me to ideas that helped shape who I became intellectually, from *Fassbinder's Berlin Alexanderplatz* to Musil's *Man Without Qualities*. Outi Korhonen, who shook up my Cola bottle and forced me to read Heidegger just to be able to argue about socks on the floor. Without her, my idea of "what is thinking" would have remained much narrower, and I would be a different person. Stacy McKee, who was doing an MFA in writing at Emerson while I was getting my law degree and let me peek at her notes. Benjamin Swire, for being not just a great writer and reader and friend, but for giving me a day job that let me pay for my son's circus school while I worked on *The Ugly*. Omid Pakbin and Omega Point for an amazing book trailer and lots of other help, Stefan Sagmeister for his support, and Mike and Andy Zaremba, for helping me get the word out through Vancouver Real and my thoughts in order through Float House. I solved several plot problems while floating in their sensory deprivation tanks. (Seriously dear reader, if you're in Vancouver, go float yourself.)

I also owe a debt of gratitude to Bread Loaf Writers' Conference, for nominating the prologue of *The Ugly* to the *Best New American Voices* anthology and giving me hope, and for all the fantastic people whom I met at Bread Loaf: Mark Powell, who has been giving me good advice for years and whose own books are a joy to read, Pete Duval, whose photography (and short stories) are out of this world, and my fellow waitrons—Debbie Kuan, Laila Lalami, Laura van den Berg, Nina Swamidoss McConigley, Gibson Fay-Leblanc—who a decade later went out of their way to help despite deservedly becoming far more famous since.

And finally, most importantly, my family—my parents, for a lifetime of support and love, Tania Xenis, who puts up with my Ugli side on a daily basis and generally makes life much better, and my son Samson for being the coolest kid in the world.

ALEXANDER BOLDIZAR was the first post-independence Slovak citizen to graduate with a *Juris Doctor* degree from Harvard Law School. Since then, he has been an art gallery director in Bali, an attorney in San Francisco and Prague, a pseudo-geisha in Japan, a hermit in Tennessee, a paleontologist in the Sahara, a porter in the High Arctic, a police-abuse watchdog in New York City, an editor and art critic for *C-Arts Magazine* out of Jakarta and Singapore, and a consultant on Wall Street. His writing has won the PEN/Nob Hill prize, represented Bread Loaf as a nominee for *Best New American Voices*, and been shortlisted for a variety of other awards.

Boldizar currently lives in Vancouver, BC, Canada, where his hobbies include throwing boulders (to make pools in the river behind his home for his son to swim in) and choking people while wearing pajamas, for which he has won a gold medal at the Pan American Championships and a bronze at the World Masters Championships of Brazilian Jiu-Jitsu. For several years, an online Korean dictionary had him listed as its entry for "ugly."

CPSIA information can be obtained
at www.ICGtesting.com
Printed in the USA
LVOW07s1319121017
552122LV00033B/271/P